WASTING BY DEGREE

Wasting by Degrees

CONOR BOWMAN

ASHFIELD
Press

This book was typeset by
Gough Typesetting Services for
ASHFIELD PRESS
an imprint of
BLACKHALL PUBLISHING
26 Eustace Street, Dublin 2.
(e-mail: blackhall@tinet.ie)

© Conor Bowman 1998

A catalogue record for this book
is available from the British Library

ISBN 1-901658-14-7 hbk
ISBN 1-901658-13-9 pbk

Printed by
Betaprint Ltd.

For Sylvia and Hannah

Acknowledgements

Cutting to the chase I'd like to thank a number of people who made this book happen.

Blackhall Publishing who agreed to take it when other people told me to go elsewhere and perform certain personal acrobatic feats (or words to that effect). In particular Gerard O'Connor, Tony Mason, Jackie Donohoe, Tara (the girl who presses the buzzer at the front door) and Linda Kenny who did all the publicity.

Thanks to my parents who have always given me great support in my endeavours. My father is the best architect in the whole world but doesn't realise it. My mother stood by me for years in the face of school reports which said "Disruptive" and "Could do better" (phrases not intended to be read together, I discovered later).

In no particular order I would like to thank: the "real" Dixton Larkin for letting me use his name; Johnny Packham for things I would rather not say; all at EMI Studios Baghdad; my next-door neighbour Helen Cody for reading the book while it was still only a broadsheet; Henry Murphy for inventing the wheel; Great Aunt Cep for agreeing to read the book and not notice my bad language; for Mark de Blacam and Chris Mullane and all in the Front Gallery who encouraged me to kick ass before it was profitable; everyone who knows me (like they say on those pukey radio shows). This book really starts on page 1.

Finally and most importantly thanks to Sylvia for all of your love, patience, understanding and encouragement. This book is really for you and Hannah, the two girls in my life.

Lots of love.

Conor
March 1998

CHAPTER ONE

'A lot of people think that "Burger Empire" is a fast food chain; that's their first mistake.'

This guy was a complete dingbat. Here they were, two eager workers lusting for knowledge and pay and their employer was visiting this kind of drivel on them within moments of giving them a job. They looked at each other and tried not to laugh. Their lanky host in his proud uniform continued:

'"Burger Empire" is a family restaurant. People expect the same kind of service here that they'd get in the Hilton.'

'Although they wouldn't expect the same kind of food,' Dixton chipped in.

'Our clients are our most valued asset and every care is taken from cow to customer to ensure that our food is of the highest possible quality. You never get a second chance to make a first impression!'

'Particularly if you're dead,' sniggered Dixton's companion.

'Please gentlemen, humour has its role in the world of cuisine but there is a time and a place. Nobody enjoys a joke more than myself but if you want to rise through the ranks in the BE family you will have to put *service* before *self* in order to succeed.'

This fellow appeared to be living on another planet altogether, with his neat haircut and his gold badge for ten years endeavour in the fake food industry. He was clearly anxious to ascertain their commitment early on, and he posed the million-dollar question as they rounded the corner into the kitchen to confront the jewel in the "Burger Empire" crown: the turbo-driven frying unit.

'You *do* see your long-term future within this industry?'

'Of course,' they answered without hesitation. What else could they say? This was the opportunity of a lifetime. It hadn't always been like this though. Dixton cast his mind back to that fateful day over a year ago. He'd been offered a place at Cambridge and couldn't believe his luck.

There must have been some mistake, he'd thought, when the letter arrived with its clearly legible postmark. His hands hadn't trembled uncontrollably while opening the envelope, no, Dixton Larkin was never a great fan of amateur dramatics and feigned surprise; he'd ripped open the letter and was genuinely gobsmacked.

He had spent the previous three years studying law in Ireland and had scraped an upper second class honour in his finals. It was the first class honour he'd fluked in Equity which had dragged the entire degree up to that grade and he'd finished in the top quarter of the class. This gave him great satisfaction for two reasons. Firstly, his grade assured him of a qualification infinitely more impressive than he actually deserved. Secondly, and more importantly, it meant that he had finished ahead of quite a number of people he hated. There could be nothing in the whole universe really more satisfying than that (except possibly winning the National Lottery). He was just twenty one and ready to launch himself upon an unsuspecting world. Law was the perfect subject to have chosen to study at university. It combined the status of a profession with a relatively manageable workload and was therefore ideal for Dixton. Nothing frightened him more than the prospect of an early debut in the job market and so the opportunity to stave off the evil day, via post-graduate study in England, provided the instant solution to a problem he'd been too afraid even to consider. Phrases such as 'an honest day's work' or 'you never get anything for nothing in this life' terrified him. At any rate, the next year was now fairly clearly mapped out.

Dixton had been brought up by his Aunt Sheila in Dublin. His parents had been killed in a bizarre road accident when he was just seven months old. Apparently they were driving home from the Grand National at Fairyhouse when they were ploughed into head-on by a horse lorry which was transporting the winner to the airport. The horse was undamaged while Dixton's parents had been killed outright. He was an only child and Aunt Sheila was his father's older sister. She was a spinster but had no hesitation in taking on the task of raising Dixton. His parents had deposited him with her on the morning of the Grand National and he'd lived with her ever since. Had he been a seven-month-old racing enthusiast things could easily have been very different indeed.

They lived in Ailesbury Crescent, a fashionable and wealthy suburb of Dublin, in a house that had more bathrooms than bedrooms for some strange reason. Most of the residents of the area looked on Dixton as an aberration in an otherwise very respectable part of the capital city. Dixton had wreaked havoc from very early on. At the age of six he had painted the windows of the Rolls Royce owned by the Chief Executive of an airline company who lived next door. Someone had been decorating a garage nearby and had nipped off for a minute or two leaving the paint and brush unguarded. Dixton thought that he was helping but the neighbours took a somewhat different view. Looking back at the event he felt that the neighbours had totally over-reacted and would have been better served turning their attention to the energy crisis which was troubling the rest of the world at the time.

Some years later he caused mayhem by selling tickets to thirty school friends to come and watch the girl at number fifteen undress through a telescope he had rigged up in the garden shed. All went well until Aunt Sheila and the girl's mother, who happened to be visiting, came down to investigate the claim of one disgruntled viewer who complained to Aunt Sheila that he wanted his money back because he'd seen.

'Nothing only an auld blouse and a pair of jeans.'

Despite his somewhat turbulent childhood Dixton had managed to get into college. He didn't have the requisite self-confidence or independent means to be a drop-out and so he stuck to the task in hand, hit the books in spots and generally muddled through. Finally Aunt Sheila had formed the impression that Dixton might make something of himself and so the bargain was that as long as he kept passing exams she would keep bankrolling his education. Dixton was in no hurry to jeopardise this arrangement.

Although he had got his act together somewhat he was still looked upon with contempt by the majority of the neighbours. They never forgave him his earlier exploits and regarded him as a middle class thug cluttering an upper class area. Dixton couldn't have cared less because, while he was scrambling his way through a law degree, many of the neighbours were falling over themselves to enrol their children in 'pretend Universities' as Dixton had christened them. These were the private third level colleges, which were sold to the public in much the same manner as detergents with slogans like: 'Looks like a dumping ground for rich ignorant children but is in actual fact a college.'.

This was the thinking person's nightmare scenario: education on a supermarket shelf. Not that Dixton was an intellectual snob, he wasn't, but it was encouraging to see people who looked down on him being immersed themselves in situations which they considered themselves above. He felt sorry for their children though, being hounded into moulded futures like frightened sheep.

As for his own education, his aunt had suggested to him quite frequently while at college, that the next logical step was the Bar or a large solicitors firm. Dixton had headed her off at the pass by suggesting further studies and she had been very impressed by this display of decisive self-advancement on his part. Talk of Dixton working his way and earning a living would be shelved for the next year at least. Aunt Sheila was rightly chuffed.

3

'I think it a worthwhile proposal that you round off your education with a Masters from Cambridge. My father, your grandfather, was a great believer in the Oxbridge tradition. He'd have been proud of you Dixton.' (Dixton was very proud of himself, but for different reasons.)

'My thoughts exactly Aunt Sheila.'

This was complete bollox. Dixton hoped to postpone hard work and elbow grease, and all those other euphemisms for hell, for an indefinite period. He'd only recently before that hit upon postgraduate studies as a way out of working, but that wouldn't stop him. Hard work never killed anyone or so they said, but why take the risk of being the first casualty? You very rarely hear of people resting to death!

Aunt Sheila was one of the old school. She believed in the values of the brisk walk, the cold shower and the rhythm method. As far as she was concerned the Pope was the only person, besides herself, with a clear view of the world and her greatest fears for Dixton were that he might meet a loose woman or stop attending Mass, or both. She wanted to keep him as far away as possible from bad influences and to her mind as long as Dixton was directing his energies towards study then he couldn't go wrong. Her views of University were much like those of Cardinal Newman however different her motives may have been.

'I don't know if I told you or not Dixton but Saint Benildus is the patron saint of Law students.'

'Oh really, that's nice.'

'Well I hardly think that "nice" is the word you're looking for there Dixton, saints are rarely if ever "nice". You should pray and ask God to make you more like Saint Benildus.'

'How do you mean like him? You mean like, dead?'

'You know very well that I do not mean that. Education is a vocation, like the priesthood, and those who dedicate their learning to God will ultimately achieve saintliness, if not in this world then in the next.'

'I'd prefer to be a saint in this world Aunt Sheila because I feel the competition for sponsorship would be less hectic.'

Dixton loved Aunt Sheila. Not only had she brought him up but, looking back on his first twenty-one years on earth, it was clear to him that she loved him too. His relationship with her was a healthy mixture of fear and affection. He was the son she never had and she was the aunt he never wanted but appreciated just the same. They provided each other with company and an interest and occasionally they even enjoyed being together. She never once made an issue of having brought him up. He didn't know whether she was unmarried by accident or design but for someone who had about ten minutes practice with children before taking him on, she'd done a great job. They didn't always see eye-to-eye, especially where religion was concerned, but Dixton would have been worried if they had.

Apart from Dixton, who took up a lot of her money and all of her patience, Aunt Sheila had one close friend, a retired High Court judge who was unmarried and lived in the end house on the town side of Ailesbury Crescent. They went for walks together regularly and swapped gardening tips. Aunt Sheila always referred to him as 'the Judge'. The Judge shared her religious fervour and this, together with a common view of the crumbling moral fibre of Western society, combined to bond the two together as platonic gardeners fighting social and moral decay with hyacinth bulbs and compost. Dixton often secretly hoped that his aunt would marry the Judge so that he could use whichever house they didn't live in for parties. He was a great believer in the ill-wind-theory.

If she was nothing else, Aunt Sheila was decisive. She was a great advocate of making choices and sticking by them. Making decisions for herself was one thing but Aunt Sheila really came into her own when making decisions for others (whether invited to do so or not). As well as applying for entry to the university itself Dixton had had to fill in a form applying for admission to a college. He hadn't a clue about any of the colleges on the list and nominating three colleges in the order of his choice was a fairly fruitless exercise. Aunt Sheila of course had very definite views.

'I think that your choice of college is crucial to the success of the entire venture Dixton.'

'So do I, Aunt.'

'Good, well that's settled then, we'll apply to Saint Edmund's College shall we?'

'Why Saint Edmund's?'

'Because it's a Catholic College and it will provide a sound base for your studies, a home away from home.'

Dixton's personal feeling on the matter was that it was pointless going to the trouble of travelling abroad to study at all if the environment awaiting him was simply a replica of the one he had gone there to escape in the first place.

'It sounds like a good idea in principle aunt but I wonder if it's really practical.'

'How do you mean, Dixton?'

'Well it seems to me (he knew he was about to start lying whenever

5

he prefaced a remark in this way) that the set of values which I have received in Ireland might well not be the ones espoused in a Catholic college elsewhere. Remember Aunt that at a university the whole point of postgraduate study is to improve one's knowledge of a subject already studied at a lower level.'

He knew that what he said made no real sense at all; however, he felt that perhaps even a vague sign of disagreement would deter his aunt from forcing her choice on him. He was wrong.

'I don't see how that makes Saint Edmund's unsuitable Dixton.'

Dixton felt the situation slipping from his control and knew that to retrieve it would take a classic flurry of untruth.

'Frankly Aunt Sheila, my difficulty is this, I feel that I have a secure grip on my religion as a result of my upbringing, (he could see his aunt beginning to glow with pride and so he pressed home his advantage) I don't want to have to spend the year defending my own values from assault by clever religious academics forcing Liberation Theology down my throat.'

His aunt looked genuinely worried. He supposed that it had been the use of the word 'Liberation' which had prompted the re-think as that always conjured up images of unshaven South American guerrillas.

'Perhaps you're right, Dixton. It would be a shame for you to be deflected from the real purpose of postgraduate study. How about some of the other colleges then?'

This was more like it.

Having avoided the pitfall of a religious college he set about trying to select ones which would prove suitable in his own mind. He considered the possibility that there might be other home-away-from-home type colleges lurking within the prospectus but dismissed this as unlikely. Aunt Sheila would be sure to know them also and would have mentioned them earlier on. There was quite a range of colleges and so Dixton decided that the best way to choose from a group of this size was by simply tossing a coin. He wrote the names of the colleges down in no obvious order on a sheet of paper then he numbered them from one to thirty two. He drew a line through the middle of the list and so created two blocks, numbers one to sixteen and numbers seventeen to thirty two. He tossed the coin on behalf of the two blocks then halved the winning block into groups of eight and repeated the exercise until he was left with two colleges; Lupin Hall and Newnham. He tossed one final time, heads for Newnham, tails for Lupin Hall. Heads it was. He opened the prospectus and scanned the contents for information on his chosen college.

'Newnham is an all female college situated on Sidgwick Avenue. It was founded in . . .'

Dixton stopped reading. It would have to be Lupin Hall. He didn't bother putting down second and third choice colleges on the form because he didn't think he'd even get an offer to go to Cambridge at all. It was more of an exercise to keep the future at bay rather than to court it.

Early on in June, after he had finished his final exams and a month or so before the offer from the university, Dixton had received a provisional acceptance from Lupin Hall. The acceptance was contingent on his being offered a place by the university when his degree results were known. Because he had put down Lupin Hall as his only choice and had ticked the box on the form which indicated that he wished to be considered for a bursary, the college invited him for an interview the Friday after his exams had finished. Despite this preliminary offer Dixton never seriously thought that he would get a good enough grade to go and so he looked on the interview as the only opportunity he might ever get to visit Cambridge. His aunt bought him a new suit (at least the trip would yield that) and put him on the plane to Stansted.

The sun was splitting the rocks as he walked to the college from the railway station in his new suit. It was a scorching June day which made the tar on the road look hazy and Dixton was more worried about the soaking armpits of his shirt than the prospect of the interview itself.

He was only here to keep his aunt happy as in all likelihood he'd be sitting the Bar exams next year in Dublin with his cronies Flannery and Mullane from the law class. His mood was fairly carefree when he entered the college through the big wrought iron gates and made his way to the Porters' Lodge to ask directions to where the interview was being held. He waited in the corridor in a leather armchair opposite a painting of a rowing crew until his name was called.

There were three interviewers. The chairperson was a kindly faced middle aged gentleman with sideburns who stood up as Dixton entered the room and stretched out his hand and smiled warmly as he shook Dixton's hand.

'Welcome to Lupin Hall Mr Larkin, I'm Professor Burton, the President of the college. This is Dr Hagar, the Senior Tutor', he indicated the man seated on his right, 'and this is the Praelector Dr Winston.'

Dixton wondered what a Praelector was but supposed it must be fairly important and left it at that. He sat down.

7

The interview lasted almost an hour and ranged in topics from Law (ground on which Dixton felt shaky enough) to his general 'interests'. He had been reluctant to cite 'watching television' and 'chasing women unsuccessfully' and so had filled the available two spaces with 'music' and 'debating'. Dixton had never debated in his life but thought that it sounded impressive. He had not envisaged being invited to elaborate.

'Mr Larkin, you state that you are interested in debating. Tell us a little about your achievements in that field?'

The question came from the Praelector. Dixton disliked him instantly and stalled for time.

'My achievements? Well, I suppose I competed and did fairly well.'

The Praelector wasn't going to be put off that easily:

'There's no need to be coy about success at *this* university Mr Larkin. Did you take part in the recent world championships in Dublin?'

'Er, yes I did.' (He hoped he wasn't shooting himself in the foot here, to use an old paramilitary metaphor.)

The Praelector closed in for the kill.

'Splendid. How did you get on? Were you a Finalist?'

'Afraid not.'

'Semi-finalist then perhaps?'

Dixton rested a hand under his chin and tapped his lips thoughtfully with his index finger.

'Well.' He was beginning to hate this Praelector fellow.

The President bailed him out.

'Frankly Praelector I think it is having the interest which counts, not how you get on. There's too much competition already in life without having to compete in your leisure activities as well. What about this music interest Mr Larkin?' He thumbed the CV. 'Do you play an instrument?'

Dixton heaved an inward sigh of relief and launched into a monologue about the guitar (an interest he really did have). He'd been playing guitar for about four years and occasionally busked in Dublin when he was short of cash. The change in topic clearly didn't suit the Praelector as he seemed only to be at ease when others were uncertain. Dixton wondered just what kind of person got their kicks from hassling people at interviews.

The rest of the hour went extremely well indeed. Dixton felt that he had made a good impression on at least two of the interviewers. His complacency however was severely dented just before he left.

'One last thing,' said the Senior Tutor, 'you realise of course that we do not have the final say as to whether or not you will be coming to Lupin Hall next autumn. While we will probably offer you a place, and

8

perhaps even a bursary, all of that depends primarily on the University being satisfied with your final degree result in Ireland. If they do not offer you a place we can do nothing about that.'

As he made his way back to the railway station to catch a train to Stansted it dawned suddenly on Dixton that he probably would not be returning to Cambridge in October. The carefree mood which had accompanied him on the trip to the interview gave way to a large dose of self-recrimination. He remembered looking at some of the other colleges on the way back to the station and thinking to himself that, for the want of a couple of months' hard work during the previous year, he had most likely blown a great chance to take part in all this. If only he'd realised sooner what was at stake.

Remembering the disappointment, which had engulfed him on that scorching day the previous June made his joy, at having been offered a place, all the greater. Here was an opportunity in one fell swoop (or in one 'foul sweep' as a taxi man once said to him) to postpone working for a living for another year at least and to participate in a way of life which would have been beyond him but for that fluked First in Equity and the fact that Newnham was an all-girls college. He hadn't been awarded a bursary but he felt sure that Aunt Sheila wouldn't let that stand in her brilliant nephew's way. While others struggled with the Bar and Law Society exams in Dublin, Dixton would be standing back and looking at life from the safety of a Masters course. Perhaps he might even get the chance to finally rid himself of his virginity. He clutched the acceptance letter as though terrified it would disintegrate if he should let go and then went outside into the shrubbery to find his aunt.

CHAPTER TWO

The college crest glared down at Dixton from above the main door of Lupin Hall. It consisted of two rampant lions one either side of a large anaemic tree with the motto of Lupin Hall written in embossed gold letters underneath 'Knowledge, Love, Truth'. Dixton thought it was a strange motto. It was in English for a start. Oh well, perhaps it was just as well, as his Latin was fairly limited despite the efforts of Mr Walsh, the Latin teacher at his old school, who had done his best and then had a nervous breakdown at a gymkhana. Dixton had fond memories of Latin class but little or no recollection of Latin itself.

He pushed the main door open and then made his way into the foyer of the building. The Porters' Lodge was on the extreme right and a couple of students were queuing to get keys to their rooms. The porter himself looked like a real tyrant and was obviously under severe pressure from having to deal with more than one person at a time. He was about fifty and wore gold rimmed glasses with one of those horrible chains, which drooped, around his jaws allowing the glasses to hang around his neck when not in use. He was quite agitated and seemed to be having difficulty in understanding an oriental girl who was looking for a room-key.

'I'm afraid I don't understand a word you're saying Miss, is your name Lee or Li?'

'My name is Lee, liiee.. liiee..'

The girl enunciated her name very slowly and was genuinely attempting to help, but this seemed to drive the porter around the bend even more.

'I know what it sounds like but how do you spell it? Is it L-e-e or L-i or what? I have a Lee in room F4 and another one in J12 but there are no first names with either of them.'

'Ah yes first name, you want my first name, my first name is Li, you want I spell?'

The porter was completely exasperated. He was making no progress at all. Finally the girl was packed off to J12 as the porter gave up trying to decide who she was. Dixton imagined the porter was the kind of fellow who peed in the cubicles.

When Dixton reached the desk the porter was at the end of his tether. He didn't even look up but barked out abruptly.

'Name?'

10

Dixton couldn't resist the temptation,

'Lee.'

Steam rose from the porter's nose as he slowly lifted his head and stared viciously across the desk. Dixton knew he had overstepped the mark.

'A comedian are we?'

'No, not really, well, sort of . . .'

'Well keep your jokes to yourself in future all right?'

'OK.' Dixton suppressed a desire to burst out laughing.

'Your real name then?'

'Larkin.'

The porter glanced down through the list in front of him and then threw a key on the desk.

'You're in El.'

Dixton was tempted to ask for directions but thought better of it. He turned towards the front door and as he reached it the person who had been in the queue behind him, a blonde willowy chap of about his own age, caught up with him.

'Sailing a bit close to the wind there, eh?'

'I suppose so.'

Never mind. Nobody likes him anyway, he's known as the Abominable Slowman. Thankfully he only works part-time.'

They both laughed and stepped outside into the sunshine. Dixton had left his luggage outside the door.

'Let me give you a hand with that.'

Between them they carried all of Dixton's luggage, two suitcases, a haversack and a guitar, to the block of rooms in the West court with the letter E over the door. Dixton's room was on the ground floor on the right just inside the door of the block.

'Just dump everything on the floor, I'll unpack it all later.'

They piled the cases in the middle of the floor and Dixton placed the guitar case carefully on the bed.

'My name is Andy, by the way, Andy Chalmers.' He stretched out his hand.

Dixton shook it. 'Dixton Larkin, pleased to meet you Andy.'

'Are you here for the LLM Dixton?'

'Yes, how did you know?'

'Well Lupin Hall seems to attract LLMs these days. Every second person here seems to be studying Law.'

'Really? I didn't know it was a law college.'

'No? Well how come you chose Lupin Hall then?'

'I tossed a coin,' Dixton smirked.

'You're joking.'

'No, honestly, I tossed a coin it was either Newnham or Lupin Hall.'

'But Newnham's an all female college.'

'That's why I wound up here, simple isn't it?'

Andy grinned, 'You know I almost believe you.'

'Great, do you want a drink of whiskey? I bought a bottle of Jameson in the Duty Free.'

'I'd love some, I've got glasses in my room. I'll be back in a second.'

Dixton was beginning to settle in already and he'd only been there for about twenty minutes.

While Andy was gone to get some glasses Dixton contemplated his new room. Although it was about a quarter of the size of the room he had in his aunt's house this room had the distinct advantage of not actually being in his aunt's house. Once he put his posters on the wall and found some space for the miniature statue of Groucho Marx the room would be perfect. Andy came back a few minutes later.

'So what's Lupin Hall like then?' asked Dixton.

'It's not too bad really. The main benefit of being a graduate college is that we don't have to put up with yapping undergraduates. All they do is whinge for home for the first year and then jump on some left-wing bandwagon for the rest of their degree and bore everybody to death.'

Dixton knew the type. They studied the exploitation of poor people on the far side of the world for four years at college and then went on to become bankers.

'What are you studying Andy?'

'"Comski" or Computer Science. I did my first degree in Exeter. That was great fun but three years was enough really. I'm sure I'll be glad to see the back of this place when I'm finished too.'

'That bad?'

'No, not really. You can have some great fun here if you want to but you've got to make a bit of an effort because Lupin is so far out of town.'

'So how does everybody get about?'

'By bicycle. It's murder otherwise.'

Dixton wondered if Aunt Sheila's generosity would stretch to include a means of transport to and from pubs for her nephew. He made a mental note to broach the subject when he wrote to her.

'What about meals. Do most people cook for themselves or what?'

'Practically no-one cooks except some of the vegetarians. The food in college is pretty good; it's dirt-cheap really. You'd be crazy to cook for yourself.'

Dixton was delighted to hear this. His domestic skills did not extend far beyond a basic understanding of can-openers and an uncanny ability to arrive home at the very moment at which food was being served. His definition of self-catering was what lonely people did in the privacy of their own bedrooms and he had no intention of learning to cook at this late stage in his life. Andy looked at his watch:

'I'd better go, I'm supposed to hand in a report to my supervisor before five. I'll see you later on. Maybe in the bar after nine or so. There's bound to be a large crew there on the first day back.'

Dixton unpacked and put all his clothes and belongings into the wardrobe and drawers. He arranged his collection of cassettes in a neat row against the wall on the desk. He loved pop and rock music and had a huge collection of cassettes at home in Dublin. He'd had to choose some essential music to bring with him and so he limited his choice to twenty tapes. He put up a poster of the Beatles on the back of the door with blu-tac and placed Groucho Marx on the window-sill. He'd taken some books with him from home and these included the complete works of WB Yeats and three or four novels by Walter Macken. He'd read them all a number of times and was currently re-reading *Rain on the Wind*.

He was a little surprised to discover that his luggage included some legal textbooks but then remembered that he'd done that for the benefit of Aunt Sheila who had helped him pack on the previous night. He supposed that she had been glad to see him take with him the tools of his trade so to speak. He had no idea whether any of the books would be of use to him during the coming year as he hadn't yet chosen his subjects. He had some information on the courses somewhere and would have to root it out at some stage and pick his subjects.

There was a knock at the door just as he finished unpacking.

'Come in.'

The door opened and a pretty girl in her late twenties with tight jeans and her hair in a ponytail entered. She was clutching a clipboard and had a black pen in her left hand. She was gorgeous.

'Hello, you must be,' she glanced down at her clipboard, 'Dixton, yes, Dixton Larkin isn't it?'

Dixton could hardly think let alone answer. He was in love. (Dixton always felt more than a little disappointed at the end of a day if he hadn't fallen in love at least once.) Dixton? That is your name isn't it?'

He woke up momentarily 'Oh yes of course, that's me Dixton Larkin. And you are?'

'I'm Liz.'

'Oh yes I see.'

'Welcome to Lupin Hall.'

'Thank you,' Dixton answered rather limply. At the same time he thought that if this girl was really serious about making him welcome then there was an entirely obvious avenue of action open to them. He could imagine her wearing jodhpurs.

'There will be a tour of the college in ten minutes so you can assemble with the others at the Porters' Lodge.'

He wasn't too keen on re-visiting the porter. The girl left the room and Dixton stood transfixed for a couple of seconds gazing at the space where the jodhpurs might have been.

About ten others were waiting when Dixton arrived some minutes later. Liz introduced them all to each other but Dixton couldn't remember any of the names after a couple of seconds except that he knew that one of the male students was called something like muesli. The porter was not behind the desk and so Dixton needn't have worried. The tour got under way and the newcomers followed their guide around the college with at least one of their number hanging on her every word.

Despite the fact that Lupin Hall was a relatively modern college, it appeared to have no shortage of funds and was lavishly furnished. The reading room, which was their first stop, was upstairs of the front foyer and its windows overlooked the front court of the college. It was sumptuously decorated the entire room was full of antique furniture and leather settees and armchairs. There was a large clock on the end wall with the date 1763 engraved on it's face. There were two oak roll-top writing desks at either end of the room and the daily newspapers were laid out in red leather folders on an enormous table in the centre of the room. Dixton was breathtaken. This kind of room wouldn't exist in Ireland for very long if students had access to it.

Their guide stood at the head of the group facing them with her back to the clock and told them a little about the room.

'The reading room is open every day from eight in the morning until eleven at night. All the daily newspapers are delivered to the college and the porters lay them out here at about five past eight. If you want any other newspaper delivered then submit the name to the porters and they will be ordered. The other main use of the room is on Tuesday and Thursday nights after formal hall. The coffee is served here before we return to the main dining room for port.'

At the mention of alcohol Dixton's ears pricked up and he began to warm to the reading room. It was apparently an ante-room to getting trashed. He had no idea that people actually lived like this, not at college anyway. One of the other students asked about the clock on the wall.

'The clock', their guide answered 'was a gift to the college from Lord Lupin himself. He presented it to the college on the date of the official opening of the college.'

'When exactly was that? In 1965?' Dixton tried to sound intelligent and vaguely recollected the brochure.

'No no, Lupin Hall didn't come into existence until two years ago. It was formerly known as University College Hall but changed it's name as a mark of thanks to the kindness of Lord Lupin.'

Dixton understood where all the money had come from to furnish the college in this expensive way. On the way to the main dining hall he struck up a conversation with another person in the tour group. Herve, it appeared, was Belgian and was studying history at Lupin Hall.

'I think I have heard of this Lord Lupin (he pronounced Lupin as Lupan) some time before.'

'Oh yes?'

'Yes in Belgium we have a phrase: "Lupan pour les lapins".'

'Oh right.'

Dixton hadn't a clue what this man was on about. He persevered however with the conversation and gathered that 'lapin' (which he was nearly sure meant rabbit) was a pet name for children and Lupan was a brand name of some garment or other for children. Hence 'Lupin pour les lapins'. Surely that couldn't be right? Or if it was what connection did it have with Lord Lupin? He did not have to wait very long to find out.

'Lord Lupin!' their guide announced triumphantly when they had gathered in a semi-circle around her in the dining hall. She pointed in the direction of the area behind them and Dixton turned around, expecting to see their loyal benefactor waving at them from a balcony or something. He was nearly right, as a huge portrait of the man, who had paid enough money to change the name of the college, loomed down at them from the wall. He looked reasonably young, though of course there was no way of knowing when the portrait was painted. Lord Lupin was sitting in an armchair in a drawing room and two marmalade cats crouched at his feet as though about to spring out of the painting. Dixton wondered if perhaps the library was called after the cats.

'Lord Lupin is the founder and owner of Lupin Nappies Limited the largest producer of nappies in the world!'

The tone in which this accolade was delivered was sincerity itself and Dixton got the uncomfortable feeling that Liz, the sexy guide with the clipboard and oodles of possibility, was completely taken in by the myth of altruistic academic benefaction. He tested his theory by catching her eye and smiling, inviting her to share with him the knowledge that she too was a healthy cynic. He met with a stony stare. He was no longer in love. Still, he supposed, what else could you expect? He ignored the remainder of the tour commentary and wondered where the next object of his desires might be lurking. He was a great fan of co-education. His old school had gone co-ed the year after he left. He always felt that this development so soon after his departure had not been a coincidence. He looked out the window.

The college was made up of three main buildings and they were arranged in a horseshoe shape. Dixton supposed that from the air, the college would look something like a giant crab.

A voice intruded on his thoughts.

'Would you like to come back to our rooms for some coffee?' asked Herve as the tour finished. Dixton accepted the invitation. Herve lived with his wife in a suite of rooms in M Block. They had got married the previous February and Karen worked in a translating agency in the town. In the living room a Belgian tricolour adorned one of the walls.

'What subjects will you be studying?' asked Herve.

Dixton realised almost suddenly that that was why he was there in the first place. He hadn't seriously thought about the whole venture in terms of learning and attending lectures and all that but he supposed he would have to think about it sooner or later.

'I don't know really Herve, I've got a list somewhere in my room and I think that I have to choose four from that.'

The couple laughed. Dixton thought that it must seem strange to them that someone would travel to another country and not have a clue what subjects he was going to study. Looking at it objectively he even thought it a bit odd himself. He would have to root out the syllabus at some stage but the exams were a long way off and Dixton wasn't unduly worried. He was offered a second cup of coffee. This was the life. He and Herve discussed rugby and then got onto the subject of foreign travel.

'I've been to Ireland once,' said Herve.

'Yes?'

'Oh yes it was a couple of years ago now, I went there camping with my parents to Kerry. I don't remember much about it.'

Dixton presumed it must have either been a very long time ago or that Herve was simply being polite. Nobody could fail to recall the horrific details of camping in Kerry. People in Kerry were a law unto themselves. All the Kerry people he'd ever met were either terribly generous or unbelievably mean. There was no middle ground. Some of them had a nose for ripping off that would leave Revenue officials stranded. He even knew of one family who were so mean that they ran their deep freeze off a socket in the house next door where a pensioner had the benefit of free electricity.

While he thoroughly enjoyed Herve's company Dixton felt a little uneasy about his wife. She hovered in the background and tutted disapprovingly to herself from time-to-time for no apparent reason. Dixton was fairly certain that Herve's wife kept a close eye on her gregarious husband and was not too happy to have to share his company with other people particularly non-studious people like Dixton. He waited until he'd finished his coffee then made some excuse about having to unpack, and left.

When he got back to his room Dixton put the suitcases away in the cupboard under the stairs in the hallway. He wondered who were the other inhabitants of E block and whether any of them were eligible females. He made his way upstairs to the middle floor and found the kitchen he hoped he would never have to use. It seemed to be fairly well equipped and each person in the block had their own locker in which to keep food. The kitchen was spotlessly clean and he thought of it as somehow an appropriate monument to the nappy empire: pristine and waiting to be dirtied. By now it was nearly five o'clock. The dining hall would be open in half an hour or so, it wasn't long to wait but he'd been travelling for most of the day and was starving. He was so hungry he could have eaten a farmer's arse through a hedge. He took a tray and queued and when he'd reached the checkout he was surprised at how little the whole meal cost. Perhaps the dining hall was heavily subsidized or maybe all the other places where he'd ever eaten had overcharged him. This seemed the most plausible explanation. He spotted a seat between two people at the end of the hall and made a beeline for it.

On his right was a very odd looking gentleman. He was one of those people who could have been anything from fifty to ninety years of age. He had a strange beard which curved outwards and upwards from the end of his chin. Dixton imagined that he was the type of person for whom minestrone would be a nightmare. He was wearing an academic gown which had slipped down his person as he sat hunched at the dining table and had come to rest just above his elbows. He looked at Dixton, as soon as he sat down, with almost a look of fright. If it had been a scene from a film Dixton's line would have been.

'You look as though you've seen a ghost old man.'

It was not a scene from a film so Dixton said nothing but instead turned his attentions to the person sitting on his left. He looked a more friendly prospect. Dixton smiled at him, half to say hello, and half out of relief from discovering someone semi-normal to eat beside. The young man smiled at Dixton then winked and nodded his head in the direction of the Rip Van Winkle character on Dixton's other side. He swallowed whatever he'd been chewing then spoke.

'I see you've been getting acquainted with one of the college institutions!'

'Pardon?'

'Professor Lynn the librarian.'

Dixton nodded questioningly to his right. The man nodded back and continued,

'He's been here for absolutely years. Nobody knows what he's professor of but I suppose that doesn't matter much in the library.'

Dixton was afraid that the old man might take offence if he heard these comments he spoke again in rather hushed tones.

'He seems a bit strange.'

The other man laughed, 'I don't know why you're whispering, he's as deaf as a post.'

'Really?'

'Yes. He can't hear a thing. Doesn't stop him doing his job though. If you have any overdue books he phones the Porters' Lodge and asks one of them to find you. Then he shouts down the phone at you to return the book.'

Dixton felt that this course of action possessed at least one fatal flaw.

'But if he's deaf, I mean if he can't hear, how does he know whether the right person is on the other end of the telephone or not?'

'That's just it, he doesn't, so he just shouts down the phone regardless of whether or not the porters manage to locate the person he's looking for. This drives the porters so crazy that they take it upon themselves to make sure that the books are returned. They know that if the books don't reach the library in the next day or so he'll be back on the phone screaming at whoever happens to pick it up. They daren't hang up on him either because he'll simply turn up and rant at them in person. It's a strange system but it works. The library hasn't lost a book in years.'

Dixton recounted the details of his run-in with one of the porters earlier on.

'Oh don't worry about him, everybody hates him. The other porter Stan is fine. Old Slowman is an insufferable git and he's not around much. He's the kind of person who would buy a knife from you, stab you with it and then sue you for breach of contract.'

'Are you studying law?' Dixton picked up on the legal reference.

'No, architecture, but we do a bit of law as well in our second year. I suppose you're another LLM bloke?'

'Yeah, there seems to be a lot of us about.' Dixton was only halfway through his meal when his new acquaintance was getting up to go. He didn't even know his name.

'My name's Dixton, what's yours?'

'Jack, Jack Miller. I'm in J10 and I'm chairman of the Sports Committee.'

Dixton heard a low growl to his right. He turned towards the librarian. The old man was having some difficulty in rising from the bench because Dixton was sitting on the edge of his gown. Dixton raised himself up slightly to free the gown and as he watched the librarian disappear with his tray he made a mental note never to keep a book out for longer than he should. Libraries were not, in any case, an essential part of his game plan for the year.

The bar opened at nine on the dot and Dixton was one of the first customers. A pint cost just seventy pence. Theoretically he could get absolutely wasted for six or seven pounds but he was fairly tired and was not in the mood to indulge in a heavy session just yet. He spotted Andy but as he was chatting up a young rather tanned lady, Dixton thought better of disturbing him.

There was a pool table in the bar and people booked their turn to play by writing their names in chalk on a small piece of blackboard dangling from a string on a nearby wall. Dixton wasn't a bad player and so he wrote his name down. There were about four people ahead of him on the list. When his turn came to play the person who had won the three previous games was a loud brash fellow with brylcreamed hair. He was wearing a multicoloured waistcoat which was rather pukey looking and a pair of those awful pleated trousers which Dixton always associated with waiters. He seemed to be surrounded by a number of acolytes and his name was Bernard something.

Dixton had been watching him playing for a couple of games and though he'd stayed on as winner, Dixton felt that the opposition hadn't been great. The mediocre are always at their best. He knew he could do better himself (to be fair though, he often thought the same of televised skating but never got a chance to test his theory). For some reason he felt an immediate animosity towards this chap. Dixton rarely disliked people on sight but he felt that the way this joker had sneered while beating the other people was a bit over the top. Normally Dixton felt it was unfair to dislike anyone other than taxi-drivers on first impressions.

Dixton broke off. His hand was shaking slightly and it was a terrible opening shot. The pack split very favourably for his opponent, two striped balls stopped at the edge of the centre pockets.

'Bollox,' he thought.

Bernard the aristoprat chalked his cue and walked around the table eyeing up various angles and taking mock shots as though he was planning the D-Day invasion instead of a shot that would be obvious to a three year old. Get on with it Dixton thought. Even though the shot was simple, and the margin of error nil, Bernard looked up from the table with the self-congratulatory air of someone who had set a new world record for freestyle farting. Dixton was sickened. He was going to lose and even worse, it would be to this dick.

The break continued and four balls were potted in a row before Dixton got back to the table. He was on the 'solid' coloured balls. He potted one in the left top corner pocket and there was a palpable gasp from his opponent's fan club. Feeling that his luck might be in, Dixton tried to pot the only other available solid along the cushion but missed. Bernard looked over at his lackeys and smiled. It was a horrible smile, sort of a cross between an Elvis Presley leer and the facial contortions of a man who had just drunk some weed killer. He chalked his cue again and prepared to finish Dixton off.

He had two striped balls and the black to pot. The first shot was difficult enough and Dixton reluctantly admitted, not openly of course, that it was a good shot. Dixton had just begun to feel that all was lost when Bernard potted the white ball by accident. While his opponent was glaring at the tip of his own cue in disbelief Dixton used the free extra shot to his advantage and cleared the table of solid balls. He had only the black to sink to win the game. The pressure was on. He lined up the shot into the bottom right pocket knowing that to miss would almost certainly mean losing. The cue ball struck the black almost dead centre and it swept towards the pocket. As it headed for the pocket Dixton realised that he'd misjudged the angle. The black ball hit the left side of the pocket and ricocheted bizarrely along the top cushion. There was utter silence around the pool table as everyone watched the ball roll slowly towards the other pocket. Would it make it? Yes, no, yes, no, yes, no, YES!

Dixton felt like hugging the person next to him but realised in time that it was his opponent. Dixton was over the moon. Bernard looked furious. The lackeys were not at all pleased. One or two of them in fact looked quite nasty particularly a large fat chap with a baseball cap and Dixton sensed that it was the type of situation that perhaps given a slight push could escalate into violence quite easily. For the first time in quite a while he felt a little vulnerable. He was an outsider here. He wasn't quite sure what his next move should be, but fate, it appeared, was at that moment wearing her kindest knickers.

'Well done.'

He heard a familiar accent congratulate him from behind his right ear. He wasn't quite sure for a second but then mentally decoded it. It was definitely an Irish accent. He turned around. His congratulator was a solid looking chap in a navy golf pullover. He sounded northern, (Belfast maybe). He hadn't noticed him before but he must have been watching the game. Bernard and his lackeys backed off. The man in the golfing pullover spoke.

'Are you Irish?'

'Yes I am, I'm from Dublin, and yourself?'

'From Belfast.' (He'd been right.)

'My name's Dixton Larkin.'

'I'm Johnny Pepper. Do you want a pint?'

'I'd love one.'

From behind, as they walked towards the bar, someone shouted from the area of the pool table.

'Hey you, it's winner stays on.'

Dixton turned for a second and faced back towards Bernard and his goons.

'I think the loser probably needs the practice.'

It wasn't a show-stopping put down by any means but it had the desired effect.

When Dixton reached the bar there were two pints settling on the counter.

'I presumed you'd want Guinness, Dixton.'

He'd presumed correctly.

21

CHAPTER THREE

Dixton had a hangover. His mouth felt as if a dog had slept in it. His first morning in Lupin Hall dawned as one of those deceptive October days. It was bright and sunny enough to remind you that the summer was still pretty recent but at the same time there was a latent chill in the air which hinted at another season.

He couldn't have cared less what the weather was like except that he had developed a recent aversion to sunlight. He had forgotten to close the curtains in his room before going to bed and so the sun woke him up at about seven. Dixton had managed to get back to sleep for a couple of hours but was now fully awake and totally aware of his hangover. He and Johnny Pepper had gone on a major bender the night before. Eight or nine pints in the college bar and then back to Pepper's room where they had demolished the rest of the Duty Free Jameson. It's tough at the top but it's very lonely in the middle.

He steeled himself for the ordeal of getting up by counting to ten and then jumped out of bed, ran to the sink and extracted a packet of Solpadine from his wash-bag. He ripped open the packet and then realised that he didn't have a glass or mug in which to dissolve the tablets. He looked frantically around the room for a suitable receptacle. His eye came to rest on the only available option, the wastepaper bin. It was a brand new and made of bright orange plastic. He managed to squash one side of it into a sort of a point and then slipped the bin into the sink and under the tap. He turned on the water. Dixton emptied the entire packet of Solpadine into the orange bin. There was an almighty whoosh like a tractor tyre being slashed flat. Dixton stared down into the bin at what looked like a spadeful of suds, closed his eyes and tipped the whole lot down his throat.

The T-shirt got soaked but the bulk of the mixture ended up inside Dixton. He felt better already, or at least told himself that he did. Although it was the first Monday of term, classes were not scheduled to begin for a couple of days. Perhaps he would mooch around the town today and get his bearings. He struggled into a pair of jeans, chose the first shirt that came to hand in the wardrobe and pulled on his runners without opening the laces. His head had begun to clear slightly but his stomach felt awful, perhaps he'd overdone it with the Solpadine. There were shower units in the corridor outside but felt he couldn't quite raise his game to that yet. He stripped to the waist and made for the sink.

The previous evening's drinking session was a little blurred; however, he did remember some of the conversation he'd had with Pepper.

'Dixton, I've come to Cambridge to achieve three things - a golfing Blue, membership of the Hawks Club and a geology degree, and all in that order.'

Pepper was a keen golfer and was determined to play for the university against Oxford. Dixton had no idea what the Hawks Club was.

He had nearly finished brushing his teeth when he heard the sound of a key being inserted in the door of his room from the outside. He hadn't yet put on his shirt and so when he heard a woman's voice:

'Hello?'

The door opened, he grabbed a towel and held it up to his chest in much the same way as he'd seen female movie stars do. A lady wearing a light green pullover and matching slacks entered. She looked a bit surprised to see him.

'Oh I'm sorry,' she said 'I thought you'd be out of the room by now, I can come back later.'

Dixton had no idea who this lady was or why she was in his room while he stood near the sink clutching a towel to his hairless chest. He answered in his best embarrassed but polite voice,

'No that's quite all right, I'll be out of here in a second.' The lady smiled,

'You're Irish aren't you?' My mum's Irish, she's from Sligo. Listen, I'll turn my back for a minute while you finish dressing.'

Dixton hurriedly buttoned his shirt and then cleared his throat to alert her to the fact that he was ready. She turned around again to face him,

'I'm Laura, your bedder.'

Dixton was stunned,

'You're my what?'

'Bedder, cleaner, Hoover-upper, I'm here to tidy the room.' All was now clear, Dixton realised that he'd misread the meaning of the term, and he smiled back.

'I'm Dixton, Dixton Larkin, I just got here yesterday.'

'Well Dixton I'm glad to meet you, I hope you'll be an improvement on the last one who had this room. He kept incense burning here the whole time. I spent most of the year hoovering up ash from the carpet.'

'I certainly hope I'll be an improvement on that.'

He'd have preferred not to know anything about the previous owner; it made the room seem somehow less his. Laura was very motherly looking. He guessed her age to be about forty fiveish and saw that she wore a wedding ring and a huge diamond engagement ring on the same finger. He grabbed a pullover from the back of the chair and made his way past her to the door.

'I'm just heading out for breakfast.'

'I won't be long cleaning the room, there's not much needs doing. See you in the morning, then, Dixton.'

He knocked on Pepper's door.

'Come in.'

He pushed open the door. Pepper was sitting at the desk writing something. He looked up.

'Oh hello Dixton, how's your head?'

'Not too bad now, but my stomach's in bits after all the Solpadine I poured into it. How's *your* head?'

'Fine, I managed to drink a couple of pints of water before I went to bed. Any plans for today?'

'Not really, I thought maybe I'd go into the town and see what it's like, find my way around, that sort of thing. Have you started studying already?' He indicated towards whatever Pepper had been writing. Pepper laughed.

'Oh God no, I just make a list of things to do every day and try to get through it.'

This sort of organisation was completely alien to Dixton. 'Oh I see.'

Pepper must have detected the reticence in Dixton's voice and was quick to reassure him.

'Don't worry it's not work or anything like that; for example my list today consists of four items.' He listed them: 'One: buy golf balls. Two: find out where the geology department is. Three: have lunch. Four: phone Clara.'

'Who's Clara?'

'She's my girlfriend, she lives in Belfast.'

'You didn't mention her yesterday I don't think.'

'Didn't I? Oh well. Look do you mind if I come into town with you?'

'Not at all, we can get a bite to eat somewhere.'

They made their way out the back entrance of the college and asked someone for directions into town. One thing they both noticed were the number of cyclists who passed them as they strolled along.

'Everyone else here seems to have a bicycle,' said Pepper.

'I spoke to someone in the college yesterday who said that it is pretty difficult to survive here without one.'

'Do you think that we should buy a bike each?'

'I don't know really Pepper, maybe the college will have some scheme for renting them out or maybe there's a second hand shop somewhere that flogs them off cheaply.'

If he could get Aunt Sheila to cough up for a new bike and bought a second-hand one, he'd have a few extra quid to spend on himself. In principal that sounded dishonest but he was sure he'd be able to cope with it.

They crossed a main road and made their way towards a bridge. Queen's College was on their left and as they walked up onto the bridge they saw a smaller, wooden bridge that was elaborately made and joined two parts of Queen's College. Dixton had heard of the Mathematical Bridge before, it was supposed to have been built by Newton or someone like that. As they crossed the bridge Pepper pointed out a pub on the right called The Anchor.

'That looks like a decent pub.'

'Oh, I couldn't face a drink at this stage.'

'No I don't mean now, but maybe as a place to go drinking some night maybe later this week.'

'Yeah maybe.' Dixton was still at that early stage of a morning after the night before when he was seriously considering never drinking again. They continued past the Anchor and on to King's Parade, a street which fronted some of the older and more famous colleges. They strolled under the sandstone archway into King's.

This was the college which was familiar to them from postcards. The two were absolutely knocked out by the architecture of the college and the whole atmosphere of the place. Most of the people that they saw around the grounds were either tourists or undergraduates. Apart from the absence of cameras the undergraduates stood out from the tourists because they all seemed to be deliberately unimpressed by their surroundings. Dixton felt that even if he owned this college he would never take its splendour for granted.

This was the kind of place which would impress Aunt Sheila no end. He bought a postcard of King's to send to her. It would reassure her that her investment was worthwhile. She could put it on the mantelpiece and say, when the bridge club committee met in her front room,

'Oh yes that's where Dixton is studying he's awfully clever you know,' but actually she would mean: 'Oh yes that's where I sent Dixton, I'm awfully rich you know.'

Dixton often thought of his aunt more as a sponsor than as a relative.

There were signs all around the edge of the vast court saying 'Keep off the Grass' and 'Only Fellows may walk on the Grass'. Dixton and Pepper needed no second invitation. They stepped over the small railing on to the grass and made their way diagonally across the court towards the chapel. A porter emerged from the lodge just inside the main gate and shouted at them to get off the grass. They ignored him. The porter disappeared.

'That's the end of him,' said Pepper 'there's really nothing they can do to stop us, we'd easily outrun him any day.'

As they looked back in the direction of the Porters' Lodge they had scarcely begun to savour their minor triumph when the porter re-emerged with a large dog on a leash. From where he stood Dixton thought it looked like an alsatian but he wasn't sure. (From a distance Dixton thought every dog was an alsatian. He'd been bitten as a child, well not exactly bitten, he'd been snapped at, which was actually worse in his opinion because all the scars were mental.) The Porter led the dog to the edge of the railing, where the two had stepped over and slipped the leash off. It was as though Dixton and Pepper were seeing the whole scene in slow motion. They looked at each other.

'The bastard,' said Pepper.

'Oh bollox,' said Dixton, 'let's leg it.'

The two boys turned and sprinted towards the corner of the court. They could hear the dog woofing in the distance behind them. It certainly sounded like an alsatian. Pepper was a couple of yards ahead at this stage and Dixton began to realise that if the dog was going to eat anyone that it would be him. He had never been so frightened in all his life. Pepper reached the edge of the court. Dixton was still on the grass and could hear the dog barking and getting closer all the time.

He saw Pepper disappear across the concrete into the chapel and thought to himself, well this is it Dix you idiot, you get accepted into Cambridge and eaten by an alsatian on your first day for walking on the grass. He reached the edge of the court and as he did there was a loud whistle, he looked behind and saw that the dog had stopped dead in it's tracks and was panting and leering at him from only a foot or so away. The Porter had stopped the dog just in time. Dixton was so relieved that he forgot his fear for a second although he was acutely aware that his hands were perspiring profusely. He stumbled the remaining few yards to the chapel door in a daze. Pepper was waiting inside the door leaning up against a pew.

'I thought we were gone there Dixton, did you see the size of him?'

'Did I what? If he'd come any closer I'd have had to marry him.' Dixton was still trying to catch his breath. 'They . . . they can't do that, not legally they can't, can they Pepper?'

'I don't know, you're the lawyer Dixton.'

The two of them stood there for a couple of minutes panting.

'I suppose it's our own fault really,' said Pepper, 'I mean, we saw the signs and everything.'

Dixton could hear his aunt's shrill voice somewhere in the back of his head saying: 'Dixton, the only person you're fooling is yourself.'.

There was a guided tour just leaving the chapel and so Pepper and Dixton were the only people left in the magnificent building. They walked on the sandstone floor up towards the top of the chapel. A vast painting by Rubens dominated the end wall. Dixton wondered if they would be able to steal it and never have to work for a living.

'What do you think of this place Pepper?'

'It's fantastic, it's a shame I didn't get accepted here, I'd love to live in a college like this.'

'Did you apply to get in here?'

'Yeah. But it's impossible to get in to the really old colleges unless you're royalty or something. Where did you apply to?'

'Lupin Hall.'

'You're joking?'

'No honestly I did.' Dixton sensed Pepper's mild amazement.

'I suppose we should go. But what about the dog?'

'Oh him, I wasn't really afraid of him.'

'Yeah right,' said Dixton, sneeringly, 'do you think he'll be outside waiting for us?'

'I bloody well hope not.'

They left King's College by the back entrance.

The town centre was a maze of small winding streets littered with book-shops. Every corner they rounded seemed to contain another college. Some were facing onto the main street, others were tucked away down alleys and had deceptively small entrances that when explored gave way to sprawling olde world buildings covered in ivy. Some of the small sidestreets seemed to have been frozen in time hundreds of years before and would have been difficult to date were it not for the card-phones which haunted every corner. It was while they were looking around Trinity Hall College that Dixton spotted a notice on a notice board.

'Look at this.'

'What?'

'Look, here, Clubs and Societies Day for the University.'

'What about it?'

'Well it's on today in someplace called Kelsey Kerridge the University sports centre. Let's go?'

'Why not, it might be fun. Listen I'm starving so lets get something to eat first all right?'

'OK.'

They made their way back out onto the main street and found a pub called the Crazy Partridge just off King's Parade. They ordered soup and a sandwich each and Dixton drank a pint of milk while Pepper had a half of Guinness. Dixton didn't know how Pepper could face alcohol so soon. The pub was just beginning to fill up with its lunchtime trade. Dixton noticed that some of the women coming into the pub were gorgeous executive types with long legs and short skirts. It certainly wasn't a student pub. He wondered if he would find any romance in Cambridge during the coming year.

Pepper had a more direct approach.

'I tell you Dixton, I wouldn't mind spending a shallow meaningless night with one of them.'

'But I thought you had a girlfriend, in Belfast, Clara, isn't it?'

'Well yes I suppose you're right, but Clara and I we have this, well, this arrangement I suppose you'd call it.'

'What kind of arrangement?' Dixton was intrigued.

Pepper explained. It appeared that Clara was a childhood sweetheart of Pepper's and that her parents and his were quite close. It was tacitly assumed by everyone (well everyone except Pepper, perhaps) that he and Clara would eventually marry when he finished studying and returned to Belfast. Pepper had spent the three previous years doing his primary degree in Edinburgh. He phoned Clara every day while he was away and when he went home on holidays he played the part of the faithful boyfriend.

'But while I'm away I do as I like and nobody is the wiser, least of all Clara.'

'But what happens when you eventually go home after all your studying is over? Won't you be expected to come up with the goods and marry her then?'

'Well if by then I haven't met and married anyone else well maybe I will marry her.'

Dixton couldn't believe what he was hearing. He stared incredulously at Pepper.

'You're not serious?'

'Oh I am. Think about it Dixton, if this girl is willing to wait for four years for me to come home and marry her then surely it would be unfair to disappoint her. Anyway that's not today's or tomorrow's problem.'

Dixton didn't know whether to laugh at Pepper or to hit him. He felt sorry for this poor girl he'd never met, stuck at home in Belfast while her boyfriend roamed Britain in search of casual sex.

'Well suppose Clara has a fling and finds someone else while you're away cheating on her in various universities Pepper?'

'Not possible.'

'What do you mean, not possible?'

'Well there's no way she will meet someone else or even think about having a fling.'

'How can you be so sure?'

Pepper looked straight at Dixton and said, in a tone of voice Dixton took to be complete sincerity or at least a superb imitation of it.

'Look Dixton there's no way I would continue going out with her, on any basis if I thought she was the type who would cheat on me.'

Dixton was dumbfounded. He'd never encountered this mix of warped logic, arrogance and geniality before. He basically liked Pepper, but his attitude towards this girl Clara who obviously loved him, was totally over the top. He remembered hearing once that the key to success is sincerity because once you can fake that you've got it made. Still, it was really none of his business how Pepper treated his girlfriends. Dixton gulped down the remainder of his milk.

'Come on Pepper, let's find this Clubs and Societies thing.' They paid their bills and left the Crazy Partridge.

Kelsey Kerridge was, as the poster had intimated, the University Sports Centre. It was a massive ugly grey building on the edge of a large park called Parker's Piece. As they approached the entrance they were surrounded by a large group of enthusiastic students proffering a wide array of leaflets and flyers. Other students simply shouted at them,

'Join the Bungee Society.'

'Come to the vegetarian barbecue.' (Dixton had heard of few more pointless concepts.) For some reason non-alcoholic beer came to mind.

They battled their way through the group of people handing out the leaflets and once inside the building they both dumped all their leaflets and flyers into the nearest bin. It was as though there was telepathy between them. Watching the bunch of multicoloured leaflets disappear into the bin reminded Dixton of the Solpadine episode. For a moment he feared that he was going to be sick, but the moment passed and he knew he was well on the road to recovery. They climbed four flights of stairs to get to the main hall which was packed with stalls representing dozens and dozens of clubs and societies.

'Jesus!' Dixton exclaimed.

'It's pretty impressive isn't it?'

'Yeah. Any ideas where to start, or are there any stalls we really want to visit? Dixton was keen to get started.

'I don't mind, all I really need to do is to make contact with the Golf Club.'

'That's exactly how I feel playing Pitch and Putt.'

Pepper missed the pun completely.

'Let's start here on the left and work our way around the hall against the crowd,' Dixton suggested.

'OK.'

There was a massive selection of stalls and most of them promised free drink at their inaugural meetings to anyone who joined now. By this time Dixton was quite open to the idea of free drink and this more or less signalled the end of his hangover symptoms. They approached the stall occupied by the Christian Folk Rock Society. An eager faced girl smiled out from behind the table.

'Would you like to join?' she asked enthusiastically.

She spoke in one of those soft sweet voices, which is often used by shop assistants to persuade you to take a replacement item instead of a refund.

'Well we're not so sure, what is this Society all about?' asked Dixton in his best I'm-lost-and-searching-for-meaning-in-this-cruel-materialistic-world voice. The girl warmed to the task of enlightening him.

'Well, we meet every week to worship God through the medium of music.' (The girl should have been a chat show host.)

'Oh, I see,' Dixton looked mildly interested.

'Well would you like to join?' she smiled.

'We're not so sure, I mean yes we would, but there's one problem, well maybe it's not a problem, we wouldn't be able to take part completely in this musical worship business, would that be a problem?'

The girl smiled understandingly.

'No of course not, quite a number of our members don't play any instruments, but still participate fully.'

'Oh, no it's not that,' said Dixton beginning to write his name and college into the ledger on the desk.

'No?'

'No,' said Pepper, 'he plays the guitar and I play the. . .'

'The triangle,' Dixton cut in looking up from his task.

'That's right the triangle.'

'Well I don't see what the problem is then,' said the girl.

'Well,' said Dixton, 'that's great then, we thought the fact that we don't believe in God would pose some problems but it's great to see that your society is pluralistic.'

The girl looked shocked.

'Well I must em, say, that there is a problem if you don't believe in God. I mean that's the basis of our Society to begin with.'

'Oh I see,' said Dixton, 'I understand now. I see that the fact that we qualify under two of the three headings isn't enough for you, we have to be Christians as well. Pluralism my foot. Come on Pepper let's take our musical talents elsewhere, how about the Hare Krishnas?'

At the mention of this rival group of soul-savers the girl capitulated totally,

'Look, you're most welcome any week, here's our address, drop in if you get a chance, we can always have a chat, talk things out. . .'

Her voice faded into the distance behind Pepper and Dixton as they laughed and made their way past the Gay Society and the Veterinary Club to the Golf Club.

'Dixton, you're unbelievable, I can't believe you said that to the poor girl winding her up like that. She looked like she was nearly going to cry.'

'Well, you're laughing about it all the same.'

'Oh I know, I mean it was funny. It's unfair but it's funny. I wouldn't able to wind someone up like that with a straight face for even a minute without cracking up laughing.'

'Oh, I don't know about that Pepper, you seem to have managed to do it for four years to Clara without laughing.'

Dixton sensed that Pepper's reaction to this dig would define the parameters of their relationship. Pepper, fortunately, took it in the spirit in which it was intended.

'OK. OK. I take your point. If we're going to spend the year together there's no point in falling out over slight differences of opinion, fair enough?'

'Fair enough.'

The moment had passed and they were definitely going to be good friends.

Pepper made contact with the members and captain of the Golf Club. Dixton eyed up a gorgeous girl in a sari who was looking after the stall belonging to the Bahai Society. Dixton was reminded of a film with

Frank Sinatra, Grace Kelly and Bing Crosby in it. Pepper introduced him to some of the lads from the Golf team.

'This is Bob Sherwin the Captain, Alastair Trent and Charlie Fletcher.'

Dixton liked the look of these golfers. Not that he knew anything about golf, he just imagined that Pepper would fit in well with them. He could visualise at least two of the three making lists each day and being fairly well organised. Charlie Fletcher looked the least organised of the three because the other two were wearing blazers. Alastair had a soft London accent. He looked like an accountant.

'So you're from Ireland too, Dixton? Did you know Johnny before you came to Cambridge?'

'No, not at all, I'm from Dublin in the south, and he's from Northern Ireland.'

'Oh right, do you live quite a bit away from each other then?'

Dixton realised that for this person who lived in England there was no distinction between northern and southern Ireland. He found that somehow refreshing and wondered if in fact the whole Irish situation seemed quite bizarre when viewed from abroad.

'Yes, we live quite a distance from each other really.'

Pepper had apparently made contact with some of the Golf Club members before he arrived in Cambridge. They seemed very friendly and all the talk was of the Varsity match against Oxford.

'This year's venue is St Andrew's, said Bob Sherwin. Dixton knew that St Andrew's was in Scotland and felt quite chuffed with himself. He wondered of what, if anything, Saint Andrew was the patron saint. Aunt Sheila would know. They chatted for a while with the Golf Club members and as Pepper and Dixton were about to head off Alastair said to Pepper.

'Eight o'clock Saturday morning outside King's then.'

'What's that all about?' Dixton asked him.

'Our first golf outing, it's on Saturday. We'll be playing each weekend between now and the Varsity match in March. The team will be picked on the basis of how we do during the year.'

'Is there a lot of competition for places?'

'Yes, there's roughly twelve in the squad and six will make the final team.'

'Only six?'

'Yes, it's quite competitive. Everyone will get to play during the year in the other competitions but the main one is the Varsity match.'

'What are your chances?'

'I wouldn't even be trying if I didn't feel I had a chance. We'll see how I get on.'

Dixton had a theory about Northern Ireland Protestants, he always suspected that they were a race who were quietly confident when it came to sport and could be relied upon to take penalties in a World Cup final. If he had to choose someone to take a penalty on his behalf to save his life Pepper would probably be as good a choice as any. He barely knew Pepper but then the section in Dixton's address book marked "Penalty Takers" was pretty sparse.

They spent the best part of the afternoon traipsing around the various stalls. Dixton joined the Home Brew Society and the Classic Movie Club. The movie club sounded excellent. They showed one film each fortnight in a theatre in the town and the line-up for the first term looked great, *Casablanca*, *Some Like it Hot*, *The Third Man*, *Brief Encounter* and *The Thirty Nine Steps*. What finally convinced Dixton to join was the fact that the Society had chosen the Kenneth More version of *The Thirty Nine Steps* instead of the Robert Donat one. He loved the scene where Kenneth More is running from the bad guys and stumbles into a lecture theatre in a girls school and is mistaken for a guest speaker who is to deliver a talk on the spleenwort. For the couple of pounds that he paid to join, Dixton would be able to see all of these old films for a mere pound each.

On their way out of the hall they stopped at a stall which had a large crowd around it. As they edged their way through the crowd they saw that it was the University Rifle Club. There were a number of firearms on the table of the stall and these were the main attraction for the entirely male crowd of onlookers. Despite the great initial interest it appeared that people were put off joining by reason of the expensive membership fee of thirty pounds. The membership book open on the table was still at page one and even that wasn't very full.

Dixton and Pepper squeezed through to the front of the crowd. There were two very smug looking male students manning the stall. Dixton imagined them as extras in *The Deerhunter*. (In fairness to them, however, Dixton always had a reasonably low opinion of people who associated with guns.) They reminded him of an officious idiot he had once seen at an Elvis Convention his aunt had dragged him to in a Dublin hotel. That particular idiot was smugly guarding an item of the 'King's' clothing which was on display in much the same way as these two were minding the rifle stall. (Dixton was an Elvis fan when he was a child but now only associated the man with golf carts and ice cream.)

Pepper obviously shared his impression of them, he winked at Dixton as if to say 'watch this' and then proceeded to talk in a loud Belfast accent.

'I'd like to join the Rifle Club please.'

The two manning the desk looked at each other and Dixton caught a glimpse of a smirk passing between them as though they were enjoying a private joke. One of them turned to Pepper.

'Of course, could I have your name please?'

'I'd rather not give my name if you don't mind.' Pepper replied in a tone which implied all sorts of previous convictions. The pair looked at each other again, this time less self assuredly than before.

'I see, and what College are you at?'

'What's this, a bloody police interrogation?' Pepper raised his voice but retained the intensity of the accent.

The two rifle club members looked more than a little worried, the person talking to Pepper became somewhat apologetic.

'No, no, it's just that we need this information in order to process your application. Do you have any previous experience with rifles?'

The words were no sooner out of his mouth than he realised he'd said the wrong thing. The crowd at this stage were listening to this conversation with varying degrees of interest, scepticism and fear. They waited for Pepper to reply.

'Experience? With rifles? Do you mean during the daytime?' The interviewer was flummoxed.

'Er, yes I suppose so.'

'No, no daytime rifle experience. How about semi automatics? Do you use them? Have you got night sights?'

The two behind the desk looked terrified. The other one baled the interviewer out.

'Listen, we're fairly new in the club, could you come back later when the Captain is here?'

'OK. I'll do that,' said Pepper calmly.

His apparently sudden mood swing made him seem even more unstable and the two looked relieved that the conversation had come to an end. As he turned to go Pepper suddenly swung back to face the stall and reached into the inside pocket of his jacket. The crowd recoiled and the two boys at the desk looked scared stiff.

'One more thing,' he said accusingly pulling out a biro and pointing it at them.

'Yes?' one of them stuttered.

'Thanks for all your help.'

They looked like they felt a death sentence had just been narrowly avoided. No sense in disappointing them. Looking around in a knowing but security-conscious fashion Pepper and Dixton made their way towards the exit like two cops from some seventies TV series. The crowd seemed to part in front of them. Once outside the hall they burst out laughing and raced each other down the stairs. When they reached the bottom of the stairs Dixton spoke.

'You're such a bastard Pepper, to think I felt bad about that Christian girl for a while.' Dixton paused for breath as they stood in the foyer.

'Oh, never mind, that will give the Rifle Club something to think about,' said Pepper.

'Or it may give them something to give to the police to think about,' Dixton said cheerlessly.

'Oh, don't be such a pessimist Dixton.'

Dixton chuckled as he recalled the shocked face of the lad who had asked Pepper about previous experience with rifles. They continued out of the building onto the pavement where a group were still handing out leaflets. It had begun to rain and it was quite a walk back to Lupin Hall. They wished they had bikes. Dixton kept a look out for potential alsatians: the price of freedom was eternal vigilance.

CHAPTER FOUR

Let me introduce you to one of the most exciting, it not *the* most exciting, courses available on this year's LLM: Asian Land Law. You'll find a course outline on page four of the syllabus booklet.'

Dixton had almost fallen asleep but the rustle of one hundred and ninety nine people turning to page four disturbed his concentration. He looked up at the lecture podium. Who was this guy kidding? Asian Land Law, it sounded about as interesting as watching paint dry. The worst thing about it was that the lecturer seemed genuinely enthusiastic. There were thirty-four subjects available and each lecturer gave a ten-minute spiel to try and sell their course. This was only number six. It was going to be a long day.

'I'm sure that many of you have a special interest in the Law of the Sea, I know I have.'

Subject number eight was taught by some brainbox who looked like he was still a teenager. Dixton knew the type; straight first class honours all the way, references, recommendations, esoteric papers published in obscure journals but had never seen the inside of a night-club. He was tempted to leave but knew he would have to pick four subjects anyway so maybe a little bit of effort now would avoid work later on. From the guided tour of the law library earlier Dixton had retained little information besides the location of the photocopier.

Some of the most beautiful women he'd ever seen were doing this course. Dixton looked around the lecture theatre feeling a little like a child in an ice-cream factory. He spotted one of Bernard's lackeys in the distance and chuckled to himself as he recalled his victory on the pool table earlier in the week.

Of the first ten or so subjects only one sounded any way promising. Dixton's textbook for criminal law in his degree had been 'Simpson & Hartley'. Professor Simpson, whom Dixton was delighted to know was still alive, was offering a course in Critical Criminal Law. It seemed interesting even if only for nostalgia value and so Dixton chalked it down as one of his four. Most of the other lecturers before lunch were awful, there was one woman with a low bassy voice who lectured on 'Law and the Oppression of Women'. Dixton didn't feel that he could stand two hours a week of self-analysis and breaking up into workshops. He identified 'The Law of International Banking & Securities' as another horror subject as he was no good at maths. He was hungry.

They resumed at two o'clock after an hour's break for lunch. Dixton had arranged to meet Pepper in town at three to get bicycles and so he would have to pick his final three subjects before then. He settled on EU Law because the lecturer was gorgeous, 'The Law of Salvage' (well how much law could there be on sinking ships?) Critical Criminal Law with Professor Simpson, and he just needed one more. He glanced at the clock on the wall, he would have to go soon. The next lecturer was the archetypal male academic, tweed suit, horn-rimmed glasses and a little absent-minded. He began: 'Well now, are you third years or second years?'.

Some loudmouth shouted up at him, 'We're LLMs sir.'

He took off his glasses, wiped them with his handkerchief and put them on again, he looked at the assembled mass.

'Oh yes I see. Well most of you from common law jurisdictions will be familiar with the concept of equitable remedies, injunctions and that sort of thing. Well that's what this course is all about.'

Dixton marked Remedies and Restitution down as his fourth choice. If he'd fluked a first in Equity, he could certainly fluke a pass in a course which concentrated on a small part of the overall subject. The lecturer seemed absent minded enough to provide the necessary easy ride through the course. Dixton had strategically positioned himself near the door of the lecture hall. He left silently. Pepper was waiting for him outside Great Saint Mary's Church on King's Parade.

'I thought you weren't coming.'

'Well here I am. I had to pick my subjects. Any luck finding the geology department?'

'Yeah. I found it all right, there are only three of us doing the M Phil. It's a really small department. I met my supervisor Dr Crowther. He seems OK.'

'So what about these bikes then?'

'Well I spoke to Charlie Fletcher from the Golf Club and he gave me the address of a friend of his who has a couple of bikes for sale. It's very near here.'

'Any idea how much?'

'Charlie said the guy is very reasonable.'

They made their way across the Market Square and headed down through a lane at the side of Sidney Sussex College to a terrace of small artisan dwellings where this friend of Charlie Fletcher's lived. Pepper rang the doorbell. There was no reply. He rang the bell again and just as they were about to turn and leave the door opened. A red haired youth in a Chelsea football shirt confronted them.

'What do you want?'

He sounded aggressive, Dixton wondered if they'd got the wrong address. Pepper took control of the situation.

'We're friends of Charlie Fletcher, he said you might have a couple of bikes for sale.'

The red-haired chap stepped out onto the pavement and glanced from side to side up and down the street.

'I think you'd better come in.'

It was just like a spy movie.

'Are you Pepper?' he asked suspiciously.

'Yes.'

'Who's he then?'

'He's a friend of mine, he needs a bike too.'

'I thought Charlie said you only needed one bike.' This bloke was obviously paranoid.

'Well you know how things are,' Dixton chipped in conspiratorially. His comment was deliberately throwaway but it seemed to convince this idiot of his bona fides.

'I know how things are, all right and I may be able to accommodate your request,' he said vaguely. Dixton responded with a wink, he felt somehow that the occasion called for it.

The hall was tiny, it was completely filled by the three men and a hat-stand. Dixton noticed that their host wasn't wearing any shoes. They followed him into the kitchen. There were books everywhere, on the table, on the floor, even blocking the back door to a height of about two feet. Each pile had a number written on a slip of paper and sellotaped to the top book.

'Sorry about the mess, I'm cataloguing all my books at the moment.'

Dixton noticed some of the titles. They were mostly science fiction. Dixton hated science fiction. He always thought that people who wrote those kind of books were somehow cheating. He remembered that when he was in his last year or so at school that the 'in' book to read was *The Hitchhikers' Guide to the Galaxy*. Dixton hadn't read it and didn't feel he'd lost out. Most of the people he knew who had read it had ended up becoming accountants.

'What about these bikes then?' said Pepper.

'They're out in the yard.'

The three of them lifted the piles of books from in front of the back door. The back yard was slightly bigger than the hall. There were two bikes locked together leaning against the wall. The red-haired book cataloguer opened the lock and stood between the bicycles steadying one with each hand. One was a black gent's bike of the type used by village policemen. The other was a brand new girl's racer.

'What do you think? Are you interested?'

'Yes, we're interested, we're definitely interested,' said Pepper 'aren't we Dixton?'

'Oh yes, we are.' Dixton didn't know if they really were interested considering one of the bikes was a girl's racer. The other bike looked OK though.

'How much do you want for them?' asked Pepper.

'Oh I don't know, say twenty quid each.'

Dixton felt it would be folly to discount the racer on the grounds of sex at that price. He wondered aloud why the bikes were being sold off so cheaply.

'They're stolen,' said the red haired student with no shoes.

'Really?' Dixton was amazed.

Pepper gave him a withering look, Dixton understood why they were being offered a bargain.

'We don't mind that,' said Pepper.

'That's all right then, as long as you understand that if you're caught, you're on your own. That's the way I work.'

'Can we talk about it for a minute?' asked Dixton.

'Sure.' The bicycle thief went back into the kitchen leaving Pepper and Dixton in the yard with the two bikes.

'What is there to talk about?' said Pepper 'two bikes, twenty quid each, we need bikes, what could be simpler?'

'They're stolen,' said Dixton.

'I know, I know. Think of them as second-hand if it makes it easier for you.'

Pepper obviously had no qualms about buying stolen property. Dixton had some basic reservations,

'What if we're caught?'

'Who's going to catch us. Look, what if we fork out a hundred and fifty quid each for new bikes and they're stolen, what would we do then?'

'Come back here I suppose and buy them back for twenty quid.' Dixton knew that it made economic sense to buy the bikes but he felt that he should consider the moral aspect of it as well, even if only to allow himself the luxury of making a wrong but informed decision. Who was it that said the Ten Commandments should be approached like a university exam in that only six need be attempted? Maybe they were right.

'OK, let's buy them. But I don't want the girl's bike.'

'Neither do I, we'll toss for it.'

They paid for the bicycles and wheeled them through the house out

39

on to the street. They tossed and Dixton lost. Still any bike was better than no bike, especially at that price. Dixton still had some doubts about buying stolen goods but they related to the risk of being caught rather than the loss to the original innocent owner. He could imagine trying to explain to some cop.

'I bought it from chap with red hair, bare feet and a Chelsea Shirt. No I don't know his name.'

They were back at Lupin Hall within fifteen minutes.

There was formal dining that night. Dixton hadn't realised until that morning and by then it was too late to put his name down. He looked at the typed list on the notice board in the foyer of the main building: it said 'full'. Dixton was disappointed. He would be at a bit of a loose end that evening as Pepper was going to a golf club meeting in town.

'Are you dining tonight?'

He looked behind him and saw that it was Jack the architecture student, whom he'd met at teatime on his first day.

'No I'm not. I didn't put my name down in time.'

'Would you still like to dine?'

'Yes, I mean I would of course but the list is full, isn't it?'

'Technically it is but someone who was supposed to be at our table has just phoned to say they won't be coming. They're stuck in London. Would you like to take their place?'

'I'd love to, but wouldn't the other people at the table mind? I probably won't know any of them.'

'You'll know me won't you? That's enough to start with.'

'OK. Thanks a million.'

'No problem, I'll just tell the head waiter upstairs so they'll have a placename put out for you. Unless of course you feel up to masquerading as medical student Alice Eliott for the evening?'

'I don't think so.'

'Fine, we'll see you here in the foyer at seven sharp.'

Dixton went out through the main door and was walking across the court to his room when he heard Jack shouting behind him from the front steps,

'Hey Dixton.'

Dixton turned around.

'Wear a jacket and tie OK?' Jack waved and disappeared back inside. Dixton was glad of the advice as he would have worn jeans otherwise. Good old Aunt Sheila and the new suit.

The foyer was mobbed. Everyone had to wear an academic gown over their suit or dress or whatever. The gowns were hanging on hooks in the corner of the foyer near the stairs. Dixton had only worn one once before and that was on the day of his graduation in Dublin during the summer. This all seemed so far removed from that time despite only being a matter of a month or two later. He remembered Graduation Day. Aunt Sheila had worn a huge pink hat with revolting plastic flowers and fruit sewn around the rim. It looked like someone had been sick all over it. The Dean of the law school had given the standard speech, end of a long hard road, beginning of new lives, opportunities, oysters, alma maters that sort of thing, Dixton knew it must have galled the Dean to see the people he didn't like in the class doing well. He had never liked Dixton, ever since someone put a box of laxatives chocolates on the top table at the Law Ball in first year. Oh well, it had given the Dean a good run for his money.

Dixton met up with Jack, he was with a group of five others.

'This is Penny, Dave, Richard, Alicia and Nathalie. Everybody this is Dixton.'

'Is Dixton your first name?' Alicia asked as they walked up the stairs to the Dining Hall. She was averagely pretty but had wonderful friendly eyes.

'Yes that's my first name.'

'It doesn't sound very Irish.'

'It's not very Irish but I suppose my middle name makes up for it.'

'What's your middle name?'

'Promise you won't tell anyone.'

'I promise,' she laughed.

'Do you really promise?'

'Yes I promise, what is it?'

Dixton lowered his voice and bowed his head slightly towards her.

'Columbanus.'

'You're joking?'

'No, I wish I were. Promise you won't tell anyone?'

'I promise, that would be too cruel,' she laughed.

Dixton wondered if she was attached.

Waiters in dress suits served sherry from silver trays in the waiting area outside the Dining Hall. Dixton took a glass. He drank it slowly. The group he was with were easy to talk to and he learned that they were all architecture students but only Jack and Penny were at Lupin Hall. Alicia and Nathalie were from Newnham (bingo), Dave was at Trinity and Richard was at Hughes Hall. Architecture was considered a postgraduate degree because you had to do a foundation course somewhere first before coming to Cambridge. Dixton had drunk three glasses of sherry by the time the gong rang for dinner. Oh well he thought they're small glasses. The dining hall looked very different. There were sparkling white linen tablecloths on the tables. Each place was laid with silver cutlery and three or four crystal glasses. There were large candelabras on each table although the main lights in the hall were also on. Lord Lupin oversaw the proceedings from his portrait with the marmalade cats.

'We're at the long table nearest to the far wall,' said Jack.

Dixton found his placename and saw to his delight that he had been placed beside Alicia. On his other side was a large American man who was examining the fish knife as though looking for a hallmark. Opposite him was Dave from Trinity. The two chairs to Dave's left had been tilted and their backs rested against the table as if reserved. They all stood behind their chairs until there was a bit of shuffling at the entrance to the Dining Hall and the President of the college entered followed by some members of staff and special guests.

Dixton watched the entourage make its way around the hall and then realised that the President was going to be sitting at their table. He sat next to Dave, so almost across the table from Dixton. The person to the president's left looked familiar. The gong rang again, the President said a short prayer in Latin and everyone sat down.

'I see you made it to Lupin Hall Mr Larkin,' the President nodded in Dixton's direction.

Dixton was amazed that he had remembered his name.

'Yes, yes I did. I wasn't sure that I would but here I am.'

'You are most welcome, I hope you have an enjoyable year.'

'Thank you very much.'

'Now I'm afraid I don't know most of these people so you'll have to introduce them to me. I'm sure you remember Dr Winston the Praelector,' he indicated the man on his left.

Dixton remembered him all right, the one who'd nearly exposed him at the interview. What a bollox. He'd have to try and avoid him if he could. It was obvious that the Praelector remembered Dixton as well. He leaned forward and smiled superciliously.

'Ah Mr Larkin, the debater from Dublin.'

Alicia turned to him,

'Do you debate? How wonderful. I'm involved in the Debating Society at Newnham, perhaps we can organise a match against Lupin Hall.'

'Well I'm sure that Mr Larkin would be delighted to get involved in that,' said the Praelector. Dixton wished he would shut up. Still it was a long way to go until the end of the year, perhaps Dixton would get a chance to even the score with this idiot before the year was up.

Apart from the early swipe by the Praelector the meal went well. The food was great and there was plenty of wine. Dixton chatted up Alicia for a while until she mentioned she had a boyfriend in Coventry.

'We see each other nearly every weekend, either he comes up or I go down.'

Dixton thought that sounded reasonably interesting. He wasn't going to strike it lucky with this lady anyway. Oh well more fish and all that, maybe he should have chosen the Law of the Sea after all.

The American on his right was called Mike Zinowsky. He was loud, obnoxious and boring which was no great surprise to Dixton who recognised him as one of the people who had been supporting Bernard during the game of pool. For most of the meal he spoke to the person on his other side though he might as well have been addressing the entire gathering given the noise level he operated at. Dixton heard snatches of the conversation, and it was like being in a small room with a slightly deaf person while they were making a phonecall.

'I come from Seattle, Seattle Washington, yes siree that's where I come from. You ever been to Seattle?'

Dixton gathered that he was studying Arabic. The man also had three brothers all of whom went to college in Seattle. What a pity he hadn't followed in their footsteps. By the time he turned to Dixton towards the end of the meal, Dixton felt as if he'd known and disliked him for years.

'So you're Irish?' he bellowed.

'Yes,' said Dixton curtly.

'Well whaddyuh know? I'm one-twelfth Irish. My great, great Grandmother was from Blarney, I'm one twelfth Irish.'

Dixton suspected that the Irish twelfth of him was certainly not his brain.

At the end of the meal the gong sounded again and everyone adjourned to the reading room for coffee. Dixton was glad of the chance to escape from Mr Zinowsky from Seattle. He drank lots of coffee to counter the wine and sherry. He hadn't drunk very much really but was wary of spawning another clanger of a headache. He manoeuvred around to talk to Nathalie.

'So what did you think of the meal?' (It wasn't much of an opening line but it was more subtle than say, 'Any chance of a snog?'.)

'Yes it was lovely. The company was good and the wine was

excellent. What more could one ask for?'

From her accent he guessed that she was French. She spoke the last sentence with a twinkle in her eye that made Dixton think for a second that maybe, no surely not? This woman couldn't be coming on to him, could she? He could remember at least a couple of hundred previous occasions when he'd misread signals and suffered great embarrassment as a result. He cleared his throat.

'Nothing more, I suppose.'

'Oh,' she said in a disappointed tone.

'Bollox,' thought Dixton, perhaps this was the only time he'd ever misread the signals and been right. He tried to think of a suitable tack to claw back the conversation to its original level of suggestion. Before he could say anything however the large American was back.

'Oh there you are?' he roared, thumping Dixton on the back. The jug of milk Dixton was holding lurched forward out of his hand and drenched the front of Nathalie's dress. Dixton was mortified:

'I'm terribly sorry. Let me. . .'

He pulled a handkerchief out of his pocket but wasn't quite sure how best to go about helping the situation without compounding it. He felt like a complete idiot. Penny who was standing nearby talking to Jack, stepped in.

'Don't worry about it Nathalie, you, can come back to my room and change.' Nathalie gave Dixton a filthy look and left with Penny. Dixton could see Jack in the background laughing away to himself about the whole scene. The American was oblivious to the damage he had done,

'What's wrong with her? Too much drink eh? Well we Irish know how to hold our drink don't we?, he guffawed and thumped Dixton on the back again. Dixton was tempted to kick his face in. Jack sensed the impending violence and stepped in between the two of them with his back to Zinowsky.

'So Dixton, how are things?'

'Not great really Jack.' Dixton put his cup and saucer down on a table, 'God I've made an awful fool of myself.'

'Not at all,' Jack consoled him, 'don't worry, she'll be fine. Anyway it wasn't your fault.'

'Yeah but she doesn't know that does she?'

'I'm sure Penny will explain everything to her. Don't worry about it. Listen what are you doing tomorrow afternoon?'

'Nothing, why?'

'Well we're a bit short for the mixed hockey team. Would you be interested in playing?'

'I've never played hockey before.'

'Neither have some of the others. We really need a goalie.'

'A goalie?'

'Yeah you'd be perfect, we'll give you all the gear and all you have to do is stand there and keep goal.'

'So you guys play ice hockey?' Zinowsky boomed. He just couldn't take a hint. He stood beside them grinning inanely.

'We play field hockey, not ice hockey,' Jack explained politely. Dixton simply looked in another direction.

'Field hockey? Jeez don't you guys play any real sports here like we do in the States? What's up with you, afraid of a bit of physical contact or what?' He shouldered playfully into Jack as he spoke. Dixton had had enough.

'That's a ridiculous statement from someone from a country whose national sport is built around television commercials.' Zinowsky was taken aback but rallied aggressively.

'Have you ever been to the States wise guy?'

Dixton was on a roll.

'As a matter of fact I have been to the States and once was enough. It's just one big fast food restaurant full of fat divorced people who can't speak English properly. I'm sure you fit in fabulously well.'

That shut him up. There was nothing like a bit of common or garden rudeness to get rid of annoying twits.

Zinowsky glowered at him in the background as Dixton resumed his conversation with Jack. He was glad that there were plenty of people around as he felt that otherwise the American would be quite capable of violence.

'OK, I'll play. Where is the match on and how do I get there?'

It was the word 'mixed' which finally won him over. He drank gallons of water before going to bed just in case.

CHAPTER FIVE

'Sorry about the shortage of shirts. We gave one each to the girls and it's first-come, first-served for the others,' said Jack.

'Not to worry,' said Dixton, slinging his gear bag on to the bench beside Jack in the Men's Changing Room.

The Lupin Hall colours were red and yellow harlequin style. Dixton wore his Herbal Tea sweatshirt. 'Herbal Tea and the Power of Prayer' was the name of a band that Dixton had formed during his last year at school. The band had only done one gig before breaking up rather acrimoniously. The dispute was about whether to split the three pounds fifty in takings between the band members to defray bus ticket expenses, or to plough it back into the band by buying a set of guitar strings. In the end they split the money and disbanded. The drummer's brother had a clothes shop and had donated the sweatshirts.

'What am I doing here?' he thought as he pulled on the sweatshirt. In Ireland only women and Protestants played hockey. Perhaps that was why Aunt Sheila had never encouraged him to take it up. Anyway, he'd seen it on television and it didn't look too difficult. He recognised two of the others, Andy Chalmers and Stan, the decent porter. Bernard emerged from the door leading to the loos. God, was he playing?

'I think most of you know each other from last season but we have one or two new players with us today. This is our new goalie, Dixton.' Jack introduced everybody. The four men Dixton didn't know were Harry Pickford who ran the bar, Niall somebody a vet student from Scotland, Sanjra from Pakistan who was doing the LLM and Simon something who was studying Chemistry.

'And this is Bernard Rainford, he's studying Land Economy. You probably know him already from around Lupin.'

'Yes we've met,' said Dixton in a reasonably polite tone. Bernard looked disdainfully in Dixton's direction, muttered something and resumed tying his laces. Sore loser thought Dixton. He wondered what the hell 'Land Economy' was all about.

'There are only two girls on the team, Penny Williams and Liz,' Jack continued, 'I know its supposed to be a mixed team but that's the best we could do at short notice. Simon, have you got the goalie's gear for Dixton?'

Jack threw the bag over to Dixton, 'There you are goalie.'

Dixton put the gear on. There were all sorts of pads for every imaginable part of his body. The most alarming one was a pad to protect his private parts. Dixton hadn't bargained on putting so much at risk for Lupin Hall.

'Don't worry, it's only a precaution,' Simon reassured him. The last time Dixton had heard that phrase was when he had had his appendix out.

'I thought that this was a fairly sedate game? It always looks very safe and relaxing on television.'

'It is generally, but Peterhouse take it quite seriously,' said Harry Pickford.

Dixton wasn't sure whether he was being wound up or not, but felt it was best to assume that he was. He put on the face mask and the gloves. He presumed that he looked like an Egyptian mummy. Still, at least he was wearing all this protective stuff, the others were only wearing shorts and shirts.

'OK,' said Jack standing up on one of the benches, 'let's do a bit of warming up, we don't want anyone getting injured.'

Except maybe Bernard, Dixton thought to himself. Dixton was almost completely immobilised by his armour and the only part he could move was his neck. He couldn't face the thought of having to take off all the gear and then put it back on. The rest of the team warmed up, Dixton rotated his neck gingerly. They probably needed to warm up more than he did because they'd have to run around a lot. All he'd have to do was to stand still. The two girls joined them. Liz looked fabulous in the short hockey skirt but Dixton couldn't bring himself to forget the fact that she was still a disciple of the nappy king. Penny looked as though she'd played a lot of hockey. She controlled the ball with her stick on the dressing room floor in an impressive manner, twisting the stick back and about. It was what cliched commentators would describe as 'great close control'. Jack told everyone what position they were playing.

'OK everybody, let's try and give Dixton a little support out there. This is his first ever game of hockey. Peterhouse are the cream of the University, rich and thick, let's get them.'

Sanjra and Andy started whooping and cheering. It was obvious Lupin Hall had a laid back non-competitive attitude to the whole thing.

Peterhouse on the other hand were as serious as an attack of herpes. For a start they had a complete set of team shirts. They also seemed to have about two hundred extra players. They were already on the pitch when Lupin Hall arrived out. The first thing Dixton noticed were two huge guys practising short corners in one of the goal areas. They were whacking the ball into the goal with ferocious accuracy and strength. Each time the ball hit the back-board there was a loud smack. Dixton shuddered with each thud. He stood with his mouth open gawping at them.

'That's your goal Dixton,' Jack said, 'we lost the toss.'

Dixton suddenly made the connection between being goal-keeper and having to keep goal. He was terrified. No wonder he was so well wrapped up. He felt too weighed down by the gear to attempt to do a runner. He walked reluctantly towards the goal. He looked back and saw Simon giving him the thumbs up sign. He felt like giving him the two fingers but the thickness of the gloves prevented him. He reached the goal and stood against one of the goalposts looking back up the field. The Peterhouse players were huddled on the halfway line chanting some song. It reminded him of the All Blacks rugby team. The referee arrived.

Dixton wished he were dead and after about three seconds he nearly was as straight from the off Peterhouse strung together a move which culminated in a vicious strike on goal by one of the opposition females. Dixton thought she looked like an East German swimmer. The Lupin Hall defence was unavailable to help him as they had barely realised the game was under way. Dixton saw the ball as it rose like a missile from the edge of the penalty area. He flailed out at it with his stick but missed completely and the ball cannoned against the post but was deflected wide. Dixton screamed, 'Where the hell is the defence?'

He wondered how long each half was in hockey. Simon approached him as he placed the ball to hit it out.

'Well done, Dixton you're playing a stormer, hit it up the left side to Jack.'

Dixton whacked the ball as hard as he could and saw it miraculously reach Jack. Perhaps Lupin would begin to get their act together now. He was wrong, they managed to string two or three passes together and then were easily dispossessed. Within moments of hitting the ball out Dixton was under siege again. This time the Lupin defenders were in place, they were simply left standing as Peterhouse played a series of one-twos around them and stormed into the box like a herd of mad cows. Dixton ran out to narrow the angle but as he lunged towards the ball with his stick the player in possession wrongfooted him and tapped the ball past him into the empty goal.

'Bollox,' said Dixton. He knew that this was going to be one of those awful days when the better team would win.

'OK,' said Jack at half-time 'we're six-nil down but all is not yet lost. I think we're capable of getting a goal ourselves.'

'You mean an own goal?' said Dixton.

'No,' Jack smiled, 'I mean a real goal. Don't look so disheartened;

you're doing great Dixton. If it wasn't for you we'd be losing by double figures.' Dixton was less than totally consoled by this compliment. There was an audible sneer from Bernard.

'Now Penny and Liz are going to change positions for the second half and Bernard is going to play up front on his own.' Surely he means 'with himself' Dixton thought.

The referee blew his whistle. Dixton thought about falling on the ground and pretending to have a fit of some sort. Maybe he'd be able to miss the second half. However there was also the possibility of getting mouth to mouth resuscitation from one of the East German swimmers. He thought better of that ploy and consoled himself on the way to the goal by telling himself that this was the last time he would ever have to play hockey. He resolved to spend the half avoiding the ball like the plague. He didn't mind losing so much as the possibility of getting hurt. They were another two goals down after a few minutes.

More goals followed, one was particularly bizarre. The ball had been played forward innocently enough into the heart of the Lupin defence and for once Dixton thought that Simon or Pickford would reach it before the opposition, considering they were much closer to it to begin with. The two defenders certainly made an attempt to get to the ball ahead of the Peterhouse attackers. The kindest thing which could be said was that they got their signals confused. Pickford and Simon went for the ball together but neither of them reached it, presumably each thought the other would leave it to them. It was like watching someone run into a mirror. There was a loud thud as they collided and the ball ran through towards Dixton. At this stage the ball was near the end of its run and so should have been easy enough for Dixton to control. It was not to be so. This was the moment the mask chose to slip down his face like a well oiled visor. Dixton couldn't see a thing. He had a vague idea of where the ball was and so he swung wildly missing the ball completely. It trickled behind him into the goal and ran out of steam just over the line. Ten-nil. Dixton lifted the face mask and saw the ball. He was as sick as a rat.

Dixton was to hockey what Churchill would have been to ballet. Someone asked the referee how much time was left and Dixton was relieved to see the referee indicated five minutes. How much worse could things get in five minutes? He was about to find out. Firstly, a penalty was awarded against Lupin Hall because the ball had been deflected up off a stick and become lodged behind one of Dixton's kneepads. Dixton felt it was the height of unfairness to penalise him for something which was clearly not his fault. He couldn't help it if the ball decided to lodge behind his kneepad. There was also the added terror of the Peterhouse forwards all hacking away with their sticks trying to dislodge it before the referee blew his whistle for a penalty. It was like one of those medieval rituals 'hacke ye goalie' or something. Dixton, to his credit, had defended himself rather well and had even managed to cripple one of the opposition with a severe chop to the ankles. In retrospect perhaps this contributed in some small way to the penalty award.

As the Peterhouse centre forward lined up to take the penalty Dixton considered the possibilities. Supposing the penalty taker decided to go left and thought that Dixton might anticipate him. Then he might go right instead. However, if he was going to go right having initially decided to go left there was always the chance that he would go left anyway in order to try and confuse Dixton. On the other hand of course he might try to anticipate which way Dixton was going to go and choose the other side then. As well as left and right there was also the option of hitting the ball straight at the centre of the goal and relying on there being a space there if Dixton went either left or right. Dixton's main priority was to avoid contact with the ball at all costs so in fact what he wanted to do was to guess which way the ball would be struck and then go the other way. He closed his eyes and went left.

The ball struck him full on the chest. It was like having a heart attack on the outside. 'Fabulous save Dixton.' Penny was standing over him and stretched out her hand to help him up. He struggled to his feet. The entire team were around him clapping him on the back and congratulating him. Considering the bruise he would have the following day he wished he'd gone to his right or stood his ground.

The second event which marked the closing minutes of the match was another goal. Not that goals were an unusual feature of this particular match, because there had already been buckets of them. What distinguished this goal was that Lupin Hall scored it and what made it a less than happy event, for Dixton, was that Bernard scored it. Dixton couldn't bring himself to feel good about this prat scoring so he looked at the goal in a more positive way; instead of Rainford scoring one goal it would be as if Dixton had only conceded nine. The final whistle blew. Dixton collapsed in the goalmouth and sat there for a little while.

'Come on Dixton, lets get changed and then we can get a drink.' Jack came down to the goal to help Dixton get up.

'Jesus that was awful,' said Dixton.

'It could have been worse, last year they beat us thirteen–nil.'

'Why didn't you tell me that before the match so I could have refused to play?'

'That's why I didn't tell you,' Jack grinned, 'It was difficult enough to get you to play in the first place without scaring you with the statistics.'

As he walked slowly towards the dressing room Dixton noticed a small group of people applauding the Lupin Hall team as they filed into the pavilion. These were the loyal travelling supporters. Dixton recognised two of them, Professor Lynn, the librarian, and Nathalie of the milk-jug incident. Oh no he thought. He took immediate action pulled the face mask back on and attempted to slink past them undetected which was impossible given the gear he was wearing.

'Well played, young Larkin,' the librarian shouted as he went past. Nathalie turned towards him and looked quizzically into the mask. Dixton rushed past into the pavilion. He reckoned from her expression that he had not been forgiven. He was relieved to be able to get out of the gear.

The general mood of the players was excellent. The improvement on the previous years score plus the unexpected bonus of a having scored a goal themselves was almost as good as winning. Dixton wondered if he'd picked a no-hope college.

'This is one of the mixed team's finest hours,' shouted Simon across the dressing room to him. Niall, the vet student who had played in the midfield, was in great form.

'I'm sure this all seems very strange to you Dixton, but when you've been in Lupin for a bit longer you'll appreciate the significance of playing on a Lupin side which actually manages to score.'

'Is it really that bad?'

'I'm afraid so. About two years ago the rugby team won a friendly and the college went absolutely bananas. They were all taken out to dinner by Lord Loopy.'

By the time he'd showered Dixton had begun to feel quite proud of himself. It was like being part of a Swiss yachting team; getting wet was an achievement. Bernard left before most of them were fully dressed.

'Off to meet his high flying father I suppose,' said Simon rather scathingly. Dixton gathered from his tone that he didn't like Bernard much. Nor it seems did anyone else.

'He's an amazing plonker,' said Jack, 'he never shuts up about how wealthy his parents are. He said his father is going to buy him a Ferrari if he gets honours in his Land Economy finals.'

To Dixton's delight everyone had a bad word to say about Bernard. It seemed that he'd been an undergraduate at Lupin Hall because he'd already done a degree somewhere before coming to Cambridge. Lupin had a number of places for 'mature' undergraduates. Bernard was unpopular partially because of his snobbish attitude towards others who were financially less well off than his own family, but mainly because

51

he was a plonker.

'If he were filthy rich but normal, he'd be fine,' said Andy, 'the trouble is he's an only child and he's spoiled rotten. He thinks he's entitled to everybody's attention and admiration because that's the way it is at home I suppose. Apparently the family was originally from South Africa and they made their fortune in the Boer War. They changed their name from Gooseneck. His father owns Wales or something.'

'He's the only student in the college who insists on being called "Mr", by us at the porters' desk', said Stan. 'Yes Mr Rainford, no Mr Rainford. It makes me sick.'

Dixton thought this last comment was particularly revealing about the fellow's character. He remembered the game of pool earlier in the term. Bernard had been livid that he'd lost. Oh well sod him, if he was going to sneer at Dixton for letting in a couple of goals he didn't deserve any sympathy. He could have everything his own way as long as he kept out of Dixton's.

'How about a "Grantchester Run" tonight lads?' said Niall. This suggestion met with general approval.

'What's a "Grantchester Run?"' asked Dixton.

'You'll find out tonight at nine o'clock,' said Jack, 'have you got a bike?'

'Yes I do.'

'Great then, we'll see you at the front gate at nine. Bring that other Irish chap with you, what's his name?'

'Pepper, Johnny Pepper.'

'We'll see you all then.' Andy was on his way. The others left shortly afterwards. Dixton was getting a lift back to college with Jack. Nathalie was gone when they got outside.

'Blast,' said Jack as they reached his rusty old Ford Escort, 'I can't find my keys, I must have left them in the dressing room.' He went back to check. The keys weren't there. They looked around the car and under it in case he'd dropped them when he had gone out to get the sticks. Still no sign of them.

'I know I had them when I got the sticks out of the car Dixton. I can't think what I did with them.'

They both circled the car thoughtfully. Jack spotted the keys, they were locked in the car lying on the back seat.

'Any ideas? My spare set are at home in Bristol, so they're sod all use. I'll have to break a window.'

'Wait a second,' said Dixton, 'are there any clothes hangers in the dressing room?'

'Probably, well yes there are, why?'

'Go get one would you?' Dixton looked up and down the road. There was little or no traffic. This was a quiet residential area off Grange Road. Jack returned with a wire clothes hanger. Dixton unwound it and twisted the hook into a small loop. He wedged the loop between the door and the insulating rubber strip and tried to manoeuvre it through the gap. After a great deal of effort the wire appeared inside the car just a couple of inches above the button.

'That's it,' encouraged Jack, 'just wiggle it a bit and bend it down over the button, a little bit more, more left, left.'

Dixton was doing his best but the wire hanger simply didn't want to be directed to the button. He twisted and levered it but to no avail. He thought about tying a shoelace to the loop and trying to lasoo the blasted button but was reluctant to withdraw the wire from the gap in case he couldn't get it back in. Jack appeared to be losing faith in this method.

'Look, I don't think we're going to have much luck with the hanger Dixton, I appreciate your trying but maybe I could phone a local garage. They might have a master key. The groundsman lives in the lodge on the other side of the road, perhaps I can use his phone. I won't be long.'

'Fair enough, anyway I'll keep trying until you get back.'

Dixton was determined to succeed, if they could do it in a cheap television series surely he could do it too? He set about the task with one last effort. He thought that if he wedged the wire between the button and the window that maybe the pressure would allow him to sort of push the button up from underneath its head instead of pulling from above.

He had almost managed to push up the button when he became aware of a car approaching him quite slowly on his side of the road. His initial reaction was that the driver was probably looking for a particular house and was driving slowly as a consequence, however as the car approached him it slowed down even more. Dixton began to feel that he was being watched. He chuckled to himself as he realised that to a complete stranger it might appear decidedly odd to see a youth trying to open a car door with a wire hanger in a quiet residential area. The car drew level with him and he recognised the driver, it wasn't a complete stranger at all, it was the Praelector. The wire slipped suddenly and the button fell back into place, 'Oh buttocks,' said Dixton.

I know what you're thinking but it's not what you think Dixton said to himself, of course it looked odd but there was a very straightforward explanation. The Praelector however had seen enough. Jack and the groundsman emerged from the lodge and were about to cross the road towards the car. The Praelector sped off after giving Dixton a look that would have turned a funeral up a side road.

'The garage are going to send someone out right away,' said Jack.

'That was the bloody Praelector, Jack.'

'Where?'

'In that car. The one that just went past.'

'We should have asked him for a lift.'

'A lift? I'll be lucky if he doesn't come back with the police, all he saw was me trying to break into your car.'

Jack thought this was hilarious, 'Don't worry, Bedford prison is only a couple of miles up the motorway we can come and visit you in the very car you were trying to break into.'

Dixton didn't see the funny side of the story at all. If he'd even bothered to stop and ask Dixton would have explained the situation to him. He was certain that the Praelector wouldn't be interested in explanations. He was obviously a first impression afficionado. Dixton was quite worried. Oh well there was nothing he could do if the old fart had already decided to hate him. All Dixton could do was hate him back. Now there was a thought.

Dixton and Pepper wheeled their bikes from the bicycle shed through the West Court to the main avenue and down to the front gate. There were six other cyclists waiting at the entrance to the college.

'Right,' said Niall 'let's split up into two teams. The simplest way is, from my left, every second person is with me.' He pointed round the group. 'Jack, Simon and Johnny Pepper, you're on my team and Dixton, Andy, Pickford and Sanjra you're the other team.'

'How does this work?' asked Pepper. Andy explained.

'There are five pubs in Grantchester, in each pub we have a relay pint drinking race between the two teams. Everyone buys a pint of their favourite beer and one person from each team starts the race on a count of three. The second member of the team can't start his pint until the first one has finished his and holds the glass upside down on his head and so on. A team has to win in three pubs to win outright and the person who is the last drinker on a team in one pub starts the race in the next.'

'What happens if you have an uneven number of people?' asked Dixton.

'Then the team that's a player short doesn't start until the first person on the other side finishes,' Niall informed him. Dixton thought it sounded like mad fun. He looked around at his team-mates Sanjra, Pickford and Andy. He hoped he'd be up to the task.

'Right, let's go,' said Pickford looking at his watch, 'It's a quarter past nine now so lets aim to start in the Red Lion at half past.' They set off. Looking around at the bunch of cyclists Dixton felt that this was the closest he would ever get to competing in the Tour de France. It only took them ten minutes or so to get to Grantchester. It was a tiny village but there was certainly no shortage of pubs. It looked like there was probably about one pub for every three inhabitants. The Red Lion was at the top of the village. It was a Friday night and so the pub was busy enough. Jack obviously knew the barman.

'Another run, eh, Jack?'

'That's right Robbie, we've even got a couple of new faces tonight.' He introduced Pepper and Dixton to the barman. He seemed like a decent sort. Everybody paid for their own pint and after a few minutes they were ready to begin. The barman counted to three: 'Go.'

Pickford started for Dixton's team and he raced Niall. Pickford was tall and fairly well built and tore into the pint with great promise. Niall was considerably shorter than his opponent but was obviously well used to speedy drinking and finished marginally ahead. Next were Andy and Pepper, they were fairly evenly matched but the marginal advantage was with the others as Dixton got ready to join the fray. As Andy finished Dixton picked up his pint but Simon was already drinking. Dixton hadn't drunk a fast pint in ages however he made up ground on Simon because Simon was a gulper rather than a swallower. The lager was not too bitter and so Dixton enjoyed the sensation of the liquid whooshing down his throat (insofar as anyone can enjoy cascading alcohol rushing past their tonsils).

The teams were neck and neck when Jack and Sanjra began the last leg of round one. Dixton was amazed by Sanjra's display of breakneck consumption. Jack was equal to the challenge until about mid pint and then he seemed to fade a bit. Sanjra slurped down the last drops then put the upturned glass on his head.

One-nil to Dixton's team.

'Great stuff Sanjra,' said Dixton, 'To tell the truth I didn't think you Muslim chaps drank at all.'

'We're not supposed to, really,' Sanjra beamed, 'but in a way that make it even more enjoyable!'

'We better get a move on, lads,' said Pickford.

'Best of luck,' shouted Robbie after them as they left the Red Lion. They mounted their bikes and rode the fifty yards or so to the Rupert Brooke. This time Sanjra and Jack kicked off. Jack seemed to have a little more energy than Sanjra this time and it was almost a dead heat for the first pairing. Andy was well beaten by Pepper and that seemed to be the turning point in round two. The teams were level. There was very little to choose between the teams and it was evident that there would be a close finish.

By the time they reached the last pub, the Bit and Bridle, it was two-all. The highlight of rounds three and four was Pickford dropping his glass in the Blue Ball, up until then it looked like himself Dixton, Andy and Sanjra were going to win three–one. If anyone dropped their glass or failed to finish the pint the round was forfeited. Pepper and Andy were the last two drinkers in the Bit and Bridle. It was the closest of the five rounds but in the end Pepper shaded it by a split decision and the casting vote of the bar owner Chris.

About midway through the cycle back to Lupin Dixton's bike went completely out of control and he crashed into a hedge. He got back on the bike and no damage was done but all of a sudden he felt really drunk. It must be the fresh air he thought. The others seemed similarly afflicted although they managed for the most part to avoid cycling into hedges. Dixton reckoned that it must be a little like drinking alcohol through a straw. Somebody started to sing and off their own bat they all joined in.

'IT'S A LONG WAY TO TIPPERARY, IT'S A LONG WAY TO GO . . .'

Dixton wondered if old Rupert Brooke had ever sung this song before he died at the Somme or wherever it was. He supposed that Cambridge probably hadn't changed all that much since then. All he'd missed really was Marks and Spencers and another world war.

CHAPTER SIX

Dixton turned up for his first lecture in Remedies and Restitution expecting to see the absent minded tweed-suited chap who had reassured him in the introductory talk. As soon as the lecture began he realised that he'd made a horrible mistake. His worst fears were confirmed by a dapper grim faced man who began the class by handing out a twenty page list of 'recommended reading'. Dixton's idea of recommended reading was other people's notes. He shivered as it became apparent that keeness was the order of the day in this subject. He hadn't even brought a pen and paper with him.

'Professor Campbell very kindly stepped in for me to give the introductory talk. I'm afraid I was away at a conference in Vienna. As a result I haven't had a chance to finalise the reading list but any additions will be ready by next week.'

He hoped that the lecturer was making a little wisecrack to break the ice, but no, it was all for real. Jesus, this was a nightmare. Oh he'd heard of reading lists before all right, but they'd always been a kind of superfluous extra, an academic garnish that was part of the overall package but never actually consumed. He wished he were sitting near the door so he could leave quietly.

'Now, I'm sending a sheet of paper around and I'd like you all to write down your names, colleges and countries of origin.'

'May I borrow a pen?' Dixton turned to a sharply dressed man sitting next to him. In answer to his request he received the kind of disgusted look he would have expected if he'd asked for permission to pick the fellows nose.

'Here, you can have this pen,' a girl behind him stretched a hand over his shoulder. Dixton smirked at the chap in the Armani suit. Sod him.

Because he was sitting near the front of the class Dixton was the third or fourth person to write down his name. The couple of people on the list ahead of him were from Canada, Lesotho and England. As Dixton was writing his name down the lecturer continued:

'Some of you may be wondering what relevance your country of origin might have, well it's quite simple. Each week, working in the alphabetical order of the countries you all represent, we will hear a prepared paper on how the issue under discussion would be tackled in that country and internationally.'

Oh God, thought Dixton, audience participation. He crossed out 'Ireland' and wrote 'Republic of Ireland'.

His experience of previous courses was that the first lecture was always fairly general and gave you a feel for the subject instead of actually dealing with some substantive matter. This was the exception to the rule.

By the time the list was handed up they were well into the lecture. Dixton tried taking notes on the back of the recommended reading list but couldn't really decide where to begin. The lecturer was not someone who paused to allow the students to take notes verbatim and it was even more difficult to synopsise what he was saying as that appeared to require a basic understanding of the subject. Dixton gave up after writing less than a page. If this was one of those subjects he'd have to work out by himself then he really wasn't interested. Perhaps he'd been a little hasty in discarding Asian Land Law as an option. Even Women and the Law began to sound attractive.

What eventually killed off Dixton's interest in the subject was the reminder about the prepared papers which the lecturer gave at the end of the class. Just as the students readied themselves to leave he held up the list.

'Our guest speaker next week will be Michel Santerre from Belgium. Michel, where are you?'

The unfortunate candidate raised his hand, it was the idiot who'd refused to lend him a pen. 'Excellent,' he thought.

'Ah splendid. Well Michel, your topic is the use of mandatory injunctions, just prepare something brief, about twenty minutes or so. No need to deal with more than five or six jurisdictions, begin of course with Belgium. We'll meet again next Monday in room 301 in the Law School.'

Dixton felt like he'd been released from prison when he reached the courtyard outside the lecture theatre. What he couldn't figure out was where was the nice old guy, Professor Campbell? Maybe he would surface at some stage and redeem the situation. At the rate the current chap was going they would cover about forty courses worth of material before Christmas. He was unlocking his bicycle when another student from the class approached him, he was very tanned and Dixton guessed he was Spanish.

'Hello?'

'Yes?' said Dixton.

'Excuse me, my name is Oscar, some of us are going for a coffee now, would you like to join us?'

Dixton was glad of the opportunity to calm his nerves with caffeine.

'I'd love to join you yes, thanks.' He relocked the bike and joined the group, he could collect it on the way back.

Oscar introduced him to the other students. There were two other men, Fraser from Canada and Carlos, also from Spain. The three girls were Monika or Marinka from Holland, Sarah who was English and Audrey, a tall blonde American. They listed off their colleges but Dixton wasn't paying any heed to anyone except Sarah. They walked around the corner to Fitzbillies coffee shop and found a long table near the window. A waitress took their order.

'So what did everybody think of that?' asked Fraser.

'Pretty heavy stuff,' said Sarah. She reminded Dixton of one of those women who were uncomplicatedly pretty and always appeared in black and white war films as the nurse with whom the hero falls in love. He liked her instantly.

'How do you manage to understand lectures here in a foreign language?' Audrey directed her question at the non English speaking contingent.

'It's not so bad,' said Oscar, 'most of us studied English at school in Spain so it's not too difficult, but for me sometimes there are new words but I don't mind so much.'

The Dutch girl spoke perfect English. 'I understood most of the lecture but I don't know what the subject is about.' Everybody laughed. Dixton knew exactly how she felt 'Well I have to say that I expected to be taught by the friendly old guy who gave the introductory lecture.'

'So did I,' said Sarah. Dixton had fallen in love with her before the waitress came back with the coffee. He decided to play it cool though, if he didn't rush into things then maybe, well maybe.

'My understanding of it is that Professor Campbell taught this course last year but he's retired now and Dr Grenville has taken over,' said Fraser.

Dixton hadn't felt so cheated since penny bars turned out to cost tenpence. He'd filled in the subjects choice form however so it was too late to ditch the course. Still, the exam was miles away. If push came to shove he could actually do some study, but it was too early to be thinking total doom and gloom. They sat chatting and drinking coffee for an hour or so. It was Fraser who broke up the coffee session.

'I've got to get back to college to train with the rowing team at lunch.'

Everyone suddenly became aware of the time and so they all left together. Dixton had hoped for an opportunity to chat to Sarah on her own but it didn't materialise. However, as they all stood outside Fitzbillies and prepared to go their separate ways Sarah issued a surprise invitation.

'I live in Gwydr street with three other girls and we're having a houseparty in a couple of weeks time. Its on Sunday night the weekend of November 15th. You're all most welcome to come. It's 27 Gwydr Street but we'll probably be in the Geldart pub around the corner until closing time. Bring someone with you if you want. Apparently the first term is fairly hectic socially in most colleges so I'm telling you all well in advance.'

Excellent, thought Dixton, the soup thickens. Perhaps romance was in the air after all.

The intervening couple of weeks went well enough for Dixton. He attended almost all of Professor Simpson's classes. He enjoyed them thoroughly from the word go. This was how Masters courses should be taught. The course was unfettered by reading lists and it was apparent that the topics would reveal themselves as the year unfolded. Dixton also found Professor Simpson's approach to exams refreshingly unenthusiastic.

'I don't believe in exams, they're of no real assistance in assessing the extent of a student's learning. Learning is a long-term enterprise, exams test memory, not understanding. At any rate postgraduate study is a time to explore and enjoy the law. There won't be any surprises in my exam next summer, no trick questions or any of that nonsense. Enjoy Criminal Law and you will have learned all you need to know.'

Dixton felt like standing up and applauding. This was the kind of attitude he had hoped to encounter in Cambridge. Professor Simpson may have been old and frail looking, but, if he lasted the year, Dixton felt that at least there would be one exam which wouldn't pose too many problems. He hadn't intended attending very many lectures but this was one course he could see himself getting out of bed for.

As an added bonus Sarah was studying Criminal Law as well. This allowed Dixton to dodge Remedies and Restitution completely but to still see her regularly. He would worry about that subject when the time came but he wasn't going to ruin his entire term by letting himself be exposed to high powered academic lectures on a regular basis. There was one EU seminar each fortnight for an entire afternoon, he would get to one or two of those if only to establish contact with someone who would provide him with notes as D-Day approached. He decided to do the Law of Salvage by thesis having discovered via a circular from the law faculty that one subject could be submitted this way instead of by exam. Despite the fact that he'd chosen the subject because the lecturer was gorgeous he sacrificed the experience of attending her classes. He had begun to feel that things might be moving on the romantic front and didn't want to over extend himself.

Back at Lupin Hall Dixton had begun to establish a routine for himself. He felt that even if he were going to do as little as possible during the year a plan of campaign would be invaluable. Some days would obviously have an inbuilt purpose, like a lecture to go to or a rugby match to attend. There would be other days however, when the temptation not to participate at all in the world would be overwhelming. What he needed was a middle ground routine which would cope with all eventualities. He made it a rule of thumb always to get up for lunch. Laura, the bedder, usually knocked on his door at about ten or so each morning. Depending on how he felt Dixton would use this as an alarm call or as an opportunity to wake momentarily, see if it was raining outside and go back to sleep. If he got up when she knocked Laura would clean the room, but if he said 'Hangover' in a loud voice she would reply 'see you at twelve' and would leave his room until the very end of her quota of rooms. It was a good arrangement from Dixton's point of view. In order to thank Laura for allowing him to sleep on he always brought her a cup of coffee from the E Block kitchen on the occasions upon which she did his room last. Dixton felt that oversleeping was a talent rather than a weakness. He imagined writing one of those self-help books and making millions. *Oversleep your way to Success in Industry* by Dixton Larkin. Sometimes he read in bed in the morning to wake himself up. There was nothing like a re-read of the rat scene in *Rain on the Wind* to get Dixton's adrenalin going.

Aunt Sheila, though technically out of range, maintained a fairly regular contact with her investment. The postcard of Kings had been well received and a letter arrived within a week asking probing questions about the courses Dixton had chosen and how his studies were progressing. Dixton replied in vague but positive terms. He didn't want to give sufficient information to make Cambridge either seem worth a visit or not worth the bother. Neither reaction by Aunt Sheila would really suit his own agenda. He always found with his aunt that the fatal mistake was to foster expectation on her part, as it inevitably led to disappointment for one or other of them. The key to keeping Aunt Sheila onside was to tell her enough to keep her happy but not enough to worry her.

Pepper seemed to spend each spare moment practicing his golf. Dixton saw him every day at some stage, either for lunch or for a cycle into town in the afternoons. They made a couple of trips into town each week, usually so Pepper could visit the golf shop on Trumpington Street while Dixton rambled through the market square from stall to stall looking for old records and good books. They held putting competitions on the carpet in Pepper's room and occasionally Dixton accompanied him out to the Corpus Christi football pitches to hit twenty or thirty golfballs from one end to the other. Dixton was getting the hang of swinging the club, although, because he was left-handed, it was difficult using Pepper's clubs. One Saturday morning Dixton was in bed at midday when Pepper arrived in to see him.

'C'mon, Dixton, it's time to get up.'

'I thought you had gone on off somewhere to play this weekend with the golf team?'

'We were supposed to be going to Royal Sussex to play but apparently the course is rained out. It was too short notice to organise another venue so we've got the weekend off.'

'Any plans for the day Pepper?'

'That's why I'm here, I've got a present for you.'

'What's her name?'

'Very funny, look, if you want it you'll have to get up and come to my room.'

Dixton had planned on having a lazy day but he was too awake now to be able to get back to sleep.

'I'll see you in five minutes,' Pepper left.

Dixton's present was a left handed nine iron golf club. 'One of the boys said this has been lying around the clubhouse for ages, nobody seems to own it so I asked the caretaker if I could have it for a friend of mine who was taking up golf.'

Dixton was delighted. Now he might be able to actually hit a golf ball instead of just churning up huge divots on the Corpus pitches.

'When are we going out?'

'Let's have lunch first, that way we'll have the whole afternoon to muck about.'

Dixton spotted Bernard in the dining hall. He was chatting up some blonde girl over the soup of the day. He wondered if anyone would actually go out with this dork. He was a clear case of the ego has landed. Dixton remembered the sneering way he'd laughed at his disastrous goalkeeping the previous week. It sickened him to remember that Bernard had scored their only goal.

'But will he score with her?' Pepper interrrupted his thoughts as though he'd been listening to them.

'I doubt it.'

'You never know,' said Pepper, 'one thing about women is that they often seem to go for the most idiotic guys, almost out of sympathy. Of course idiots are even more attractive if they're rich.'

Dixton wondered if other people might consider him to be an idiot but he felt it was a lot like the fear of having bad breath, if you were aware of the danger, you were unlikely to be a victim. He wasn't sure if that was logical or not but he found it re-assuring. It was the old question: do stupid people know they're stupid?

Herve came over to their table and joined them for a moment. Dixton hadn't seen him around for a while.

'How are things Dixton, any luck in choosing your courses?' he grinned.

'As a matter of fact yes, I've even been to a couple of lectures.'

'Don't wear yourself out, we're only halfway through the first term.'

'How is Karen?', Dixton turned to Pepper, 'Karen is Herve's wife.'

'Oh she's in good form these days, her sister is visiting at the moment and they've gone to London for the day to do some shopping. They'll probably go to a show as well and get the last train back tonight.'

Dixton thought that Herve sounded at a bit of a loose end. 'How about going for a drink later on Herve? Maybe this evening at some stage?'

'That would be great, call around after tea.' He seemed genuinely thrilled to have been invited for a drink. Dixton reckoned he probably didn't get out much.

They took their cups of coffee into the reading room. Dixton had a quick look at the papers and saw that a doctor in California claimed to have found a cure for nymphomania. Dixton hadn't even been aware that it was an illness.

'I'm going to hit that goalpost,' said Pepper taking a practice shot through thin air first.

'Rubbish,' said Dixton.

'Want to bet a fiver?'

'No way.' Dixton was a chicken when it came to relying on chance. Even if the odds appeared in his favour Dixton was reluctant to back up his scepticism with hard cash. Pepper took a few more practice shots.

'Get on with it,' Dixton goaded.

Pepper swung back the club and chipped the small white ball up into the air. It seemed to hang there for ever and then plummeted and made contact with the base of the goalpost. Dixton was well impressed.

'It's like bonking,' said Pepper, 'the longer you take the better you get.' Dixton wasn't in a position to comment with authority about either activity. Talk of the pleasures of the flesh reminded him of Sarah.

'I've been invited to a houseparty tomorrow night in town. Do you want to come along?'

'Is it strictly for lawyers?' Pepper asked.

'No, no anyone can go. It's this gorgeous girl in the Criminal class who's having it, there will be tons of women there.' Pepper was on for it.

'That sounds excellent. Are you going to bring your guitar Dixton?'

'I don't think so.' Dixton hadn't practiced much lately and anyway he wasn't sure what the lie of the land would be. Sometimes it was a great idea and went down well at parties but, as he didn't know the people well, he would leave it at home. There would be other parties. If he brought it he would have to play and there was always some idiot who would be drunk and complain if he couldn't play massive rock solos or sound like an orchestra. Invariably they were talentless gits themselves. In their sober moments these sort of morons would say things like 'People tell me I'm difficult to get to know'. Usually the answer was much simpler: people were too bored by them to make the effort.

It started to get dark so Dixton and Pepper headed back to Lupin Hall. 'Maybe we'll get out and hit a few more tomorrow morning,' said Pepper.

'OK,' Dixton felt that this was a game he could get addicted to.

He checked his post, there was a flyer from the rugby club in the college advertising an all-in bus and match ticket to the Varsity game in December for ten quid. Dixton filled in the attached slip and left it in the club captain's pigeon hole. He told Pepper about it and Pepper did likewise.

'It'll be a day out anyway Pepper.'

'Some of the lads in the golf team went last year and said it was a crazy drinking session. Would you be interested in coming to the Varsity golf game in Scotland, Dixton?'

'If you make the team I'll go, in fact I'll caddy for you Pepper.'

'You're on.'

Dixton had never been to Scotland before. Of course he was a Celtic supporter like everybody else in the Republic of Ireland but that was more historical than practical. Quite a few good bands had come from Scotland and his favourite part of *The Thirty Nine Steps* took place there.That was all he knew about the place.They met up with Herve and had a few quiet drinks in the college bar. Dixton had an early night because he was quite tired. Pepper said he'd stay on.

'I'll see you in the morning then Dixton,' Pepper said.

As Dixton made his way out the side door and into the court he saw Pepper through the window get up from where they'd been sitting and make a beeline for a couple of girls who were playing pool. Pepper had obviously invited himself to join them and Dixton wondered what kind of reception he would get. If nothing else Pepper had nerves of steel and a neck to match.

On Sunday morning Dixton got up at nine. The sun was trying to emerge from behind some clouds without much success but at least it wasn't raining. He thought that November was probably a winter month but, apart from a bit of frost the previous week, the weather was still all right. He felt totally refreshed and was very proud of himself for having had an early night. He decided to go for a cycle. There was no reply when he knocked on Pepper's door. He was probably still asleep.

Grantchester looked completely different in the daytime. Not that he was in a position to make a comparison really because all you could see there at night were the lights of the pubs. He cycled past the Bit and Bridle, the scene of the climactic last leg of his first "Grantchester Run". It was a bit like being a member of a team which had lost the cup final and then passing by Wembley on your way somewhere else. He pictured himself and the rest of his team doing a lap of honour clutching a massive pint glass.

The main street in the village was deserted except for an old lady walking her cat. Dixton had never seen a cat on a lead before. He thought it looked very funny. It was like a scene from a cartoon. For some reason he thought of *Miss Marple* films. He cycled through the village as far as the church at the other end and leant his bike against the wall of the church grounds while he dismounted and tied his shoelaces. He looked over the wall at the headstones, it reminded him of his parents. It was bizzare really – he'd never actually missed them, in the physical sense. It was as though he'd always known they were gone without ever registering the change of circumstance. As he stood there Dixton got the feeling that he was being watched. He turned and looked behind him. There was a small shop on the opposite side of the street and a pretty young lady was standing outside it beside a red pill-box. She looked to be about mid twenties and was dressed quite formally, as if she were on her way to church. Dixton wondered for an instant if she were staring at the church or at him. She was definitely staring at him. Dixton felt quite chuffed. He was glad he'd shaved. The girl continued to stare at him intently. Dixton was a firm believer in love at first sight but it had never happened to him in reverse. He was basking in this new sensation when the moment turned somewhat sour. The girl was joined by a chap who came out of the shop, he was reading a newspaper. As he drew level with her she pointed over in Dixton's direction and shouted in a loud high pitched voice,

'Felix, I do believe that's my bicycle.'

Dixton was the first of the two men to react, he grabbed the handlebars and began to wheel the bike smartly back towards the village. This was no time for the standing start. Felix threw the newspaper into the girls arms and started across the road after Dixton. Dixton looked over his shoulder and began to run on the pavement with the bicycle to build up enough speed to hop on. Felix looked a lot bigger now as he approached and began to get into his stride, Dixton glanced back again. He was still on the pavement but unless he got aboard now he'd be caught. He mounted the bike just as the pavement ended abruptly and nearly ruptured himself. He began to pedal furiously but was in the wrong gear and had to stop pedalling and change down about four gears before he could start to make any real progress. At this stage he knew that Felix had almost caught him, he could hear the footsteps quicken considerably as the runner reached the peak of his sprint. Dixton closed his eyes and pedalled like the mischief. Who was this chap Felix? Some sort of vigilante? For some reason he suddenly remembered the voice of Professor Simpson.

'What is the function of prison? Punishment or rehabilitation?'

Dixton couldn't give a flying shag what the purpose of prison was but he knew that he was one gear change away from finding out. He felt the chain slip,then it caught and, faster than castor oil through a cat, he was away. He accelerated at the same time as his pursuer began to tire. He put his head down and his legs pumped like pistons. He gave one final glance back. Felix was in the middle of the road, bending with his hands on his thighs, catching his breath. Dixton kept cycling, there was always the chance they might have a car. He was fairly sure he wasn't followed back to Lupin.

He was soaked in perspiration (men perspire but women apparently 'glow'). He put the bike away in one of the lesser used bike sheds. He could feel what he presumed was adrenalin, rushing through his body. What had begun as a beautiful dry Sabbath had degenerated into a man-hunt. He would go and see Pepper, after all it was his contact who had led them to the dodgy merchandise to begin with. As he prepared to knock on Pepper's door it opened and a woman emerged. She blushed traffic light red when she saw Dixton. It was Alicia, the girl with the boyfriend in Coventry. She muttered something and hurried past him out the door of the block. Dixton pushed the door open. Pepper had his back to him and was shaving at the sink wearing only a pair of boxing shorts.

'Did you forget something, sexy?' said Pepper.

'Yes,' said Dixton 'I forgot what a sleazebucket you are Pepper.'

Pepper turned around, his face was covered in shaving foam. He chuckled.

'I see you met Alicia, she's a lovely girl isn't she?'

'I met her at the beginning of the year at formal hall. Did she mention her boyfriend in Coventry to you by any chance?'

'Oh, old Georgie, yes indeed she mentioned him all right. It appears he had to work to finish some project or other so he couldn't make this weekend.'

'So what did you do? Buy a timeshare?' Dixton was wildly jealous.

'Well Dixton let's just say we were two lonely hearts far from our loved ones and we consoled each other. She came to Lupin to borrow some notes from Jack and wound up getting a tutorial from me. Women love being in bed with me because I make them look good.' Pepper winked. It was difficult to stay mad at him because there was absolutely no point. Dixton remembered why he'd come to see him in the first place.

'Well, while you were busy consoling each other from the waist down, I was trying to save myself from being savaged by some lunatic called Felix.' Dixton explained what had happened. Pepper was more philosophical about it than helpful.

'Well at least you still have the bike.' I'm sure they didn't get much of a look at your face. From what you say she was more interested in the bike and all this Felix fellow will be able to identify is your backside and the soles of your shoes.

'I think I should dump the bike Pepper.'

'Are you mad? That's the last thing to do. There's nothing to gee-up these sort of maniacs more than a hot trail. The bike would be covered in your fingerprints and even if you wiped it the cops could carry out forensic tests and track you down. You can't sell it either. No the thing to do is to keep it but make it unrecognisable.'

'You mean paint it or something?'

'Yeah, we'll make it so different that no-one will ever suspect. Let's leave it in the shed for a couple of days and then tackle it.'

This plan sounded like madness to Dixton but he was desperate for some sort of way out. At any rate it was probably the least logical course of action and that always held a certain attraction. He needed the bike more than it needed him.

'So what about this party then?' said Pepper.

'It's on tonight, we're all meeting up in the Geldart pub.

'I'm really looking forward to it,' said Pepper. He grinned, 'You know, I'd almost forgotten how good it feels to be unfaithful.'

Dixton was looking forward to the party too. Maybe he would strike it lucky with Sarah. It was finally time to see if Fate had discarded her most cruel cardigan.

CHAPTER SEVEN

Sex, Dixton reckoned, was the most unusual of all human activities. It was the only physical endeavour where you were considered a beginner rather than an expert if you did it on your own. It was about six hours since Dixton had lost his virginity. He looked at the sleeping form beside him in his Lupin Hall single bed. Oh God, what had he done?

Drusilla Hobbet was a formidable woman. She was a student nurse in London and a friend of Sarah. Dixton had met her in the Geldart and she had taken an immediate shine to him. He successfully avoided her until well into the night. However, by the time Sarah began to succumb to the charms of a chap called Martin (who *had* brought a guitar to the party), Dixton was sufficiently drunk and desperate enough to take whatever else was on offer. That turned out to be Drusilla. He couldn't remember much of the conversation they'd had, but he'd obviously avoided insulting her enough for her to make the trek back to Lupin and spend the night with him. As for the evil deed itself, Dixton remembered enough of it to know that he definitely wanted more, but definitely not with her. Virginity is the sort of thing which has to be tackled head on and so it had been. However Drusilla was built more for comfort than for speed and Dixton's next problem was how to break the news to her that he only wanted a test run. He was faced with the Coyote Syndrome, she was lying on his arm and he was more inclined to chew it off than to wake her. There was no way of knowing what enthusiastic activity she might have in mind for launching the day.

Up until the previous couple of hours Dixton had never really had to consider the mechanics of lovemaking. He had a fair grasp of the essentials but, like most things he'd experienced for the first time (with the possible exception of breakfast television), the practice was very different from the theory. He had always thought from what he'd read that it was essentially a natural effortless exercise which yielded a maximum of pleasure with a minimum of mess and noise. The reality was quite different. Sure it was enjoyable, but it certainly wasn't effortless or silent. Dixton hadn't been so out of breath since he ran the last leg of the four by one hundred relay on the under thirteen team at school all those years ago. Still, all things considered, it was a milestone in his adulthood which had threatened never to materialise amid quite a number of false starts.

Drusilla stopped snoring and so Dixton guessed she was awake. He was right.

'Good morning darling,' she sort of half yawned, half spoke as she turned towards him in the bed and flicked the hair back from her face. Dixton began to remember why he'd avoided her so diligently when he was sober. It wasn't that she was ugly but she was attractive in that sort of subjective way that would appeal to a small minority consisting perhaps of herself and her parents. Good looks weren't everything of course, but the absence of them narrowed down the list of redeeming features. Dixton racked his brains to try and think of something appropriate to say.

'Oh hello,' was the best he could come up with at short notice. Drusilla however wasn't short of conversation.

'It's great to wake up beside someone and feel totally at ease. I feel like we've known each other forever, don't you Dixton?' she fluttered what might have been false eyelashes. Dixton nearly choked (though not on the eyelashes).

'Well, er yes, it certainly seems like a long time, doesn't it?' How the hell was he going to get rid of her? He looked at the clock on the bedside table, it was ten past eight. He leaped out of bed and then realised that he was naked. He grabbed his jeans from the back of the chair and held them strategically in front of him.

'Oh, I don't think there's any need for shyness between us at this stage,' she smiled suggestively.

'Do you always get up this early?'

'I do, actually,' Dixton lied, 'I normally go for a jog at about eight every morning and then head off to lectures after breakfast.'

'I could do with some breakfast myself, I have a very big appetite,' she spoke like someone from a dubbed Swedish porn film. Dixton shuddered and pulled on his jeans.

'Do you always go jogging in your jeans?' she laughed.

Dixton realised his mistake and hopped over to the wardrobe to find a pair of shorts. He just wanted to get away from her and think out his next move.

'Come back to bed and I'll help you get fit,' she patted what little space there was beside her in the bed. Dixton felt seasick.

'Oh no, I'm afraid not Drusilla, I have to train for the hockey team, we've an important match coming up next weekend.'

'Great, I love athletes, there's nothing worse in my book than wasting a good body when you could be indulging in some physical activity,' she leered.

'I feel the same,' said Dixton. 'Oh bollox,' he thought. He felt he would have to take a fairly direct approach. He silently rehearsed the line as he was putting on his running shoes.

'So,' he said decisively, 'you're off back to London then are you?' He waited for her to take the hint and respond. She missed it completely.

'No, I don't have to be back at work until after lunch tomorrow. I can stay in Cambridge tonight and get the first train back in the morning. It would be a shame to waste the little time we have together.' Dixton certainly felt that it would be a waste of any time to spend it together but he knew somehow that that wasn't what she meant.

'That's great but . . .' he struggled to invent an excuse.

'But what darling? Surely you don't have anything else planned for tonight?'

He detected the apprehension in her voice and tried to confirm her fears.

'It's uncanny Drusilla, if it were any other night of the term there wouldn't be a bother in the world, it's just that I've been invited to dinner by the parents of a friend who are visiting. We're going to the Garden House Hotel.'

'Oh.' She was obviously disappointed.

Great, he thought, that's that. She rallied however and tried to launch him on a guilt trip.

'I see. Well if someone else is more important to you than me, than us.' In retrospect this was the moment he should have put in the boot and finished it cleanly; however, he took the easy option.

'Of course it's not like that at all Drusilla, you know I'd love nothing more than to spend the evening with you. It's just that, well let me be blunt about it Drusilla, both of his parents are dying of cancer. Of course they could last another few months, maybe even a year but I know they've been looking forward to this night. Their lives, or what's left of them, are built around looking forward to small events which to us might seem minor but for them well, it's a reason to go on as it were.' He knew from her expression that she'd swallowed the entire story. He'd really surpassed himself this time. There was nothing like a well placed lie to snatch back the high moral ground. All that nonsense about honesty being the best policy, the only real way forward was pro-active fibbing.

'Oh Dixton, how could I have been so selfish?' she was nearly in tears but for all the right reasons.

'I don't know Drusilla,' Dixton consoled her perversely, 'I just don't know. We all have weaknesses.'

It wasn't so much a question of not letting the grass grow under your feet, as of actively planting poison ivy. The possibility of a scene had been avoided. He was still congratulating himself when he remembered that he was supposed to be on his way. He jogged on the spot for effect and aimed another well disguised hint in her direction,

'Listen, just pull the door after you when you're leaving will you?'

'But, but, won't we be spending the day together at least Dixton?'

'I wish we could but I'm going to be spending most of the day at the library. I'll only be free for a short while in the afternoon. I have a degree to get you know.' Make it all sound as plausible as possible.

'Well if that's all the time we can have together we'll just have to manage it somehow won't we?' She spoke in that resilient tone of voice popular with practical people for whom the solution was always "making do".

'Well I suppose so but I can't promise much Drusilla. Perhaps we could meet up in town for a drink or something around four or so.' He was slipping a little bit but he'd have to make some effort however little he intended following through.

She smiled encouragingly, 'Love isn't a question of promising little or much Dixton, it's about trusting someone enough to let them in over the walls we hide behind.' (Oh puke.)

It reminded Dixton of those awful cards with the 'footprint' messages that girls exchanged at summer camps. He resisted the concurrent urges to laugh and be sick. They arranged to meet outside Kings College at four o'clock. As he turned to leave he stabbed her expectations with a scimitar fashioned from fatigue and cowardice.

'Listen Drusilla, I may not be able to make it, of course if I can then I will, but just in case I don't, thanks for everything and well goodbye.'

Her face fell and Dixton reckoned that, for the first time in the whole conversation, she had finally got the message. He didn't wait around long enough to give her time to respond. He jogged out of the room and out the back door of the building to the next block. Pepper's door was ajar; he entered the room and saw that Pepper wasn't there. His clothes were still neatly folded on the chair and so he reckoned that he'd probably just gone to the loo. Pepper returned after a moment.

'What are you doing up so early, Dixton?'

'I had to escape, she's in my room.'

'Who's in your room?'

'She, it, whatever her name is, Drusilla Hobbet.'

Pepper squinted questioningly at him, 'You don't mean that girl from the party, the one that kept going on about Marxism in the National Health?'

'I'm afraid so, Pepper.'

'Well she may have stayed with you but surely you didn't, I mean you didn't, you know. . .?'

Dixton could barely bring himself to look Pepper in the eye,

'Of course not, there's no way I would, nothing of the sort, what kind of person do you think I am?' he protested vehemently but there was no fooling Pepper.

'You did!' he laughed triumphantly, 'I knew it. As soon as that idiot with the guitar put the movers on Sarah you seemed to give up the hunt altogether. Now that you mention it I did see old elephant what's-her-name closing in for the kill just as the canapés finished. Oh God Dixton how could you?'

Dixton knew that there was no point in trying to fool Pepper, he was a man well used to the below the waist vagaries of college life himself.

'I know, I know. Look that's all over with now. My latest problem was trying to dissuade her from staying for another night. She thinks I'm going out to dinner with two terminally ill people tonight and that's why I'm not free.'

'Do you think she believed you?'

'I'm certain she did.'

'Oh, that's even worse.'

'Why? What's wrong with that?'

'Well if she believes everything you say she'll think that last night was a declaration of your undying love for her.' Dixton gulped, she'd certainly mentioned the word 'love' all right, but he found it hard to believe that it was meant in a permanent way. Surely not?

He recounted his conversation with her.

'What do you think Pepper?'

'I don't know Dixton. The worst kind of one night stand is where one of the parties isn't aware that it *is* a one night stand.'

'What are you saying Pepper?'

'Nothing really, just don't presume that you've heard the last of the elephant. They've got awfully long memories.'

Dixton felt that Pepper was exaggerating the possible dangers. If Drusilla had any doubts about the shallow nature of his affections for her, surely she would realise that it was all over when he didn't turn up that afternoon?

'Considering I'm fully awake now Dixton how about going to that cafe at the end of Barton Road for breakfast?'

'OK. I hope you've got money because there's no way I'm going back to the room yet.'

'It's OK, I've got money, don't worry.'

The mention of money set Dixton thinking about Aunt Sheila and the allowance she had calculated for him for the term. He would have to be careful enough with what he'd left as he had to fly home for Christmas in about four or five weeks and also take into account buying a present for his aunt. It wasn't that his allowance wasn't adequate, it was just that Aunt Sheila didn't classify alcohol as a legitimate expense and so there was an appreciable gap between how much he had and how much he needed. Still, he'd probably manage. They had a huge breakfast and when Dixton returned to his room at about half past ten Laura was cleaning it and there was no sign of Drusilla.

'I see you had company last night,' Laura grinned.

'How do you know? I mean, what do you mean?' said Dixton, beginning to blush.

'Don't worry, you didn't leave any sordid evidence lying around or anything like that. I met her.'

'You met her?'

'Oh yes when I knocked there was no reply so I let myself in. There she was sitting in the armchair waiting patiently for her boyfriend to return.'

'She said I was her boyfriend?'

'Well she didn't exactly use those words.'

'Jesus, I'm glad to hear it.'

'All she said was that she was your girlfriend.'

Dixton couldn't believe his little ears.

'What? You mean she thinks that I'm her boyfriend now after one night of . . .'

'Mad passion?' Laura suggested.

'Yes, well no not really, sort of but not exactly.'

'Oh well you have to pay the price for having your wicked way,' she laughed.

'I hope I've seen the last of her, anyway,' Dixton thought out loud.

'I very much doubt it Dixton. Take it from me, call it female intuition, this girl has it bad for you. She even left a note for you.' A single sheet of his own notepaper was folded and lying on the pillow. It had his name written on it. Dixton didn't want to read it. After Laura left, however, his curiosity got the better of him. He opened the note.

'My darling Dixton. Thank you for last night. I know it is the beginning of something beautiful and precious for both of us. We are so lucky to have found each other, a new life awaits us. I shall count the minutes until our next meeting.'

'I hope you've got a bloody calculator,' Dixton thought. He had no intention of ever seeing this woman again. Surely he'd made that clear to her? The note was signed with dozens of kisses; Dixton crumpled it up and threw it in the bin. He didn't want to even think about Drusilla any more. As far as he was concerned he'd had a fling and that was all there was to it. There was an element of hesitation however, fuelled by what Pepper and Laura said, that perhaps Drusilla might not get the hint. He decided that there was nothing he could do except hope he'd seen the last of her. Perhaps he should have been more blunt with her, but then there was always the likelihood that Sarah and her friends would react against him on her behalf and that was something he wanted to avoid if at all possible.

He showered and got dressed. There was a Criminal lecture on at eleven but he decided to skip it in case he ran into Sarah. Drusilla mightn't be far behind her. He'd been so preoccupied with getting rid of her that he didn't have time to have a hangover. Given the choice he'd take a hangover any day. He occupied himself quite productively for the rest of the day. He did his laundry and wrote letters to Aunt Sheila and to a friend of his from college in Dublin who was emigrating to the States to work as a lawyer on Wall Street. The prospect of ever having to work for a living himself did not appeal to Dixton at all. So many of his classmates had gone on to do their solicitors apprenticeships in small offices up and down the country. They got paid a pittance to do the donkeywork for people who would never have got into college themselves if there had been any competition when they left school. He wasn't sure where he would end up himself but he knew he would hate to have to work for someone else. The prospect of looking over his shoulder all the time and asking permission to go on holidays filled him with horror. It would be like being back at primary school. He practised with his guitar for a while and wondered if he was too old at twenty-one to become a rock star. He put the strap of his guitar over his shoulder, stood in front of the mirror and pretended he was in the Beatles. No matter how much he tried to reassure himself that he'd seen the last of Drusilla, he was reminded of Pepper's phrase about the worst kind of one night stand and Laura's observations from meeting her. What if she returned? That was such a nightmare scenario however that it didn't bear thinking about. He was probably worrying needlessly - at least he hoped so.

After tea that evening he visited Herve. It was a while since he'd been to see him and they chatted for ages and listened to some CDs which Herve had bought in the market square the previous week. His wife was out.

'You seem a little bit on edge, Dixton,' Herve observed, 'is everything all right?'

'Yes, I'm fine, well mostly fine. I seem to have landed myself in a bit of a mess with a girl I met at a party last night.'

'Would you like to talk about it?'

'Well there isn't much to tell really. I'm sure there's nothing to worry about but some other people seem to think I may not have heard the end of it.'

'I don't quite follow you.'

Dixton explained in general terms what had happened. Herve was very definite about the course to follow if Drusilla re-appeared.

'You must tell her that you are not interested, apologise for having wasted her time and say your goodbyes. It's very important that you don't send out the wrong signals.'

Dixton felt that this advice, though sincerely meant, was somewhat impractical. From the little he knew of Drusilla he felt that the time for signalling had gone and his best option was to simply lie low for a while and hope she disappeared back to London to nurse the sick. Dixton knew that this was the logic of a coward; however, he'd have ample opportunity to live dangerously when he began to pay tax.

The 39 Steps was showing at the Arts' Cinema so he took himself off to see it to help him forget about Drusilla Hobbit. He was poignantly reminded of her though for some reason when the hero of the film was being pursued by the baddies and had to cling onto the underside of a railway bridge. On his way back to Lupin Hall he spotted a sign in a jewellery shop window which said 'Ears pierced while you wait.' Dixton wondered if there was any other way. At about ten o'clock he made his way over to the bar to meet Pepper for a drink.

'Any sign of the elephant?' Pepper asked unhelpfully.

'No. Don't tempt fate by even mentioning her name. I think I've seen the last of her.'

'Maybe you're being too hasty Dixton, why don't you give it a chance?' Pepper laughed, 'you might regret giving her the elbow so quickly.'

'I think that's unlikely Pepper. I know enough about her to make a final informed decision even at this early stage.'

'I hope for your sake she realises she's been dumped Dixton. With all this note business it looks like she's pretty keen.'

'Can we drop the subject, Pepper?' Dixton was getting a little bit annoyed.

'OK, OK,' said Pepper, 'how about another pint?'

It was unlike Dixton to get unduly worried about anything, that was what worried him most about all this. He was normally unflustered about things but then overly keen women to whom he sacrificed his virginity were not a normal occurrence.

'Listen, Dixton,' Pepper said, 'why don't you come out to the University golf course with me in the morning. I'm sure we'll be able to get a set of left-handed clubs for the morning. The sooner you get out on a full course the better.'

'Do you think I'm ready for that?'

'No-one ever is, there's a first time for everything, but then in view of your recent experiences you don't need me to tell you that,' he laughed. Dixton let the jibe pass.

'That would be excellent Pepper. Maybe in the afternoon we can do something about disguising the bike so I'll be mobile again.' Golf sounded like the ideal tonic he needed to take his mind off more hazardous physical exertions.

He awoke the following morning to the sound of someone knocking on his door. He looked at the clock, it was nearly ten. He remembered that he was going out golfing.

'Hang on Pepper,' he shouted. He stumbled out of bed in his boxer shorts and Winnie the Pooh T-shirt. He unlocked the door. Oh fuck. It was The Elephant. He tried to close the door but he was too slow, she was 'in like Flynn' as the phrase goes. Within nanoseconds her arms were around his neck and she was kissing him wildly. Considering it was all one way traffic it was still fairly hot and heavy stuff. From Dixton's point of view it was like a sneak preview of drowning. He finally managed to prise himself away from her. He decided to put on his jeans before she could rip off his shorts.

'Oh Dixton, how I've missed you. Last night was hell without you, I didn't sleep a wink thinking about you, about us, about everything. It's all happened so quickly that I can hardly believe it. We've got so much to talk about, plans to make.'

Dixton was stunned. He had no idea how to react to this avalanche of lust and affection. He got dressed and tried to figure out what the hell he was going to do.

'You haven't said a word Dixton, is there something wrong?'

He seized the opening,

'As a matter of fact there is Drusilla, you see. . .'

'You don't need to say anything darling,' Drusilla pressed her index finger against his lips in a sort of reverse shush, 'I know exactly what's wrong. You're battling with all the same emotions I am, love, panic, decision making, raw physical need.'

Dixton gulped.

'Well certainly some of those emotions seem familiar. Listen Drusilla.
. .'

He couldn't get a word in edgeways,

'No you listen Dixton, it's all arranged. I spoke to the matron on the phone last night and explained everything, she's given me tonight off. I told her, well,' she hesitated coyly, 'that I'd met someone. We can spend that romantic night together that I know we both wanted so badly yesterday.'

'Well yes, you see that's it really Drusilla, I'm not altogether sure about all of this,' Dixton was trying desperately to work his way up to laying his cards on the table. Drusilla laughed.

'Of course you're not sure, I'm not sure, no one ever is. The thing to do is to nurture the flame. Tonight will give us a chance to do that.'

'Well you see Drusilla, the real reason I said I couldn't see you last night was because . . .'

'Because you put the well-being of other people before your own, isn't that why Dixton?'

'Well yes I suppose so,' he said weakly.

He clearly wasn't going to be able to get through to her directly. He would have to think of some other way. He thought of just escaping from the room and never coming back but that wasn't really feasible. He went over to the sink and ran the tap for a shave. What had he got himself into? Laura had been right, this girl had it bad. His main difficulty was going to be getting rid of her quickly as he feared the bonding potential of another night spent together. However keen she was now would multiply overnight especially if she stayed. Sleeping together wasn't the problem, it was what might happen when they weren't asleep that would land him in even deeper waters (if that was an appropriate phrase). He finished shaving and turned around. Drusilla was sitting on the bed and gazing starry eyed at him. Oh God.

'What are your plans for today darling?' she asked suggestively.

'Er, nothing really.'

'Great, then you're all mine?'

'I suppose so.'

Dixton couldn't see an immediate way out of spending the day with her. He couldn't pretend to have another engagement or she would smell a rat. He wanted to dump her as painlessly as possible because he knew how Sarah and the rest of the women who knew Drusilla would react. Women were romantics at heart and they seemed to live vicariously through each other's relationships. If he soured the ground with Drusilla he could forget about getting anywhere with Sarah. Even from a purely academic point of view he wouldn't be able to show his face in the Criminal Law class again if he ditched her overtly. Hell hath no fury like the friends of a culled elephant.

'I suppose I could show you around the college.'

'That would be lovely.'

(At least she couldn't jump on him out in the open.)

They spent the rest of the morning traipsing around Lupin Hall. Dixton took her everywhere he could think of, from the Dining Hall to the laundry room and even up along Grange Road to the University Rugby ground. He hoped to tire her out and at the same time hatch an escape plan. He would have to think of a way to get rid of her without incriminating himself. He thought about staging a family death, say Aunt Sheila's, and pretending he had to leave for home right away. There was always the danger that she would decide to accompany him in his hour of grief; no, that was too risky a course to take. He needed outside help. The opportunity arose after lunch when they were back in his room.

'I think we should go out for a meal tonight, Dixton.'

'That's a super idea.'

'We'll go to a small romantic restaurant, my treat.' Dixton was tempted by the prospect of a free meal but resisted.

'I wouldn't hear of you footing the bill Drusilla, no no, I have an even better idea. Why don't I book us in for Formal Hall tonight here in Lupin?'

'Oh Dixton, could we really? I've never dined at a Cambridge college before, but I've nothing to wear.'

'Don't worry about that at all, you're fine as you are. All you have to do is put on an academic gown over your ordinary clothes and no-one will know the difference.'

'Oh Dixton,' she threw her arms around him and tried to kiss him on the mouth. Dixton evaded service by feigning a coughing fit. He made for the door.

'I'll just nip out and put our names down, I'll be back in a second.'

'OK my darling,' she blew him a kiss, 'missing you already.'

Dixton launched himself into Pepper's room. Pepper was practising his putting on the carpet.

'Pepper, Pepper, you've got to help me, she's back.'

'Who's back? The Elephant?'

'Yes her, she arrived back this morning, she's taken another day off.'

'I warned you Dixton, this girl wants your body.'

'She can have it but not till I'm dead. Listen you've got to help me get rid of her.'

'Oh I don't know Dixton,' Pepper grinned, 'you can't expect me to break my back for cross border relations now can you?'

'I'm desperate Pepper.'

'Well you must have been, to wind up with her.'

'Look Pepper, quit joking, you have to help me out.'

'What do you want me to do?'

'I don't know, anything, just drop in to my room in a while and say we'd organised to go somewhere today. I'll pretend that I'd forgotten and then you do a bit of insisting and hopefully I'll be able to persuade her to leave.'

'OK Dixton, just this once, but if it works, you've got to take me out drinking for the night.'

'I promise, just bale me out. Leave it for a little while and then call round and make it look authentic.'

Dixton returned to the room and spent the next three-quarters of an hour or so resisting Drusilla's amorous advances. Every time she moved in for the kill he pretended he had to look at something or jot something down. The last thing he needed was to succumb to the desires of the flesh. He tried to think of her as the most repulsive woman imaginable and that proved even easier done than said. He glanced at the alarm clock. Where was Pepper? Finally there was a knock on the door. Dixton gave Drusilla what he hoped was a who-can-this-be-disturbing-our-romantic-tête-a-tête? look.

'Come in,' he said in a sort of exasperated, annoyed voice. The door opened.

Dixton nearly wet himself. Pepper was dressed in a huge duffel coat. He had a large rucksack on his back and a kerchief around his neck.

'Dixton what the hell is keeping you? I've got the geology department car outside. We're off to France.'

Drusilla looked as if she'd been whacked in the face with a stuffed weasel. It was imperative to maintain the momentum of the charade. Dixton put on his most indignant tone:

'Pepper how dare you burst in like this? Drusilla and I were enjoying each other's company and we would appreciate some privacy.'

'But we're off to France!'

Dixton tried not to catch Pepper's eye for fear of making them both laugh. He tried to authenticate Pepper's claim by a reverse comment.

'But that trip to France isn't until,' he racked his brains for the date 'until the week of the 17th, Pepper.'

'Well what date is it today you idiot?' Pepper countered.

Dixton looked at the small calendar on the desk, he picked it up. 'Today is only the...' his voice trailed off in a defeated tone, 'the 17th.'

'Right you are then, let's go.'

Dixton played his next card, make her part of the decision making process and then use his own veto. (That old trick.)

'Well Pepper this is outrageous, I mean Drusilla has taken the day off to make up for last night, we have a wonderful evening planned, I don't know what we're going to do.'

'You're the only one who can speak French, Dixton. We need you. You gave us your word.'

Dixton saw that the groundwork had been sufficiently laid. He rounded on Pepper.

'Drusilla and I will have to talk about this Pepper. Give us a chance to sort it out and come back in a while will you?'

'OK,' said Pepper, 'but remember, we're relying on you.' He shut the door behind him as he left. He'd played an absolute blinder. From here on in it was up to Dixton. He turned to Drusilla, she was still obviously stunned by the latest turn of events.

'The bastard, who does he think he is?' said Dixton, 'Imagine springing this on me at this stage? He should have told me well in advance. Well there's no question of my going with them at this late stage and that's that.'

Drusilla looked relieved, she smiled at him.

'That's right Dixton, stand your ground and don't let them push you around.'

'Dead right,' said Dixton, 'what do I care if he fails his bloody degree.' This had an instant effect.

'What do you mean Dixton?'

'Well it's not my problem if he can't get his research done in time for the deadline.'

'What deadline? What do you mean Dixton?'

He could see that she was curious. Hopefully he could turn her curiosity into guilt.

'Well he's doing some thesis or other about raised beaches on the south coast of England and the north coast of France. I'm supposed to be his interpreter for the visit to the Geological Institute at Calais.' (Gosh that sounded good.) Drusilla had a conscience and it was clearly starting to nag her.

'If I weren't here would you go with him, Dixton?'

'Well, er.' He feigned shyness.

'Answer me honestly Dixton, there can be no lies between us.'

'Well, yes, I suppose I would but there's no way I'm going now that you are here. An evening with you is much more important than Pepper's degree.'

Drusilla was clearly worried somewhat by the possibility of being the cause of Pepper's failure but at the same time she was a mass of female hormones in the grip of love and didn't want to lose her man. She took hold of both his hands and stared intensely at him.

'Dixton, you can't be a slave to others, you've got to live your own life, make your own decisions.'

'You're right Drusilla.'

'I know I am,' she sighed with relief.

'OK. I'm off to France.' He deliberately misunderstood her and used it as the opportunity to make his escape.

'But, but . . .' she protested.

'No, you're right Drusilla, I gave my word and I'd be wrong to break it.'

He pulled out a holdall from under the bed and began to throw clothes into it like a person anticipating a police raid. Drusilla was cornered. If she pressed him to stay now she would be signing the death warrant for Pepper's degree. Perfect. It was like asking someone how they were so they'd return the compliment and give you the chance to tell them you were sick.

'I couldn't have made this decision if you hadn't been so understanding Drusilla.'

Dixton looked up momentarily from his packing. She was nearly in tears. He felt a little bit mean but surely this way was better in the long run. By the time she got a chance to come up with another few days off work he would have gone home for Christmas and once there was the guts of a month distance between them she would have got the hint. At worst if she reappeared he could always say he'd met someone else when he was in France and she would blame herself even more. Pepper arrived back.

'I'm glad to see you're coming with us Dixton.'

'Well I wouldn't be if Drusilla hadn't been so accommodating.'

Drusilla was still trying to recover from having her words twisted and thrown back in her face. She looked miserable.

'I really envy you guys heading off to France,' she half sobbed.

'Well it's not going to be a holiday at all,' said Pepper gravely, 'there's a lot of work to be done.'

Dixton felt sorry for her. He could sense however that she was beginning to get the whiff of conspiracy. In order to compound the deception he threw her a bogus lifeline.

'If you didn't have to work you could probably have come with us,' he said. As soon as he'd uttered the words he knew he'd made a mistake. Drusilla fluffed herself up and wiped her eyes,

'That's a great idea, I'm sure I could get another day or two off work.'

Dixton could see Pepper behind Drusilla's back, mouthing obscenities silently at him. Oh no, he had undone all their good work in one sentence. His mind raced trying to think of a clawback.

'That's great Drusilla. Have you got your passport with you?'

'No,' she stopped short' I didn't even renew it when it expired last year.'

The two boys heaved a sigh.

'But I thought you didn't need it for EC countries,' Drusilla was down but not out. Pepper saved the day,

'Technically you don't but my supervisor told me that we won't be able to take geological samples back through customs without export control visas on our passports. That applies to everyone in the car.'

'Oh,' her face fell.

'Well that's that,' said Dixton, 'I suppose we'd better make tracks.'

'Yes, we're picking up Shinners in Dover at nine,' said Pepper enthusiastically.

'I'll go on out to the car.'

Dixton turned to Drusilla, 'Sorry about all this Drusilla, maybe it just wasn't meant to be between us.'

'But you'll be back soon won't you?'

'Oh yes, we shouldn't be more than a couple of weeks.'

'A couple of weeks?' she was incredulous.

'At the outside three weeks, a good investment of time now will avoid having to make further trips later on in the year. I'm certainly not going to make myself available at the drop of the hat for the year for trips like this. I have my own studies to think about.'

'Will I see you again Dixton?' she was clearly on the ropes and the canvas beckoned invitingly.

'Oh yes, if I'm ever up in London I'm sure we'll bump into each other.' (He felt he was safe enough saying this given a population of about eight million.) He shepherded her out of the room and into the court. Pepper was revving Jack's car in the avenue of the college. Dixton slung the holdall over his shoulder.

'Well goodbye Drusilla,' he put on his Spitfire pilot's voice.

'Goodbye Dixton.' She made a poor Vera Lynn.

He turned and ran towards the car. Pepper opened the passenger door. There was a screech of tyres as they sped down the avenue. They looked at each other and started roaring laughing.

'The Bit and Bridle?' suggested Pepper.
'Bloody right. It's on me.'
The two non-virgins headed for the hills.

CHAPTER EIGHT

The whole episode with The Elephant seemed to be a portent of evil to come. Although Dixton had managed to extricate himself from the situation with Pepper's assistance it was not all freewheeling from mid-November to Christmas. Certain matters, which had been successfully shelved since the beginning of term surfaced, much like reluctant drowning victims, just as Dixton was beginning to believe that he might have been blessed with more than the applicable EU quota of good fortune.

'I suggest that you contact me as a matter of urgency on extension 3348,' the note in his pigeonhole read. It was signed, 'Alice Hindley'. Dixton couldn't figure out who this person might be. He tackled Stan the porter to see if he might be able to help.

'Oh yes, Miss Hindley, she's one of those whatdoyoucallthem tutors'

'A tutor?'

'Yes, is she your tutor Dixton?'

'I don't think so, I mean I don't know, this is the first I've ever heard of her. What do you suppose she wants?'

'I dunno, maybe it's for one of those orientation sessions, you know the stuff they do for foreigners?'

'What do you mean "orientation"?'

'Oh you know, when they explain to you how to get the hang of our money and use the cardphones,' Stan laughed.

'Oh feck off Stan, it's a bit late in the term for that now really isn't it? Even if she did think I was a helpless idiot. No there must be more to it than that.'

Despite his flippant attitude Dixton was a little bit worried. What could this woman want with him? Surely he wasn't going to have his term ruined by someone raising the topic of study? Perhaps it wasn't about study at all but about something more sinister such as bicycle theft. The only thing to do was to brave it out and volunteer no information until absolutely necessary. There was nothing more annoying really than misplaced self incrimination. He phoned extension 3348 and was given an appointment for the following morning at nine.

'Jesus this must be serious,' Pepper said when Dixton told him how early in the morning the appointment was.

'Do you think it could be about the bike Pepper?'

'No way, they couldn't know about that. Anyway if they did, the police would be questioning you, not some college tutor. No, it's got to be about studies or something like that. I bet you haven't been up for nine o'clock very often in the last couple of months. In my experience if someone wants to see you first thing in the morning they either want to shag you or give out to you.'

Pepper's observations turned out to be accurate but unfortunately there wasn't any sign of early morning love and affection when Dixton knocked at the tutorial office door the following day.

'Ah Mr Larkin do come in, take a seat.'

Miss Hindley was a tough looking self contained woman. Dixton figured she was in her mid forties. She wore a grey two-piece jacket-and-skirt type suit and her hair was done in a bun which kind of sat on top of her head and looked a little like a jam-jar which had been painted with glue and then dipped in fur. Her face bore no sign of either friendliness or pity and this put Dixton on his guard instantly. He could see why she wasn't married.

'I suppose you are probably wondering why I have asked you to come and see me,' she began.

'Well, yes, as a matter of fact I had . . .'

'Mr. Larkin I'll come straight to the point, you've been brought to my attention by the Law Faculty. Apparently your attendance at lectures has been appalling and you've failed to submit an outline to the faculty on the subject matter of your thesis.'

This was so blunt that it could have passed for a Soviet agent. Dixton was relieved that at least it wasn't anything to do with bicycle theft. When he tired of the initial relief he tried to defend himself by that age-old ploy of delivering untruth with indignation.

'I beg your pardon, not only have I begun researching my thesis but any classes that I've missed have been. . .'

His opinion was obviously surplus to Miss Hindley's requirements, and she cut across him like a Grand Prix driver.

'Look Mr Larkin, I'm not interested in any of your pathetic excuses. From what I can gather you were rather fortunate to get into Cambridge in the first place and mark my words you will be very lucky to leave here with a degree of any description unless there is an instant change in both your attitude and your workrate.'

Dixton was shocked, who did this jumped up trollop think she was? Didn't she know who she was dealing with?

'Perhaps I have missed a couple of classes,' he said defiantly, leaving the "whats-it-to-you?" part unsaid but implied.

This woman was no tulip.

'I'll tell you exactly what business it is of mine Mr Larkin. I'm your tutor, despite the fact that you are the only student who has ever failed to meet with me even once during the first term and have ignored all my notes and invitations to that effect thus far.'

'I don't for a second doubt that you are my tutor but I don't remember ever getting any notes or invitations,' Dixton protested. She ignored him and continued.

'Because I am your tutor I am held vicariously liable in some bizarre way by the college authorities if you fail. If you succeed in your exams the system merely claps itself on the back and applauds the selection process. Failure by any of my students reflects badly on me and while you may be afforded the luxury of failing into oblivion, I have to remain here and try to protect my reputation. If things do not change, and change quickly, then I will have no hesitation in exercising my influence to have the Exam Board refuse to let you take the LLM exams.'

She sounded as if she meant every word and Dixton thought better of challenging her on the spot. He imagined she was the kind of woman who would not indulge in idle threatening. Even if he had been able to think of a suitable tack on which to stand his ground it was unlikely that he would have been given the chance to air it. It was clear that he had been invited there to be talked at tather than talked to. He wished he were back in bed.

She wasn't finished.

'Before you go Mr Larkin, here is the name of the supervisor for your thesis in the Law of Salvage. She handed him a piece of paper.

'I expect you to go and see him within the week without fail. He will advise you as to the standard of work required and will decide on the basis of your outline whether the topic you have chosed is a suitable proposition to put to the faculty for approval.'

It was like getting planning permission.

'Good day to you Mr Larkin, I trust that I will not have further cause to reprimand you between this and the exams.'

That was the only sensible thing she'd said all morning.

As Dixton left the office he felt that for the first occasion in a long long time the system had begun to get the upper hand. He glanced at the slip of paper.

'Robert Feldman, room three, Peterhouse College.'

He wondered what this geezer would turn out to be like. He closed the door of her office behind him as he left and noticed the nameplate 'Alice Hindley'. It came back to him now, yes he had recieved some mail from her during the first term all right but he'd binned it all, thinking that she must be the woman from the Christian folk/rock society. He smiled to himself. Still this telling off business was serious, maybe the honeymoon was finally over. He'd certainly never bargained on having to get his arse into gear this early, if at all.

'That's complete bullshit,' said Pepper, 'they can't stop you taking the exams just because you skip a couple of classes.'

'I'm not sure either but she seemed to know what she was talking about and she was bloody serious.'

'Oh don't worry about her Dixton, this will all blow over.'

'Well the faculty obviously chases up students who don't attend classes.'

'I'm sure they get tired of that pretty quickly, these boys don't give a toss as long as the fees are paid and the port doesn't run out.'

'That's easy for you to say, Pepper, you don't have to do any exams, just collect a few rocks and rattle off a couple of essays. If this dragon was telling the truth they could prevent me from taking the exams at all.'

'Not a chance, she's bluffing Dixton. She knows you're not going to fail the exams, no-one fails out of this place. That's why it's so hard to get in here in the first place, everyone wants to study in a university where no-one fails.'

Dixton felt that this logic was somehow warped.

'What about all these students who commit suicide each year in Cambridge, Pepper? They hardly do it to celebrate getting first class honours do they?'

'Undergraduates Dixton, undergraduates. It's a different story for them but postgrads don't fail at Cambridge. They work on the theory that if you've got a good grade elsewhere then eventually you're going to get a job and so they let us in here so that they can churn us out with postgrad degrees at a rate of knots and rely on us to cough up as alumni fairly shortly afterwards.'

This seemed vaguely plausible. The problem about the thesis still remained however, and Dixton would have to come up with a topic and then approach this supervisor Fieldmouse or whatever his name was.

'Look Dixton, if you're still worried about the bike we can sort it out this afternoon.'

This cheered Dixton up somewhat.

'OK, how do you suggest we disguise it?'

'Trust me, no-one will ever recognise this bike when we've finished with it. We'll give it a new identity.'

'Like those witness protection programmes?' grinned Dixton.

'Dead on. We'll go into town and buy a few essentials.'

'Excellent.'

The Law of Salvage could wait a little longer. Who did that joker think she was fooling with her nine o'clock starts and her vicarious liability?

A shadow loomed in the doorway of the bicycle shed and a deep voice boomed.

'What the hell is going on here?'

Dixton nearly jumped out of his skin, Pepper leaped up with the aerosol can still in his hand. In doing so he sprayed Dixton's shoes pink. This was it, caught in the act disguising stolen goods.

'I hope we're not interrupting anything,' the door opened fully and they saw that it was Jack and Andy.

'You bastards,' said Pepper, 'we thought it was the Praelector or someone.'

'I could go and get him if you like,' grinned Jack, 'how are you getting on with the painting?'

'Not too badly,' said Pepper aiming the can in their direction playfully.

'Take it easy with that stuff Pepper,' said Andy.

'I wish you'd told him that before he ruined my shoes,' said Dixton.

'Shouldn't you pair be wearing masks or something?' asked Jack.

'Don't worry about the fumes they're good for you,' Pepper replied.

'Bollox,' said Dixton coughing into a handkerchief, 'I read somewhere about some guy who owned a garage and died at about thirty from petrol fumes.'

'But this stuff is different,' said Pepper, 'it's the only form of aerosol which is ozone friendly.' He shook the can vigorously and the ballbearing in the can made a noise like a football rattle. He resumed spraying.

'I find that hard to believe. Look if you ever want anything painted properly ask an expert. Like me,' Jack chipped in.

'You're too late this time. Anyway don't worry about the spray-paint, maybe it's not great for the atmosphere but its good for bikes.' He stood back to admire his handiwork.

'Well, what do you all think?'

Dixton was unimpressed.

'I think it looks, oddly enough, like a girl's bike which has been sprayed pink because it's stolen. In fact it's more conspicuous now than it was before.'

The manufacturer's lettering on the frame was clearly legible through the thin coat of paint. Dixton wondered if it was an omen or punishment of some sort. He'd hung onto the bike after the incident in Grantchester mainly because of Pepper's theory that if he dumped it the police would be sure to track him down. Now the bloody thing was luminous pink and certain to get him caught. Jack and Andy thought the whole thing was very funny.

'You probably won't even need lights on it Dixton,' grinned Jack 'in fact you can hang it on the Christmas tree when they put up on the traffic island in the avenue next week.'

'There's no way I'm cycling this bloody thing outside of this shed,' said Dixton, 'I'd be picked up instantly for either theft or soliciting.' He wasn't quite sure which would be more embarassing socially.

'OK, OK,' said Pepper, 'maybe it's not the perfect disguise but have any of you got a better idea?'

'What about scorching the frame with a blow torch?' Andy suggested.

'No way, you'd melt all the gear cables, unless anyone here is confident enough to strip down the bike first and then reassemble it?' Jack queried.

There were no takers for the title of amateur bike mechanic.

'The only other thing I can think of is to cover the frame with rolls of sticky plastic tape,' Pepper volunteered.

Dixton's abiding memory of sticky tape was a three-legged race at school when he was about seven. Some idiot teacher came up with the bright idea of taping the teammates together. After they'd lost the race Dixton and 'Fizzer' Kelehan spent almost an hour trying to unravel the tape from around their ankles without scarring themselves for life. Ever since he'd discovered Aunt Sheila once waxing her legs her pain threshold had gone up in his estimation.

'I've got a couple of rolls in my room, we use them on the hockey sticks.'

Jack went to fetch them.

An hour later the bike was unrecognisable. Black and amber tape covered it from brake-pad to handlebar. Even some of the spokes were taped to mask the light pink paint.

'A masterpiece,' said Pepper.

'Excellent,' said Jack.

'What do you think?' asked Andy.

'Bloody hell,' replied Dixton, 'it looks like an escaped tiger.'

'But do you like it?'

'I love it,' said Dixton.

They'd put so much collective effort into the bike at this stage that it was difficult not to think of the bike in an affectionate way. Pepper left the shed and returned with four cans of beer.

'I think it's time we officially christened this bicycle,' he said, handing them one each.

91

'To the Tiger,' said Jack.

'To the Tiger.'

'You'll turn into a zookeeper Dixton if you're not careful,' laughed Pepper.

'How do you mean?'

'Well you'll soon have a huge collection of animals, first The Elephant and now a Tiger.'

The others roared laughing, Dixton knew that the time had come to defend his integrity as wittily and as intelligently as possible.

'Fuck off the lot of you!' he said shaking the can vigorously and spraying them with the contents.

Dixton spent a little while practising the guitar in his room once or twice during the next week or so. Herve had told him that there was a concert in Lupin before Christmas and that anyone who wanted to could get up and perform.

'Maybe you can sing a couple of Irish songs, Dixton.'

'I don't know Herve, it's a while since I practiced properly and anyway I'm not sure if I'd have the nerve to play in public.'

The tips of his fingers had softened considerably since the last time he'd played and they hurt like crazy for the first couple of sessions but gradually became re-accustomed to the wire strings. From time to time he tried to work out songs from the radio by ear. He wasn't a good guitar player by any stretch of even his own imagination but he found that if he sang loudly enough then the bum notes and chords were less noticable.

'I MET MY LOVE BY THE GASYARD WALL . . .'

Anyway wasn't that how most modern bands succeeded? Some of them had so much high-tech equipment and money behind them that they were either made to sound great by computer or hyped beyond belief. Either way the result was the same, massive sales to a public who were conditioned to accept the word of some DJ as gospel. In Dixton's opinion the posters and adverts were invariably more impressive than the bands themselves. A million pounds worth of amplifiers was enough to flush any band into the Top Ten. Oh well. Perhaps he should try to write a song and perform it at the Christmas concert. Yes, that's what he'd do. He looked out the window and saw Bernard and Liz, who'd given the guided tour on his first day, strolling across the Court deep in conversation. Water certainly finds its own level. He resumed playing the guitar with newfound resolve.

Sarah wasn't at all pleased with Dixton. As soon as he saw her at the next Criminal lecture he knew that she'd put two and two together and come up with the word 'bastard'. However gullible Drusilla might be, her best friend was certainly a great deal more perceptive. She didn't have to say a word for Dixton to realise that whatever chances he might ever have had with her were now well and truly destroyed.

'FRAUD,' said Professor Simpson. Dixton thought he was being spoken to so he looked up, Professor Simpson continued.

'Fraud takes many forms. It is also a Tort, I am sure you are all familiar with such terms as "fraudulent misrepresentation". The basic element in all crimes or torts of fraud is that someone tells lies to achieve some advantage.'

Sarah turned around and stared at Dixton. It was a look that would have melted cheddar. He'd certainly burned his boats with her. She obviously wished he'd actually been in one of the boats at the time. It really wasn't turning out to be a good week. He remembered that he'd been told by that Hindley woman to see his supervisor in the Law of Salvage before the week was out. It was Friday morning now and so he'd better get the skates under him as Aunt Sheila used to say. If ill fortune had taken a liking to him Dixton thought he'd see if he could get it over with as quickly as possible.

He strolled through the market place after the lecture and bought a second hand book called *Play golf in two weeks*. Dixton felt that even if it didn't help him to play in two weeks he might learn something from it. He wondered if you could sue the author for misrepresentation if it took you longer than two weeks to get the hang of the game. Still for fifty pence in a market stall Dixton reckoned he couldn't go far wrong. The market was quite busy.

'D-cup bras, two for a pound.'

It reminded him of trips down the country in Ireland with his Aunt Sheila to see relatives in Galway. There was a wonderful market there on Saturdays. For the first time since he'd come to Cambridge, Dixton was homesick. When he realised that that was what this emotion was he was surprised. Surely he couldn't be missing Ailesbury Crescent and the prospect of being pressganged into doing some gardening. How could he be yearning for accountability in the matter of allowances and the horror of saying the rosary with his aunt while *Match of the Day* was on? The feeling passed but Dixton remained surprised. He set off for Peterhouse College.

'I hope you're not heading for the library Dixton?' someone spoke from behind him, he turned around and saw that it was Penny from Lupin wheeling her bicycle with a basket full of shopping. A French loaf peered curiously out of the basket at an awkward angle.

'Pardon?' he replied.

'I said I'd be disappointed if you were going to the library to study or anything like that this early in the year.'

'No, no, I'm just heading in to Peterhouse to meet someone.'

Dixton hated making small talk, what he really wanted to know was how Nathalie was getting on. He hadn't seen her since the hockey match. Penny wheeled her bicycle beside him.

'Are you going to the Christmas dinner next week?' she asked.

'I hadn't really thought about it, will there be many people there?'

'I should think so, it's a fairly big affair, Lord Loopy will be there.'

'Oh,' Dixton said in a disinterested tone. Anyway he had planned on going to the Varsity Rugby game in London with Pepper.

'Never mind if you can't go,' she said putting one foot on the pedal and beginning to mount, 'I just thought you might like to know that Nathalie will be there, but of course if you can't be there you can't.' She winked at him as she went past waving a hand in the air behind her.

'Byeeee.'

Dixton wasn't sure whether she had been the bearer of good tidings or was simply alerting him that Nathalie would be there as a warning not to turn up himself. He couldn't figure women out at all; they weren't interested in football, always went to the loo in pairs and seemed to spend a fortune on cosmetics in order to look natural. Whenever the opportunity presented itself to Dixton to form an attachment to one of them he seemed to scare off the decent ones and attract the psychopaths.

Peterhouse looked beautiful, there were some leaves on the lawn in the main court and a ray of evening sunlight beamed through the arch leading into the next court. Two students in monks garb were strolling around the court deep in conversation. His aunt would have loved this, it would be like having a sneak preview of an enclosed order. Aunt Sheila had an idealised view of all things religious and wasn't shy about sharing those views with Dixton.

'Enclosed orders have a higher calling Dixton, they devote their lives to God free from the fetters of materialism and immorality. They are spared the pettiness of human interference.'

All the same if enclosed orders were televised, Aunt Sheila would beat a path to the cable company in her nightie with her subscription.

He found room three. The door was slightly ajar. There was no reply when he knocked. He turned to go and as he stepped back out into the court he almost collided with a smiling fair haired man who was clutching three bottles of whisky. He had a bottle in each hand and the third was wedged against his chest by the other two.

'I'm terribly sorry,' Dixton apologised.

'Not to worry,' said the man, 'no harm done.'

They squeezed past each other and then the man called after him.

'I say, you weren't looking for me, were you?'

Dixton returned from the court, the man with the bottles had nudged open the door of room number three and was standing inside on the carpet still clutching the whisky.

'Are you Mr Feldman?'

'Yes, that's me.'

'I'm Dixton Larkin.'

'Dixton Larkin yes mmm, well Dixton Larkin make yourself useful take one of these bottles will you before I drop them all.'

Dixton obliged.

'Where do you want me to put it?'

'Oh anywhere really, look why don't we open that one. Leave it on the desk and fill that jug with some water in the bathroom across the hall, while I put these away in the cupboard.'

When Dixton returned Mr Feldman was sitting in an armchair on one side of the electric fireplace. He indicated towards the armchair on the other side.

'Sit down there and let me get you a drop of this stuff. Leave the jug on that ledge there.'

Mr Feldman got up and went over to the desk. There was a small grating noise as he broke the seal on the bottle. Dixton looked around the room. It was quite large and served as a study–cum–bedroom. There was a low bed, neatly made, in one corner and the opposite side of the room was dominated by a huge mahogany desk. The walls were decorated by about ten or so framed pictures, five of which were a set of nineteenth century legal caricatures. The other pictures were paintings and prints of what seemed to be very similar seaside villages.

'It's Mousehole in Cornwall, that's where I'm from originally. I haven't been back there in years but I keep the pictures to remind me of it. I'm sure if I ever did go back for a visit I'd remember all the reasons I left there in the first place then I'd probably have to get rid of the paintings.'

'Do you want some water with that?' he placed a half full whisky glass in Dixton's hand.

'Yes, please.' Dixton rarely drank whisky, he always found that what he gained in warmth from it he lost in taste buds. This smelled sweet though.

He took a sip expecting to cough his guts up like they predictably always did in the films. It went down like honey.

'Good isn't it? I have a deal with the cellar keeper here, whenever he goes home to Edinburgh on holidays he brings me back a couple of bottles of this stuff and whenever he gets too drunk to drive to Steeple Morden I let him sleep on my floor. Here have another drop.'

He leaned forward and refilled Dixton's glass. Dixton liked him instantly.

There was an easy air about this man which made it seem perfectly natural that they should be sitting either side of an electric fire in late November drinking expensive Scotch in Peterhouse. Mr Feldman took a large gulp of whisky and leaned forward.

'Now Dixton Larkin what exactly was it you wanted to see me about?'

Dixton was a little taken aback.

'But hasn't Miss Hindley been in touch with you?'

'Never heard of her who is she?'

'She's a tutor at Lupin Hall, she told me to come and see you about my thesis topic in the Law of Salvage. Apparently I've missed the date for having the topic approved.'

'Oh, I see, one of those. Well don't you worry about deadlines or any of that nonsense, Dixton Larkin. A thesis in the Law of Salvage isn't the kind of thing that answers to deadlines or tutors. You pick the topic and I'll get it past the Board. There's always another Board meeting you know - it gets those chaps from John's and Magdalane out for the free lunches. More whisky?'

Dixton was flummoxed. There he was getting his knickers in a twist over this Hindley woman and her ultimatums when all he needed to do was keep his head and let things take their natural course. This was ideal.

'Mr Feldman?'

'Call me Robert, please; "Mr Feldman" always reminds me of mangy solicitors: "Dear Mr Feldman, your ex wife would like an account at Harrods".'

'Well, er, Robert,' Dixton was totally unfamiliar with the concept of a mixture of first name terms and authority, 'what about the thesis then, what topic should I choose?'

'Been to any of the lectures?'

'No,' Dixton said rather sheepishly.

'Excellent, I always find that any exposure to taught courses completely dulls the senses when it comes to creative writing. You're much better off relying on your intuition in situations like this. What's the first thing you think of when you hear the term "salvage"?'

'I don't know, em, the Spanish Armada I suppose, I know it's not directly relevant but . . .'

'Nonesense, of course it's relevant, "The Law of Salvage: an analysis of the Spanish Armada by Dixton Larkin". There you are, that's your thesis topic.'

'But what about . . .?'

'What about this Hindley woman and the Board? Don't give them a second thought. Leave the Public Relations side of things to me. First I'll write a note to your tutor and that'll keep her quiet. The Board meet before Christmas to consider the Phd viva results, I'll lob in your proposal for approval and they'll rubber stamp it. That way everyone's happy.'

'Thank you ever so much for all your help.'

'I've done nothing, you've chosen the topic and that's the first step. Drop in and see me after Christmas if you have any difficulties. My advice would be, read around the topic on a casual basis whenever you get a chance and then write the bloody thing in one go as close as possible to the end of the year. That way you don't give yourself a chance to brood on it and make pointless changes.'

Dixton got up to leave. He felt quite light headed.

'Thanks again for your help, I'll drop in and see you again in January.'

'Are you sure you won't have another drink?'

'Oh no, no thanks, I've probably had too much already. Oh all right I will.'

They finished the bottle and Dixton got back to Lupin at about half past seven that evening. It was the earliest Dixton remembered going to bed since he'd been a child.

CHAPTER NINE

'Come on Cambridge, get the finger out, it's a scrum not a bloody siesta.'

Dixton found himself entering into the spirit of things in Twickenham right from the kick-off. The second Tuesday in December; a battle date laid out by more than a century of tradition. The cold blue December sky provided a dry canopy for this annual set-to. The name 'Oxford' was never uttered by the true supporters of the light blues; it was always referred to as 'the other place'.

'Referee, REFEREE,' Pepper screamed into his ear as yet another penalty decision suspiciously went the other way. Dixton looked around the stadium and chuckled to himself. Here he was cheering his team on in the Varsity match next to an Ulster Protestant. This would bring tears to the eyes of thousands of Irishmen and Irishwomen who had fought for centuries to achieve a separate identity from 'the Brits'. Sod them. When your team was losing by six points history could screw itself quietly in the corner for all the attention it was going to get from Dixton Larkin.

'Did you see that? Did you see that? He was miles offside,' Pepper took every refereeing decision as a personal insult, 'I've seen dyslexic rabbits who know more about offside.'

There was a capacity crowd. Dixton was glad he'd seen the notice from the rugby club all those weeks ago. Tickets would have been impossible to get on the day. The hawkers were flogging stand tickets for five times their face value. The two boys had seriously considered selling theirs and going on the trash but sense prevailed; there would be plenty of opportunity for that at the Christmas dinner at Lupin Hall that evening. He was looking forward to seeing Nathalie again. Despite the fact that he'd had a crush on Sarah and an ill-fated romance with The Elephant, Dixton felt that Nathalie was the kind of woman he would really get on well with. Of course the milk-jug incident had proved to be a minor setback but Dixton was sure that all was not yet lost on the Nathalie front. There was also the concert which was scheduled to follow the dinner. Dixton had put a lot of work into his song and was itching to air it to the general student body in Lupin. Although he was a bit nervous about the prospect of performing in public he felt that a couple of well placed drinks would sort out the nerves.

'It's a penalty, it's a penalty, look Dixton are you asleep or what?'

Pepper elbowed him into the ribs.

'I can see it's a penalty Pepper. What are they going to do with it? That's what worries me.'

'They'll run it Dixton, I can feel it.'

'Rubbish, they'll kick it, points on the board, points on the board.'

At that very moment the man sitting in front of Dixton decided to stand up and do a bit of shouting.

'Oxford, Oxford.'

Dixton was furious, he couldn't see a thing. Pepper was to his left and had an unobstructed view.

'What did I tell you, Dixton?'

The man in front of Dixton persisted in standing up and shouting, 'Oxford, Oxford' and he started clapping his hands above his head in time to his own ranting. Dixton poked him in the back with his match programme.

'Hey, would you mind, would you mind sitting down?'

The man turned around and glared at him, 'As a matter of fact I would mind.'

'Well, whether you mind or not would you just do it?' Dixton felt sufficiently strongly enough about the issue to retort agressively. He put on what he hoped was a mean expression. It was always difficult to judge these things. The man rose to the challenge.

'I suppose you're a Cambridge supporter?' he sneered. Dixton knew he'd either have to put up or shut up. He decided to put up.

'We'll considering I'm wearing a Cambridge jersey, that's hardly a major observation. Who are you? Inspector fucking Morse?'

As soon as he'd said it he knew he'd hit home. Fortunately things didn't get the chance to turn nasty because at that moment the crowd around them errupted. Cambridge had run the penalty and scored a try. The man delivered another glare and sat down. Pepper and Dixton jumped up and down and screamed in the idiots ear for the remaining ten minutes of the match, 'CAMBRIDGE, CAMBRIDGE'. It drove him crazy. A drop goal in injury time sealed victory for the light blues.

They had forty minutes to kill before their train left. Pepper wanted to visit Soho but there wasn't time. Dixton had only seen it on television and it struck him as a rather sad amalgam of neon signs, expensive suits and disappointment. He supposed it was a bit like a closet which heterosexuals queued up to get back into. Real England was here in a greasy spoon cafe opposite Liverpool Street station; uneven doorstep slices of rye bread on the sideplate; the Beatles on the radio and an old man in a Chelsea shirt rolling a cigarette under a no-smoking sign.

'What about this song then Dixton, when are we going to hear it?'

Jack was sitting opposite them on the train back.

'You'll have to wait until tonight like everybody else Jack, it wouldn't be fair to give you a sneak preview.'

Dixton knew how the Beatles must have felt around the time of the release of their first single: will they, won't they, like it? In actual fact he hadn't quite finished it, he needed a second verse. He was however most proud of the chorus and if needs be he could always just repeat that a couple of times. His thoughts were interrupted by a loud voice bellowing in the passageway of the carriage:

'Oh it's the Irish contingent and their left-wing fan club.' It was Bernard. He was quite drunk and was followed closely by Zinowsky who of late appeared to be his best friend. In fact the earlier members of Bernard's merry band seemed to have disappeared altogether and Zinowsky might have been his only friend at this stage.

'Ignore him,' Jack said quietly. Bernard drew level with their seats and continued.

'What were you lot doing at Twickenham? Planning a terrorist attack?'

Dixton was tempted to whack him there and then but resisted. What was to be gained from doing that? At any rate there would be too many witnesses. 'A crime without witnesses is indeed a difficult crime to prove.' (Professor Simpson.)

'Sod off and die,' Pepper said.

'Oh it speaks,' Bernard sneered, 'Hey, Pepper have you knocked off any more attached women this term?'

'Just one: your mother!' Pepper retorted.

It was an excellent reply. Bernard reddened. Pepper started to laugh and that made Bernard even more furious. He muttered some weak jibe about Dixton preferring rugby to hockey because there was no goalkeeper. Despite this parting remark it was clear that the round had been won by them. Zinowsky glared at them as he passed and said nothing. He was a proper lapdog.

'Watch yourself with him,' Jack warned, 'he's dangerous.'

'We're quaking in our boots,' laughed Dixton. He was glad he'd kept his cool and allowed Pepper to cut Bernard down with a sharp comment rather than get physically involved himself. They arrived back in Cambridge in plenty of time to make it to the dinner.

Dixton stood in front of the mirror in his room and straightened his tie. Yes, he thought, Dixton you *are* a handsome devil. He wasn't sure if he was fooling himself or not but it certainly made him feel more confident. He had always been amazed at the type of man which women found attractive and had no idea whether or not he was good-looking himself. At any rate he reckoned that the best he could do was to shave and put on a suit. Even boxers looked good in suits. Pepper arrived.

'OK boy, are you all set?'

'As set as I'll ever be, how do you think I look?'

'Not too bad at all. Are you sure what's her name will be there?'

'Nathalie? Well I don't really mind whether she's there or not.'

'Like hell,' Pepper laughed, 'Come on or we'll be late. Are you all right for money?'

'I've got twenty quid.'

'More than enough. Seventy pence a pint, that's nearly thirty pints.'

Mention of money reminded Dixton that he had almost eaten up his allowance for the term and there was still another week to go before going home. It would be a close run thing but he was relieved that he had the other half of a return ticket which would get him to Dublin. The car park was jammed full of expensive cars and the lights of the tree on the traffic island were blinking on and off indecisively.

'I'll get the gowns Dixton, you hang around near the bottom of the stairs where I can find you.'

Dixton looked around the foyer. It was packed. It seemed that every person who had ever gone through Lupin Hall had returned for the Christmas dinner. It was one of the nights when students could bring guests and Dixton recognised one or two faces from the LLM classes of people from other colleges. He spotted Sanjra and Niall the vet across the foyer. Sanjra was wolfing back the sherries and Niall was chatting up a gorgeous tall girl. No sign of Nathalie. Pepper returned.

'Here you go, it was murder getting them I had to grapple with some old dear to get the last two, she was probably head of the old girls network.'

'Thanks Pepper,' Dixton put on his gown.

Zinowsky pushed past them on his way up the stairs to the dining hall. Dixton turned sideways and made his passage a little more difficult.

'I could have clocked him and Bernard on the train earlier on Pepper.'

'Just as well you didn't or things would have got completely out of hand.'

As they began up the stairs themselves Dixton noted that the Praelector was directly behind them. He hoped they weren't destined to share a table again.

'There's that cute little one who helps out in the college library' Pepper nodded in the direction of a red haired girl talking to the President of the college directly outside the dining hall.

'Don't even think about it Pepper,' Dixton warned, 'remember Clara.'

101

'Clara who?' Pepper winked at him.

The dining hall was covered in Christmas decorations and everybody's place setting included two crackers and a paper hat. Only about three people put on the hats initially but after a glass or two of wine most joined in the spirit of the occasion.

They were in the middle of the first course before Dixton finally located Nathalie. She and Penny were at the other end of the hall but if he leaned to his left Dixton had a clear view of her back. Penny was seated opposite her and Dixton caught her eye. She must have said something to Nathalie because she turned round and gave him what appeared at that distance to be a smile. She turned back to Penny and they both seemed to be laughing. You never know, he told himself.

'Could you pass the salt please?' Professor Lynn, the librarian was sitting on Dixton's right. Dixton obliged.

'A fabulous win today for Cambridge eh?' the librarian continued.

'Yes, yes it certainly was,' Dixton replied. He had no interest in pursuing a conversation with the deaf librarian. He had more pressing things on his mind, namely how to catch another precious glimpse of Nathalie through the gap between the two waiters serving the peas.

'Were you at the game yourself?'

'Pardon?' Dixton really didn't want to talk while he was busy eyeing up a prospective elopment partner. However it would have been rude to ignore Professor Lynn. The question was repeated.

'Were you at the match Mr Larkin?'

'Yes I was Professor, I enjoyed it thoroughly.'

Dixton spoke quite loudly so that he could be heard. It must be awful being deaf, he thought. The main course was served while they spoke fairly superficially about the Varsity game. He thought he saw Nathalie looking over at him once during the meal but wasn't sure. Pepper meanwhile was chatting up the librarian's assistant on the opposite side of the table. Dixton could barely hear any of their conversation above the general hum in the room but caught one brief snippet. Pepper was laying on the charm with a shovel.

'The thing is, I really miss home you know, it's not having anyone to really talk to, if you know what I mean?' What was worse was that he was might be believed. Oh well. Lord Lupin was the guest of honour at the Christmas dinner and a number of people made speeches welcoming him.

'It is a great honour and pleasure to welcome our benefactor here this Christmas to our midst,' said the Praelector. Dixton thought it would be the ideal time to start a food fight, but he was on shaky enough ground in college at the moment as it was, so he simply switched off from the Praelector's speech and looked over in Nathalie's direction instead. She had turned sideways in her chair so he saw her profile. God she was breathtakingly beautiful. His view was obstructed by some idiot who moved his chair back to talk to someone at the table behind him. The speech droned back into his wavelength.

'Benefaction and sponsorship are the only way in which a college of this size can manage to function. If it were not for your generous help Lord Lupin how we would make ends meet?'

'Stick two people into the same nappy,' someone heckled.

The room errupted into laughter. The Praelector looked sternly around the dining room but couldn't locate the culprit. He continued his speech as though nothing had happened and this made the situation even funnier. His speech ended with a promise to show Lord Lupin the new 'Lupin fountain' which had been built in his honour since his last visit. Everybody except Lord Lupin looked thoroughly bored. Dixton had seen some workmen erecting the fountain earlier that day. It was a little like the wet paint syndrome for royalty.The meal was nearly over when Bernard got up from a nearby table to go out to the loo or something. As he passed their table Dixton muttered under his breath.

'Bloody idiot.'

'Yes he certainly is.' Professor Lynn commented as though he had heard Dixton's remark. Dixton had deliberately muttered under his breath and was amazed that Professor Lynn had heard. After all he was almost totally deaf. He looked up in time to see the Professor give him a knowing wink. Surely he couldn't have been pretending to be deaf? Just then however, in answer to his query, the Senior Tutor leaned down the table towards the Librarian and said in a rather loud voice.

'I say, Professor Lynn, have you finished that report on the proposed changes to the library?'

The old man cupped a hand behind his ear.

'Eh, pardon, what's that Senior Tutor?'

The Senior Tutor repeated his question two or three times and then gave up. The librarian turned back towards Dixton and gave a little smile.

'To amend the old saying Mr Larkin, if you get a name for staying in bed in the morning, people soon get the message.'

The old codger. So he wasn't deaf at all. It was perfect; feign a blemish and inefficiency will soon be accepted as normality. Dixton chuckled away to himself until the end of the meal. He remembered the first time he'd met the librarian, in this same hall in fact. He wondered if he'd said anything awful about him on that occasion. Still not to worry, this was quite funny. As the librarian got up to leave the dining

103

hall Dixton gave him a coded seal of approval.

'GOODBYE Professor,' he roared.

Dixton pulled a cracker with Pepper across the table. Pepper won some stupid tiny plastic motorbike. Dixton spotted Penny and Nathalie exiting into the corridor and promptly got up to head them off via the double doors.

'Oh Dixton, fancy seeing you here,' the astonishment in Penny's voice was almost authentic. Nathalie, however, seemed genuinely surprised and not unhappily so. Dixton was stuck for something to say for the first time he could remember. Penny opened the way for him.

'Goodness is that the time? I've got to rehearse my sketch with the rest of the girls from the hockey club. I'm sure you two have lots to discuss.' She hurried off leaving Dixton and Nathalie staring uneasily at each other.

'Perhaps we could go for a drink?' she suggested. Dixton remembered for the first time that she was French. Gosh what a cutie pie.

'Yes, yes of course we could get some coffee in the reading room.' He instantly felt awkward. He shouldn't have mentioned the reading room in view of his strike rate with milk in that venue. It was unlikely that Nathalie had forgotten such an assault on her ankles and one of her dresses.

'Perhaps not the reading room,' Nathalie laughed.

'I'm terribly sorry about that, I mean it wasn't like it seemed, it really wasn't a very good start, I don't mean a start of anything, just well you know. . .'

'No need to explain, I know that it wasn't your fault. Perhaps we could start all over again with something less dangerous than milk.'

Dixton felt as though he'd just won the national lottery. It was a strange warm feeling, like everything going right without his really having to try. It was as if some huge screen which had separated him from his destiny had been demolished by accident. He was in love. The bar was less crowded than was usual after formal dining. Most people had gone to change for the concert or to rehearse their acts.They perched themselves on two of the high stools.

'What would you like to drink Nathalie?'

'Some wine please.'

Dixton thought that it sounded very French to order wine at a bar so he rowed in.

'Wine for two please, Pickford.'

Pickford grinned, 'Would you like a bottle of wine or two glasses?'

'Oh definitely a bottle,' Dixton replied. It could be a long evening.

'OK Dixton, any particular type?'

'Em.' Dixton knew a few of the basic categories, red, white, rosé, and anti-freeze but beyond that he wasn't too discerning. When he drank wine it was usually free and so it was the quantity rather than the label which interested him on those occasions.

'Could I see the wine list please?'

He selected a bottle of Chateau Margaux. It sounded vaguely familiar and Pickford certainly looked impressed. Nathalie opened her purse.

'Oh no Nathalie, you're not paying for this, it's my treat.' Dixton pushed the cash she'd put on the bar counter back towards her.

'A chit please Pickford,' Dixton took a pen from his pocket and hovered it over the slip of paper waiting for Pickford to read the price out from the list.

'That's forty five pounds please.'

Dixton nearly choked, 'I beg your pardon Pickford, how much did you say?'

'Forty five pounds, Dixton.'

Dixton tried to look as unshocked as possible. This was probably the most expensive wine in the whole world. For that kind of price you'd expect shares in the vineyard. Still this was not the time to appear either cheap or poor.

'No problem Pickford,' he signed the chit and handed it over. He would have to scrimp on lunch between now and going home to balance things out. Anyway, even if nothing happened between Nathalie and himself she was well worth splashing out a few pounds on.

'This wine is gorgeous Dixton, do you know a lot about wine?'

'Eh, not really,' he didn't want to get drawn out into the open on the subject if he could avoid it at all, and he decided to talk about something else.

'Oh I see they've got the stage all set up for this concert.'

'Oh yes, it looks fabulous.'

At the far end of the room Jack and a few others were stomping on the makeshift stage to ensure it was safe. Dixton still hadn't managed to think of a second verse but he hoped that something would occur to him in the course of the evening. Sanjra joined them at the bar; he ordered a large gin and tonic. Dixton introduced him to Nathalie.

'Are you looking forward to Dixton's song?' Sanjra asked her.

'I didn't know he was going to sing; Dixton you never mentioned this, what are you going to sing?'

'Oh just a song I wrote myself,' Dixton tried to mask his embarrassment with bravado.

'Oh that's wonderful, I didn't know you could sing.'

'He can't,' Pepper quipped, joining the group at the bar counter. He was accompanied by the assistant librarian.

'This is Dawn everybody, Dawn this is Sanjra, Dixton and . . .'

'I'm Nathalie.'

Dawn shook hands with everyone and then so did Sanjra. He was well gone at that stage.

'Oh great, you've got some wine, Dixton.' Pepper picked up the bottle.

'You'll hardly drink all that on your own. Pickford two more glasses, please. Sanjra will you have a glass?'

'OK,' Sanjra beamed.

'Three more glasses Pickford.'

Pepper filled the three glasses and poured the remainder into Nathalies glass. Dixton gawped at him. Pepper caught his look.

'No more drink for you boy, you need all your wits about you for this singing business.'

'I'd better go and get my guitar. I'll see you in a while Nathalie?' Dixton said in a cross between a question and an expression of hope. He was a bit put out that everyone had descended on him just as he was making progress. Maybe she wouldn't stay. Her reply reassured him greatly.

'I'll be here Dixton, remember the next drink is on me.' She smiled and he lost himself in her big brown eyes for a second.

'Right-ho, I'll just go and get the em, the guitar.'

'Let me introduce to you, ladies and gents, all the way from J block, the Lupin Hall Morris Dancers.'

Jack was MC for the evening and he stepped aside from in front of the stage to allow the first act of the evening to get under way. Dixton had just returned to the bar in time for this introduction. The place was now completely full and people were still streaming in carrying chairs from the kitchens of their accomodation blocks. The Morris dancers were not quite on form, this was largely due to the restrictions imposed upon them by the size of the temporary stage. Dixton stood just inside the door leading from the front foyer and did his best not to laugh.

'Excellent eh?' a voice beside him said. It was the college chaplin. Dixton couldn't remember his name but twigged who he was from the collar.

'Oh yes, yes,' he agreed. He thought of the vicar as one of those horribly optimistic people who invariably see some good in everything, especially when it's crap.

The first act finished with the lead dancer stepping off the front of the stage by accident and landing on the pianist. The audience enjoyed at least this part of the performance and applauded loudly, Jack stepped back into the limelight to ensure continuity.

'Next we have "The Academics", a jazz quartet comprised of members of staff. Please give them a particularly warm round of applause.'

The place erupted into applause and cheering as the Senior Tutor led the quartet on clarinet in a recognisable version of *When the Saints go Marching in.*

Dixton looked through a gap in the crowd and focused on the group of people gathered at the bar. He wasn't sure if he could make out Nathalie or not but he found the effort somehow comforting anyway. As the jazz band finished, his attention was drawn back to the stage as Jack tried to stop Bernard clambering up onto it. It all happened too quickly though and Bernard suddenly appeared on the stage clutching the microphone. He was even more drunk than he'd been on the train.

'Hello, hello, everyone,' he tapped the microphone unnecessarily four or five times, 'hello, Lupin Hall do you read me?'

'Get off dickhead,' someone shouted. There was a roar of support of the sentiment from the crowd. Bernard ploughed on undeterred.

'Did you hear about the two Irishmen who went to Twickenham? One said to the other "hey Paddy, I don't remember the two keepers being sent off do you?" Speaking of Irish idiots I have to say that . . .'

'Sod off Bernard,' someone roared. By this time Jack and Andy Chalmers had climbed onto the stage and physically removed Bernard.

'I'm terribly sorry about that ladies and gentlemen,' said Jack, 'our next act is a man some of you may know as the reserve mixed hockey goalkeeper, one man and his guitar, Dixton Larkin.'

Dixton's arrival on stage was greeted with a slightly reticent reaction by the crowd. It was clear that they were unsure about how he was going to react to the comments from Bernard, which had so obviously been directed at him and at Pepper. Dixton put them at their ease immediately.

'I haven't brought any racist jokes with me here this evening, I thought I'd leave that to some public school git who can't hold his drink.'

His dig at Bernard was greeted with fierce applause and much cheering. He could see Lord Lupin and the Praelector in the West Court through the window. Heading for the Praelector's residence for a few tipples no doubt.

Dixton continued, 'I've always felt that our college lacked something which is essential to ensure the identity of Lupin Hall as an institution of learning.'

'Double beds,' Niall the vet shouted. Everyone laughed.

'Even more important than that, a College Anthem. That is why I decided to write one and to sing it here this evening.' He strummed the guitar and began.

'Here at Lupin we're a family, the Praelector's like a father to me,
Miz Hindley's like a mother, cause she treats me like a child.
Beaten at sports every single week, a twenty five year losing streak,
We live our lives on the off peak, and the cheap beer drives us wild.

CHORUS

We are Lupin, nobody knows us
No other college ranks academically below us,
Even the t-shirts and the maps they sell in the market square don't show us.
We are Lupin, the college that time forgot.'

Dixton hadn't written a second verse so he repeated the chorus. When he'd finished the place went crazy. People stood up and cheered. There was a chant of: 'We want more, we want more.'.

Dixton regretted not having prepared any more songs to sing. At the same time he didn't want to disappoint anyone either. He launched into a reprise of the Lupin Anthem and was prevailed upon to repeat the chorus over and over until everybody in the bar was singing along. When he finally left the stage he was exhausted. He knew how Elvis must have felt. All that was missing was a golf cart. He made his way through the crowd to Pepper, Dawn and Nathalie.

'Well done boy,' Pepper clapped him on the back, 'what are you having to drink?'

'Dixton, I am really impressed,' Nathalie leaned forward on the stool and gave him a peck on the cheek. He felt himself blushing but hoped no-one would notice.

'Here you are.' Pepper handed him a pint.

The next act was a fairly timid chap called Burns studying English who recited a poem he'd written himself called *The Weasel*.

'This is about as interesting as unblocking your ear with a biro,' said Pepper.

'I'll have to go pretty soon,' said Dawn. Dixton saw a look of alarm descend over Pepper's face.

'Er, maybe we can go for a walk around the grounds before you go,' he suggested.

'At eleven o'clock at night?' she asked.

'Well I just thought that maybe you'd like to see around the college, it's different at night and well. . .'

'Perhaps some other time Jonathan, thanks for a wonderful evening but I really must be off,' she finished her drink.

'At least let me call you a taxi,' Pepper was desperate not to let the opportunity slip away completely.

'Oh all right,' she sighed.

'See you in a while then.' Pepper gulped down what was left of his pint and hurried out after the assistant librarian.

Her boss isn't deaf and she's certainly not dumb, Dixton thought.

'I should be going back to Newnham quite soon,' Nathalie remarked.

'Oh,' said Dixton disappointedly.

'It's not that I wouldn't prefer to stay here with you it's just that our house mistress is quite strict and she locks the doors at eleven thirty. I had hoped to move out of college residence this year but I was a little late in looking for accomodation. I'm going to move out after Christmas.'

'I see.'

He wasn't sure whether he should ask to walk her home or whether she was giving him the brush off. He decided she was worth risking rejection over.

'Would it be all right if I walked you back to Newnham?'

She took his hand and squeezed it.

'I thought you would never ask,' she smiled. Dixton was on cloud ten.

They left Lupin and walked out the back gate to Grange Road. When they were crossing over to Sidgwick Avenue Dixton risked his entire life and took her by the hand. She responded by intertwining their fingers. Dixton heaved an inward sigh of pure relief and elation. At the gates of Newnham they stood facing each other holding hands for what seemed like ages.

'I really must go in,' Nathalie said as they saw the lights in the Halls of Residence begin to go out one after the other.

'OK,' he said reluctantly.

'OK,' she said.

'Goodnight, then Nathalie.'

'Goodnight, then Dixton.'

He let go of her hands and his mind started racing, this was the moment to declare his affection, or was it? He knew that in a matter of seconds they'd have to part and whatever would happen between them in the future might well depend on how he handled this particular

109

moment. He took hold of her right hand as she turned to go and pulled her gently towards him. He was prepared to back off at the first sign of resistance but at the same time knew that he had to take the initiative. His eyes searched hers for the go-ahead but he was more afraid of overlooking the signals than of misreading them. When her face was right in front of him he leaned in, closed his eyes and hoped for the best. It was the most wonderful kiss ever in the history of the world. It may have lasted seconds or years, probably seconds, then it was over but still happening.

'See you tomorrow,' she whispered as she opened the side-gate.

'See you tomorrow,' he said back but she was gone and somehow still there. He floated back to Lupin Hall humming the *Wedding March* out loud. Maybe it was a bit premature but he didn't care.

Dixton approached the main building through the archway near the bicycle shed. It was quite dark and a figure stepped out of the shadows.

'Well, Romeo I suppose you and your friend Pepper think that you can make an idiot of me in front of a crowd of people and get away with it.' It was Bernard.

'Look Bernard, why don't you just go and sleep it off. It's late.'

'Hey, wise guy, there's no need to be condescending.' Another figure loomed out of the archway blocking his way.

'Zinowsky what are you doing here? I thought you'd be off somewhere raising sponsorship for a brain transplant.'

'Well I think it's time someone taught you a lesson,' Bernard leered.

Dixton knew that this situation was going to turn nasty pretty quickly, he would have to adopt the old cowards approach: 'defence is the best form of defence'. He turned and sprinted back the way he'd come. It took the others a split-second to react and he rounded the corner past the sheds and doubled back into the East Court.

He took refuge against the ivy covered gable wall of the tutorial office building and listened out for the sound of anyone following him. He waited in the darkness for a short while and then tried to sneak across the Court. The light in the Court was quite dim but he could make out the shape of the Lupin fountain from the Christmas lights draped around it and he could hear the water splishing. He made a break for it across the open space and peered around the corner. He could make out the shape of a couple of people coming towards him and so he quietly turned back to go around the accomodation blocks instead. A hand grabbed the neck of his pullover.

'Thought you'd get away from us, did you?'

Bollox, it was Zinowsky. He tried to struggle free but this ape had a very firm grip on him. Dixton was dragged back out into the middle of the Court near the fountain. The sound of voices drew close and it was clear that Zinowsky might not have much time in which to rough him up. Dixton drew little solace from this as he saw Zinowsky's fist draw back in the moonlight preparing to punch him in the face. He ducked and felt the punch fly past his ear, then Dixton put his head down and charged forward. He bulldozed Zinowsky full in the chest and forced him to topple backwards. There was a huge crash as the newly concreted fountain collapsed under the weight of years of McDonalds convenience food and milkshakes. The water supply to the fountain which had been politely controlled to a trickle gushed up from the base like a delinquent fire hydrant.

'And this, Lord Lupin, is the fountain,' the Praelector announced triumphantly, nudging the nappy king ahead of him around the corner just as the catastrophe unveiled itself.

Dixton wished the ground would open up and swallow him and it did, he plunged through some plastic sheeting into a shallow trench to one side of the statue. He flailed out and tried to stop himself falling but only succeeded in dragging the Christmas lights (still lighting) with him. The kind and generous benefactor of Lupin Hall rounded the corner in time to see a statue of himself arse end up as Dixton tried to extricate himself from the tangle of pipes and wires in the trench while enmeshed in a set of Christmas lights. Meanwhile the water gushed onwards and upwards delivering a heavy downpour on the Praelector and Lord Lupin on its way back to earth.

'Lord Lupin, I assure you there's a perfectly simple explaination for all this,' the Praelector grovelled.

'Yes Praelector, I suspect there is, the words "Piss-up" and "Brewery" spring to mind.' Lord Lupin turned and headed for the dry comfort of his Rolls Royce.

Dixton sensed that the Praelector was absolutely livid.

'Larkin, there's no point in trying to conceal yourself in that trench, I can see you perfectly well.'

'But, but. . .' Dixton protested vainly. He looked around for someone to share the blame with but Zinowsky had disappeared.

'My office tomorrow at nine o'clock sharp Larkin.' Dr Winston turned on his heel and marched after their fleeing benefactor.

Dixton remembered Pepper's words.

'There are only two reasons why someone wants to see you first thing in the morning.'

It didn't take a Noble Prizewinner to figure out which reason applied here.

CHAPTER TEN

Dixton looked out of the small window. He hated flying. The fact that people like Ferdinand Magellan had successfully circumnavigated the earth, centuries before the invention of the life jacket, did nothing to allay his fears about meeting his demise somewhere above Kidderminster. He knew that planes were able to fly but that didn't mean he had to believe it.

'Would you mind terribly moving your seat forward please?'

The lady in the row behind him had stuck her knee into his back for most of the journey and was now asking him to give even more ground. He was too tired to argue and pressed the button in the arm of the seat, straightening it instantly. His chest was thrown forward while his head seemed to stay where it was. The perfect illustration of self-inflicted whiplash. He didn't even have the energy to scream. His meeting with the Praelector earlier in the week in the aftermath of the Christmas Concert had drained him completely. He'd arrived in good time for the meeting; the Praelector had been about twenty minutes late.

'Sorry about that, Larkin, but the College Disciplinary Committee meeting ran over time.'

Dixton gulped silently.

The Praelector sat down in the chair behind the mahogany desk. The chair was facing the window; he swivelled around sharply.

'Larkin, you're a problem student and at Cambridge we do not tolerate problem students. Oh yes, there are off-the-wall writers, low-grade actors, top-class mad scientists, these we embrace wholeheartedly on the basis that, however eccentric they may be, they all possess one common characteristic; usefulness. The determining characteristic of problem students is that they have no usefulness whatsoever. Do I make myself clear?'

Dixton wasn't sure whether to brazen it out or to feign helplessness. He suspected that whatever course of action he adopted would be the wrong one.

'Not really.'

Dr Winston leaned his elbows on the desk and allowed his fingertips to tap quickly against each other. He smiled patronisingly.

'Well, let me make myself more clear then. You are not wanted here, your sort is not wanted here at Lupin Hall. I have to say that I opposed your admission to this college from the word go. Even at your interview I suspected a degree of subversion which you have subsequently gone on to display time and again. Now do I make myself clear?' (It was beginning to become as clear as a Foxes Glacier Mint.)

Dixton felt that he would be doing himself a disservice by not defending himself. He was already standing so he couldn't suddenly stand up indignantly. He took out a handkerchief and blew his nose; at least it gave him a couple of seconds to think. It was a losing battle but he attempted a defence.

'I think that 'subversion' is a rather harsh term to use, Praelector.' (Tackle him on specific words and get the overall tenor of the allegations reduced, that the trick.)

'Subversion is a harsh term, Larkin, but then these are harsh times and we must not shirk from calling a spade a spade.'

'Well, by the same token I think. . .'

'No, that is your problem, or at least one of them, Mr Larkin. You do not think. Otherwise you would not have attempted to steal a car outside of the hockey grounds, you would not have failed to attend your lectures, you would not have had to be spoken to by your tutor.' He was on a bit of a roll. Dixton attempted another intervention.

'In fairness, Praelector, I can explain. . .'

'Explanations are of no use at Cambridge, what we seek are solutions. Perhaps you feel that you can also explain your reprehensible behaviour during the last twenty four hours, Mr Larkin. You threatened another student in my presence on the stairs before the Christmas dinner, ridiculed the College and members of its staff in a pathetic ditty and then rounded off the evening by assaulting a student, wrecking the statue of our benefactor, and drenching Lord Lupin and myself. You then had the temerity to try to avoid detection by hiding in a trench.'

Put in those terms it sounded fairly damning, Dixton looked down at his shoes.

'Yes, well I do admit that perhaps. . .'

'Perhaps what, Mr Larkin? Perhaps now the adjective 'subversive' seems somewhat more appropriate? Is that it?'

Dixton had never felt so isolated in his whole life. What he wouldn't give to be back in good old Remedies and Restitution class. He felt that it was only a matter of time before he was blamed for the Moors murders and the disappearance of the *Marie Celeste*. He tried to make light of the situation in his head but he knew that this was fairly big biscuits. There was a pause before the Praelector delivered the final kick in the teeth.

'No-one has ever been sent down from Lupin Hall before. Even Hedley Woofpath, who was caught with drugs in the seventies, was allowed to remain but then of course he was a rugby Blue. Our short but proud history has never had to suffer the humiliation of one of our students being sent down.'

Dixton was terrified. Surely they couldn't send him home? That kind of thing never actually happened, or did it? Aunt Sheila would kill him. What about Nathalie? What about Pepper? He felt his entire life slipping away from him in much the same way as you know when your team is losing by a thousand points and the referee looks at his watch that the game is still on but to all intents and purposes, fruitlessly over at the same time.

'The Disciplinary Committee have heard my recommendation that you be sent down. They will reconvene on Friday morning to make a final decision. Reports will be sought from various sources but you needn't pin any hopes on them. You may rest assured that the game is up Larkin. Problem students may be easily noticed but they are equally easily forgotten.'

Dixton felt gutted. What the fuck was he going to do? He was too sick for words. He looked at the airsickness bag as he recalled the parting words of the Praelector.

'There is a ton of bricks balanced finely over your head, Mr Larkin and it is about to come crashing down. You may expect a letter from the Committee on Friday officially informing you of their decision. Good day to you Mr Larkin.'

'They're complete bastards,' Pepper said when Dixton filled him in that afternoon.

'I know, I know, but there's no point in trying to off load the blame at this stage, anyway there's more to all this than Bernard.'

'OK so maybe Winston doesn't like you but those scumbags haven't helped. To think that we could have taken them on the train, Jesus it makes me sick, why don't we sort them out now?'

'Look Pepper, I'm up to my neck at the moment but there's no need to bury myself completely. The final decision won't be until Friday morning.'

'Yea, you're right Dixton, maybe the Committee will let you stay.'

'Maybe they will.'

The next couple of days were a nightmare. Dixton had always considered himself to be even luckier than a clairvoyant black cat but it seemed that he had miscalculated horribly. It had crossed his mind during the interrogation to implicate Bernard and Zinowsky but he had no intention of trying to drag others down with him. Whatever else he was, he wasn't a snitch.

Nathalie was his greatest consolation that week and also his greatest possible disappointment. Just when he'd found someone to love it seemed that he was to be served with an exclusion order.

'Don't worry, Dixton, they can't separate us forever.'

'Oh no, I know that once you've finished your degree and trained with some large firm in Paris we may meet up again at the tercentenary celebrations at Lupin. I'll be able to sneak up behind you in my wheelchair and clank romantically against your zimmer frame.'

'Don't be silly,' she laughed, putting her arm around him. They sat on a bench in the Newnham College grounds near the grass tennis courts.

'We can write and I can come and see you in Dublin.'

It all sounded horribly thin and unlikely to Dixton. If it weren't for the fact that Nathalie was hell bent on comforting him he would have taken a policy decision to be inconsolable and signed up for the Foreign Legion that Tuesday. It was important to make the most of these last few days whatever happened. The news spread around Lupin Hall within hours. Dixton Larkin was on death row and the Governor of the State hated him. During the next couple of days people either avoided him altogether or went out of their way to approach him and offer support.

'I hear you're in a bit of bother at the moment,' Professor Lynn whispered to him in the corridor outside the recreation rooms on Wednesday morning. Outside it had begun to rain maniacally.

'I'm afraid so, Professor,' Dixton replied dejectedly.

'Chin up, eh?'

'What?'

'Where there's life there's hope and all that,' the librarian punched him playfully in the arm. It was the kind of comment you heard at Wimbledon in the first round when the last British competitor in the tournament is two sets down and losing five love in the third but wins a point with a lob. Dixton felt that the Praelector was probably right, the game was up. Who did he think he was? Coming to Cambridge under the false pretences of a scraped two-one? Who was he fooling?

On Thursday after lunch Herve invited him to drop in to his rooms for a drink. Dixton sat in an armchair swishing whiskey around in a large tumbler and staring at the melting ice clinking aimlessly around the edges.

'You must be positive Dixton,' said Herve, Dixton looked up.

'Why bother?' In twenty four hours or so I'll be winging my way back to the Republic to face charges of treason against my sponsor.' It was the first time he'd really articulated his deepest fear out loud, Aunt Sheila would kill him. Karen came in carrying shopping bags.

'Oh Hello, Dixton.'

He knew from her tone that she disapproved of whatever it was that had happened. She disappeared into the kitchen.

'Don't worry Dixton, most people know what really happened.' Herve tried to make up for his wife's disapproval, 'Zinowsky has been spotted wearing a medical collar but no-one has any sympathy for him, or Bernard.'

What galled Dixton most was that no charges were being levelled at them. He, Dixton Larkin, the victim of an unprovoked attack was being treated like a criminal while his attackers were at large and enjoying not only diplomatic immunity but also the benefits of the NHS. Pepper was as defiant as ever about the whole affair and threatened to sort out the other two if Dixton were sent down.

'If they ever set foot in Ireland they won't get a welcome from either community.'

Pepper's heart was in the right place but good intentions couldn't save Dixton now. They had a quiet drink in the Bit and Bridle in Grantchester on Thursday night. Pepper cycled the Tiger while Dixton borrowed Jack's bike. The pub was empty as the local drinkers were in training for the weekend. They played darts for a while but soon lost interest. Dixton was reminded of the darts game as the plane began to swoop down from the clouds over Dublin Bay towards the Airport.

'There's a note in your pigeon hole, Dixton,' Stan the porter said sombrely the following morning as he was going off duty. The Abominable Slowman was just beginning his shift and he leered condescendingly at Dixton. He would be delighted to see the end of Dixton at Lupin Hall. There were one or two people hanging around the porters' desk and even they stopped and looked expectantly in his direction as he opened the small white envelope bearing the university crest. Dixton read the note five or six times before the message registered.

'Dear Mr Larkin,

In view of the seriousness of recent events which have occurred in the College grounds, involving a number of our students, the Board has conducted an investigation in to these and other matters which have been brought to our attention. An application has been made to have you expelled from Cambridge. However, in the light of some character references which have been submitted on your behalf it has been decided to allow you to continue your studies at this University subject to the following conditions:

1. any further incidents of misconduct on your part will result in an immediate reconsideration by the Board of the application to have you expelled;

2. your supervisor and tutor have been requested to submit monthly progress reports to the Board;

3. compensation is to be paid by you at the beginning of next term in respect of damage to College property.'

At Dublin, Dixton noticed small patches of thin ice on the runway as they touched down. He checked to see if his skates were secure.

Aunt Sheila was standing at the front of the crowd in the arrivals lounge, clutching a set of rosary beads. 'We heard there was fog.'

'Hello, Aunt Sheila', he said kissing her on the cheek. She reeked of some perfume that smelled like aftershave. Perhaps it was aftershave. Aunt Sheila pocketed the rosary beads carefully and gave him a peck on the cheek. Dixton could hardly remember the last time he'd been glad to see her. When the greetings were over Aunt Sheila enquired on behalf of the entire arrivals lounge at a volume which would have put a megaphone to shame.

'How is Cambridge? How was your first term?'

Dixton had decided hours before to lie at all costs about the state of play at Lupin. At the slightest sign that all was not well he knew that she would take action to remedy the situation and that had to be avoided.

'Couldn't be better, Aunt Sheila, I never knew there was so much more to learn about the law.' (That at least was true enough.)

A huge 'Welcome' sign written in Christmas lights dominated the vista as they stepped outside the main building and approached the car park. Dixton knew that this time at least he was not going to be in Ireland longer than the Christmas holidays, however it could all have been horribly different. As he sat into the passenger seat of his Aunt's BMW he wondered who had bailed him out with the character references. They negotiated the large roundabout to the entrance to the airport and followed the sign for the city centre.

'Tell me everything, Dixton,' his aunt prompted.

'Well, the lectures are tough going but I'm managing to keep up with the secondary reading so far.'

'Glad to hear it, you can never do enough secondary reading, Dixton, the mind is a razor but it must be sharpened regularly.'

'I suppose so, Aunt.'

The lights of oncoming traffic hurt his eyes but they did nothing to deflect his aunt from her direct line of questioning.

'I presume you've been to mass each Sunday?'

'Yes,' he lied.

'Religion is the backbone of our culture, Dixton.'

(Dixton had always thought that European Structural Funds were.)

'Yes, Aunt Sheila.'

His aunt glanced at the digital clock on the dashboard.

'If we hurry we'll make seven o'clock mass.'

Dixton knew that he was well and truly home.

His room was much as he had left it. The only additions were a couple of Opus Dei calendars which his aunt had obviously left out to help him get the New Year off to a proper start. She never let up. Oh well. The bed covers had been changed recently and the room had a warm homely feel to it, which wasn't all that surprising given that it was his home and the radiator was on full blast. Dixton was glad to be back in Ailesbury Crescent. It was old familiar territory; a Sherwood Forest haven safe from the clutches of the Praelector; a protected supply route in the war theatre of the North Atlantic; a snug packet of cotton wool in the pharmacy of life. God, he really missed Nathalie. Still, only two and a half weeks to go. He wished someone would invent an alarm clock that would allow him to sleep uninterrupted through times of hassle and wake him just in time for the next cuddle with the girl he had fallen madly in love with. His thoughts were interrupted by his aunt's voice. 'Dixton,' she shouted up the stairs, 'Dixton, come down and decorate the tree.'

This was a phrase he had come to fear every Christmas for as long as he could remember. What sounded like a fairly simple procedure was in fact a two or three day event. When Dixton reached the end of the stairs his aunt was clutching a fairy in one hand and had covered her eyes with the other. The bare tree sat calmly in the special Christmas tree barrel, unaware of its fate.

'I can see the red stars, Dixton, they are there, there, there,' she took her hand down from her eyes and pointed dramatically at the lower regions of the tree.

Every year she had this vision of the locus of each decoration from the previous year. Her rationale was that this visionary feat ensured continuity in the decoration of the tree in Ailesbury Crescent. It ensured continuity all right; the bloody decorating went on forever.

'Here?' he said hopefully, holding the white angel with the bell on its head (there were two white angels).

'Oh Dixton,' his aunt said in an exasperated tone. She clutched her hand to her eyes once more and sighed with the utter confidence which characterised every aspect of her life, 'under the short strip of blue tinsel.'

Dixton was reminded of a surgeon during an operation barking out commands, 'Scalpel, suture, plasma, tinsel, crackers, white angel with no bell.'

There was no point in arguing the logic of the procedure with Aunt Sheila. Up to Christmas Eve itself he would make adjustments at her request. Despite the fact that the first time the item had been put on the tree she had been equally vehement that that was its correct place, Aunt Sheila blamed Dixton for having to make any adjustments at all. Her stock put down was, 'Well, who put it there in the first place, eh?' (That was Aunt Sheila for you; often wrong but never in doubt.)

'I've put your name down to sell holly on Christmas Eve in Grafton Street.' They were in the study with a huge roaring fire insulating them from the torrents of rain outside. Aunt Sheila was reading *The Messenger*. Dixton looked up from writing a letter to Nathalie.

'What, on Christmas Eve, Aunt? Put my name down where?'

'With the Timid Sisters of the Assumption. All the holly sellers are meeting at two o'clock tomorrow afternoon outside Bewleys.'

'But I was hoping to. . .'

'Never mind hoping, Dixton, it's 'doing' that helps those in need, there's too much 'hoping' in the world and not enough 'doing', that what I always say.'

It was the first time Dixton had ever heard her say it and once was enough. There was no real way out of this holly business. In fairness to his aunt it could have been lot worse, he remembered that when he was about fifteen she'd volunteered his services to play Joseph in a crib in the City Centre for an afternoon. The original Joseph had mumps or something and Dixton had been a snap replacement. Everything went well enough until the wolfhound who was standing in as a donkey took quite a liking to one poor woman kneeling at the crib and then. . . . Oh well there was no point in indulging any more than necessary in fantasies about the possible hazards of farmyard animals. Holly sounded reasonably harmless although the Timid Sisters of the Assumption could probably be relied upon to complicate even the apparently simplest of tasks. Dixton had a deep suspicion of charities administered by religious orders. How did they know what percentage God meant them to spend on administration costs?

It was pitch dark when he arrived back to Ailesbury Crescent. He'd spent the previous eight hours in a pub drinking with Mullane and Flannery. He crept up the stairs, step eleven and sixteen were the ones to watch. He'd obviously undercounted or something because as he tiptoed over what he believed to be a danger step he heard a loud yawning creak like a tree falling. Suddenly the light came on the landing and there was Aunt Sheila in her night-dress with her hair in curlers, clutching a golfclub.

'Oh thank God it's you, Dixton,' she said in a voice that was just this side of hysterical.

'Of course it's me, Aunt Sheila.'

'Where the hell were you until now?'

'Selling holly,' his own voice sounded strange to him.

'Until one in the morning?'

'It's a very slow mover,' he countered weakly.

'Have you been drinking?' she snapped.

'No,' he slurred.

'We'll discuss this in the morning,' his aunt turned on her heel and went towards her own room. Dixton opened the airing cupboard door by mistake but finally found his bedroom. He imagined his aunt well capable of whacking an intruder with the three wood. He closed the door. He pulled his jeans off and threw them over the end of the bed. All the change fell out of his pockets.

'Bollox,' he exclaimed.

'Dixton, language please,' his aunt warned from her room across the corridor.

'OK, Aunt Sheila, Happy Christmas anyway.'

'Happy Christmas yourself. Go to sleep. We're going to all four masses tomorrow to make up for this drinking business.'

As he drifted off to sleep Dixton felt certain that as usual Christmas would be a total fucking disaster.

CHAPTER ELEVEN

Cambridge was covered in snow. It was as though some omniscient bedder had thrown a virgin linen sheet over the university, the town and its inhabitants. The Backs were resplendent; Queens, Saint Catherine's, Clare, Kings and Trinity Hall presented white carpets to the river and any footprints which spoiled the scene were quickly filled in by eager flakes waiting overhead for the opportunity to fall down and be counted. January felt like heaven and looked like Christmas.

Dixton had come back a couple of days before term started proper. It was a move prompted more by boredom with Dublin than by the prospect of stealing a march on his law class and hitting the books early. Despite his continued distaste for study, the fourth of January saw him in the Squire Library looking through journals for a starting point for his essay on the Spanish Armada which he hoped to disguise as a passable attempt to satisfy the requirements of the LLM exam board. He hoped to do the research now and write it all up in a rush near the end of term as Feldman had suggested.

The library was mostly empty except for a couple of students who looked young enough to be still at school. These, Dixton presumed, were the lawyers of tomorrow. He found it difficult to imagine that he might ever be a lawyer himself. How could he ever expect to don a wig and gown and represent people in Court? What about the age old dilemma which faced all criminal lawyers and with which the public seemed obsessed, namely: how could he represent someone whom he knew in his heart would be unable to pay his fees?

'Not only must justice be done but justice must be seen to be believed,' someone had doodled on the inside of one of the law journals. Dixton wished he'd thought of that phrase himself.

'Can I help you?' a mop topped girl with thick glasses asked. Dixton had been thumbing through the journals near the issue desk and he must have seemed a little lost.

'Oh not really, I'm just looking for some material on the Spanish Armada.' She must be a library assistant he thought. The girl looked at him somewhat oddly,

'The Spanish Armada? But that's history, this is a Law Library.'

'Oh yes, I know,' said Dixton, 'but its all tied in with salvage and the law of the sea and all that.' He hated having to explain himself.

'Oh, I see, international sea carriage, maritime salvage, the Utrecht Conventions on intellectual property rights at sea and that recent case on heritage dispute resolution under the Brussels Directive?'

'Exactly,' said Dixton. He hoped he'd remember enough of that spiel to get started on the essay.

'You need shelves 8, 9 and 10 in Bay Y,' she said confidently.

'I need a drink,' Dixton muttered under his breath.

He followed the librarian up a winding staircase at the back of the issue desk and onto the next floor. Dixton had never been in the Squire Law Library before and was surprised that it was this big. Still, he thought, if they're going to number the sections all the way from A to Z then they probably need the space. Bay Y was a small room off the main body of the library floor. There was a fabulous view out over the backs.

'If you need any further help don't be afraid to ask,' the librarian smiled as she left the room.

Dixton knew how the children CS Lewis wrote about must have felt when they first stepped into the wardrobe. He'd never been here before and he wondered how he was ever going to get back safely to where he'd come from. It was shelf upon shelf of maritime law, a table, a chair, three red biros and a refill pad. He didn't know where to begin. A quick glance told him that the books were organised alphabetically. He looked up 'Spanish Armada', 'Salvage' and 'Help'. Out the window a boy and a girl held hands and trudged through the snow past the silver trees leading to the back gate of Kings College. Only a couple of more days and he'd see Nathalie again. He set about the task of getting his essay up and running with an enthusiasm which he normally reserved for nights out on the town. He was going to treat himself that evening with a trip to the Film Club to see *Casablanca*. He already felt he'd earned it.

'Funny seeing you back this early,' Laura the bedder said when Dixton met her in the corridor one morning later that week.

'Couldn't keep me away from Lupin,' he grinned.

'From what I hear they certainly tried,' Laura said gravely.

'So you know all about that business then?'

'Who doesn't? Everybody was talking about you at the Christmas Dinner. Some people don't think you'll last another term!'

'What do you think, Laura?'

'I think you'll be fine if you want to. It's all down to you, isn't it really?'

'I suppose so.' Dixton was glad of the few words of support. He'd buried himself in the essay for the first couple of days and hadn't thought about the bigger picture.

'Anyway they fixed the fountain,' Laura laughed

'So Lord Lupin's up and passing water again?' Dixton quipped.

They both broke up laughing at this and sat on the stairs for a moment.

'You'll be all right Dixton Larkin,' Laura said giving him a pat on the backside as he got up to go to his room.

'Hey, I though it was the students who were supposed to make passes at the bedders, not the other way round,' Dixton grinned.

'Some people need encouragement. Speaking of encouragement, any sign of Drusilla lately?'

'Thankfully not, Laura.'

'Oh that's right, its that lassie from France, whatshername, isn't it?' Laura grinned knowingly.

'You bedders don't miss a trick, do you?'

'You can't beat the Christmas Dinner for information.'

Laura picked up the hoover and headed upstairs. Dixton went back to his room and got his shower things. He was supposed to meet Nathalie's flight at Stansted Airport at three that afternoon. He wondered if she would have changed during the time they were apart. Maybe she'd see through him and think he was an idiot, or worse still see through him and spot someone else to fancy. He put on a double dose of deodorant to bolster his confidence.

Stansted Airport was the perfect Thatcherite symbol of irony; a space-age edifice built as a launching pad to the Canaries for middle-class Britain in the winter, while the government sought to increase the VAT on fuel to kill off the pensioners and the poverty stricken. Dixton stood beside the 'Arrivals' sign and waited for flight AF318 to touch down. He'd never waited for anyone at an airport before, it was an experience reserved for lovers and relatives. There was always the chance that the flight would be delayed or would crash and so the sacrifice was waiting for the flight rather than being on it. A family of about eight had crowded on to a row of seats next to Dixton and the children, who ranged from about two to ten, seemed to take turns asking their mother: 'Will Dad be home soon?' Dixton found the whole scene touching yet intensely annoying. One of the small screens changed from flashing the arrival time of Nathalie's flight to flashing 'Landed'.

The first people out into the arrivals lounge were all met by someone and gradually the exit door was obscured by a large crowd of people and a fleet of trolleys at varying degrees of full or empty. Then Dixton spotted her. She was approaching the door between a red woolly hat and a bag of duty free being waved about by some idiotic woman. Nathalie was looking around expectantly as she wheeled her trolley into the arrivals lounge. At least that's a good sign, he thought. As soon as she saw him, she smiled (another good sign) then she abandoned her trolley altogether and ran towards him. It was like something from a film except that when they began to run into each other's arms they weren't very far apart to begin with so the effect was less dramatic, and of course neither of them got up to full sprint. Nonetheless it was perfect. Dixton gave her a huge kiss before she could even say hello.

'You left your trolley behind you,' he said awkwardly when the kiss was over.

'Who cares, there's nothing worth stealing in my luggage,' she laughed.

'I really missed you,' Dixton said, laying his heart on the line. She held him at arms length and twinkled her eyes at him, 'Not half as much as I missed you.'

'Game set and match,' he thought. At least he'd progressed to the quarter finals. He retrieved her luggage and they held hands as Dixton wheeled the trolley to the ticket counter in the airport railway station.

'The train you want is leaving now Sir from platform one,' the ticket man said as Dixton paid.

'Come on Nathalie or we'll have to wait another hour for the next one.'

They grabbed the luggage from the trolley and sprinted down the platform. A British Rail Official was just getting ready to wave the train off with a flag and the automatic doors had already closed. Dixton flung himself at one of the buttons and pressed furiously, the door opened and they scrambled aboard.

'How is Aunt Sheila?' Nathalie enquired when they'd safely ensconced themselves in the carriage.

'Jesus, don't ask, Christmas was a nightmare.'

'She can't really be all that bad, Dixton', she grinned.

'She can if she really wants to.'

'Well, if she does visit, you'll have to make the most of it and show her around.'

'I suppose so.'

'What did she say when you told her about me?'

'Em, Er.', Dixton stalled.

'I see, you didn't tell her about me did you?' Nathalie seemed a little put out.

'Well, to tell you the truth, I wasn't sure whether there was any point.'

'How do you mean?' she asked guardedly.

'Well, I don't know, I suppose I thought you might decide over the holidays that you'd had enough of me.'

'Well, I haven't, and, unless you do something silly like spill milk over me or get sent down I won't.' Nathalie looked across the table at him and grinned.

They leaned in spontaneously across the table and kissed. It was just the sort of soppy moment that Dixton would have cynically dismissed out of hand if he'd seen others do it. However it was different when he was involved himself, it was just sort of, well you know, different; acceptable and different.

When they arrived back at Newnham, they went to the Porters' Lodge. 'I've just got to pick up my keys,' Nathalie said. Dixton waited with the luggage. She emerged dangling a set of keys in her hand. 'OK, lets go. You've got to see my place. I've got lots of cases to move.'

'I thought men weren't allowed into the rooms at Newnham?' Dixton queried.

'They're not,' she answered.

'Then where are we going?'

'4 Clopton Way, I've got a room in a house that the College owns. I've finally moved out of rooms here.'

'But won't they object to you bringing a strange man back with you, even if it is only to double as a porter and carry your luggage?'

'Poor old Dixton,' she laughed. 'It's a College House but there are no restrictions. I'll be sharing with two other girls but College has no say in what visitors I have.'

'Oh,' said Dixton.

'Yes, Oh!' she smiled mischievously.

The house was roomy with a large back garden and the makings of what probably used to be a pond. Nathalie's room was at the back of the house and had a splendid view across the back garden over the back wall and on to the river which ran behind the house and on out towards Grantchester.

'What do you think?' she asked when all the luggage had been carried up the stairs and stacked on the floor.

'Not bad at all. It's much bigger than the rooms at Lupin.'

'Do you like it?'

'Yes, of course I do.'

'How much do you like it?' she asked.

'What do you mean, how much?'

'Enough to stay tonight, in case I get cold in my new surroundings?'

'Definitely that much,' he answered without hesitation. (A spot in the semi-finals began to look more likely.)

'Its a pain in the arse, that's what it is, Dixton, a great big pain in the arse.' Pepper and Dixton were leaning over the bridge near the Anchor Pub throwing stones into the Cam.

'What can I do about it Pepper? I had to pay the money otherwise they wouldn't let me back into College. Winston is only looking for an excuse to wreck my year here.'

'So how are things now financially?'

'Not great. I've got to pay for my accommodation bill for the term and it'll leave me with sod all to survive on. That's the end of most of my allowance for the rest of the year.'

'Bollox,' said Pepper.

'That's my swearword,' Dixton smiled.

'Well now I know why you use it so much. There must be something you can do to earn a few quid.'

Dixton skimmed a stone into the river, it bounced five or six times then landed on the concrete jetty beside the pub.

'Excellent shot, but what are you going to do, Dixton? I'm sure I could lend you some money but not much.'

'No, way,' said Dixton, 'I wouldn't dream of taking money from you, you've got enough to worry about yourself without lending me money. Don't worry, I'll think of something.'

'How about betting whatever you have left on a horse or something?'

'I don't know anything about horses.'

'Me neither.'

They lobbed a few more stones into the river and then headed back towards Lupin.

'How are things with Nathalie?' asked Pepper.

'Couldn't be better, how about you and Clara?'

'Well, I saw her over the 'hols' and things were OK but I'm beginning to think its not a great idea this long distance thing.'

'Really?' Dixton asked mockingly.

'No, really,' said Pepper, 'I seriously suspect that she's seeing someone else.'

'No?' Dixton smirked.

'I'm serious boy.' Pepper turned to him and looked genuinely concerned. 'God only knows what she's been getting up to behind my back all these years.'

'Probably the same things as you've been getting up to behind her back for all the same years,' Dixton grinned.

Pepper pushed him into a lamp post. Dixton narrowly avoided serious injury.

'Hey, what's that for?'

'For being right.'

'So you're going to break it off with her then and do the decent thing?' Dixton suggested.

'No way, I'll give her a dose of her own medicine, if she's going to have a good time I may as well enjoy myself for the rest of the year too. We'll probably be married next year so we'll finally be together and faithful!'

'I give up,' said Dixton.

'Bollox,' said Pepper laughing.

'Bollox is right,' Dixton laughed back.

They walked down Grange Road. Dixton felt something damp land on his hair. He brushed his head with both hands: snowflakes.

'I suppose that bastard Bernard went skiing for Christmas. I hope he had an accident,' said Pepper.

'And what about that ape Zinowsky,' growled Dixton. 'If I hadn't ducked that time he'd have punched me into next week.'

'What really gets to me is that both of them got off scot free. The Praelector wasn't interested in how the row started, just what happened to that stupid fountain,' Pepper said.

'Yeah, when I think of the roasting he gave me and not a word said to those two bastards.'

'Never mind, Dixton, its a long road between now and the end of the year, we'll get them back somehow.'

'Whets the use, Pepper? If there's even a sniffle out of me this term, I'll be sent down.'

'Look up there,' Pepper pointed into the sky. The snow had quickened.

'What? I don't see anything except snow,' Dixton craned his neck.

'Its a ton of bricks which will come crashing down about your ears,' Pepper mimicked the Praelector's upper class gravely accent and laughed.

'Oh sod off, Pepper, race you to the Hat and Feathers.'

'You're on.'

The two sprinted down Grange Road and on to the Hat and Feathers. The traffic lights were against them and the snow was now torrenting down like blanched cornflakes.

'Two double whiskeys, please,' Dixton ordered as they leaned panting against the thick wooden counter.

'Don't worry about those two idiots, Dixton, we'll get them back for all that fountain business.'

'Promise?'

'Promise.'

They clinked glasses before downing their drinks in one go.

The first two weeks of the new term flew past like the mischief. Dixton's rush of energy early on had been a good investment of time and the desk in his room held two huge piles of photocopied material relating to the law of Salvage. Some of the references he'd come across had a fairly tenuous link with his essay title but that would mean he would have to be imaginative when it actually came to writing, or rather inventing, his magnum opus. College life got back into swing quite quickly and he attended a couple of lectures in order to keep his hand in. Professor Simpson was, as always, both entertaining and practical and Dixton saw from his folder of notes that he'd only missed two or three lectures in criminal law. The latest topic was obscure offences which, though seldom now tried by the Courts, were nonetheless still alive on the statute books.

Some of the more notable included: 'Having in one's possession any dog or cat or the plumage or skin thereof, knowing same to be stolen', or the bizarre offence of being one of 'two or more persons armed with any offensive weapon or under disguise, carrying away any illicit malt or spirits'. Dixton's personal favourites were the promotion of unlawful meetings by 'sound of drum, horn, music, fire or shouting' and 'taking or destroying rabbits by night.'

In any event the classes were never dull and the most recent pearl of wisdom from their criminal law mentor was his advice that: 'As it is in wine, so it is in murder; no body, no satisfaction.' Dixton thought that was brilliant and he was certain that it was original. Sarah and Co seemed to have pretty much forgotten Dixton's dealings with The Elephant and so all was well on the criminal front.

Dixton continued to avoid the Remedies and Restitution lectures, more out of fear than disinterest. Whatever steps he felt able to take in his other subjects, Remedies and Restitution remained a complete mystery to him and Dixton preferred it that way. He would face that problem whenever he could no longer continue to avoid it and even that would be too soon.

Sanjra had become an EU Law enthusiast and that suited Dixton.

128

Dixton had brought him back a bottle of Jameson Whiskey after the Christmas hols and this sealed the deal.

'You don't mind giving your EC notes to me every now and again, do you?' Dixton enquired sheepishly at the beginning of term.

'Of course not, my friend, you have introduced me to the delights of distilled spirits and the least I can do is to give you my notes.'

'I really appreciate it, Sanjra, I'm afraid I've avoided the seminars for too long to suddenly appear at them now.'

'Do not worry, Dixton, you will pass this exam because I know that you have that great gift which so few men possess.'

'You mean intelligence, charm, analytical faculties?' Dixton suggested, feeling quite flattered.

'No,' smiled Sanjra, 'you are able to read my writing!' He chuckled away to himself.

'I shall be eternally grateful,' said Dixton and he meant it. The exams were going to be a major problem whenever they finally came around. At least he'd started to get things budging, if not exactly rolling.

'Hey, Dixton, are you coming on the beer with us to the Anchor to-night?' Jack pushed aside his dining tray and leaned across the table.

'No, I can't tonight, I'm afraid, I'm going to the Arts' Cinema.'

'On your own?' queried Andy laughing.

'Maybe, maybe not,' Dixton prevaricated.

'Rubbish,' said Jack, 'the romance of the century is still going strong then?'

Dixton shrugged his shoulders, feigning nonchalance.

'Next thing you know, you'll be meeting her parents,' laughed Andy.

'Or she'll be meeting your aunt?' Pepper joined in the slagging as he sat down beside Dixton.

'Are you coming with us tonight?' Pepper asked.

'No, 'fraid not, Pepper, love and romance and the big screen call,' Dixton said proudly.

'Oh, *Emmanuelle 9* is it?' Jack joked in his best Mancunian accent.

'No, its not *Emmanuelle 9*,' said Dixton sharply.

'*Emmanuelle 10* then?' laughed Pepper.

'Sod off the lot of you.' Dixton dipped his fork in the water jug and started flicking water at the three lads.

'Watch it,' Jack whispered a warning, 'the Praelector's sitting behind you.'

Dixton nearly wet himself. He turned around slowly, expecting the worst. The table behind him was empty.

'You bastards, for a moment there I nearly believed you.'

'Only winding you up, Dixton,' said Andy, 'but, speaking of the old bugger, any contact since you've come back?'

'No, I see him from time to time but I avoid him like the plague.'

'You're better off doing that,' said Jack, 'anyway he's too busy organising this new Debating Society. They're debating against some other college this week.'

'Well, we'll be here talking all week if we don't hurry up,' Andy observed.

'OK lads, the Anchor it is,' Pepper rallied the drinkers.

'See you later, maybe?' said Dixton.

'Yeah, we'll probably be back for a few final pints in the College bar,' Jack smirked looking at his watch, 'only another seven hours drinking till closing.'

Dixton watched them head off. He didn't envy them even a little bit and that surprised him a lot.

It was a French film *La Parapluie* by some well known director Dixton had never heard of. It was a fairly simple plot full of the usual eight or ten minute scenes where all the characters did was blow unfiltered smoke up at the ceiling in a dingy boarding house room. The only bit Dixton enjoyed was where the hero got on a train and managed to get his suitcase onto the luggage rack despite the bullying efforts of a huge sailor who had got on the train after him and tried to steal the last space on the rack. Nothing in the film really hinged on this scene but for Dixton it was the only part of the whole film which justified even turning up in the cinema, never mind actually paying to watch the film at all.

'What did you think?' Nathalie asked excitedly.

'Excellent,' Dixton lied. (No point in upsetting her when the damage to his optical senses had already been done.)

The only redeeming feature of the film had been its length, it ran for an artistic sixty-six minutes. In actual fact it could have been quite easily ended at any of about forty points after the opening credits.

'Really, did you really enjoy it, Dixton?' Nathalie was delirious.

She linked her arm in his and skipped along Kings Parade. Dixton couldn't quite raise his game to skipping but quickened pace enough to keep up with her. He supposed that his lying about enjoying the film and being believed thus making Nathalie happy was what marriage guidance people termed a 'bonding experience'.

He left Nathalie at the door of 4 Clopton Way. Her architecture class was going to London early the next morning to an exhibition so he didn't stay over. As he approached the entrance to Lupin, he saw a flashing blue light. A policeman was standing beside the open driver's door, leaning his elbows on the roof of the car. He had a two way radio in his hand. It didn't appear that there had been an accident or anything so Dixton edged past the panda and towards the main gate.

'Dixton, Dixton,' he heard someone calling his name but couldn't make out where it was coming from. Next came a sharp rap on the rear passenger side window of the police car. Dixton peered in, the policeman stopped talking into his radio and looked across the car.

'Pepper? What the hell are you doing in there?' Dixton exclaimed as he saw Pepper's face pressed up against the window. The policeman closed the door of the car and walked around.

'Do you know this gentleman Sir?'

Dixton hesitated.

'Well, er, yes, well he's a friend of mine.'

By this time Pepper had rolled the window down. It only opened a couple of inches.

'Dixton, Dixton, you have to help me,' he slurred.

'I believe this gentleman is a friend of yours Sir?' the policeman addressed Pepper.

'Yes, yes, of course he's a friend of mine, he's my lawyer.' (Pepper was totally plastered.) The policeman straightened up, visibly impressed to be in the presence of a lawyer. Dixton thought of laughing it off or doing a runner himself, but realised that Pepper was wearing handcuffs and suddenly felt quite sorry for him.

'Are you his lawyer, Sir?'

'Yes, yes, I am, I'm his em . . .'

'Lawyer,' prompted Pepper.

'Yes, lawyer,' conceded Dixton, wondering if you could be disbarred before you were called to the Bar.

'I'll be taking him to the station, Sir, if you wish to follow us there.' The arresting officer got into the car.

Dixton quite liked being called 'Sir'. He felt he should say something legal to seize the moment and bolster his credentials.

'What allegations are being levelled against my client, Constable?' (It sounded like an authentic enough inquiry.)

'I'm his client,' chipped in Pepper.

The policeman looked back at Pepper and then turned around to Dixton.

'Well, Sir, it concerns a matter of a taxi.'

'That's right, I got run over by a taxi,' Pepper's face lit up in recollection.

'What?' Dixton exclaimed, 'are you all right? Why wasn't an ambulance called? And what the hell are you doing in handcuffs?'

'Well, Sir, he wasn't exactly run over by a taxi, we received a complaint from a taxi driver that two of his passengers had got out without paying the fare.'

'Oh, that's right,' Pepper grinned inanely, 'we did a runner from a taxi.'

'Oh,' Dixton felt less confident than ever about his decision to pretend to be representing Pepper. What if this thing went to Court and all that business? A second policeman emerged from a cul de sac opposite the Lupin Hall Gates.

'No sign of the other bloke, Sarge.'

'Never mind, we'd better get back to the station. We'll see you at the station then, Mr?'

'Larkin, Dixton Larkin.' He'd have to cycle.

'My cigarettes, Dixton, get my cigarettes from the room.' Pepper's voice trailed off past the Hat and Feathers as the panda car headed away down Barton Road.

He parked his bike outside the station. The clock in the hallway said eleven twenty three. The officer on duty was reading a copy of *Ben Hur*. He was a weedy policeman who looked totally out of place. Dixton supposed that they only had a minimum height requirement, not weight, for recruiting cops. Still, whether tall, small, decent or bastards, they all had power of arrest. Dixton adopted his legal tone of voice.

'I'm here to see Jonathan Pepper, I'm his lawyer.'

The duty officer put down his book, face down on the desk. Dixton could see he was on the verge of sniggering, but did his best to contain himself.

'His lawyer, Sir?'

'Yes, that's right.'

The little shit, who did he think he was, doubting Dixton's bona fides? Still, the fact that Dixton was wearing jeans and a multicoloured jumper must have smacked of deceit. Dixton ploughed on however, it was imperative that his cover not be blown. Not now, there was too much at stake; Pepper was inside in handcuffs and the Tiger was outside lying unlocked against the sign saying 'Parking Prohibited'. Dixton decided that attack was the best ploy.

'I see you're reading while on duty,' he sneered, looking down at the upside-down cover of *Ben Hur*. The policeman was quite taken aback.

'I beg your pardon, Sir?'

'I said I see you're reading while on duty, is that station policy in Cambridgeshire?'

'No, no, of course its. . .'

'Don't bother making excuses, I won't tell anyone, but get out a pen and paper and write down your name and number for me.'

The poor idiot was so taken back that he unquestioningly followed Dixton's orders. He handed the sheet of note paper to Dixton. Dixton read it a couple of times to himself and made a couple of satisfied noises.

'Aha, am ham, uh hum.' He folded it carefully and placed it in his inside coat pocket. He tapped it meaningfully from outside and nodded to the policeman.

'Just routine, in case there's any difficulty with the custody record.'

The frightened cop nodded back almost gratefully.

'And now, if you don't mind, I'd like to see Mr Pepper.'

The officer disappeared for a second and re-emerged at a door into the hallway.

'Through here, Sir.' He ushered Dixton into an empty waiting room.

'The arresting officer is finishing the photographing and fingerprinting, when he's finished with that you'll be able to see your client.'

Fingerprinting, photographs; what the fuck was that all about? Dixton thought they only did that to criminals. He racked his brains in the criminal law section, yes, perhaps doing a runner from a taxi could be construed in some perverse way as being a crime. He sat down and thumbed through some magazines on fox hunting.

The door opened again and a large pot bellied man in his late fifties, wearing a maroon polo necked jumper and slacks, entered. He sat down on a chair facing Dixton and gave a short friendly smile. Dixton smiled back, then looked back down at the fox hunting magazine, ugh.

'I hope my taxi will be all right, it's parked outside,' the polo necked man broke the silence.

'I'm sure it will,' said Dixton looking up. God, I wonder is this *the* taxi driver.

'Are you here to make a statement too?' the taxi man enquired. As he spoke Dixton noticed that he had a small birthmark shaped like Japan under his left ear.

'Yes, well sort of . . .'

'A couple of buggers did a runner from my taxi without paying, but they caught one of them hiding in some shrubs.'

It certainly sounded like Pepper.

'That's great then, I mean great that they caught one, not great obviously that they did a runner,' Dixton muttered placatingly.

'It's probably some middle class student who could easily afford the fare you know, it's always the same.'

'Oh, I see.'

Dixton felt that things were not looking so good for Pepper. Once this chap swore up then it would be carpets. Still, he looked a kindly enough sort. Dixton wondered if there was a chance he could help Pepper out even at this late stage.

'Well, I just got a phone call to say a friend of mine was being held here. They didn't say why exactly but I can guess, I suppose, its drunk and disorderly or something.'

'Oh, the demon drink,' said the taxi man sympathetically.

'Well, I suppose its the same old story, the Irish Disease.' Dixton adopted what he hoped was a rueful tone. He could see the taxi man becoming more interested, he must have known one of his passengers was Irish. (Bingo).

'Is that what they call it?' he was trying to draw Dixton out on the subject.

'Well, disease or no disease, of course it's wrong to commit a crime, any crime, whether drunk or sober.'

'True enough,' nodded the taxi driver in that tone of voice which Dixton usually associated with the clergy. He allowed another short silence to follow and then stuck out his neck.

'Still, I suppose you can't blame someone for trying to forget their worries, bad news often prompts people to get drunk and do silly things.'

'Bad news?' the taxi driver sat up, all the better to nibble at the bait.

'Oh, yes,' Dixton shook his head. 'My friend, for example. He hasn't taken a drink for almost three years and then today he got word that the blood donor they'd found in the States for him has died so the operation has to be put off yet again.'

'Operation? What kind of operation?' the driver was clearly startled.

'Oh, I don't understand the medical jargon but its something or other to do with the central nervous system. God only knows what else they'll find when they go in. Still, its no excuse for committing a crime of any sort, however trifling, eh?'

'No, no of course not,' the taxi driver was deep in thought and after a short pause he reignited the conversation.

'But can't they find another donor? I mean to say, surely with all the advances of science?' He was quite emotional. Dixton was finding it difficult to keep a straight face but he knew what was at stake. He began to sense the possible release of the Lupin One.

'Well, you would imagine so, but then how many people do you know with blood type 'G minus'?'

The taxi driver put his head in his hands. The door opened. 'Mr Hammond, we're ready to take a statement from you now.'

'You'll never believe this, Dixton, the fucking taxi driver offered me a lift back to Lupin, free of charge. I met him in the corridor and he said he wouldn't be pressing charges.'

'Really?' Dixton smiled. They were back in Pepper's room having doubled up on the Tiger to get back to Lupin after Pepper had been released. Pepper was still quite drunk.

'Would you really have appeared in Court for me, Dixton?'

'I suppose so, but I'm glad it didn't come to that.'

'I still can't get over the taxi driver, what do you think happened?'

'I'll tell you in the morning Pepper.' Dixton got up to leave, Pepper was falling asleep in the chair.

'Oh, by the way, Pepper, who was the other person with you in the taxi?'

'Can't remember, I think it was Andy, or maybe it was Jack, I'm not really sure.'

'OK, Pepper. Goodnight so.' Dixton was half way out the door when Pepper called him back.

'Dixton, Dixton, do you know what?'

'What?' Dixton turned around, Pepper had flopped down on the bed.

'You're a fucking excellent lawyer,' Pepper laughed.

'Goodnight, Pepper.' He closed the door quietly but Pepper had already begun to snore.

Dixton was opening the door of E Block when he was stopped in his tracks by a familiar voice.

'Larkin, just a moment, I want to speak to you.' It was the Praelector.

How could he know about this police station business so quickly? Dixton nearly collapsed with fear as he turned to face his assailant.

'Yes?'

'Tomorrow night, eight sharp, Queen's College, you're on the debating team.'

'Pardon?' Dixton was overcome with a mixture of relief and disbelief.

'It won't be world championship quality but I'm sure as usual you'll have no difficulty in lowering your standards.'

Dixton didn't have time to refuse, the Praelector was gone and

Dixton's relief seemed sufficient to carry him to his room. He could worry about the speech tomorrow when he found out what the topic was.

CHAPTER TWELVE

Dixton sat down in exhaustion and simultaneously the audience rose to its feet as one for a standing ovation. He couldn't believe it. He had delivered what he hoped would be his only speech ever and the audience were applauding themselves out of their knickers for him. The only plausible explanation was that the crowd shared his complete ignorance of the topic. He had begun with a couple of weak jokes and ended with even worse anecdotes. However it seemed to have done the trick. His team-mates had piled on the statistics while he had supplied the necessary antidote. At any rate it had worked despite the worst intentions of the Praelector. Dixton spotted Nathalie standing outside the door of the hall, she must have arrived during the speech. She was smiling proudly up at him.

'And now to present the Rigby-Walpole Trophy to Lupin Hall; Colonel Walpole.'

Syrah Manalgi, a computer science student, was the Lupin Captain and he stepped forward to receive the trophy. Dixton saw that the Praelector's face was crossed with a mixture of pride and hatred. As the team passed the trophy between themselves, the Praelector approached them.

'Well done, Syrah, well done, Martin,' he shook hands with the other two. It was an awkward moment. Dixton stretched out his hand but the Praelector turned away.

'Never mind him, congratulations, Dixton.'

He felt a friendly clap on the back and turned around. It was Feldman. Dixton was delighted to see him.

'Excellent show, one of the best speeches I've ever heard, it meant nothing of course, but sounded superb. Have you ever thought of politics?' he laughed.

Dixton pumped his hand.

'Thanks ever so much for showing up, how did you know it was on?'

'Just spotted your name on a poster and wandered in. I missed most of the debate.'

'You didn't miss much,' said Syrah. 'Dixton was excellent, he really was, the rest of us were pretty boring I have to admit.' Dixton thought it was decent of his own captain to compliment him like that.

'Are you coming to the College bar for a drink?' Colonel Walpole interrupted them.

''Fraid not,' said Syrah, 'I've got a project to hand in by Friday so I hope to get a couple of hours done tonight.'

'Typical computer student,' said Feldman.

'I'm on for a drink,' said Dixton.

'Good chap,' said the Colonel, 'I'm buying.'

Nathalie met up with them outside the door of the hall. 'Well done, Dixton,' she gave him a kiss on the cheek. 'Oh, I see you've got a fan club as well,' laughed Feldman. 'Not really,' Dixton was semi-embarrassed.

'This is Nathalie. Nathalie, this is Mr Feldman.'

'Robert, please,' his supervisor shook hands with her. '"Mr Feldman" is so formal it always reminds me of. . .'

'Your solicitor?' ventured Nathalie.

'Yes, my solicitor,' he was amazed, 'but how?'

'Dixton told me.'

'Oh did he? And what else did he tell you?'

'Oh, nothing much, just something about Scotch whisky.'

Feldman roared laughing, 'God, is nothing sacred?'

They reached the College bar.

'Three double scotches,' Feldman ordered, 'and that old geezer down there who pretends he's a colonel is paying.'

'Anyone for more?' Mr Feldman held out a tilted bottle of ten year old whisky.

'God no,' said Dixton putting a hand over the top of his glass, 'I really couldn't.'

'Nathalie?' his supervisor offered.

'No, no, really, thank you but I think we should be going soon?'

When the College bar shut in Queen's the three of them had gone back to Feldman's rooms in Peterhouse. Dixton was quite merry at this stage while Nathalie had prudently sipped the same drink for most of the evening.

'Yes, I suppose you had better make a move soon,' Feldman smiled. 'I've got a nine o'clock lecture in the morning myself.'

As Feldman retrieved their coats from the bed, Nathalie strolled around looking at the paintings of the small Cornish village. 'Pretty, isn't it?' Feldman said, helping Nathalie into her coat.

'Very, is it somewhere near here?'

'No, I'm afraid it's not. Cornwall is always at least two worlds away.'

'Do you ever visit there?' Nathalie helped Dixton button up his duffel coat. He had begun one button too low.

'Haven't been back for years, Nathalie,' Feldman swished what was left in his glass, 'haven't been back for years.'

Dixton thought about having another drink but knew that he was only about two or three measures the safe side of comatose and he remembered the rather sorry expression on Pepper's face that morning in the aftermath of the taxi incident.

'Robert, thanks a million for having us around.'

'Not at all, Dixton, I really enjoyed the company. As your supervisor I'm glad that you're still with us this term. I think it was a bit touch and go there before Christmas, wasn't it?'

'How did you know about all that?'

Dixton had deliberately kept his close call from Feldman in view of the help he'd given over the essay business.

'Your librarian, Professor Lynn, contacted me the week before we broke up for Christmas and we sent in a joint reference.'

Dixton almost burst into drunken tears. 'So it was you and Professor Lynn who saved my life?' he stammered.

'Well, I wouldn't exactly use those terms, Dixton.'

'You've never met my Aunt Sheila, Robert.'

'No, I suppose I haven't.'

'Thanks ever so much, Robert,' Dixton gripped him by the shoulders in a show of emotion and gratitude.

'No problem, Dixton, I'm more than glad to put in a word for you any time.'

'Thank you very much,' Nathalie turned to him as she whooshed Dixton out the door ahead of her.

'Not at all Nathalie, you take care of him, I need him sober sometime around May for the thesis in Law of Salvage.'

'He'll have me to deal with as well as his aunt if he doesn't behave,' she smiled.

'To the Spanish Armada then Dixton,' Feldman raised his glass.

'To the Spanish Armada.' Dixton roared back, shouldering the 'pull' sign on the door. 'It's stuck, Nathalie, the bloody door's stuck. I've pushed it but it won't open.'

'You're supposed to push from the other side,' she said gently.

'I know, but we have to get outside first before we can do that,' Dixton spoke with the utter confidence and logic which only ten year old Dalwhinnie in vast quantities can inspire.

Dixton had just come out of a criminal law lecture when he spotted a familiar figure looking in the window of Ryders and Amies Shop on the corner of Great Saint Mary's and King's Parade. 'Pepper,' he called. There was no response. He made his way across the street and approached the love machine from Belfast. He saw however that all was not well. 'Hey Pepper, what's up?' Dixton tapped him on the shoulder. Pepper turned around slowly.

'Oh hello, Dixton, were you at a lecture or something?' Pepper spoke in an unusually distant tone.

'Yeah, just been to one, hey, what's the matter? Got a free evening and only four women to choose from?' Dixton tried to cheer him up.

'That's what's wrong,' Pepper sighed disconsolately pointing at the shop window.

'What? The Corpus Christi blazer? What's wrong with that?'

'No, dumbo, the list, look at the notice board.'

Surrounded by blazers, crests, cuff-links, and scarves of the various colleges was a small notice board with a number of notices tacked to it. To the left of the Ladies Hockey Tournament cancellation notice was the University golf team to face Oxford in the Blues Game over the Easter break. Pepper's name wasn't on it.

'Bollox.'

'Jesus, I'm really sorry, Pepper.'

'I can't believe it, Dixton, I just can't fucking believe it.'

'But I though that. . .'

'So did I.'

'So I suppose this means that. . .'

'Probably.'

'Well, you never know.'

'Suppose not.'

'Come on, Pepper,' Dixton tugged his friend's sleeve, 'let's go for a drink.'

Even being undercharged for their drinks didn't raise Pepper's spirits any. Dixton thought that this was the worst thing that could have happened to Pepper besides being killed by a stray bullet at a Poll Tax march.

'Its not just the golf, Dixton, its the Hawks Club as well, its all just slipped away from me in one stroke of a pen.'

'I know, I know, its awful, especially the Hawks Club bit,' Dixton shook his head in sympathy, 'what exactly is the Hawks Club?'

Pepper looked up in disbelief.

'You're joking, you honestly don't know what the Hawks Club is?'

'Of course I'm joking Pepper I know what it is I just can't quite take it in that you're not going to be a member that's all.'

Dixton knew that this was not the juncture of their relationship at which to seek in-depth explanations. His silence would be of more value than his ignorance to Pepper at a time like this. Whatever this club was Dixton appreciated the significance of it now to his friend. Pepper's heart was on the golf course, not in some destitute quarry chipping for geological samples in the pouring rain. The Hawks Club was his Valhalla and he'd been shown a glimpse of it and then gone blind.

'It's all I ever really wanted out of this place. Pepper spoke in a wistful distant tone. 'First I get landed in educational outer space, Lupin Hall, and now this.'

'But what about your performance so far this season, wasn't it good enough to get you on the team or what?'

'Obviously not. I played well enough up until Christmas but I had a dodgy round at Wentworth last weekend. Still I was sure I'd done enough.'

'Maybe they made a mistake, maybe someone typed up the list wrongly.' (Dixton was clutching at sand bunkers.)

'No way, there are so few people in the club that they wouldn't make a mistake like that. Anyway the Captain of the club always informs the Blues team members personally, before the list is put up. There hasn't been any mistake.'

'So what happens now?' Dixton felt totally helpless in a situation where he desperately wanted to offer some consolation to Pepper.

'I don't know, Dixton, I don't bloody well know.'

'Another pint?'

'Yeah, another pint.'

4 Clopton Way was a gorgeous house. It seemed so totally fair that Nathalie had managed to get a room there. The other girls in the house were decent. The true litmus test of that was their attitude towards him any time he stayed over.

'Great to have a man about the house,' Sally the botany student said across the breakfast table one morning about a week after the news about Pepper not making the team.

'Oh he's not too bad, I suppose,' Nathalie smiled, playing footsie with Dixton under the table.

'Hi Dixton,' Hannah the other occupant of 4 Clopton Way was tying her hair back with one of those bunchie things as she arrived into the kitchen. It never ceased to amaze him how women were able to manipulate their hair without seeing it. It was a bit like the unseen Latin text.

'More toast anyone?' said Sally as the triple toaster zinged and coughed up.

'I'll take one of those.' Hannah spread some thin cut marmalade on a slice, folded it and bit into it before heading out to a lecture.

Hannah was from the south coast somewhere near Rye. She was studying English. Both she and Sally were attractive but Dixton didn't think of them in that way. Nathalie was the only woman in his world. There was something odd about that line Dixton drew in his head almost unknowingly when he reached the point with a woman of no longer seeing her in terms of a potential romance. Somehow it made everything seem easier when he was around them. They became no-go areas without the grief. Once you thought of friends as lovers it could only lead to trouble. However, the reverse did not apply. As apart from Pepper, Nathalie was his best friend. It really was great to have a partner. He wondered how he'd ever coped on his own. Masturbation was definitely the triumph of circumstance over ambition.

'Lets go shopping,' Nathalie suggested.

'I don't have any money,' Dixton's finances were stretched to the absolute limit. The fountain compensation was wreaking its full revenge and it wasn't Easter yet.

'Don't worry,' she rummaged around in her wallet and produced a credit card. 'There,' she announced triumphantly, 'we don't need any money, not yet anyhow.'

'OK, let's go shopping, you've twisted my arm.'

'But I didn't touch your arm, Dixton,' a look of alarm passed over her French features.

'Its a figure of speech.' Dixton leant over and kissed his left index finger and deposited the kiss lightly on her nose. He loved the intrigue and confusion of cross-cultural romance.

Why were women's clothes so much cheaper than men's? Dixton glanced around the shop at the rows and rows of dresses or frocks or skirts or whatever they were called. '£20 reduced to £15.' Everything seemed to be priced in multiples of five pounds. He wondered if it was because there were more women in the world that their clothes were cheaper. A man would get nothing worthwhile for fifteen pounds in a menswear shop. No wonder women bought so many clothes. They were dirt cheap. Nathalie had disappeared into a 'communal fitting room' (whatever that was) to try on her fourth skirt of the same size and colour from the same rack. He couldn't see what the big deal was. Women's clothing seemed to be the only area of measurement where constants were variable.

'What do you think?' Nathalie exited into the lingerie aisle, doing a twirl.

'Fabulous, it looks as well, if not better, than the first size ten, navy blue skirt you tried on about half an hour ago.'

'Oh Dixton, you're no help.' She stood in front of the mirror and shifted from foot to foot. 'I think I'll try the other one on just one more time.'

Nathalie disappeared back into the fitting room. Dixton strolled away from the lingerie aisle so he wouldn't look like a pervert. Two sales assistants were leaning across the desk talking to a tall gorgeous blonde girl who was wearing a mini skirt which could have passed for a belt. February seemed an odd month in which to wear a mini, even to Dixton.

'I can't get over the change in you Mandy,' one of the sales assistants addressed old long legs.

'Well it's all down to Nigel you know,' she leaned in towards them.

'He told me that I'm at a cross in my life you know. It's as if my life is in the shape of a cross,' she drew an imaginary cross in space with a discarded security tag, 'your life starts at the bottom, down here and then you gradually move up. At the moment I'm on this bit here.' She made a motion indicating the horizontal part of the cross.

'Yeah, on that bit there,' the other sales assistant nodded sycophantically.

'Now my life choice, that's what Nigel calls it, my life choice is to go from side to side along that bit of the cross as I have been doing. . .'

'As you have been doing, yeah.' Shop assistant number one was really on the ball.

'. . . or to find the opening here,' she indicated again, 'and go up straight for it, no nonsense, don't take no for an answer.'

That's obviously Nigel's game plan thought Dixton.

'Amazing, its really amazing, Mandy.' The shop assistants gazed in awe at her.

'So you've no regrets about chucking in the job then?' ventured assistant number two.

'Absolutely not, you see this is all part of my life choice, Nigel wants me to groom myself for the takeaway revolution.'

'The takeaway revolution? What's that?'

'Well,' Mandy looked at both sets of her pink fingernails, 'Nigel says that hotels and eating out and restaurants and all that are a thing of the past. Fifty-nine percent of all British families eat takeaways, an average of. . .'

As Mandy of the mini skirt's voice drifted off out of his interest wavelength, Dixton forgave Nathalie all of her skirt try-ons. He always felt that Nature had a cruel way of combining beauty and stupidity. It was a bit like the grotesque sight of local authority housing in award winning villages. Nathalie emerged again, 'I think I prefer the first one.'

Sanjra's notes appeared from a cursory glance to be excellent. Dixton had photocopied most of them at this stage and apart from one or two plus the three week period of lectures to go after Easter, he had a full set. He'd copied them well in advance so as to cause Sanjra's study plans the minimum of disruption. EU Law was a maze of outrageous cases about import restrictions on cheese and obscure directives on the size of fishing nets. In footballing terms it was the European Bureaucracy Cup played in a series of away games in Brussels and Luxembourg with Irish supporters, a French referee and German sponsors. Still, the exam was only around the corner and Dixton would have to learn this rubbish off by heart. He finished photocopying the last page and thumbed through them to check that the originals were all in order. Thank heavens for photocopiers, it must have been very difficult to be a waster before their invention. He gathered all his notes up and went down the stairs from the tutorial offices to the ground floor. As he passed the administration desk one of the secretaries called him over.

'Dixton, have you got a moment?'

'Yes' he retraced his steps.

She was one of the younger and prettier of the secretaries and he thought her name might be Rose. She looked slightly embarrassed, he faced her over the reception desk.

'I know there's never a good time to mention money but your College bill is running a little high lately.'

'I know, I know. Listen, things are tight at the moment but I hope to get some funds together soon.'

'Look, if it were up to me you'd have unlimited credit but I'm afraid that he's been asking questions about your account,' she pointed up at the ceiling to the tutorial office.

'The Head Tutor?'

'No, Dr Winston, the Praelector. He's told us that your bill has to be cleared by the end of the Easter holidays or else. . .'

'Or else what? What could they do to him?'

'I don't know but anyway I thought I'd warn you in advance.'

'Thanks, Rose,' he shrugged his shoulders and smiled. He had no money in his bank account and another full term to run after Easter plus whatever arrears were now building up. Jesus, if it hadn't been for that fucking fountain. Oh well, there was no use crying over spilt milk or shattered benefactors.

It was definitely Spring. After a couple of false alarms the daffodils had come through and Dixton supposed that if he ever plucked up the courage to go and visit Grantchester in the daylight that lambs would be frolicking in the nearby fields or whatever it was they did in Spring. He sauntered up College Avenue on his way back from the last criminal lecture before Easter. As he wheeled the Tiger in through the side gate to the East Court he spotted Sanjra on his way into the College Library. He'd give back the notes to him now while it was in his head. As he pushed open the door to the library building he heard someone out of breath behind him. It was Professor Lynn carrying a box of books.

'Let me help you with that Professor.'

'No, that's fine, young Larkin, just hold the door open will you?' The old guy edged past him and in towards his office.

'Do you need a hand opening the office door?'

'If you wouldn't mind.' The office door was locked. Dixton tried the handle about forty times nonetheless.

'The key is in my left side jacket pocket,' said the librarian, almost collapsing under the weight of the books. Dixton rummaged in his pocket and they were home and dry. As he turned to leave the office Dixton suddenly remembered what Feldman had told him a couple of weeks ago. He should have thanked the librarian sooner but come to think of it, he hadn't seen him since, until now.

'Oh, Professor,' he said.

'Yes, Larkin, what is it?' the librarian looked up from unpacking the box.

'I can't thank you enough for that reference you sent in on my behalf before Christmas.'

'Oh that?' the librarian dismissed the issue with a wave of his hand, 'don't mention it, everyone deserves a second chance.'

'Yes, I suppose they do.'

''Specially when they haven't properly used up the first one, eh?' the librarian grinned.

'I meant to mention it to you earlier but I haven't seen you for a while.'

'Been a bit ill for a couple of weeks on and off, damn flu. You spend your youth beating it and your old age dreading it. Still, not to worry, I'm right as rain now. Are you looking forward to the rugby match on Saturday?' (England were playing Ireland in the Five Nations.)

'Yeah, I am, I hope we don't win by too much,' Dixton laughed

'No chance,' countered the librarian, 'I only hope your side have the decency to turn up.' He chuckled away to himself but his laugh converted into a cough.

145

Sanjra was in the reading room at one of the computer terminals. Dixton could barely see him over the piles of books. Even for Sanjra it was a bit early in the day to be studying.

'Hi, what are you up to?'

'Oh hello, Dixton,' Sanjra looked up.

'I saw you going into the Library so I brought your notes.' He handed Sanjra an envelope.

'Oh thanks but there's no rush. If you like you can keep them for a bit longer.'

'No, no, I've copied them all, thanks ever so much.'

Sanjra leaned back in the chair and rubbed his eyes and yawned.

'You look wrecked,' Dixton stated the obvious.

'I know, it's this bloody essay.'

Dixton picked up a page from one of the piles and read a couple of lines.

'"Land Economy"? This is taking secondary reading a bit far isn't it?'

'No, it's nothing to do with my own study.'

'Then what's the essay for?'

Sanjra looked more than a little embarrassed. 'I'm . . . I'm typing it for someone else.'

'Who?'

'Never mind who.'

Dixton spotted a folder of notes propped up against one of the books, he picked it up.

'Rainford, Bernard fucking Rainford!'

'OK, OK, it's for Bernard.'

'But why? I thought you disliked him as much as I do.'

'I do, but it's just. . .'

'Just what? Do you have to write the essays for him?'

'No, no nothing like that. . .'

'What? What is he doing asking another student to type his essays?'

Sanjra seemed a bit upset by this line of questioning so Dixton laid off.

'Listen, Sanjra, I'm sorry, it's none of my business, forget I asked.'

'Its OK, Dixton, you may as well know. My family at home in Pakistan are not very wealthy and so every term I send them my grant cheque. My father had an accident at work and so he can no longer earn money. Bernard offered to pay me to type his essays.'

Dixton was stunned.

'This is outrageous, who the hell does he think he is? God or someone? Look Sanjra, I'll give you some money if you're short.'

'Listen, Dixton you are very kind but no thanks. I know how it seems but. . .'

'But nothing. This is unfair, it's exploitation. I'll bloody well give him a piece of my mind when I see him.'

Sanjra looked alarmed. 'Oh no, Dixton, you mustn't say anything to Bernard,' he implored. 'As well as the essays I hope. . .'

'You hope what?'

'Well perhaps if I can help him now he may be able to use his influence to get me a job when I finish at Cambridge.'

Dixton felt that any optimism Sanjra might have in this regard would be better directed elsewhere. Still, however unfair the situation may have seemed to him it was clear that Rainford had really done nothing wrong. If the arrangement suited both of them then who was he to interfere?

'Of course I won't say anything if you don't want me to, its just that, well you know.'

Sanjra grabbed him by the wrist and looked beseechingly up at him, 'Don't say anything to him please!'

'OK, OK, Sanjra, I won't say anything, don't worry.'

'Thanks Dixton. I've got to get back down to this.'

Dixton ambled out of the Library into the Court and began to feel guilty about borrowing Sanjra's notes himself.

'Young Larkin!'

Dixton heard the librarian's voice as he was about a third of the way across the Court. Professor Lynn was leaning out of his office window.

'Yes Professor?'

'That game on Saturday, the Five Nations.'

'Yes?'

'I normally watch them at home, care to join me for this one?'

'I'd love to, where?'

'53 Hayfield Lane, its just behind the fire station in Newnham.'

'Great, I'll be there.'

'About two o'clock, kick off is at a quarter past.'

'Right ho, Professor.'

He was looking forward to it already. He felt privileged to be invited and even more privileged at being one of the few people for whom the librarian ceased to be deaf.

CHAPTER THIRTEEN

The College bar was almost full. The Lupin Hall Women's Squash team was celebrating a famous landmark - Penny had been selected to play against Oxford. It was only a half Blue but for Lupin Hall that was a tremendous achievement. Dixton and Nathalie had spent the afternoon cycling to Wrestlingworth and back. Dixton's legs felt like they'd been used by all four members of a relay team in the same race. Nathalie appeared as unruffled at the end of the trip as she'd been at the beginning.

'It's good for you, Dixton, you need to be physically fit to be mentally strong.'

'You sound like my aunt, "brisk walks, and a spell with the Christian brothers" that's her panacea for all ailments.'

'I'm really looking forward to meeting your aunt.' Nathalie sounded as if she meant it. Dixton couldn't think of anything he'd look forward to less.

'Do you want a drink?' he shouted above the melee as they made their way towards the bar.

'No, I've got to get back home pretty soon, my term assessment is this week and the project has to be in by Friday.'

'I'll see you home.'

'No need,' she pointed over his shoulder. 'I think someone else is more in need of your company than I am.' Pepper was playing pool on his own and looked like he was losing. 'Byee,' she kissed Dixton briefly. The squash team whooped and cheered.

'See you tomorrow?'

'Meet me for lunch in the Red Wolf.'

'OK, see you.'

Pepper cut a lonely figure silhouetted against the backdrop of the squash team's celebrations. Dixton's heart went out to him. He'd never seen his friend as low as he'd been these last couple of weeks. Pepper and he hadn't even discussed the golf team for days and that worried Dixton more than anything. At least if Pepper was ranting and raving about something it was better than complete silence. You were always better off spitting something out than letting it gnaw away inside.

'Do you want a game?' he suggested cheerfully. Pepper shrugged his shoulders.

'Set them up,' said Dixton 'I'll pay.' He took a fifty pence piece out of his pocket and flicked it over to Pepper to insert in the table. Pepper sort of caught the coin but it slipped through his fingers and disappeared into one of the pockets on the table. That said it all.

'Hey, Dixton, Jonathan, how are things with you two?' Herve spotted them across the room and came to join them.

'Not too bad, Herve.' Dixton answered for both of them but Pepper didn't even look up. Herve didn't notice that Pepper was depressed or, if he did, it didn't deter him.

'Listen, the Lupin Hall Ball is on at the beginning of June and we're looking for a theme. Any ideas?'

'I don't know, what do you think, Pepper?' Dixton tried to gee Pepper up a bit.

'Don't know, don't care,' Pepper said firmly.

Herve looked a little put out. Dixton tried to signal him with his eyes to back off. For a moment he felt that Herve was going to put his foot in it and ask what was up. That was all they needed.

'Never mind,' said Herve, smiling politely, 'I'm sure we'll come up with something.'

'See you then, Herve,' Dixton urged him to leave them alone. He retreated prudently. Pepper was so far down in the dumps that Dixton could imagine him climbing over twenty naked women to get to a bottle of sleeping tablets. The squash team were singing *For She's a Jolly Good Fellow*.

They played a game of pool but Pepper's heart wasn't in it. Dixton deliberately fluffed a few shots and left easy opportunities for Pepper to score but even then his friend lost easily. As Dixton potted the black to win the game, Pepper broke his silence.

'What really galls me, Dixton, about this golf business is that it's completely beyond my control now. There's absolutely nothing I can do to change the situation. There are no more practice matches, I can't play any better or try any harder than I've done already. It's so frustrating but there's absolutely nothing I can do.'

Dixton doubted if Pepper ever cried about anything but he'd never seen him so close before to breaking up. Even faced with the possibility of a criminal prosecution Pepper had been able to laugh at it. This was something much deeper. To face this in a light-hearted way would have meant trivialising everything he'd worked for, everything he'd come to Cambridge to achieve and everything he'd ever wanted to be. Damn.

'It looks like Ladies squash will be our only taste of a Blue this year, eh?' Zinowsky had come up behind them and was leaning against the blackboard.

Dixton reacted first and stepped in between Zinowsky and Pepper just as Pepper picked up the pool cue and turned to hit him.

'Fuck off, Zinowsky,' said Dixton.

'Steady on boys, I hope nobody's going to start a fight,' the American sneered. Pepper looked ready to explode but Dixton was determined not to let it happen.

'I'll kill you Zinowsky, just give me a chance,' Pepper fumed, he lunged forward but Dixton held him at bay.

'Come on then,' Zinowsky beckoned him over provocatively. Dixton didn't know how much longer he could keep them apart.

The rest of the people in the bar had sensed the tension and their singing had been replaced by silence as everyone focused on the corner of the room where the pool table was. There was an atmosphere that you could have cut with a chainsaw. Dixton stood sideways between the two men wondering what more he could do. The moment was shattered by the sound of Jack, Andy and Niall the vet bursting into the bar through the double doors. Jack assessed the scene instantly and came over and put his arm around Pepper's shoulder.

'He's not worth it, Pepper, you can't let some fat American ruin your evening.'

'Its OK by me if you want to chicken out,' Zinowsky taunted. 'You see this?' He pointed to the vulgar crest on his blazer. 'I got this playing for my University back home, you'll never know how good that feels.'

Dixton looked at Pepper and back to Zinowsky. He hoped Pepper wouldn't blow up. Pepper looked at Zinowsky and then calmly put down the pool cue.

'Surely you mean for playing with yourself at university?'

Zinowsky reddened and moved close. Dixton shouldered him aside. The crisis passed.

'Come on Pepper, Dixton, we're going into the Anchor in a while for a few pints,' said Niall.

'OK,' said Dixton. Zinowsky had turned reluctantly and was now on his way out of the bar.

'Bikes and cash at the back gate at eight sharp,' announced Jack.

Dixton was oceans proud of Pepper for keeping his cool. This was a strange country, he thought. It was hard to believe that a nation which spawned such greatness as the Beatles and Thomas the Tank Engine could produce such a bastard as Bernard or tolerate a dickhead like Zinowsky. The single most unrewarding thing in life (apart from walking a girl home to discover she lives with her parents) was to work towards something and to see it slip away at the last moment. He'd come to Cambridge to lose his virginity and gain a degree: one down (albeit in dodgy circumstances) and a long way to go to the other. For Pepper, however, things were quite different. It was like passing someone else's house when their phone is ringing; there was absolutely nothing you could do about it. Suddenly the whole world seemed jaded. It was as if the bigger picture had slipped by unnoticed. Dixton wondered what might be in store that would lift Pepper out of his depression. A couple of months ago they'd both been imbued with a sense of invincibility, nothing could rattle them, individually or collectively, for more than an instant. Christmas, the fountain; debt, Rainford, Zinowsky, the Praelector, and now the loss of Pepper's Blue, had all combined to head the pair of them off at the pass. Much as it must have been in the aftermath of the First World War, it was almost impossible to look back beyond those events and believe that everything was or could be all right ever again. He was dying for a pint.

'What's the story, Pepper?' Dixton met him in the bicycle shed. It was quite chilly out and Dixton was wearing his Arran jumper. Pepper seemed in better form.

'We've only got the Tiger between us.'

'What about your bike?'

'It's in the geology department, they'd locked the car-park.'

'We could double up on the carrier,' Dixton suggested.

'No way,' Pepper smirked. 'I was almost too drunk to notice on the way back from the cop shop but I nearly did myself a mischief.'

'What'll we do? It must be nearly eight.'

'You tell the others to go on, its five past now, we'll see them in the Anchor. You can go ahead if you like, I think I know where there's another bike that's unlocked.'

'Not at all, I'll wait for you.' Dixton cycled around the College to the back gate and told the others they'd catch up. When he returned Pepper was pumping up the back tyre of a red mountain bike.

'What's up?'

'Slow puncture, I'd say. It'll get me there and back.' This was true camaraderie: co-operative thieving.

'I wonder what's going on here?' Dixton exclaimed as they approached the crossroads at the end of Sidgwick Avenue. A small crowd of people had gathered in the middle of the road.

'An accident?' Pepper thought aloud.

'Maybe, let's slow down.' They braked slightly as they got nearer.

'Isn't that Jack, Andy and the boys?' asked Pepper

'Yeah, stop and see what's going on.' Dixton tipped his shoes off the road to compensate for having no back brake. They'd almost ground

151

to a halt when Jack warned them off.

'Hey lads are either of you cycling stolen bicycles?' he roared with a laugh. Dixton saw that two uniformed police were at the centre of the knot of people; it was a checkpoint. 'Cycle like fuck, Pepper,' he urged under his breath. They'd both almost come to a halt at the edge of the group and had to change direction with very little notice. Pepper almost collided with the back wheel of Andy's bike.

'We'll see you at the Blue Boar,' Dixton roared as they pedalled past furiously. Anything to throw them off the scent. Whatever trouble he'd been in so far, getting caught with the stolen bike would finish him altogether. They cycled like crazy into the middle of town and then wheeled the bikes down the towpath behind Magdalene.

'Jesus, that was close,' said Dixton.

Pepper looked at him stonily and then started laughing.

'What? What are you laughing at, Pepper? If they caught us with the Tiger we'd be fucked altogether.'

'I know, I know, the thing is though, they didn't catch us, did they?'

'Yes, but they nearly did.'

'Nearly never wet the bed.'

Dixton was flummoxed. 'I just don't understand you, Pepper. Half an hour ago you were ready to beat someone's brains in with a pool cue and now you're laughing because we were nearly caught by the cops. What is it with you?'

'You don't see, do you Dixton?'

'NO, I bloody well do *not* see!'

'It's an omen, our luck has changed. It's a sign that better things are to come. Police checkpoints like false pregnancy scares are sent to try us.' Dixton wasn't sure why but it all seemed funny and suddenly he too was laughing.

'You know what it means though?' said Pepper gravely.

'What? What?'

'I'm afraid it's cheerio to the old Tiger.'

'What do you mean?'

'We can't keep it now, we've got to dump it; now, here, tonight.'

'Why?'

'Forensics, fingerprinting, DNA, all of that stuff.'

'That's what I said months ago, after the Grantchester incident and I think I remember being shot down as a scaremonger. Suddenly you think of the same pitfalls and its a real live danger.' Dixton was indignant.

'But that was before either of us had a police record. They have my fingerprints now, remember?'

It really was the end of the line for the Tiger. They both stood back and admired the vehicle for one last time. It had served them well but now, like the secret agent whose cover has been blown, it was more of a liability than an asset. They took a wheel each and lifted it onto the thin railing. 'One, two, three.' They heaved it into the Cam across from the Spade and Beckett pub. There was a loud splash and the Tiger was gone.

'You know what, Dixton?'

'No, What?'

'You're still an excellent lawyer,' Pepper smirked.

'And you're a bloody awful client.'

'You know what else, Dixton?'

'No, what else?'

'I think I know the perfect way to get Zinowsky back for everything.'

'My Dear Dixton

I know that Easter is almost upon us and it is a salutary reminder that the exams cannot be far behind. All the mental conditioning that has been carried on throughout the winter months is now about to face its finest hour. The Apostles were in much the same position when faced with the task of carrying on their Master's work after his Ascension. I know that the solid background which our Catholic home has given you will stand you in good stead. It is only the very foolish or the very evil who would waste the opportunities with which you have been blessed. The distractions of the flesh are unspeakable (yet so very real in any place in which young rash people of opposite sexes are gathered without supervision). However, I know that our happy home has been a springboard, as it were, into mature early adulthood for you. People may laugh at the devout inhabitants of our small island yet remember it was Ireland and her monks who carried the torch of the one true faith when the rest of Europe lived in fear of the Vandals. The power of prayer is a powerful ally but a terrible foe. I enclose a selection of holy pictures to inspire you in your exams. Please let me know what your plans are for the Easter break (you notice I do not use the word 'holiday'). I have won two tickets to Lourdes by paying the gas bill on time.

Yours Aunt Sheila.'

What did she mean 'Easter is almost upon *us*?' *She* wasn't facing blindly in into Remedies and Restitution or scrambling to meet the deadline with an essay on the Spanish Armada. That was the odd thing about guardians, they were willing to claim credit for the victories but absented themselves from the defeats and blamed their charges one

153

hundred percent. Steeping the whole letter in religious beliefs was further evidence of the series of opt-out clauses at Aunt Sheila's disposal.

Sometimes Dixton was an agnostic on the subject of his own atheism. If there really was a better world out there, somewhere in the ethereal beyond, surely it would be reachable by Inter-Rail? On the other hand, the grand we've-all-been-hoaxed theory was a bit too successful if it were true to be actually true if you know what I mean. He thumbed through the holy pictures: Saint Valance of Thermos looked like the patron saint of licenced premises. Why was she sending him this stuff? Much as he loved his aunt, her obsession with the topics of keeping your faith and losing your virginity was a little bit draining. Why was it always so difficult to imagine members of your own family ever having sex. ('My dad? Maybe, but my mother? No way.') Aunt Sheila was his parents. Perhaps her letters and her views only meant that she was playing a blinder as both. He folded the letter and smiled. Even though he didn't believe in God he hoped that if there was a heaven (which of course there wasn't), that it would at least have cable TV (which of course they didn't have at home).

The last Saturday before the Easter Holidays was one of those clear warm March days which, in seasonal terms, is neither fish nor fowl (to mix metaphors horribly). The sun was making a valiant effort to get through. Dixton emerged from E Block with the purpose of a man destined for cornflakes. Laura had been able to clear his room earlier than expected because he'd been up and out by ten o'clock. He had a good feeling about today and though he hadn't planned to do any study or anything like that, he decided to take the day on from the pre-lunch side for a change. He took the first meaningful strides towards the main building.

'Larkin, Larkin, you bastard.'

Zinowsky's American twang cut across the court like a bolt from a crossbow.

'I'm gonna get you for this,' the large Yank loped across the grass towards him. Zinowsky's movements struck Dixton as dictated more out by necessity than choice.

'What's up with you?' he asked calmly. This had the desired effect. Zinowsky went ape.

'What's up with me? What's up with me?'

'Now you're asking the same question I asked,' Dixton smiled.

'Look you little shit, I've had about enough of your back talk, you're responsible for this and I know it,' Zinowsky stuck his fat hand into

Dixton's chest.

'For what? I haven't the faintest idea what you're talking about. Now if you don't mind, I'm on my way to breakfast.'

Dixton sidestepped past Zinowsky and began walking towards the main buildings. Zinowsky caught up with him and stood in front of him again. 'You're not going anywhere until the damage is paid for.'

Dixton began to get a little worried. The court was empty and Zinowsky looked liable to force the issue. The scene was disturbed by the appearance of Pepper at the kitchen window of J Block. (Pepper's room was in G Block.) 'Hi there, Zinowsky,' Pepper mimicked an American accent.

'What do you want?' Zinowsky shouted back.

'Oh nothing, I've just been helping the bedder bring in a hydraulic pump to clean your room,' he grinned broadly. The penny dropped and Zinowsky's face empurpled from the neck up. He started towards J Block.

'You wait there, you hear? You just wait there,' he screamed.

'Byee,' Pepper waved and then, as an afterthought, gave Zinowsky the two fingers. Zinowsky sprinted/loped quickly across the Court. What the hell was happening?

Dixton reckoned that Pepper would either wait for Zinowsky and have his brains battered in or else attempt to escape out through the back of J Block. He legged it around towards the back of the blocks. There was no sign of Zinowsky or Pepper. He approached the back door of J Block and as he did he heard Zinowksy's dulcet tones raging down the back stairs. If he couldn't catch Pepper he might settle for Dixton. Bollox. He looked around frantically for a place to hide. He edged back the way he'd come. Suddenly a hand grabbed his shoulder and whisked him into the narrow alley between the laundry room and the wine storeroom, it was Pepper.

'Jesus Christ, you nearly gave me a heart attack.'

'Sorry, Dixton, but I had to be quick, Zinowksy's not a happy bunny.'

'That's putting it mildly.'

'Shssh,' Pepper put a finger to his lips. They scrunched themselves up in the narrow passageway as Zinowsky rushed past. 'Let's make a run for it,' urged Dixton.

'Wait a sec,' Pepper listened out.

'Bernard, Bernard, you stay there, I'll go around the front,' Zinowsky's voice boomed.

'Fuck it, there's two of them now,' said Pepper.

'I suppose we could always go out and reason with them or have it out for once and for all?' Dixton suggested. They looked at each other and simultaneously laughed and said 'yeah right', disbelievingly. The whole year was so precariously balanced now that discretion was definitely the better part of cowardice.

'This way,' Pepper inched his way further back into the passageway, Dixton followed. He hadn't a clue where they were going. The narrow opening gave way to a slightly wider space between the laundry and the boundary wall of the College. It was a mini cul de sac. The boundary wall was about six feet high.

'What about in here?' Bernard's voice came from the other side of the buildings. They didn't have much time.

'C'mon, give me a leg up,' said Pepper.

Dixton knitted his hands and Pepper put his left foot into the human stirrup.

'Jesus, Pepper, hurry up,' he weighed a couple of tons.

Pepper sprung upwards and as he did, Dixton boosted his foot up after him. Pepper gripped the top of the wall and heaved himself up. Dixton stared up at his friend's disappearing rear end and wondered how the hell he was supposed to climb the wall. It made him wish he'd bought that handbook, *Learning to Jump Twice your own Height*. He heard Bernard's voice again, it came from the passageway.

'Mike, I think he might have gone down here, hurry up.'

Oh fiddlesticks. Pepper had left him in the lurch. Dixton took two steps back and ran towards the wall, jumped but was unable to get a hold. A green plastic hose crept over the wall and edged towards him. Dixton grabbed it and tugged, it gave a little and then became taut. He pulled himself up the wall until he was about three or four inches from the top. He let go suddenly and snatched at the rough block, pulled himself over the wall and whisked the hose after him. There was an even larger drop on the other side and, as he let go, he closed his eyes and thought of the Safety in Industry Acts. He landed on a mixture of chicken wire and nettles. Pepper rescued him from the entanglement, grinning. They could hear Zinowsky and Bernard on the other side of the wall.

'There's no way he could have got over this wall, not on his own, it must be two metres high.'

Dixton hated people who measured in metres, it was always the sign of a real gobshite. The voices stopped. Dixton glanced around at his surroundings, they were in a wood, or at least on the edge of it. Pepper had tied the hose around a tree and the knot had tightened so much that the area around the knot was now white.

'At least we got away from them,' Pepper said as he helped Dixton dust off his pullover. Miraculously Dixton's face hadn't got stung, just the back of his right hand.

'Yes, I suppose there is that,' he said, 'I just want to know one thing though?' he glared at Pepper.

'Yes?'

'Why the hell were we running from them in the first place?'

It hadn't struck Dixton until now that he had absolutely no idea what this was all about.

Pepper grinned even more.

'That's an excellent question, Dixton, a really excellent question.'

'Well,' Dixton was nonplussed, 'have you got a really excellent answer?'

'Yes, I have, but first you've got to see this.' He took Dixton's arm and led him into what looked like an unhelpfully thick hedge.

'What the. . .?' Dixton protested but he realised almost instantly.

The hedge gave way to a clearing and it was so unexpected and spectacular a sight he was devastatingly and utterly silenced. It was a swimming pool. Not an ordinary cheap-hotel-mock-mosaic-tile-too-much-chlorine pool but an awesome work of art. It was like something out of ancient Greece. The pool was surrounded by a marble walkway and the cool azure water rippled so finely that the pool might have been empty. At each corner were impressive busts of God knows who but impressive nonetheless. At one end an aperture in the surround contained white marble steps into the pool. Across the pool they saw a vast grass avenue lined with trees leading to a house.

'Where are we?' Dixton gasped.

'I'm not sure exactly but I think it's the grounds of the graduate house for Gonville & Caius.'

'This is incredible. How come those bastards have a pool?'

'Come on, let's sit down, Dixton, I'm out of breath after all that.'

They spotted a bench beside a garden shed of some sort. They had a side view of the pool but could not themselves be seen from the avenue or the house. Dixton looked at Pepper expectantly.

'So? What happened?'

'You won't believe this but I'll tell you anyway. Remember I said I'd thought of an idea to get at Zinowsky?'

'Yeah.'

'Well, I finally got my chance to put the plan into action today. You know that Zinowsky always take a shower in the morning?'

'No, I didn't, but then his washing habits never really interested me.'

'Well, this morning when he was gone down to the ground floor to have a shower, he left the door of his room open.'

'So?' Dixton was getting impatient.

'So I went up into his room and put my plan into action. I carried up a bucket of filthy water from the pond behind the Presidential Lodge.'

'Didn't anyone see you taking the water?'

'Nope, I did it at night and left the bucket in the shed behind J Block. Anyway, I carried the bucket into his room and left it on the table behind the door with a long piece of string attached from the bucket to the door handle.'

'Oh, the old bucket and piece of string ploy. Surely he. . .'

'Listen, will you? Then I closed the door behind me.'

'How could you close the door behind you? Surely the bucket toppled over?'

'Oh no, the bucket stayed where it was, I'd left more than enough slack in the string so the door could open and close without disturbing the bucket.'

'But that defeats the whole purpose of the trick? I mean unless the string is tight the bucket won't fall off the table.' Dixton was really beginning to feel that his escape had been pointless.

'Yes,' Pepper laughed, 'that's just it, the bucket didn't fall off,' when Zinowsky returned to his room he found the set up and assumed . . .'

'That someone had tried to play a trick on him and had made a hash of it?', Dixton pitched in.

'Exactly, and what do you think he did then?'

'How do you mean?' Dixton was puzzled.

'With the water, what do you think he did with the water?'

'Brought the bucket out to the bathroom and poured it down the bath to get rid of it.'

'Wrong, the bathroom is two floors down and he's standing there wearing nothing but a towel.'

'Maybe he drank the fucking stuff, what do I care?' Dixton became freshly aware of the nettle stings.

'Relax,' Pepper calmed him, 'it's important, what do you think he did with the water?'

'OK, so he pours it down the sink in his room, that's the most obvious thing to do, what do I care what he did with the water?'

'Correct, however there's one thing he doesn't know,' Pepper smiled, inviting the question. Dixton obliged.

'Which is?'

Pepper reached into his jacket pocket and took out a small bag. He opened the bag and tipped it out onto the ground. 'He doesn't know that I've removed the u-bend from the sink.'

Dixton recognised the white u-shaped plastic pipe.

'That's a master stroke, Pepper, absolutely amazing stuff.' The two looked down at the u-bend again and exploded with a laughing fit which had both of them almost weeping hysterically at the genius of the plan. Dixton couldn't get over the excellence of what had happened. This was the perfect way to get back at that plonker. He who lives by the fountain shall die by the sink. Pepper wiped his eyes and, while still laughing, continued.

'Do you know what was underneath the sink, Dixton?'

'No, what?'

'That stupid blazer with the crest for inter-State tiddlywinks,' he smirked.

'But how come that was there? Its a stupid place to put a blazer,' Dixton exclaimed.

'I put it there for safekeeping,' said Pepper.

'Safekeeping?'

'Yes, of course. It was originally hanging over the back of the chair, which was beside the table, and I moved it out of harm's way in case the bucket toppled over. 'Oh well.'

'Abso-fucking-lutely excellent!' Dixton said in astonishment. Pepper had surpassed himself, All the grief Zinowsky had caused both of them had vanished down the drain. Brilliant. People hate being outsmarted by others but what really drives them berserk is being outsmarted by themselves.

'How do we get back to Lupin, Pepper?'

'I don't know, let's stroll around here for a while and take the long way back. It'll give Zinowsky time to cool off or should I say 'dry off'. Say this would be a great place for a barbecue.'

They broke into loud guffaws again which carried across the swimming pool and resounded in the ears of the marble busts. This was more like it.

In 4 Clopton Way one evening a couple of days later Dixton and Nathalie found themselves alone in front of a March log fire. Dixton was sitting on the floor of the sitting room leaning against the end of the sofa gazing into the flames when Nathalie came in with two glasses of Sainsbury's wine. She seemed to read his thoughts.

'Do you miss your parents?'

'I suppose I do, sort of. I never really knew them I suppose. It's hard to remember them at all sometimes,' he said sadly.

'What do you remember of them?' she asked gently.

'It's funny really but the only thing I really remember about them or

159

our house is the sound of laughter. I can't really separate the voices or even be sure it is their laughter I recall. It's strange really.' He lost himself in the flicker of the fire again feeling puzzled and alone.

'We must make the most of our time together Dixton.' She sat down beside him. Dixton might have cried and if he did she was there to comfort him.

Professor Lynn's house on Hayfield Road was a lovely quaint old cottage. He'd been married but his wife had died a few years before. There was a lovely old photograph of the two of them on a pier at some resort.

'That was just after the war,' the librarian remarked as he brought a tray of coffee and biscuits, 'Brighton was where we honeymooned'. Dixton felt as though he had been admitted to the librarian's other life. He was touched.

'She's very pretty, Professor.' He couldn't think of anything more appropriate.

'Yes, she was, no wonder she chose a handsome devil to marry.'

What could have been an awkward or a sad moment passed in an easy way, which convinced Dixton that true love was definitely forever. A Judy Garland album cover was propped up against a bookcase beside the record player, the record still on the turntable. It was the only thing which seemed to be slightly misplaced in the front room, everything else was neatly stacked or shelved. There were hundreds of books arranged in alphabetical order of the author's surnames. Every available space had been filled. The television was on, with the sound turned off, waiting for the match to begin.

'I've got something I think might interest you, young Larkin.'

The librarian stood on a footstool and reached for a red ledger on a shelf populated by reference books. He blew some dust off the cover of the book and opened it to reveal a title page with old embossed lettering. Dixton was definitely interested.

'It's only an idea, Larkin.'

'I think it's a great idea.' The screen flickered as the Irish and English teams raced out onto the pitch at Lansdowne Road.

Stan the porter alerted them on Saturday evening.

'Dixton, Pepper, there are a couple of messages for you in the pigeon holes.'

The notes were from the Praelector. They were to see him in his office on Monday morning, together.

'What do you think he wants, Pepper?'

'Its fairly obvious, what he wants, but don't worry?' Pepper ripped the note up and threw it in an ashtray in the reading room.

'You mean the bucket business?' Dixton was a bit slow on the uptake.

'Of course, Dixton, but he'll have a tough time linking us with the crime.'

'Us? I didn't do anything.'

'Ah, but he doesn't know that, does he?'

'Look, Pepper, we really can't afford any more trouble, well I certainly can't anyway.'

'Relax,' Pepper was totally calm, 'say nothing and see what tack he takes. Its my hunch that he'll be fishing for info, that's all.' Dixton was always suspicious of other people's hunches but Pepper was spot on.

'This is a very serious matter.'

The Praelector spoke up from his faithful swivel chair while looking over his glasses at the same time. They said nothing. 'I don't know if you realise just how serious this is?'

The two looked at each other and then back at the Praelector.

'No, Praelector, I don't,' they announced in unison. He was beginning to lose his cool.

'I didn't come down in the last shower.' Again silence. He was clearly getting nowhere.

'A student's room has been broken into and great damage done to his personal effects and to the room itself. I know that you two were involved in some way.'

'In what way exactly, Praelector?' Pepper put the boot in.

'I don't know what way exactly, Mr Pepper but I'm going to find out,' Dr Winston exploded. It was excellent to watch. He ripped off his glasses and stared madly at them across the desk. Dixton remembered the humiliation he'd suffered in this very room only a couple of months before, he wasn't going to let the opportunity slip either.

'Then perhaps you should wait, Praelector, until you do find out exactly. Otherwise these groundless allegations you are making might be construed as defamatory.'

'Don't you play the smart-assed lawyer with me, Larkin.'

'I think we should leave before you lose control of yourself, Praelector,' Pepper said calmly. They turned to leave.

'I'm warning both of you,' the Praelector shouted as they opened the door. 'I'm bloody well on to you! You see if I don't nail the pair of you.' The senior tutor, Dr Hagar, was standing outside the door in the corridor, he entered the room as they left.

'Perhaps this is not a good time?' he ventured meekly.

161

As Pepper and Dixton got to the landing halfway down the stairs, they turned and looked at each other.

'Yes!' Dixton clenched his fist and punched the air in triumph.

'About bloody time someone else was on the receiving end,' said Pepper.

As if to confirm Dixton's suspicion that things had begun to look up, a letter from Feldman arrived the same day. It had been hand delivered.

"In view of your financial circumstances, etc. I have secured offer of a job for the Easter for you with the Crown Prosecution Service in Strawford. If you're interested phone my secretary in the Law faculty. I'll forward details if reply is affirmative.

Robert."

Dixton phoned immediately and said yes about fifty times.

'I'd like to welcome you all to E Block for the inaugural meeting of the revived "Port and Stilton Society".'

Dixton looked proudly around the room at the small but cramped gathering. They were pushing it a bit for the size of the room but what the heck. He wondered where Pepper was. Penny was sitting beside Andy on the floor. Jack, Sanjra, Stan the Porter and Niall the vet were crowded on to the bed while the radiator was a seat for Nathalie. The desk top held seven unopened bottles of port and two huge full Stilton surrounded by plastic knives and paper plates.

'It gives me great pleasure to ask the President of this revived Society, Professor Lynn, to take the floor and to formally launch this new era in the Society's history.' He gave a small handclap and everyone followed suit. Professor Lynn rose from the only armchair in the room and straightened his bow tie before standing with the sink at his back to address the meeting. He cleared his throat.

'Ahem . . . Mr Secretary,' he nodded at Dixton, 'Port Officer (Niall), Stilton officer (Nathalie) and members. It is nearly twenty years since the last meeting of this Society. That meeting was held in Emmanuel College boat club before the great river battle of 1976. In those days our Stilton Officer took the train to Ashwell once a month to the premises of Moorcroft and Sons, Grocers in the High Street. It was only two weeks ago I remembered that I had the old minutes book and I approached Mr Larkin to talk about reviving the Society. It is, in my estimation, wholly appropriate that now, at a time when Lupin Hall seems to be heading in the direction of corporate sponsorship for education, that some effort should be made to preserve the past of this infant College before it becomes swallowed up in the anonymity on which other sponsored Colleges seem to thrive.'

Dixton looked at the others, there was rapt attention etched across their faces. Where the hell was Pepper? The Librarian continued.

'The aims of this Society are twofold: firstly, we must undertake to meet on a monthly basis to drink port and to eat Stilton and secondly, we must devote ourselves to the task of keeping alive the original name of the College instead of the name we have been conditioned to adopt. Let us fill our glasses therefore and make the traditional toast of the Port and Stilton Society.'

Dixton handed around the glasses of ruby port. Sanjra made as if to begin drinking before everyone else but a look from Penny stopped him. Professor Lynn stepped forward slightly from the basin end of the room and raised his glass out in front of him at about eye level.

'To University College Hall, may she prosper and triumph.'

'To University College Hall, Triumph and Prosper.'

It always amazed Dixton how people could never remember things accurately in groups. The librarian downed his drink in one and the others followed suit. Niall, the Port Officer refilled the glasses. There was a frantic knocking on the door and Andy and Penny had to stand up to let Pepper in. Nathalie had begun to cut the cheese. Pepper fell into the room breathlessly. 'It's! I'm. . .' he began.

'Take your time, Pepper, catch your breath, what is it?' He calmed him. All eyes in the room were on Pepper.

'What happened?'

'Pepper, are you OK?' Dixton spoke on everyone's behalf. Pepper looked up, still pretty breathless. 'Here, drink this.' Professor Lynn proffered a glass of port.

'No thanks, Professor,' Pepper straightened up. 'No booze for me for a while.'

'Are you sick or something?' Dixton was anxious.

'No, never been better. I can't drink because I'm in training. Cameron's got pneumonia, I'm in the team for the Blues match.'

Dixton dropped his paper plate full of oatcakes and Stilton and threw his arms around Pepper.

He wouldn't be able to caddy for Pepper because he'd be engaged by the Crown Prosecution Service for the duration but so what. At least now Pepper's dream would come true.

CHAPTER FOURTEEN

'The Crown Prosecution Service is at the coalface of the system of justice in this country. We are the footsoldiers of the legal army. We rely on the co-operation of the police force and the esteem of the British Public; in short, we are the watch dogs of our society, sanctioning when necessary and admonishing where appropriate.'

James Gobbil was a dickhead. Dixton noticed this almost immediately. He was the head of the CPS and proud of it. Dixton wasn't sure how the rest of the staff felt. The offices of the CPS were on the second and third floor of a restored mill on the outskirts of Strawford. The village itself was pretty, even in the early April rain, and its most attractive features were the old stone work bridge and the girl on the cash till at the corner shop. Dixton had taken the bus out from Cambridge bus station at a quarter to eight that morning and was wrecked tired by the time he arrived at the offices. Early starts had never figured highly in his priorities.

'And in here is where you'll be working,' Mr Gobbil ushered him into a pokey little office overlooking the mill-wheel. The occupant of the room was a dapper balding man who was wearing a blue thin pin-stripe suit and a labour party tie.

'This is George McInnes, he's responsible for the Peterborough end of things here,' Gobbil chuckled pointlessly.

Dixton noticed that the head of Strawford CPS wore a bunch of keys clipped to one of the belt holders on his trousers – ugh. It reminded him of the headmaster of a primary school. McInnes looked decent enough though, he stood up behind the desk and shook hands with Dixton.

'How do you do, Dixton isn't it?'

"Yes, Dixton Larkin.'

"Well, I'm sure that you two are anxious to get down to work, I'll see you at coffee then Dixton, don't let him work you too hard eh?'

Again the ridiculous chuckle as if he had second sight and immediate access to in-jokes which hadn't even been created yet. Dixton imagined Gobbil was the type of pathetic authority figure who felt that he was paying his employees too much even though they weren't his employees and he wasn't paying them at all. Gobbil turned to go but spotted a crystal clock on one of the shelves near the door. He picked it up and set it down again after checking the shelf for dust.

'Expensive stuff George what?' he winked at Dixton, 'I pay these fellows too well, you know that's what it is, ha ha.' Ha-fucking-ha-fucking-ha Dixton thought.

'Pull up a chair Dixton, clear all that stuff onto the floor.'

Dixton was a bit nervous. The idea of a job for a couple of weeks didn't bother him, in fact, the prospect of clearing his debts at Lupin and having enough left to see him through the summer term was excellent. It was just that, well, frankly, he'd never seriously considered the possibility of actually having to work before. Work was something other people's parents did or their brothers emigrated for. Dixton knew that of course the world didn't run on happy hours and free lunches but at the same time the whole system had functioned so well up till now that he almost felt he was intruding by getting a job himself. He'd have enough hassle sorting himself out for the exams next term. Perhaps he should have gone to Lourdes with Aunt Sheila and then studied for a couple of weeks. No, there was always the danger of peaking too early. Anyway he really needed the money.

'So you're studying Law at Cambridge?'

'Ish,' he replied evasively.

'"Law-ish"? that sounds like what I did at Birmingham. The core subjects without the core knowledge. That sort of thing,' McInnes grinned.

Dixton looked across a pile of charge sheets for dangerous driving and smiled back. He wasn't sure how to take this guy.

'Now Dixton,' McInnes looked around the room inquisitively, 'what will we get you to do first? Ah yes, over there,' he pointed to a large filing cabinet, 'second drawer.'

Dixton leaped to his feet and tugged at the drawer handle – it was locked.

'Here,' McInnes threw him a set of keys. Dixton fumbled for a while and then found the right key. He opened the second drawer, now what?

'OK Dixton, I'm putting you in charge of everything in that drawer for the next three weeks.' Oh fuck. Dixton's hands were shaking. He hadn't even looked in the drawer.

'All right get to it,' McInnes prompted. 'Two sugars, loads of milk for me.'

Dixton lifted out the kettle from the drawer.

'Rule number one in this business,' said McInnes

'Yes?'

'Never let Gobbil know anything.' McInnes whipped *The Guardian* out from under the pile of charge sheets.

'Now, what do you know about horse-racing?'

The set-up at Strawford was quite simple, everybody went about their business and ignored Gobbil while he ignored his own business and poked his snout into everybody else's.

'I'm Ted Carpenter, this is Myrna Wellsley.' A huge hand gripped his in the Slug and Cabbage pub at lunchtime. Miss Wellsley reminded him of a famous actress, he couldn't remember what her name was but she was always either a dentist's receptionist or an alpine barmaid. The entire staff of the CPS seemed to migrate each lunchtime to the same venue.

'I'm Dixton Larkin.' He was slightly embarrassed about being there at all as his job description seemed as bogus as his interest in the law.

'You're George's new assistant eh?' a wiry man with an imitation Rolex nodded accusingly across the salt and pepper at him.

'That's right Andrew,' McInnes came to Dixton's defence. 'Dixton is here to clear up the mess you boys made of the Peterborough Magistrates List.' The man with the Rolex reddened.

'With the greatest of respect George, I don't think you can lay the blame at our feet.'

'Why not? I'm sure the next rotation will throw Newmarket Juvenile my way.'

Dixton was glad of the support and the threat of ridicule by the man with the false watch receded. McInnes took a large bite of his salad sandwich and washed it down with the last of his pint of milk.

'C'mon Dixton, let's get back to the mess,' he said with a straight-laced expression. Andrew looked most put out.

Back in the office McInnes explained the politics of the place.

'Ted Carpenter's about the best of them, he's married with two kids and a wife who plays bridge six nights a week. He and Myrna have been knocking each other off for years although they try to disguise the fact by making moves on other people at the office parties. Andrew is a junior prosecutor who couldn't get the Yorkshire Ripper convicted with a confession. He has notions of getting Gobbil's job someday.'

'And will he?'

'Not a chance, even Gobbil's too smart to allow that to happen. There's bad blood between Andrew and me because I always get posted to his section after he's made a balls of it.'

'Do you like working here?' Dixton stacked the law reports in order on the shelf behind McInnes' chair.

'It's a job. I don't mind it really. Sometimes I think I'd like to go out on my own, run an office, that sort of thing, but there are too many headaches attached to working for yourself. I wouldn't mind a soft job like Robert Feldman.'

166

'Do you know him?' Dixton hadn't given much thought as to the connection that had gotten him the job.

'We went to college together.'

'So that's how?'

'Yep, he asked me did I want an assistant for a couple of weeks.'

'I really appreciate your help, I mean with the job and all, I'm sure I'm not much use to you, am I ?'

'Of course you're useful, who picked the winner in the two thirty five at Kempton on Monday?'

"Well I suppose. . . .'

'Nonsense, you're a huge help.' McInnes looked at his watch. 'Time for another teabreak.'

'OK.'

'We're in court tomorrow so fill in a lunch allowance form – you can get one from Myrna. The other thing is, here's my address.' He handed Dixton a piece of paper. 'No sense in getting the bus while I drive from Cambridge every morning.'

'So they're fine to work with are they?' said Nathalie. They were sitting in the kitchen of 4 Clopton Way having a late supper.

'Yeah, McInnes is great, we just muck about during the day and if there's work to be done he gets through it really quickly and then we do the horses.'

'Do the horses?'

'Yes, betting you know. We pick a couple of horses every day and I place the bets in the village during the lunch-hour.'

'Don't they mind? I mean the people who are in charge, what do they think of this horsey betting?'

Dixton spooned three sugars into a fairly moderate mug of coffee. 'They don't know, or if they, well *he* really, does know, he never says anything.'

'You mean Mr Gobbeel?'

'Gobb*il*.'

'Gobbil, he is the boss yes?'

'Sort of. He's a dickhead really.'

Nathalie scrunched her eyes questioningly. 'Does that word mean what it sounds like it means?'

'Yes,' Dixton laughed, 'it certainly does.'

'And tomorrow you're going to Court?'

'Yeah, Peterborough Magistrates.'

'Will you be back much later than usual?'

'No, I've got a lift from McInnes. He lives near the Abbey Stadium so I don't have to get the bus anymore.'

Dixton was looking forward even more to payday at the end of the week. Dixton glanced at the clock on the wall. 'Look, I'm going to go around to Lupin to see Pepper. He's off to Scotland tomorrow for the Varsity game. Do you want to come with me?'

'No,' she smiled, 'you go, I'll see you tomorrow evening.'

'Are you sure?'

'Yes, go and give him some encouragement and wish him "bon voyage" from me.'

Dixton rinsed his mug and put it upside-down on the draining board.

'I expect a special word of encouragement myself before I fly home next week,' she winked, sexily.

'Count me in,' said Dixton kissing her on the forehead as she sipped her coffee.

Pepper was packing a holdall in his room.

'All set, Pepper?'

'Hope so.' Dixton thought he looked nervous but confident, if that were possible.

'Where are you staying?'

'Some hotel attached to the golf course – it's the Royal something.' His clubs were ranged on the floor and had obviously been polished.

'When does the match start?'

'Saturday. The final singles matches are on Wednesday.'

'How do you feel?'

'Great. A bit edgy though, because I haven't played for a few weeks. That's why I'm going tomorrow. I'll get two days practice before the thing begins.' He picked the clubs up one by one and placed them carefully in the golf bag. The last club was the putter. He twirled it around and then eyed Dixton mischievously.

'One last game?'

'No problem,' Dixton rolled up his sleeves, 'ten pence a point?'

'Ten pence a point.' Pepper put the wastebasket on its side. Dixton lined up the first shot.

It was pouring rain when they were driving from Cambridge but by the time they'd reached Peterborough it had stopped. Dixton wondered whether the clouds decided when to stop spilling rain or if it was just a natural thing like peeing; you were finished when you were finished. The Courthouse was a redbricked building with vast superfluous steps leading up to a set of revolving doors which seemed designed to deter

168

the prosecution of people on crutches. Dixton sat in the front seat. McInnes was on his feet cross-examining a man accused of stealing a compact disc player from a BMW.

'Are you calling me a liar?' the Accused retorted indignantly. McInnes clicked his pen coolly and then cut him to shreds,

'Oh no Mr Collins, I'm not calling you a liar,' he smiled vengefully, 'I'm accusing you of something much more serious than that, I'm suggesting that you are deliberately telling untruths under oath which is perjury and infinitely more serious than the common or garden lying I'm sure you're used to normally.'

The Accused was one of those thugs who go on foreign holidays because the standard of spoken English in the nightclubs suits them better. A short butt of a man in his forties, he wore a denim shirt open to the crotch displaying a chest that looked like it had been knitted by craft workers as a joke. Dixton was enjoying himself thoroughly. The morning was a series of people trotting out pathetic excuses for having committed pathetic crimes. Dixton remembered that there was a time in England when you were innocent until proven Irish, however this was small time stuff on a big scale and all home nationals. Cans of lager stolen from off-licenses; breach of community service orders; one person had even killed a cat with a cricket bat and was being done for breach of the peace. He should have been given a medal. Dixton hated cats.

McInnes treated each case with the seriousness it deserved and Dixton noted that he never put the boot in unless someone got stroppy or rude. McInnes greatest talent was his quick verbal reaction and just before lunch he used it to great effect on a solicitor who was trying to do a deal. They were outside the door of the court thrashing out an agreement before the case was called. He introduced Dixton as his legal assistant grade two case screener. The defending solicitor was an obnoxious git in a green suit.

'Listen McInnes, you can't prove any more than the hoover and you know it.'

'Well that's that then, thanks Denis,' McInnes turned on his heel and smiled at Dixton.

'I can't advise my client to accept that; do you think I'm a complete idiot?' the snot suited man sneered after him. McInnes spun around.

'It's probably too early to make a long term diagnosis.'

'What did you think of your first trip to court ?' They were driving back to Strawford. Strangely it had begun to rain again as they reached the motorway just outside Peterborough. The windscreen wipers were going like mad and the articulated trucks seemed to go by even more quickly than they did in the dry.

'Great, I don't know if I'd be any good though.'

'Nonsense, it's as easy as getting sick once you get the hang of it,' McInnes swerved to avoid an overtaking juggernaut.

On Saturday morning Dixton strolled into town. His first paycheque cleared his debt at Lupin Hall and with the little bit left over he'd decided to buy Nathalie a present. She'd effectively fed him for the last couple of weeks so as to keep his college bill as low as possible. He was sorry she was going back to France for the rest of the Easter break but he'd have to manage. Love was such an odd emotion, it kind of sneaked up on you like the Revenue and then took over your whole life. He'd never been happier, he had a job, a girlfriend and some cash left over. The exams were the only hurdle between him and the end of the year. A group of Japanese tourists were photographing King's College to death. Dixton spotted the porter who owned the alsatian and he hurried past towards the market square.

'Oh Dixton, its absolutely wonderful,' Nathalie threw her arms around him and kissed him passionately.

'Is it really for me?'

'Well what use do you think I'd have for a four foot high stuffed teddy bear?' Dixton laughed.

The bear was sitting on a chair with its head resting tilted back on the upper door of the fridge. Nathalie was deliriously happy.

'It's wonderful Dixton, really wonderful.'

'I'm glad you like it, I think he's kind of cute.'

'Like you Dixton,' she smiled.

Dixton blushed.

'Er, what time is your flight this evening?'

'Don't worry about my flight,' she took him by the hand and led him towards the stairs in the hall, 'let's see if we can practice our take-off together.' Dixton looked over his shoulder at the bear – it had toppled on to the floor.

"Cambridge under pressure" read the headline on the sports page on Sunday. It seemed that the number one and two pairings had been expected to do well but had failed to hold their own. Pepper's match had been halved and gave them a half point but they were well behind after the first days play. "It reminds this writer of the 1978 Varsity Match at Royal Troon." That kind of writing reminded Dixton of how crap sports journalists can be sometimes. Dixton knew someone from his old school who had gone on to be a sports journalist, he was sufficiently shallow to go very far in his chosen trade. That idiot seemed to collect clichés and then spit them out at random regardless of the sport. "Hapless keepers", "weary supporters" making "long treks", "feasting their eyes" on "spectacles" which "would grace any final" made Dixton want to puke with excitement. These jokers were simply note takers of other peoples achievements; brushes in the great toilet of life. Dixton prayed that Cambridge would get their act together. Back in E Block the piles of photocopied material on the Law of Salvage were beginning to look more daunting.

Lupin was very quiet. Most people seemed to have gone home for the break. Bernard and Zinowsky were nowhere to be seen. Rumour had it that they'd gone to Lanzarote for a holiday. Rich bastards, good riddance to them, Dixton thought. In an uncharacteristic display of organisation he spent Sunday night getting the lecture notes into some sort of order. He felt as though he'd achieved quite a lot by simply putting them into separate piles and rewarded himself with a pint in the college bar with Herve.

'How is your studying going, Dixton?'

'Not too badly, I feel as if I'm beginning to be ready to be about to start.'

Herve eyed him suspiciously.

'And how's the Ball coming along?'

'Oh, the Ball?' Herve threw up his hands in despair, 'there's so much organising to do it's incredible. The tickets go on sale the week term begins again.'

'Count me in for two.'

'OK.'

'Oh, by the way, what's the theme this year?'

' It's Horror Films' said Herve proudly.

'Fantastic.' (He had no idea whether it was fantastic or not.)

McInnes and Dixton arrived late each morning and left early. Gobbil strutted around from office to office, checking up on everyone else and doing nothing himself. He was like an unemployed walrus with his sideburns and his vile tweed jacket. He wandered into McInnes' office on the Monday of Dixton's second week. Dixton was gazing out the window at the churning mill-wheel. A ray of cold sunshine was about to be devoured by the giant cogs.

'How are things in the engine-room of the CPS?', Gobbil guffawed.

McInnes looked up from his desk.

'Do you want something, James?'

171

'Just checking that all is well in every corner of the nest.'

'I thought nests were round,' Dixton quipped in. Gobbil was put off balance slightly, McInnes held in a laugh and rummaged in a drawer in his desk. Gobbil composed himself.

'Ah Dixton, just the man I came to see. We've got a new grade three executive librarian's assistant starting next week and I want you to help him organise the new library.'

Dixton wasn't impressed, he wanted to continue working with the CPS by continuing not to work under McInnes' supervision.

'I have great plans for the new library, men.' Gobbil addressed both of them without looking at either of them. He spread his hands out in front of him like a 'B' movie producer promising the world.

'All England Law Reports, Criminal Reports, Textbooks, Periodicals . . . yes I have great plans for the new library.'

'You'd think he was co-ordinating the Normandy Landings,' Dixton swiped after their leader had left.

'Oh, take no notice of him, he'll forget about the whole thing as soon as some new stupid idea overtakes him.'

'I don't know anything about libraries,' Dixton said. How true that was.

'Well, it'll be something different for your last week if it does come off,' McInnes smiled.

Dixton had the distinct feeling that "work" was about to rear its ugly head. He went down to the corner shop to get a paper and find out about Pepper.

'Well, how are they doing?' McInnes unplugged the steaming kettle.

Dixton flipped the pages back and forth, the sports section was sandwiched between the appointments page and package tours.

'It's looking a bit better. They're only two points behind now, Pepper won his matchplay and they're doing better overall.'

'What's this chap Pepper like?'

'He's great.'

He'd never had to think about how he felt about Pepper until now. Friendships were always difficult things to explain to third parties without seeming twee or feeling disloyal.

'What about putting a bet on them to win?' McInnes suggested.

Dixton mulled over the idea for a second.

'Why not, it's not beyond the realms of possibility at this stage.'

'I'm sure we'd get good odds.'

'I'll put a couple of quid on after lunch.'

'Oh listen, if you get a moment on your way back, will you pop into the filing room and get me these.' He handed Dixton a list. Previous convictions didn't always appear on the computer so the only sure way to check was with the file.

The filing room; home to the sordid biographies of thousands of people who wouldn't pay parking fines. Dixton was always amazed at the size of this room. Aisle after aisle of shelves stocked with brown manila folders in elastic bands. It was the ideal place to hide away for an afternoon, he'd keep that in mind for the following week if things got too rough in the library. The first few files he'd found easily enough but there was a chap called McGregor who might be under "Mac" or "Mc" or "Mcg" or even under "G". He pulled out a couple of "Macs" and flicked through them and as he did he thought he heard the door open. He looked around the corner but saw nothing and continued his search. He found the file at last and walked around to pick up the pile he'd collected first. A noise caught his attention. He wasn't sure but it sounded like a voice. Perhaps he was mistaken. He put the files under his arm and made for the door. There it was again, definitely someone's voice. This time it was louder and appeared to be emanating from the other end of the room. He thought it sounded like a groan but wasn't sure. He wondered if perhaps it was Gobbil. He edged around between shelves sixteen and seventeen. There it was again, however this time it spoke.

'Oh yes. October 10th last year, armed robbery in Stevenage.'

Dixton was flummoxed, what the hell was going on? The voice was so close now he knew it must be coming from the next aisle. He peered between two files called "Eviston" through to the other side. Jesus Christ! Ted Carpenter was sitting on a chair with his back to Dixton. He had a file open and was reading aloud from the list of previous convictions.

'December, aggravated burglary, oh ho yes here's a good one, January this year, unlawful entry, yes, yes, yes.'

Dixton knew that people sometimes found the law interesting but this was crazy. This poor demented nutcase sitting on a chair reading previous convictions aloud to himself – what was he like? Suddenly everything became clear. Miss Wellsley's head came into view to the side of the chair. Oh-my-God! Dixton felt the urge to explode laughing. So thats the attraction of the previous convictions. Miss Wellsley looked up in Dixton's direction but the files were too close together to allow him be seen. It was as if she'd sensed his presence.

'February 3rd, Assault with a deadly weapon,' Ted Carpenter was in ecstasy. 'Oh yes, yes, yes, more, more.' Miss Wellsley's head disappeared and the groans intensified. Dixton picked up the files and made his escape. He quietly opened the door into the corridor. A portly figure was advancing towards the filing room. It was Gobbil (aptly enough thought Dixton).

'Everything all right Dixton? I see you've been busying yourself in amongst the files.'

'Eh, yes, I have. Interesting place the filing room.' Dixton blocked his way to the door.

Well there's a couple of things in there I've got to pick up.' Gobbil tried to sidestep him. Dixton matched his steps like one of those sidewalk encounters.

'I wonder if I could ask you something?' he stalled.

'Yes of course Dixton, What is it?'

'Well,' Dixton's mind raced, 'this new library. I'd quite like to see the room but I'm not sure where it is.'

'Oh its just beside Andrew's office, third on the left next floor.'

'Oh it's on this floor is it?' Dixton mustered his most stupid look.

'No,' Gobbil laughed, 'next floor third on the left.'

'Fourth on the left this floor?'

'Come on,' Gobbil abandoned the filing room trip, 'I'll show you.'

'I don't want to put you to any trouble,' Dixton lied.

'No trouble at all.' He jangled his keys and looked important. That's all this plonker needed; a diversion couched in terms of helplessness. Dixton chuckled to himself remembering members of staff on active duty elsewhere in the building. It was true what they said about oral sex, it was dark and lonely work.

Since the Port and Stilton Society's inaugural meeting nothing of note had invaded Dixton's Calendar. He wasn't sure what lay in store in the final term however, by all accounts, once the exams were over the fun would begin. He missed Nathalie like crazy and counted the days to her return. Once you found an interest outside of yourself there was no real going back. Dixton was really in love for the first time ever, everything else had been only an undress rehearsal. The Crown Prosecution Service was going to help him survive financially for the rest of the academic year but, apart from that valuable aspect of things, Dixton was also beginning to get slightly interested in the law. It was more the prospect of Court appearances which attracted him. Perhaps he *would* be a lawyer someday. He'd have to avoid the future head-on at some stage. A postcard arrived from Lourdes. Aunt Sheila seemed to be enjoying herself. He pictured her standing in the middle of thousands of invalids, organising them all. If Aunt Sheila had been there when the loaves and fishes were being handed out, she'd have demanded steak. He always feared for the safety of crowds when Aunt Sheila was about.

"Whenever I came across Jonathan Pepper he was holing outrageous chips from bunkers – this is a player to watch for the future."

Dixton changed newspapers for Thursday to get the result of the Varsity Match. Cambridge won by half a point and Pepper was 'Player of the Tournament'. Dixton was vicariously proud. McInnes entered with a pile of files.

'How did they get on?'

Dixton showed him the paper, 'We won our bet.'

'Splendid? Your mate Pepper seems to be quite a player.'

'On and off the golf course,' Dixton muttered.

'I heard that,' smirked McInnes, 'I can't help thinking about the filing room business. I met Ted in the front office and I could barely keep a straight face.'

'You didn't say anything though did you?' Dixton was alarmed.

'Don't worry, I'll store the information for use at a future date after you've left.'

'Jesus, don't say I told you.'

'Of course I won't. Anyway Gobbil was looking for you, he asked me to get you to drop into him after lunch.'

Gobbil's office was like an advertisement for self-congratulation. There were framed certificates everywhere. "Diploma in Inter-personal Skills" caught Dixton's eye. The desktop was almost clear except for a paperweight with a blue paperclip embedded in the centre. How marvellous, Dixton thought. Gobbil's grey beard was carefully manicured which would give a stranger the first impression that he was an organised meticulous man. In actual fact he was a prize plonker. Gobbil was like an out of season Santa Claus; uncommon but stupid. He rose as Dixton entered and smiled inanely.

'Ah Dixton, the very man I wanted to see. Our grade three executive librarian's assistant will be here on Monday, and I wanted to brief you on my plans for the new library.' He produced a sheet of paper from a drawer. It was a map. He laid it on the table and pointed with a pencil.

'Now, my suggestions are these . . . the Criminal Law periodicals are published monthly, the Annual Law Review is published. . .'

'Annually?' Dixton helped.

'Yes annually,' Gobbil beamed. Dixton switched off.

'Wankfest,' said McInnes.

'What?'

'Wankfest – that's what it is, all these maps and instructions, going over rubbish instructions twice. Gobbil's life is built around all these stupid pointless exercises. The only description for them is "Wankfest".'

Dixton agreed. It was a new word which could only have been coined to describe Gobbil and his entire life.

Pepper returned to Lupin about three days after the Varsity Match had finished.

'I thought you'd be back sooner,' Dixton met him in the foyer as Pepper was retrieving his key from the Porter's Lodge.

'I got delayed,' Pepper winked, 'celebrations.'

'Don't tell me you found some Scottish lassie to celebrate with?'

'Yup, Heather Campbell, the sexiest girl in the highlands.'

'I thought you went to Scotland for the golf?' Dixton shouldered him as they both tried to get through the main door at the same time.

'We won, didn't we?'

'Then off to the nineteenth tee I suppose?'

'The nineteenth bed more like,' Pepper grinned.

'You're sick.'

'She's coming down for the Lupin Hall Ball.'

'Who, Heather?'

'Yeah.'

'What about Clara?'

'What about her?'

'I give up Pepper, you're such a letch.'

'How's your French coming on?' Pepper licked his lips and laughed.

'Fuck off.' It was great to have Pepper back.

Dixton's final week in the CPS was spent in the library organising things with Hector Fleming the new grade three executive librarian's assistant. Hector was a thin soupy looking earnest sort with a lifetime subscription to dandruff. He wore a waistcoat with a single breasted black suit every day and this gave his scalp ample opportunity to display itself on his shoulders. He was devoted to books and each volume of the 'All England Reports' was treated like an old school friend. It was quite sweet really.

'I think I'd like to put the 'Criminal Law Journals' on the middle shelf, here where the sun will catch their glossy red covers.' (That sort of thing.)

Dixton constantly felt like laughing at Hector's precious attitude but he admired nonetheless the complete pleasure he seemed to derive from his work. What should have taken a day and a half to do was going to certainly require more than a week as every shelf was measured and every volume cross-referenced and entered first in a ledger and then in a computer. Dixton did the computer work as it seemed a shame to expect Hector to sully his hands with electronics. He didn't speak much but when he did it was either something quite incisive or absolutely insane. Gobbil popped in to see them each afternoon to see how his masterplan for the library was unfolding. On one occasion he picked up a crumpled copy of his own map and tried to match up the shelves and the books with it. It soon became apparent that all was not as he had hoped. Gobbil wandered around double checking with the map looking pained and questioning at the same time as if trying to make a point. Finally when he was unable to prompt a justification or explanation from either of them he cleared his throat and spoke patronisingly.

'The map, or rather *my* map and the layout do not seem to tally. I wonder why that is?' His tone invited a retreat rather than an attack. Hector Fleming was up to the task. He looked up momentarily from the ledger.

'Oh that's because we've discarded your plans altogether.'

Gobbil stared into space with a startled expression. There was no follow on conversation or come-back remark, he just left. Dixton was impressed. Another phrase from Hector caught Dixton's attention during the week when they were stacking periodicals. It began to rain heavily and the raindrops smacked off the double glazing like water ball-bearings. Dixton stood with his elbows on the sill, his head resting on his hands gazing out on to the carpark. He could see that one of the "reserved" spaces was empty. Hector stood beside him.

'It reminds me of when I was a child, sitting in the washing machine with my cat.'

Dixton looked around sharply expecting to see a grin or a smirk crossing Hector's face. Not a bit of it. It was said in all sincerity. What a little star.

'So you're leaving tomorrow?' George McInnes spoke to him at lunch in the Slug and Cabbage on the Thursday.

'Yeah, afraid so. It's down to the books for the next month or so for these bloody exams.'

'Never mind, I'm sure you'll do well. Do you want more coffee?' McInnes headed for the bar counter.

'Please.'

Dixton looked around him at the other CPS employees. Ted Carpenter and Myrna Wellsley were deep in conversation, possibly planning their next foray into the filing room. Dixton chuckled to himself. Gobbil was ranting away about some new computer system.

'It's got three hundred megabyte techno overdrive,' or something like that. No-one was listening. Hector was nibbling at a sandwich and reading *Brighton Rock*. He turned the pages and held the book with the same hand; ingenious. Dixton pictured him inside a washing machine. Andrew with the false Rolex was away for the day, presumably making a horlicks of the Newmarket Juvenile List. McInnes returned and rattled a cup and saucer.

'There you are,' he put them down in front of him.

'How are things in the library?'

'Well, Mr Wankfest hasn't been to see us for days, so I suppose that's a good sign.'

'Excellent, listen I wonder if you could get a couple of files for me this afternoon if you're not too busy.'

'No problem. I'm sure Hector won't mind if I skive off for awhile.'

Winter, Winthrop, Winolta, too far. Dixton went back along the shelf looking for the file "Gregory Winchester" – ah there it was. Another file caught his eye as he pulled Winchester down from the shelf. Oh, what's this . . .? Fate drew level with him and winked.

The paycheque on Friday would see him through the last term. He was delighted that he'd had this job. Really he'd had to do very little but it was time well not-spent as it were. The sun shone rather unexpectedly for the whole day. McInnes bought him lunch and Gobbil made a speech.

'We are losing a valuable member of our team today. Dixton Larkin is returning to Cambridge to sit his Masters Degree exams, the library is up and running and will be a testament to Dixton's work here when he leaves. The Crown Prosecution Service is at the coalface of the System of Justice in this country . . .' He droned on. Dixton caught McInnes' eye behind Gobbil's back, he was mouthing something derogatory, it began with the letter W. He'd be sad enough to leave this behind him but more out of distaste for the month ahead than out of a desire to work here forever. McInnes gave him a copy of the latest edition of Simpson and Hartleys' *Criminal Law* as a going away present.

'You never know, you might be a lawyer someday,' he'd said. Gobbil was still at it.

'In short we are the watchdogs of our society . . .'

CHAPTER FIFTEEN

Post-Easter Cambridge is a different kettle of fish. The faculty library entrances are cluttered with bicycles for the first time all year and hoards troop through their doors at the end of the day having achieved varying degrees of successful preparation. The river seems to flow more quietly in deference to the situation and the licensed premises compensate with whist drives for busloads from out of town. Tourists begin to descend in serious numbers, completely oblivious of the crisis unfolding behind the sandstone facades and plaques to benefactors. The May sunshine arrives in earnest bringing its unwelcome companion - the exam term.

'This is the last meeting of the Port and Stilton Society before the exams,' said Dixton addressing the troops, 'Professor Lynn can't be with us this evening as he has the 'flu' again and Stan is on duty so there's just the six of us tonight. It was decent of Jack to let us use his room.'

He looked around the faces. It was like pre-jump pep-talk in a parachute club; everyone had a job to do and was scared to bits about doing it. He wondered if he'd make a good secret agent. Only two bottles of port had been drunk this evening although all the cheese had, as usual, disappeared.

'When do we reconvene after the exams?' Andy asked.

'I finish May 20th,' said Nathalie.

'I'm the same day,' Jack spoke.

'How about you, Pepper?'

'Oh I've no exams but the essay deadline is May 23rd.'

'Is that a Friday?' asked Andy.

'Yeah.'

'OK Friday the 23rd it is,' said Dixton. 'Whose room?'

'We can meet at our house,' offered Nathalie. Dixton glanced over at her, what a cutie.

'That's that then.' He raised his glass. 'To University College Hall.'

'To University College Hall,' they chorused.

'Prosper and triumph.'

'Prosper and triumph.'

Jack looked at his watch.

'I'm afraid I've got to turf you lot out. I've an early start in the morning.'

There were no protests and it was clear that exam fever was about to grip this remote outpost of the educational system.

The weeks of lectures after the Easter holidays flew. Professor Simpson wound up his course with a fabulous lecture on "Assault with intent to Ravish" and everyone gave him a round of applause at the end of the hour. Sarah smiled at Dixton across the room and he felt that this subject at least hadn't ended too badly for him. It was only a few short months ago that he had been terrified at the prospect of seeing her in the aftermath of 'the Elephant' thing. Now at least they could be civil to each other. Professor Simpson rapped his knuckles on the desk. The beginnings of chatter and the clicking closed of ring-back binders stopped abruptly. The old Professor struggled to his feet, (Dixton noticed for the first time that he'd become very thin) there was hushed silence.

'The year is over ladies and gentlemen. This course, for what it has been worth, is finished. My time as your teacher and yours as my students, is at an end.'

Some members of the class began to shuffle uneasily. It was as though the old guy was working himself up to tell them he was about to die. It was even more dramatic than that.

'You know my view on exams, they test memory not intelligence and therefore they are to a large extent irrelevant, particularly at post-graduate level. I have been very fortunate to be able to lecture you in the twilight of my career and I have enjoyed every moment of this year even more than most of you can possibly imagine. There are exams to do, scripts to be corrected, results to be given out, parents to disappoint, bank managers to placate and so forth. My exam will consist of six questions, four of which must be attempted.' He stopped for a moment, adjusted his spectacles, and then continued.

'You might for example be asked at question one "What are the maximum sentences applicable to the following offences?" . . . Write a short note on any case in which each was applied . . .' He stopped again and looked down on the class smilingly.

'I suggest you take a note of these.'

Mayhem ensued as bags were opened and folders clicked, pens were lent and paper shared.

Afterwards Dixton asked Professor Simpson to sign his new copy of Simpson and Hartley. He opened the cover on the way down the steps to the courtyard to see what he'd written, "To Dixton Larkin, Lawyer and Scholar". Dixton felt a complete fraud on both counts.

'Fancy a break?' Pepper pushed open the door of Dixton's room in E block.

'Yeah I'm sick of this essay, I've got so much material I don't know where to begin.'

'Leave it for a while, let's go for a walk. How's Nathalie?'

'Up to her ears in frontal elevations.'

'That sounds interesting,' Pepper smirked.

'It means drawings of the front of buildings, you sick puppy.'

'Oh well never mind, c'mon, I've got something to show you.'

They walked through the arch round to the back of the accommodation blocks towards the laundry room. Pepper led the way.

'This is where we hid from Zinowsky isn't it?'

'Yeah, come into this passageway, I've got something to show you.' It sounded vaguely criminal. They edged their way between the buildings.

'Ta-dah,' Pepper announced. A ladder lay up against the wall.

'A ladder?' exclaimed Dixton.

'Oh you clever boy, yes a ladder. What do you think it is? A train track doing community service?'

'OK, smart arse, what's it for?'

'For climbing over the wall to the swimming pool. We'll be able to go swimming whenever we want and no-one else need ever find out about the pool.'

'I hate to sound obvious but what's to stop other people using it?'

'Sod all people come down here anyway, but if anyone does. . .' Pepper produced a length of wire cable from his jacket pocket and strung it across the entrance to the passageway from where they were standing. Two nails had been conveniently driven into the walls on either side and Pepper wrapped the wire around them.

'A piece of wire strung across the entrance at waist height? Yeah that'll really fool the general public,' Dixton sneered.

'Take it easy I'm not finished,' Pepper reached down to the base of the ladder; a small metal sign lay face down on the ground.

'Here we are,' he announced triumphantly showing the sign to Dixton before hooking it to the wire. "50,000 VOLTS: DO NOT TOUCH". It had obviously been stolen from some transformer in the vicinity. Dixton had to concede that it was a good ploy. They climbed the ladder and both sat atop the wall then hauled the ladder up and lowered it on the other side, wedging it into the chicken wire and nettles. When they were both safely trespassing on Corpus Cristi grounds, they smiled in self-congratulation. It was like being a child again, with the added experience of knowing that the difference between right and wrong really is whether you're caught.

'Here, have a drink,' Pepper proffered a hip flask of brandy when they were safely ensconced on a wooden bench out of sight of the buildings at the top of the property.

'Thanks,' Dixton spluttered as the alcohol went down the wrong way. Pepper thumped him on the back making matters even worse. When he'd got his breath back Pepper handed him a small envelope.

'What's this?'

'Read it, I got it in my pigeon hole this morning.'

Dixton unfolded the small piece of notepaper. It was an anonymous note typed on a computer. He read it aloud.

"Don't think we've forgotten you. When the exams are over you'll be sorry you ever came to Lupin Hall."

'Who's it from?'

'Two guesses.' Pepper took the piece of paper back and folded it.

'Rainford and Zinowsky?'

'Who else? The anti-foxhunting lobby?'

'But anonymous notes, that's a bit low,' Dixton commented.

'It's just their style, particularly Bernard, he never has the guts to do anything in the open.'

'But what do you think it means?' asked Dixton. Pepper screwed up his face into a quizzical expression and put on a dumb voice.

'I don't know, Dixton but from a cursory glance I'd say that it means two things; firstly, they haven't forgotten us and secondly it would appear that after the exams we'll be sorry we ever came to Lupin Hall.'

Dixton shoved him off the end of the bench.

'I bloody well know what it says, what I mean is what do you think it really means? You know what I mean,' he said indignantly.

Pepper scrambled back on to the bench giggling annoyingly.

'OK, OK.' He shielded himself as Dixton threatened to shove him off the bench again.

'I think I know what you're saying, Dixton.' Pepper put on a mock serious face.

'Well?'

'Who cares what these plonkers mean? We'll be ready for them as soon as the exams and everything are over, in fact I'd quite like a go at them now. Don't worry about them.'

'Well I suppose *I* mightn't have anything to worry about anyway.' Dixton said inviting the query.

'Why? What do you mean?' Pepper looked at him.

'Well, the envelope is addressed to you and there's no evidence to suggest that the "you" in the note means "you" plural, it might just mean "you" singular.'

'What do you mean "you" singular?' Pepper was in the early stages of getting worried.

'I mean "you" Jonathan Pepper, Setter of Buckets, remover of u-bends – singular.' Dixton was enjoying this.

'Wait a minute, we're in this together remember?'

'I remember nothing,' Dixton smiled, 'show me that letter again.'

Pepper handed it over, Dixton opened it.

'From a cursory glance I'd say this letter means two things. Firstly, "you" singular have not been forgotten by them, you see there "we",' he pointed at the typescript, '"we" plural I suppose it means, what do you think? And, secondly, it would seem that after the exams "you" singular will be sorry that "you" – again singular – ever came to Lupin Hall.'

He folded the letter, put it back in the envelope and handed it back to Pepper.

'You're not serious?' Pepper looked at him. Dixton tried to keep a straight face but couldn't. Pepper gave a half scowl/half sigh and shouldered Dixton then got up himself and made for the ladder. He shouted back over his shoulder,

'Well "you" fucking singular better hurry or "I" singular will get over the wall and take the ladder with me.'

Dixton started after him. He was slightly worried about the note but reckoned that Pepper and he had every chance of being invincible again once they recovered from the exams. Whatever the writers of the note did mean, they were definitely going to have to deal with "you" plural.

The Law of Salvage was a nightmare. Although he'd photocopied buckets of information, Dixton had never undertaken an essay of this length before and he had no idea what standard was required. The recommended length of this essay was "five to ten thousand words" whatever that meant. He sat staring at the essay title for a whole morning without writing a word. The problem with this essay was that because his title was so original he wouldn't be able to simply plagiarise from existing texts. He felt at a total loss. Leaving the title page sitting forlornly on the desk he went to meet Nathalie for lunch in Newnham.

'Nothing? You've written nothing?'

'Well not exactly completely nothing,' he defended himself.

'How much have you written?'

'The title.'

'The title? That's all? Listen Dixton, you promised me that you would start the essay today.'

'I will, I will, it's just that I don't want to peak too early.'

Nathalie smiled, 'Oh, I don't think that's ever been a problem for you in any other areas of your life.'

'I beg your pardon? I don't know what you're talking about,' Dixton feigned shock. He speared the main course with his knife and twirled it around.

'God, I hate fish.'

'It's not fish, it's chicken,' Nathalie decoded the food.

'Well it must have drowned then 'cos it tastes like fish.'

'Stop fidgeting Dixton and go and write that essay.'

He loved it when she was authoratative. He kissed her on the cheek, stuffed a couple of cheese quarters in his pocket and got up.

'OK. I'm off to do my essay,' he said definitely.

'I'll believe it when I see it,' Nathalie laughed. He really was in love with her. Halfway up Sidgwick Avenue he reached into his pocket for the cheese. Bollox, it had melted into the lining.

Two days later the essay was finished. "The Law of Salvage with Particular Reference to the Spanish Armada" would never be viewed again in such a vague way. It took Dixton the guts of twelve hours solid to sort it out, but he'd done it. The essay began with a concrete set of aims which were all achieved in full in the course of the essay. This was because the introduction had been written last. Dixton felt that if he set up the readers' expectations in the beginning and fulfilled them totally by the end then the essay was, at face value at least, partly successful. Feldman had been right in his advice all those months ago; read like crazy, then write like crazy, then submit before you give yourself a chance to worry. It was the only way. He felt sure that the essay was so obscure that it could not be validly queried as being *too* obscure. Who would dare criticise it's vagueness without exposing themselves to ridicule as either being totally ignorant of this specialized area, or, worse still, an expert in an area so obscure as to be laughable? Perfect. He submitted it on the Wednesday of the week before the exams were scheduled to begin. He was utterly chuffed with himself. He wasn't the only one.

'I'm so proud of you, Dixton,' Nathalie smiled. They were in the living room of 4 Clopton Way.

'Well,' he shrugged his shoulders, 'you never get the results unless you do the work. As the old Irish proverb goes: "a good start is half the work".' He put on his especially most proud look.

Nathalie looked at her watch.

'Perhaps we'd better go to bed early then if we want to get half the work done?'

Dixton needed no second bidding, after all he deserved a treat after his efforts.

'I'll make the cocoa.'

Pepper had two weeks in which to submit his essay and still had plenty of time to go golfing. He returned to Lupin with his clubs slung over his shoulder at lunchtime on the warmest Saturday so far that year. Dixton's window was open so he shouted to Pepper as he passed.

'Oh hello Dixton,' Pepper poked his head in over the desk.

'Studying hard I hope?'

'Don't you do any work at all?' Dixton threw an eraser at him.

'I've got boxes of samples in my room so I'll just about get the essay done in time but I've got enough notes to see me through. How are you getting on?'

'Well the first exam is on Monday, it's European Union Law.'

'Oh I know all about that,' Pepper grinned, 'I went out with a wee Italian lawyer in Crete one year.'

'Very funny.' Dixton was impressed and also not impressed at all.

'OK fine, no more talk of my vast range of sexual experiences, how are you fixed for the exam?'

'Not too bad, Sanjra's notes are excellent.'

'That reminds me,' said Pepper, 'I saw him going into the library just now with Rainford, I didn't know they were friendly.'

'They're not. I bet I know what that's all about. Remember I told you about the essay business?'

'Oh right, I do remember something about that but wasn't that supposed to be handed in ages ago?'

'He was typing a few of them. I wonder how he's getting on.' He put down his biro and went out to join Pepper.

'I think I'll go across to the Library.'

'I'll come with you,' said Pepper, 'you never know, there might be a row.'

Sanjra was sitting at one of the computer terminals typing furiously with two fingers.

'How are things Sanjra?' Dixton asked cheerfully.

Sanjra didn't even look up but continued to type. Dixton squatted down.

'Hey, what's the matter? Are you all right?' He waved his hand between Sanjra's face and the screen. Sanjra stopped typing and looked pathetically up at Dixton.

'It's no good, I'll never finish it on time.' He was crying.

'Is this one of Rainford's essays?' asked Pepper.

'Yes,' sobbed Sanjra. 'This is the last one. It's supposed to be in by four o'clock but I'll never finish it in time. Bernard has just been here telling me to re-write some parts of it.'

The original typescript was on the desk beside Sanjra. Someone had slashed a red pen across two paragraphs on the top page. Dixton thumbed through the pile, most pages were similarly afflicted.

'I thought you'd typed this ages ago?' said Dixton.

'I did, but he only had time to read through it this weekend because he was away on holidays and now he says I've got to type in the corrections before the deadline today.'

'Well that's not too bad,' said Dixton encouragingly, 'just get the original up on the screen and you'll fly through the corrections, I'll read it out to you if that's any help?'

'That's just the problem,' Sanjra was distraught, 'someone has erased the original – from the hard disk – and I don't have a copy. I thought I'd be doing all this weeks ago.'

'Never mind that bastard,' said Pepper, 'let him fail, so what if it's not in on time, it's *his* essay so it's *his* problem.'

Sanjra was horrified.

'No, no you don't understand. I gave my word. So much is at stake. I must finish it, I must finish it.' He set about his two-fingered typing again. Pepper and Dixton looked at each other. They had to do something to help. Sanjra was supposed to be studying for his own exams, not typing an essay in Land Economy for some rich slugpuss.

'Come on Pepper,' Dixton motioned to him to leave, 'Sanjra don't worry, we'll sort this out somehow.'

Sanjra looked up at Dixton.

'You have your own worries, your own exams, this is my worry.'

'We'll be back soon,' said Dixton pulling the door of the library shut behind him.

'This is Rose, Rose this is Sanjra, up you get and let a real expert at that computer.'

Dixton had managed to secure the help of Rose from the tutorial office, she'd been tidying her desk and preparing to go home. Saturday was her half day. Sanjra looked dazed.

'But this is not, I cannot, I mean, you see. . .'

'No buts Sanjra, up you get, I know what this is all about and Dixton has promised me two free tickets to the Ball, now where's this essay?'

Rose rolled up her sleeves and set to it. She was like an express train. Sanjra gazed in wonderment at her racing hands and then examined his two wounded index fingers. Rose flicked through the pile of pages slashed in red.

'Come back in an hour and I'll have it for you then.'

The three boys went their separate ways to get some study done. The sun was shining unfairly in the East Court as if mocking their tasks. When they returned the essay was neatly stacked with each page numbered.

'There you are Sanjra,' Rose smiled, 'I told you it wouldn't take me too long. You'd better get a move on if it's to be in by four o'clock.'

It was a quarter to.

'Don't worry Sanjra, Pepper chipped in, 'just write the address of the Land Economy Department on it and I'll drop it in. I've got the geology car.'

Dixton looked at Pepper.

'This *has* to be in on time, I know you don't like Bernard but the essay has to be delivered intact, there's too much at stake.'

'Would I do anything to Bernard's essay?' Pepper pretended to be shocked at the suggestion.

'I don't want to get into trouble,' said Sanjra as he finished writing the address on the envelope.

'No-one's going to get into trouble,' Dixton soothed.

'*You* always seem to,' Rose quipped as she left the computer room in the library, 'don't forget the tickets.'

'I won't,' he shouted after her. Pepper the courier headed for his trusty Ford Transit van.

That evening Pepper and Dixton had a pint in the college bar.

'Did you deliver it Pepper?'

'Bang on four o'clock.'

'Thanks ever so much, we'd never have got it there on time otherwise.'

'No problem,' Pepper slurped the head off his pint.

'I can't get over that bastard Bernard. You know he's still bragging that his dad's going to buy him a Ferrari if he gets an honours degree.'

'Speaking of Italians, that woman I went out with in Crete, well she . . .'

'Shut up Pepper.'

Since the confrontation in his office with Dixton and Pepper, the Praelector had been curiously conspicuous by his absence around the college. It suited Dixton's purpose not to have to look over his shoulder in the run up to the exams but at the same time he was wary of the Praelector's dislike of him and felt it would not be long before their paths crossed again. On Monday morning, the day of the EU exam, Dr Winston re-surfaced at breakfast in the dining hall.

'Sorry for interrupting your breakfasts,' he tapped on a cereal bowl with his spoon while he stood near the cashier's desk.

'I say, sorry to interrupt you all,' he repeated, 'I know most of you are rushing off to exams this morning but I just want to take this opportunity to wish you the best of British.'

Dixton stifled a laugh. Most of the students were anything but British. Winston continued.

'We, the staff that is, are all rooting for you in your exams, I know all of you. . .' he stopped momentarily and then glared down at Dixton, '. . . or at least *most* of you, will not let the college down.'

Dixton stared back at the Praelector and gave as good as he got in terms of intensity and unblinkingness. The inference was clear, the Praelector evidently felt assured that Dixton would fail the exams. Well he'd show him a thing or two. On the way down the stairs to the foyer he was suddenly gripped by massive self-doubt. Perhaps he'd fail his thesis and his exams, maybe the Praelector was right. There was no time for that sort of rubbish now; EU law awaited in the Senate House. He spotted an envelope in his pigeon hole, it was a good luck card from McInnes. Jesus this was it, the exams were finally here. He collected his pens and last minute cram notes from his room and then headed into town on Pepper's bike in a rare light shower of apprentice rain.

The exam hall was packed with lots of people he didn't recognise. This was hardly surprising given his attendance rate at the lectures. He consoled himself by thinking that perhaps quite a few of the candidates might also have been absentees, like himself, so in a way, even if he had attended the lectures there would still be some faces he wouldn't know. It was a fairly thin point but straws and clutching were the order of the morning. He spotted Sanjra eight or ten rows ahead of him – that cheered him up a bit. That was the thing about exams; you finally got to see the identity of your competitors and cringe as they asked for more paper before you'd even read the questions.

The questions, happily enough, bore some resemblance to the areas he'd crammed over the previous four or five days. That was always a bonus. He remembered all those apocrophyl stories you hear in college about exams, people going in and writing one word as an answer and getting first class honours. That was complete bollox. In his old university at any rate if you tried that lark they'd give you the benefit of the doubt and presume you were stupid. You might even be covertly encouraged to switch to Psychology (or indeed, actively head-hunted by the Engineering faculty). Whatever else happened you wouldn't pass and he doubted if it were much different at Cambridge. He decided to have a whack while events were pretty fresh in his mind.

'How did you get on?' Professor Lynn called to him as he passed the library door on his way into lunch.

'Not too badly I think, if they accept my theories on cheese import restrictions I might pass.'

'Don't worry Young Larkin, I'm sure you did fine.'

Dixton was slightly blasé about it but he secretly felt that he'd done OK. At the same time he knew that the subject which was most likely to drag him down was about to surface for the first time since he'd chickened out of it all those months ago; Remedies and Restitution was on Friday. He remembered for some reason the conversation he'd had in January with Laura the bedder. He'd managed to see out the year but that would be completely meaningless if he failed the exams.

'How are things going?'

'Not too badly Aunt Sheila.'

'I hope you're working hard and of course at the same time. . .'

'Playing hard?' he suggested down the telephone line.

'That's right, praying hard, all the brains in the world won't get you anywhere if God isn't on your side.'

'I know, I know,' he tapped the phone box with his free hand and watched the credits click down.

'I don't know if I told you,' his aunt continued, 'but Saint Benildus is the. . .'

'Patron Saint of Law students,' he mouthed completing the sentence with her.

'I hope those pictures I sent you of various saints have proved useful?'

He visualised her sitting on the telephone seat at home staring up at the picture of the Sacred Heart.

'They certainly have Aunt Sheila.' He didn't dare tell her that one of them was folded four times over and keeping the desk in his room steady.

'The judge and I were talking just the other day, and it seems that a niece of his is in Bruges doing International Relations and she'll be coming back to Dublin this summer. She's about your age.'

'Oh that's great for her,' he said sarcastically.

'There's no need to be so dismissive,' his aunt said sharply, 'as soon as the mind has been educated, the heart is ready to learn.'

He had no idea what that phrase meant but he knew exactly what his aunt meant by it. As far as International Relations went he felt he was doing his little bit already with Nathalie.

'I've got to go now Aunt Sheila,' he said as the credits clicked down to one unit.

'God bless you Dixton.'

'Bye, Aunt Sheila.'

'I think his niece will be home in July.'

'Good-BYE Aunt Sheila.'

She was some cookie. She'd organise the world from a pay phone if she got the chance.

'Watch those fucking nettles Pepper.'

Pepper was manoeuvering the ladder down into swimming pool territory. Dixton sat on the wall beside him in a pair of shorts, a T-shirt and slippers.

'Don't worry Dixton, it's all under control.'

'Speaking of under control, how's your essay?' Dixton swiped.

'How's your Remedies and Restitution?'

'Touché.'

They clambered down the ladder and inched their way in the darkness theough the hedge and towards the pool. The place looked gorgeous and an eighty percent moon was reflected perfectly on the surface of the pool like a trap-door into the water.

'Are we mad or what?' Dixton exclaimed, 'it's one o'clock in the morning.'

'Look,' said Pepper, slipping off his running shoes and unbuckling his jeans at the same time, 'if these jokers aren't going to use their own facilities we may as well.'

There were marble steps down into the water and the two trespassers stood on the top one wiggling their toes in the water.

'Jesus it's cold,' said Dixton.

'Rubbish, it'll be lovely and warm once we get in.'

In fairness the night air was warm anyway so they reckoned it couldn't be too bad in the water.

'One, two, three,' Pepper counted then crouched down and dived. Dixton made as if to join him but held back. Pepper plunged in.

'Come on you wimp.' Pepper treaded water in the middle of the moon's reflection. Dixton closed his eyes and flopped in. Jesus it *was* cold.

Dixton had to admit that he felt totally invigorated by the midnight swim. He brushed his teeth in front of the mirror in his room and watched drops from his swimming togs trickle down the radiator. It was the first time he'd swam in years. Up until then he'd always written off swimming as a totally pointless exercise - what was the use of pitting your meagre frame against millions of gallons of water with the very real chance of death in the offing? He'd revised his view tonight. The single most pointless physical exercise in the whole world he now reckoned was dying. Aunt Sheila always said that it was important that people should die with dignity. It was a bit like asking someone to smile while they're being mugged. All this talk of death focussed his mind on Remedies and Restitution.

'Who are you?'
   'I'm Dixton Larkin.'
   'College?'
   'Lupin Hall.'
The exam invigilator looked like one of those awful breed of men who take buying shoes seriously. Dixton had been nervous enough in the run up to this exam but once he got inside the Senate House he was a complete wreck. Into the bargain this twit was insisting that there was a desk for Dixton somewhere on the left hand side of the room. Dixton had already been up and down that aisle three times and now all the seats were occupied so there was no immediate sniffle of a vacancy.
   'Name?'
   'I SAID Dixton Larkin.'
   'College?'
   'STILL Lupin Hall,' Dixton's nervousness was giving way to a bout of anger closely shadowed by outright panic.
   'Look are you sure you are registered for this exam?'
For some reason Dixton's brain freeze framed on a person in the shower being stabbed.
   'OF COURSE I'm registered, look down through your BLOODY list!'
Half the exam hall turned to look, someone said "Shhhsssh" rather loudly.
   'What's all this about?' A tall rather elegant looking man in a mismatched jacket and corduroy trousers had slipped into the hall behind them through the main door. The invigilator smartened up a bit but manitained his sarcasm.
   'This "gentleman" is lost, or rather, his desk is.' The new arrival cut across him and addressed Dixton in a kind voice.
   'Now Mr?. . . Mr?'
   'Larkin, Dixton Larkin, Lupin Hall.'

'Yes, Mr Lakin (he didn't pronounce the r in Larkin), now what subject are you submitting for today?'

'Remedies and Restitution,' Dixton said confidently.

'Really?' the mismatched dresser was incredulous. He reached into his breast pocket and withdrew a pair of half-reading glasses. He peered over them at Dixton.

'I'm afraid I don't recognise you at all. I'm Peter Grenville, I taught the course this year but I'm afraid you don't look at all familiar, are you sure you're registered for this exam?'

Dixton wondered if he died in Cambridge would he be buried in Grantchester? It would be great to be buried at a vantage point from which all the pubs would be visible. A desk was procured and an exam paper photocopied. Whatever snippets he'd learned at the last moment, hoping to jot them down immediately, had vanished. An hour into the exam Dixton began to feel sick. His head hurt just behind his eyes as if some person were trapped there and attempting to kick his or her way out with hobnail boots. His stomach was on the point of churning but lacked sufficient material to do so. Allied to these symptoms his answerbook bore all the hallmarks of mediocrity. He had stooped lower than ever in exam terms and copied the questions verbatim from the exam paper in order to fill space. He'd made a stab at two of the questions but the other "answers" were simply the inky manifestation of complete ignorance. In one question a scenario had been outlined whereby: "A" buys land from "B" who doesn't own the land at all and "C" who does own the land allows "A" to build on the land even though "C" knows that "A" doesn't know that "B" didn't own the land. Dixton's task apparently was to advise "A". His answer, though perhaps somewhat unorthodox, was at least heartfelt and genuine.

'Discover the identities of "B" and "C" and then kill them.'

He'd had enough, they could keep their complex problems and their straightforward esays and do what they bloody well liked with them, Dixton Larkin was finished with this exam. He was sick and he was leaving.

The invigilator smirked as Dixton approached. It appeared to Dixton that there were about four invigilators because at this stage his eyes simply wanted to be plucked out or to absorb morphine in massive quantities.

'Leaving early are we?' the invigilator smarmed.

'I don't know about you but I am,' Dixton replied weakly. If he was going to be afflicted with seeing everything in double for the rest of his life he hoped he would be adequately compensated by always being able to choose the right one to assault physically. He stumbled towards the idiot (or however many of him there were) and on towards the door.

'Are you all right?' a voice he didn't recognise descended on his inner ear. He looked around to his left and a small man with a white pointed clipped beard and an academic gown, (or perhaps two small men with white pointed clipped beards and academic gowns) stood at his side. Maybe he was dead. He collapsed on the floor. When he came to Dixton was sitting on a chair outside the Senate House and the small man with the gown was standing beside him smiling benignly. The clock on the church across the street informed Dixton that he'd been out cold for a couple of minutes.

'How do you feel?'

'Much better,' he lied. It was always difficult to know when other people really wanted you to be frank about your own health.

'It's very stuffy in there,' said the man.

'Yes, I'm afraid I left rather early.' Dixton began to make excuses.

'It happens to us all now and then,' the man smiled reassuringly.

'How do you mean?' Dixton wasn't sure if he meant that everybody leaves an exam early sooner or later in their life.

'They never open the windows in there, it's some old tradition originally designed to stop people from agricultural backgrounds getting assistance from friends outside whistling in code.'

'Really?' It had never occurred to Dixton.

'Anyway the important thing is that this bout of illness is not allowed to upset your examinations.'

Dixton was mildly interested, perhaps they'd let him resit in the Autumn or something.

'You mean the resits?'

'I'm afraid there are no resits in the LLM.'

Bollox, so this was it, one chance at the roundabout and he'd missed it and ended up on the swings. His whole Aunt flashed before him and he realised that the game was finally at an end, he'd swash no more buckles on the ocean wave of life, his goose had come home to roost and volunteered itself for the Aga cooker.

'I'll write a note on your behalf and make sure its seen by the right people.'

This was little consolation to Dixton. He wished for the the only time ever in his life that he was a member of the Free Masons.

'Thank you,' he said weakly in a disappointed tone.

'Don't mention it, and whatever you do don't worry, everything will be all right.'

'Don't you believe him Dixton?' Nathalie folded a damp facecloth and laid it across his forehead back at 4 Clopton Way that afternoon.

193

Dixton was stretched out on the sofa in his underwear.

'Oh, I don't know, I don't deserve any help anyway, I mean even if I hadn't been sick I probably wouldn't have lasted much longer in the exam than I did.'

'Oh Dixton, don't be such a pessimist,' she consoled, 'you've only got one more exam so do your best in that, I'm sure they'll take everything into consideration.'

Dixton was gutted by his own performance. Why did he get sick? Was it just nerves or what? He replayed the events over and over again wondering would things have been any different if there had been a desk and an exam paper for him when he arrived. Was he really sick or was it only psychosomatic or whatever the word was? What was the word? With his luck Professor Simpson's paper would be substituted with completely different material and his cover would be blown even further. The only certainties in life were death and nurses. What a mess.

Dixton emerged into the brilliant sunlight of King's Parade. The Criminal paper had gone as hinted at by Professor Simpson and Dixton felt guilty about ever having doubted him. Still it was too little too late as far as the exam board would be concerned; Remedies and Restitution had caught him on the hop and savaged him. Some tour guide was pointing out King's College Chapel to a bunch of tourists. Perhaps that's all he'd really been at Cambridge - a tourist taking in the sights but leaving no meaningful trace of his visit after him. What would his legacy here be? "Dixton Larkin LLM: Fail?" It reminded him of the day he'd come for the interview almost a year ago. On that occassion he'd left with the impression that he had missed his opportunity, never dreaming for a moment that he'd actually suceed in getting a place here. Now he was facing an even greater disappointment, not an opportunity missed, but an opportunity received and wasted. His Aunt would kill him.

'Silence everyone,' Andy stood on a chair in the front room of 4 Clopton Way, 'no slurping there at the back.' Penny giggled and half a mouthful of port slobbered down the front of her jumper.

'You *are* an idiot,' Jack laughed, nudging her with a plastic knife in an attempt to get her to jettison the other half mouthful in a similar manner.

'SHUT UP,' Andy shouted laughingly, 'NOW,' there was relative quiet, 'now, the Port and Stilton Society is proud to announce that there will be a special port drinking session the evening of the College Ball. Professor Lynn and Stan the Porter have very kindly presented the Society with a cask of vintage 1956 port.'

'The cask is being kept in the College wine cellar for safekeeping until the evening of the Ball,' Professor Lynn spoke from the sofa beside the piano.

'Excellent,' said Andy, 'my task, as chairman of this particular meeting is to encourage everyone to forget about the exams. They're over and out of our control now. So let's concentrate on the summer term.'

Everyone raised their glasses and drank to the summer term.

'I think we've finally sorted out the mess with the University Authorities over boat house facilities,' Jack addressed the meeting. 'We will be allocated a berth for the college punt in the Darwin boathouse.'

'I didn't know we had a college punt!' Niall the vet echoed the thoughts of most. Jack explained.

'Well we had one in the eighties and it was destroyed by a fire in the woodshed while it was being varnished. After that there was the problem apparently that our lease in the Emmanuel boat-house had run out and college weren't prepared to renew it as they'd have to invest in a new punt. So we wound up having to rent public punts and making do. Then last year some graduate club donated a punt to the college but of course there was no place to put it.'

'So where is it?' asked Pepper.

'Its going to be delivered sometime next week from the maker's yard in Ely.'

'Excellent,' said Andy, 'more port anyone?'

The meeting broke up at about two in the morning some eight bottles of port later. Dixton helped Nathalie clear up.

'You were very quiet this evening, Dixton.'

'Was I?' he said absentmindedly.

'You're not still worrying about the exams are you?'

'No, no, nothing like that.'

Nathalie stopped brushing the crumbs off the top of the piano with a duster and said worriedly.

'Is it us then? Is there something about us that you're not happy about?'

Dixton put his arms around her and kissed her all over her face.

'Of course not, I've never been as happy as I am with you. I suppose I'm just tired after the exams and everything.'

He knew that Nathalie would worry about him if she thought that he was worried. That was what lovers did. They took on two lives with twice the grief in the hope of finding twice the happiness. Ever since they'd been going out he felt he could talk to her about anything. She was the only one he'd ever talked to about losing his parents. She was the most wonderful woman he'd ever met and she loved him back. He remembered how before he'd met her he had always imagined that he was the type of person who would would never meet someone he could consider spending his life with or that if he did they would definitely leave him. He loved Nathalie to death and she loved him back. There was no point however in worrying her needlessly about the latest development. But he was quite worried about it himself. A good luck card from his aunt disclosed the horror that the Praelector had very kindly sent her an invitation to the graduation.

'The scumbag.' Pepper said as they sipped pints on the verandah of The Anchor overlooking the river.

'I knew he was up to something, he's left me alone all term since I paid my college bill.' Dixton finally saw the bigger picture.

'He thinks you're going to fail so he's invited your aunt to the graduation in order to land you in the shit.'

'Maybe I *will* fail,' Dixton said disconsolately.

'Rubbish, no-one fails out of here, we've had this conversation before.' Pepper tried to cheer him up.

Dixton remembered the conversation well. It was all too easy to accept myths when you didn't have to play a starring role yourself to disprove them. Dixton stuck a pound coin in the fruit machine and pressed the button. The words "YOU LOSE" flashed on and off. Fate, it appeared, had decided to don her most condemnatory balaclava.

CHAPTER SIXTEEN

'When do you think flies turn upside-down before they land on the ceiling?' Dixton addressed Pepper and Jack in the Emmanuel Boat-house.

'What?'

Pepper was holding the stencil while Jack sprayed the paint over the neatly cut out letters. Jack was so intent on not messing up the boat's name that he didn't even look up but replied nonetheless to Dixton's query through his white facemask.

'They don't turn upside-down at all in mid-air,' he said confidently. Dixton hopped down from the large wooden chest he'd been sitting on, it had the initials LK on it.

'What do you mean they don't turn upside down? How do they end up with their feet on the ceiling then?'

'Flies don't have feet,' Pepper was beginning to warm to the conversation.

'Why don't they have feet Pepper?' Dixton was now standing over them and he twisted his neck to try to read the name on the new college punt.

'They don't need feet,' Pepper said, 'a bit like a fish.'

'Fish? What have they got to do with flies?' Jack finished spraying and put down the can before giving Pepper the nod to take the stencil away.

'Fish eat flies,' said Pepper in a matter of fact documentary tone much like the innocent newsreel voice-overs you hear replayed on nostalgia programmes. ("Well goodbye Mr. Ghandi.")

'Never mind fish and flies, have a look at this,' Jack announced. The three lads stared like midwives at their latest production. The punt itself was a shiny brown varnish and the name was emblazoned neatly across the back in black paint "GRANTCHESTER RUN".

'What do you think?' Jack invited a comment on his handiwork.

'Excellent,' obliged Pepper and Dixton in unison.

'When'll it be ready to launch?' asked Dixton.

'Tomorrow or the next day. I don't want to take any chances with the paint,' said Jack.

They locked the boat-house behind them as they left but not before one last, proud look at their very own punt drying in the company of some really pathetic Darwin College craft. As Jack put the key in his pocket and checked the padlock one last paranoid time Dixon resurrected the earlier conversation.

'But they must turn upside down at some stage?'

'I know how they do it.' Pepper clapped his hands.

'How?'

'They turn the room upside-down and walk on the floor,' he grinned.

'Pathetic,' retorted Dixton, teed off at having been taken in even a little bit.

'Look boys . . .' Jack held up his hand like a traffic cop in a gesture of omniscience.

'What?'

'I know the real answer to this question.'

'Well?' Pepper prompted him while Dixton was already working on appearing unconvinced. Jack ran the fingers of both his hands back through his hair like a fifties character then delivered his pearl of wisdom.

'They don't turn upside down at all because they walk up the walls to get to the ceiling - they never actually land on it.'

'Bullshit,' said Pepper.

'Rubbish,' said Dixton although he had to admit secretly that it sounded totally plausible.

'How do thermos flasks know whether to keep something hot or to make it cold?' Pepper ventured. They turned out of the boat-house grounds and headed for Lupin. It was going to be a great summer term.

'So how did the exams go?' Feldman asked as he poured himself a large one in the middle of the afternoon. Through the window two girls in short white skirts were playing lawn tennis.

'Don't ask,' Dixton was trying to forget the exams at least for a while.

'Are you sure you won't have a drink?'

'No thanks I'm fine, I'm supposed to be going punting at five with a few of the lads from Lupin.'

'There's no law against drunken punting,' Feldman laughed.

Dixton's mood had been solemnised however by the mention of the exams. He looked around the walls of the room at the various paintings of Cornwall and wondered if you had to do exams to become a smuggler. Feldman refilled his glass and then sat down in an armchair which was bathed in sunlight streaming in through the diamond-shaped windows. Dixton began to wonder why Feldman had sent him a note inviting him to visit that afternoon.

'You're probably wondering why I sent you a note and invited you round this afternoon Dixton?'

'No, not at all.'

'Well anyway, the thing is,' he slurped a huge mouthful of whisky before it could escape down the side of the glass, 'I've got a bit of news for you.'

'Yes?' Dixton sat up in his chair. This was it, he'd failed the exams and they'd asked Feldman to break the news to him. That was why he'd been offered a drink.

'It's only a little bit of news but nonetheless I think you should know. You passed your essay. I can't say by how much or anything like that because I don't know but I made an enquiry and there you are. Of course, I don't know about the other exams but . . .'

Dixton wasn't sure how he was supposed to feel. Of course he was glad to know the essay had been all right but at the same time it only served to shorten the available time between now and the inevitable news that he'd failed at least one exam. He knew that Feldman's motives were well intentioned but really exams were the last thing he wanted to hear about.

'What's the matter? You look pale,' Feldman commented.

'Oh nothing, I'm fine. Look, thanks a million for letting me know, it's a weight off my mind.'

'I thought it might be.'

'Well listen I'd better go now, we're launching our new punt at five.'

'Goodbye then, Dixton.'

'See you, Robert.' Dixton pulled the door behind him. Bollox. He really wished he'd been told nothing whatsoever about the exams. Good or bad. Come to think of it he'd never really been worried about the essay at all.

'Stand back,' Jack warned. Pepper jumped back as the raw new varnished hull of their very own punt slid past his bare feet and down the slip into the water.

'Hey that was close,' Pepper laughed.

Quite a crowd had turned out for the launch. Andy, Sanjra, Pickford, Niall the vet, Penny and everyone else from the Port and Stilton Society. Stan the Porter was on duty but managed to sneak off for half an hour. Professor Lynn launched the craft and showered everyone with cheap fizzy cider in the process. It was a glorious event. They'd drawn lots for the maiden voyage and Pickford, Sanjra, Penny and Professor Lynn were the first four people to climb into the "Grantchester Run". The Darwin boat-house was situated at the end of a small tributary of the

Cam and so they punted up that for a hundred yards or so and then out into the river. Pickford stood on the back of the punt and appeared an expert with the pole. Professor Lynn sat in the middle looking around him rather proudly.

'The old boy is really enjoying this,' said Niall the vet.

'Yeah it's no harm for him to get out and about like this, I'm sure he gets bored to tears in the library,' said Andy.

'Was it really his idea to revive the Port and Stilton Society?' asked Pepper.

'It certainly was,' smiled Dixton remembering the afternoon he'd spent at Professor Lynn's house some months previously. He remembered the photograph of the Professor's wife on the pier at Brighton. It had reminded him of his parents. There was an unspoken bond between Dixton and the librarian, they both missed people they'd lost. Even looking at the Professor now he seemed years younger than that first evening at Lupin when Dixton had sat on the edge of his gown by accident. Maybe he'd opted out of life when his wife died or maybe people had just not made the effort to involve him in things outside of himself. At any rate he'd made a great job of launching the punt. Dixton resolved to keep in touch with the librarian after he left Cambridge. The maiden voyagers were embraced out of sight by a bend in the river.

'Dr Winston is not pleased,' Jack announced. It sounded like the title of a play.

'How do you mean?' asked Andy.

'Well,' Jack turned slightly to get the benefit of the evening sun and sat on the edge of the slip-way with his feet almost touching the water.

'He called me into his room this morning and said he'd never heard about the new college punt until the other day. He wanted to know if we needed anyone to launch it.'

'The nosy bastard,' said Pepper.

'Go on,' prompted Andy.

'Well, he went on and on about being extremely busy himself and I could see he was leading up to offering his services so I cut him short.'

'What did you say?' asked Dixton.

'I told him the Sports Commitee had already ruled him out because he was so busy and that we'd been able to secure the services of Professor Lynn to launch the punt.'

'Excellent,' said Andy, 'what did he say to that?'

'What could he say? He just shut up and then I left.' Jack smirked.

Dixton didn't think he could have attended the launch if the Praelector had been involved. It still galled him to think of that bastard sending tickets to Aunt Sheila for the Graduation. God, he was going to have to face the humiliation of all that business after the exam results. She'd go bananas when she knew he'd failed.

'Look,' said Niall the vet, 'they're coming back.'

Dixton hopped to his feet. He Jack, Pepper and Andy were next.

'Do you want to have a go, Dixton?' Jack shouted to him. Dixton was sitting at the front end of the punt. Jack was doing a great job with the pole but Dixton was dying for a go. Two other punts passed them going the other way. It looked dead easy.

'OK.'

He edged past Andy and Pepper which was quite difficult given the size of the craft. At one stage the punt lurched to one side and Dixton grabbed on to Pepper and they both nearly fell in.

'Jesus Christ be careful will you,' Pepper screamed. The moment passed and Dixton swapped with Jack. Andy moved up to the front and Jack sat with Pepper in the middle. Dixton stood on the warm wood in his bare feet and pushed the pole down into the river bed.

'Bollox, it's stuck,' he panicked.

'Pull it up at an angle,' Jack shouted instructions. The punt moved sleekly away from the pole and Dixton had to lean over at an unnatural angle in order to grab hold of it again. He managed to grab it, and this combined with Jack paddling backwards, allowed him to retrieve the pole. Whew.

He got the hang of it after a while. The trick was to make short stabbing pushes and then to use the pole, as it resurfaced, as a rudder. By dragging it to the left or the right you could steer the punt. They punted past King's and Trinity Hall. Students adorned every available wall space and seemed to be watching a boat race instead of enjoying the evening sun. Some of the college punts which passed them were manned by people wearing college blazers. It was idyllic. The Backs were a hive of riverside activity with punts passing by, pretty women in short skirts dangling their legs in a provocative manner and exam-weary students forgetting their woes and planning a night out. This was heaven. They swished under the Bridge of Sighs (aah) and on towards Magdalene Bridge. Here the colleges were literally built on the river banks and the walls rose out of the Cam and blossomed into windows. Everything seemed to be perfect until Dixton felt drops of water land on his head. Rain. He looked up but the sky was totally blue.

'What's that?' said Andy.

'Stop spraying us with water,' Pepper grinned looking over his shoulder at Dixton.

'I'm not doing anything,' Dixton protested as the punt slowed down.

'Yeah right,' Jack said disbelievingly.

Suddenly there was an almighty thump as something landed in the water near the punt on Jack's side. It took them a couple of seconds to figure out what it was, then there was another.

'Water-bombs,' Jack shouted, 'quick Dixton get going.'

'Look out,' Andy shouted as six or seven plastic bags full of water hurtled down on them from the windows of St John's College. Dixton shoved the pole down into the bed of the river but they were almost at a standstill now and completely vulnerable to attack from the air. Where was the Rifle Club when they needed them? One water-bomb landed between Pepper and Andy and soaked them. Another narrowly missed Dixton's head. That would have been fatal. They moved out of range as one final bomb hit the side of the punt and rocked it slightly.

'That was bloody dangerous,' said Andy, 'who are those jokers anyway?'

'No idea,' said Jack, 'they probably just attack punts going past knowing we've no way of defending ourselves.'

'Well they drenched Pepper and me,' said Andy ruefully.

'They just missed my head,' said Dixton, 'I'm sure I'd have fallen in if they had hit me.'

'Well at least we got past them, we're out of range now,' Andy grinned.

'Until the trip back,' reminded Dixton.

It dawned on them collectively that they had a return journey to make.

'They'll be waiting for us,' said Jack.

'Did anybody notice how high up the windows were?' asked Pepper.

'Second or third floor maybe,' said Andy.

'Let's pull in here for a few minutes,' said Pepper, 'I want to get to a shop.'

They tied up the punt to the jetty on the other side of Magdalene Bridge and waited for Pepper.

'What's he up to?' wondered Jack.

'I've no idea,' said Dixton,

Pepper returned with his purchases.

'Here, hand these around,' he said giving Jack a plastic bag.

'It's full of carrier bags,' said Jack dumbly.

'I know, just hand them around, there should be two or three of them for everyone.'

'What do we do with these? Fill them up with water and throw them back at the bombers in John's?' smirked Andy.

'Spot on,' said Pepper, 'they've all got handles so trail them in the water when we get near and then sling them up at the windows.'

'We'll never reach,' said Dixton.

'Don't be so pessimistic,' said Pepper, 'we only have to be lucky once to do major damage, I'm sure there are books and everything near those windows. They'll never expect anyone to fight back.'

'Well let's not all throw together,' said Jack, 'or else the punt will capsize.'

'Good thinking,' said Pepper, 'let's start at Dixton's end and throw one bag each in turn.'

Jack untied the painter and pulled it into the boat. He reached for the pole which was still lying on the jetty.

'I'll punt if that's OK,' said Pepper.

'No problem, are you sure you'll be able to manage?' asked Jack.

'If Dixton can do it anyone can,' Pepper smirked.

'Watch it,' said Dixton, 'or I'll rock the punt and you'll fall off.'

'Better not,' warned Pepper opening a bag at his feet. 'Look, paddle for a bit while I get this organised.'

The others were all facing away from Pepper and so they couldn't see what he was doing. Dixton paddled while Jack and Andy kept an eye out for waterbombs. The Bridge of Sighs came into view and they entered the territorial waters of St John's College. (It was quiet, maybe too quiet.)

'Watch out,' shouted Andy. A waterbomb thundered out of one of the windows and landed beside the punt, splashing Dixton.

'OK Dixton, you throw first,' Jack said in a cautious voice.

'Which window is it?'

'Third from the right, second floor,' said Andy.

Dixton trailed the bag on the far side of the punt, then stood up and slung it up towards the window.

'Look out,' someone shouted and this was followed by a laugh as Dixton's missile landed harmlessly against the wall of the building below even the first floor windows.

'Now you Jack,' said Dixton, sitting down abruptly.

'Take it easy,' said Pepper from the stern.

Jack's effort was somewhat more successful in one way at least. It seemed to be about the right height except that it burst in mid air and the plastic bag flittered back down to the river. Their assailants had gotten over the initial threat of defence and a squad of waterbombs showered down on them. Pepper had stopped punting and the "Grantchester Run" had come to a complete standstill. Andy stood up. They were now almost directly below the window of their attackers and were more vunerable than ever. A direct hit was scored on Dixton.

'For God's sake Andy, throw the damn thing,' yelled Dixton.

Andy Chalmers had bided his time until he was sure and now he swung the bag back and forth a couple of times to build up momentum, then guided the bag up and over his head letting go at just the instant when it appeared he was going to topple over. The bag sailed up in a horrible looping arc into the evening sun and then disappeared in through the window. Bullseye. There was a roar of horror from the room.

'Yayhh,' shouted Dixton.

'Fab,' said Jack.

'I don't believe it,' said Andy.

'Watch it,' screamed Pepper. Dixton had just pushed the punt away from the wall using the paddle and not a moment too soon. There was a big "plop" to the side of the punt and then a green object resurfaced and bobbed.

'It's an apple,' said Jack, 'I hope they only throw fruit.'

'Lets get out of here,' urged Andy. There was a scream from above and as they looked up a bright blue missile descended on them. It hit the edge of the stern and smashed. It was a bottle of ink. The water turned navy around the punt.

'The bastards,' said Dixton, 'they're serious about this.'

'I'm sure no-one has ever fought back before,' said Jack. 'Pepper, hurry up. Let's go.'

'In a second,' said Pepper, 'I'm nearly ready, anyone got a lighter?'

They turned to look at Pepper and saw that he had sellotaped some long thin objects around the shaft of the pole.

'What the fuck are they?' asked Dixton.

'Fireworks,' said Pepper cheerfully. 'Thanks,' he said as Andy threw him a lighter. A deodorant spray was the latest missile to strike the punt. Because they were almost level with the wall they were somewhat difficult to hit but they would have to go out into the open to get around the bend to the Bridge of Sighs.

'Let's go, Dixton,' Pepper shouted.

Dixton jammed the paddle against the wall and levered the punt out into the open. Another two or three feet and they would be sitting ducks for the people upstairs. Pepper shoved the pole deep into the water and pushed them out into mid-stream. There were hurried shouts from above as they moved out into clear view. An orange splattered in the bottom of the boat between Jack and Andy. More waterbombs followed. Pepper gave them one final push into the main body of the river and then pulled the pole out of the water altogether. He rested the wet end of it in the punt and aimed the end with the fireworks up at the window. He held Andy's Zippo lighter in one hand and lit the touch papers. There was utter silence for a second, then an audible fizzle followed by a fabulous

WHOOSH as three of the four fireworks launched themselves up at the window. There was mayhem in the room, they could only hear it but they knew it was going on. Someone slammed the window shut as the fireworks blasted into the windowsill. There was a direct hit just below the window and then some of the ivy began to catch fire slowly.

'Jesus Christ,' exclaimed Andy as the fire began to gather momentum.

Someone opened the window in a panic and doused the ivy with water. The nozzel of a fire extinguisher appeared over the sash and the ivy was soon smothered in foam. After a couple of seconds the potential inferno had been snuffed out. There was a vicious black mark around the underside of the window.

'You could have killed someone,' said Jack as they moved under the Bridge of Sighs.

'Oh well,' said Pepper, 'you win some, you lose some.'

When the initial shock was over there was celebration in the punt. Andy opened the only bottle of beer they had with them and handed it around. Pepper managed to light the final firework as they went past King's and it flew up into the Cambridge sky exploding in colour as the sun was going down behind Grantchester. The punt had been properly launched. They headed back to the Darwin boat-house where the next crew were waiting to take over.

'How was the punting?' asked Nathalie when Dixton let himself into 4 Clopton Way.

'Excellent,' he grinned.

'We don't have any punts at Newnham,' she sighed.

'Well maybe I'll book it for an afternoon this weekend.'

'Oh Dixton,' she threw her arms around his neck and kissed him, 'that would be really great.'

He imagined himself in a boater and striped blazer punting all the way to Grantchester. A life of ease would suit him perfectly. None of this working nonsense. He remembered his chat with Feldman.

'Oh I passed the essay,' he said in a disinterested voice as Nathalie took his hand and led him into the kitchen.

'You don't seem very pleased about it.'

'Well I don't know. . .'

'You're still not worried about that exam you got sick in are you?'

Dixton didn't reply.

'Oh you are a silly boy,' she smiled, 'you're never satisfied. Well,' she twinkled her eyes suggestively, 'almost never.'

As Nathalie put on the kettle he wondered what his aunt was doing right now. Probably she was choosing an outfit for the Graduation that wouldn't be. Nathalie put a mug of coffee in front of him on the table and the steam rose into his chin almost scalding him. He jumped momentarily.

'That's more like it,' said Nathalie, 'fluff yourself up. We're got to think about costumes for the Lupin Ball. It's on Friday week.'

Friday week, that was the day before the exam results. Damn.

'I've bought a fabulous new hat for the Graduation, Dixton.' His aunt was on course for a day out and her tone of voice, when he telephoned her later that week, was a fusion of unbridled enthusiasm and investment reaping.

'Well the results aren't officially out for another week Aunt Sheila' he tried to bridge the gap between her hopes and his fears.

'Not to worry Dixton, when the work has been done the rewards will come, that's what I always say. Now I've organised accommodation. We'll be staying at the Garden House Hotel.'

'You mean that *you'll* be staying there Aunt?' he corrected her.

'No, *we'll* be staying there, the Judge has very kindly offered to accompany me. He hasn't been to Cambridge in years and I don't mind telling you we're both looking forward to this trip. It's amazing the power of prayer Dixton, you only have to trust in God and He'll guide you wherever. . .'

'Look Aunt Sheila,' he stammered, 'there's probably something I should tell you. . .' He'd have to warn her off, there wouldn't be any Graduation, at least not for him.

'Yes?' he detected reticence on the other end of the line, 'Yes? What is it Dixton?'

He hesitated, and the silence from his aunt translated into sirens clanging in his own head. Surely he owed it to her to put her in the picture? He'd done absolutely no work and he was going to fail at least one subject, there would be no graduation and he'd wasted his time and her money and the year had been an unmitigated educational disaster.

'You'll have to get a taxi from the Railway Station to the Hotel.'

'Oh that's no problem, in fact you can get one for us and meet us at the station.' His aunt's voice re-exhibited its earlier signs of enthusiasm. He'd chickened out of his responsibility, he'd opted out in the face of the truth, he'd confronted his own destiny by turning his back on it, capitulated at the first sign of war. So bloody what? It had bought him another week's grace. He could live with that. As Dixton stepped out of the telephone booth into the foyer of Lupin Hall he collided with the Praelector. Dixton thought of apologising then realised how little he

206

thought of the Praelector, and didn't. Dr Winston gazed sneeringly over his half-glasses at Dixton.

'Ah Larkin, I hear you had some difficulties in one of your exams. Pity,' he smirked. Dixton didn't answer. Winston continued.

'I'm certainly looking forward to the exam results next week which I'm sure is more than you are doing.'

He chuckled like a comic-relief pig. Dixton was tempted to knee him in the groin. It was an urge that came over him all of a sudden like an erection but he resisted. He'd have to keep his mouth shut and his powder dry. Winston was a complete bastard for sending his aunt the tickets. There could be no doubt as to his motive. Dixton would have to look back through Professor Simpson's notes to see whether or not murder was a crime.

King's Parade was thronged with tourists. There must be thousands of people filing past these Colleges every day during the summer season Dixton thought. Pepper had gone in to Ryders and Amies to pick up his Blue's Blazer for the Hawks Club Annual Dinner. Dixton sat on the window sill of a post-card shop and watched the world go by. People were funny, they all went about their own business in vague hurried ways oblivious to everything else. Japanese tourists shot Kodaks from the hips and Americans were invariably audible before being visible. People fascinated Dixton, there was such a variety and yet certain standards applied across the board, certain norms pervaded entire societies. However, while the mores of the Western World underpinned the primacy of the individual, eccentricity (which presumably is the epitome of individualism) was universally frowned on. His mind leaped to greater questions such as the thermos query Pepper had raised in the boathouse but his attention was really only properly captivated by a tall oriental girl in a short blue skirt. Sod eccentricity and thermos flasks; sex was where it was really at. Jesus he was beginning to sound like Pepper. Pepper at any rate still sounded like himself as he emerged from Ryders and Amies.

'God did you see her Dixton? I'd say she's a short iron shot from the bunker and in in one eh?'

The blazer was wrapped in cellophane and Dixton could just about make out the crest. Pepper patted the parcel.

'This is my year at Cambridge Dixton, I've done it, the Blue's team, the Hawks Club.'

'And what about the degree?' Dixton asked.

'I couldn't care less about it, I really couldn't. Nothing they can

207

give me in that place there,' he nodded in the direction of the Senate House, 'can even touch this and even if I. . .'

'Fail?' interjected Dixton.

'Yeah, even if I fail the stupid geology degree nothing they can fail to award me in that same Senate House can take this away from me, not now, not ever.'

Dixton knew Pepper meant every word. He wondered how Aunt Sheila would react if he approached her by saying something like, 'Well I know I failed the exams but I made a lot of friends.' For the first time ever that he could recall, he shuddered.

They walked back from town to Lupin Hall and stopped in The Hat and Feathers for a pint. They found a seat outside.

'Let's go out in the College punt tomorrow Pepper.' He wanted to get more practice before making a trip with Natalie.

'Why not? The good weather is supposed to hold until after the weekend. We can book at the porters' desk.'

'Is Heather still coming down for the Ball?' asked Dixton wiggling two fingers in his pint to fizz up a head.

'Yeah, God I'd nearly forgotton.'

'So she's still coming then?'

'Oh yes, a wonderful night in store for old Heather on Friday' Pepper grinned. Dixton couldn't help but laugh, Pepper was incredible. They finished their drinks and headed back to Lupin.

'Where's the punting book?' Dixton asked Stan. The porter reached under the counter and brought out a ledger.

'Are there any slots for tomorrow?' asked Pepper.

''Fraid not lads, it's booked up but I could give you any time on Thursday.' Stan turned the ledger around to face them.

'OK how about two o'clock? How does that suit?'

'Great, we'll take that then, two to four.'

Dixton signed his name and as they turned to leave the porters' desk, Rainford and Zinowsky came down the stairs from the reading room. Stony stares were delivered but nothing was said at all.

'C'mon Pepper let's go,' Dixton said, opening the main door. As they exited into the Court they heard Bernard's upper class voice barking instructions.

'Ah Stan, I'd like a word with you please.'

'Yes Mr Rainford' Stan replied scathingly. The door closed behind them.

'They've been very quiet lately,' said Dixton.

'Yeah, despite their note a few weeks ago,' Pepper replied.

'Maybe they'll try something at the Ball,' Dixton suggested.

'Yeah, maybe,' said Pepper.

'Do you fancy a midnight swim tonight Pepper? It's a while since we went over the wall.'

'Great idea Dixton, look why don't you bring Nathalie along? I'm sure she'd enjoy it.'

'What? So you can play gooseberry?' Dixton laughed.

'No no Dixton, it won't be like that at all, I'll bring someone with me too.'

'But Heather isn't arriving until Friday,' Dixton reminded him.

'I know, but Martha's here,' Pepper smirked sleazily.

'Who's Martha?'

'Oh she's a secretary in the geology department. I met her when I was handing in my essay. I'd say she's pretty keen.'

'Oh they're *all* keen,' swiped Dixton.

'Yes indeedy Dixton, you're right there. Race you across the Court.'

The sun shone brilliantly and flickered down at Cambridge between the towers and steeples of the colleges and their chapels. Thursday afternoon on the river was like owning a dream and being able to take part in it at will. There were quite a lot of other punts out but once they'd negotiated the Lammas Land bend they had the river to themselves. Two people were cycling along the tow path in the distance.

'I really enjoyed that swim last night,' Pepper was manning the pole.

'So did I, Nathalie's all keen to do it again soon,' said Dixton.

'Is she now? And what about swimming, is she interested in doing that again?' Pepper grinned.

'Fuck off, you know what I mean Pepper,' Dixton rocked the punt and Pepper nearly lost his balance.

'OK, OK,' Pepper pleaded, Dixton steadied the punt again. They passed under a small bridge which was overhung with ivy. It reminded them both spontaneously of the assault with the fireworks. Dixton chuckled out loud.

'Thinking of fireworks, what did you make of Martha?' Pepper skilfully navigated the punt around a row-boat which was mysteriously anchored in the middle of the river near the turn into Grantchester Meadows.

'Not bad.'

'Not bad?' Pepper countered, 'how could you call a body like that "not bad"?'

'Well, I suppose she was all right to look at,' Dixton said in a throwaway tone. In actual fact Martha was a sex goddess who looked like she'd stepped out of a film and was ready to hop into bed with a motive other than sleep. Sex appeal was all right but Dixton wouldn't have liked to rely on her for conversation. Still he supposed, Pepper didn't want her for her mind, only for what she didn't mind.

'Do you want another beer?' he asked Pepper.

'Yeah, open one for me will you?' Pepper slowed the punt down and shifted his feet. The surface of the punt was quite hot under the mid-afternoon sun. Dixton wondered if the heat could be described as "relentless". The bottom of the carrier bag with the beer was soaking. Blow, he thought, I must have spilled one by accident. Dixton lifted up the bag and assessed the damage. The bottom of the punt in that section was stained. He put the bag under the bow, the stain would dry out. About two minutes later he looked again but the situation was worse, it certainly wasn't a beer spillage.

'What's up?' Pepper called out.

'I'm not sure, there seems to be some water in this section.'

'Probably from the paddle,' Pepper suggested.

'No, it's worse than that.' The section was now covered in a shallow pool of water. Dixton scooped some of it out with his hands and threw it into the river. After a few scoops he seemed to have sorted it out when he noticed that there was a leak between two of the boards. He stuffed his hanky into it. He noticed that the cyclists were still on the tow path.

'Everything all right?' Pepper asked.

'There's a small leak, I've jammed it up but I don't know how long it'll hold, maybe we should turn around.'

At this stage they were at least twenty minutes fast punting away from Grantchester and about half an hour from home. Pepper turned the punt around.

'Bollox,' Dixton said as his hanky came unstuck and floated back towards him. He climbed into the other section and tried to re-insert it. The water was coming in much more quickly now. It wasn't just between the two pieces at the joint anymore. On both sides of the board the river was seeping in. He bailed the water with his hands as quickly as he could but it was useless. The water was coming in so fast now that even if he had a bucket or something he doubted whether they'd make it back to the boat-house.

'Pepper it's no use, head for the shore, I think she might sink.'

Pepper used the pole as a rudder and turned towards the river bank. They were at one of the widest points but should have had no trouble making it. Suddenly there was a dull clunk as if someone had struck a wooden door with a boxing glove. Dixton's feet were drenched as water flooded over the narrow partition board between the next section and his. The board in the bottom of the punt had come loose altogether and water gushed into the craft. Pepper realised the seriousness of the situation and shouted 'Abandon ship,' as Dixton toyed with the idea of stuffing his shirt into the breech.

'Come on Dixton, jump for fuck's sake, leave it.'

Dixton's last thoughts were of the beer as they both jumped into the Cam seconds before it would have rushed up through the "Grantchester Run" to engulf them. Dixton felt he was going to drown as his tennis shoes filled with water and hampered his swimming. He thrashed about for a bit then managed to kick one off. He closed his eyes and did what he thought was the doggy paddle. His progress was halted by bullrushes in his mouth. He'd reached the shore. Pepper was there slightly ahead of him and helped to drag Dixton up on to the bank. They sat breathless for a while on the muddy grass. Dixton's jeans were wrecked and filthy and he'd lost one of his tennis shoes. Pepper was fully clothed but looked quite shaken. They sat up without speaking and looked out on to the river where the punt should have been. The paddle was caught in the current and was drifting back towards Grantchester; the pole had lodged in the mud on the other side of the river and swung out into the water with the current like a delinquent needle on a gieger counter.

'Jesus,' said Dixton.

'What the hell happened to the boat?' Pepper asked rhetorically.

Dixton was the first to hear it. It was faint at first but then it got louder as the wind gusted up the river towards them.

'Is that someone laughing?'

'It certainly sounds like it.'

Dixton looked back down the river. On the opposite bank about two hundred yards back towards the town two figures stood beside bicycles laughing their heads off. Initially they weren't sure but then it all became clear.

'Rainford and Zinowsky,' growled Pepper.

'Do you think they had anything to do with this?' it suddenly dawned on Dixton.

'The bastards.'

'How could they? Surely there's no way that. . .?' Dixton still found it hard to believe.

'The absolute bastards,' said Pepper, 'I noticed the two cylists but I didn't really think they were following us. No wonder they've been so quiet lately. Planning this.'

'But how could they sabotage the boat?' asked Dixton.

'Easy,' said Pepper, 'as easy as removing a bloody u-bend.'

The two cyclists waved, then mounted their bikes and headed back into town. The wind carried their guffaws back to Pepper and Dixton as they prepared for the five mile walk back to Lupin with only three tennis shoes between them.

CHAPTER SEVENTEEN

'What's happened to us? We used to love each other.'

'We still love each other, it's ourselves we hate.'

Dixton adored these old movies but it seemed to him that most black and white films end in tragedy. Was that true? Maybe they only discovered happy endings when they stumbled on Technicolor. He switched off the TV.

'Ready?'

Nathalie called as she came down the stairs flanked by Sally and Hannah who'd helped her put on her costume. Dixton struggled to his feet from the sofa. This werewolf costume was a nightmare. He chuckled to himself at the pun. Nathalie wore a flowing black dress with a huge starched collar that pointed up at the ceiling on either side like a series of spearheads. She wore false eyelashes that looked like combs.

'Woof woof,' Sally mocked as Dixton picked his way carefully past the coffee table towards the bottom of the stairs.

'Lay off,' said Dixton, 'it's bloody murder in this outfit.'

'You look great,' grinned Hannah.

Dixton wished he had a pair of scissors to cut his way out of the costume.

'Never mind them,' Nathalie coaxed, 'I think you look wonderful.'

Dixton wasn't convinced.

'Why couldn't you have been the werewolf?' he snarled.

'Because *you* wouldn't fit into the dress,' Hannah laughed. Oh well, sod them, he'd have to make do.

'Who are you supposed to be anyway?' he lifted the head of his costume off and put it under his arm.

'I,' said Nathalie, twirling around, 'am Cruella De Ville.'

'She's not in a horror film.' Dixton protested.

'Well she is a sort of horror character.' she countered.

'*One hundred and one Dalmatians* is not a horror film.'

'She can say it was a horror remake' Sally began take-off clearance on the most obvious of all jokes "One hundred. . . .'"

Her voice trailed behind them as they went out to the waiting taxi.

'We don't really need a taxi,' said Nathalie as they got in, 'it's only up the road.'

'There's no way I'm walking up Sidgwick Avenue in this outfit.'

'Where to?' the cab driver eyed them up in the mirror, 'the Dog

Pound?' He chuckled away like a maniac to himself as Dixton gave him directions. He was one of those annoying people who repeat punchlines to themselves slightly aloud for ages after the joke has been and gone and find it as funny as ever each time. '"The Dog Pound", ha ha ha.'

Lupin Hall was ablaze with coloured lights. A huge sign flickered on and off over the main gate, "Nightmare on Barton Road", like a cinema display hoarding. It was a balmy June night with a warm breeze which seemed to shroud the college making it pleasant to be outside. A centaur checked their tickets and ushered them into the West Court. There were Draculas everywhere; it was as if someone had photocopied the guests. Even some women were dressed up as Dracula (they looked particularly out of place). Here and there were Frankenstein masks and the odd Adams Family lookalike but for the most part it was a mass of velvet capes, fangs and brylcreamed hair. What was this? A Ball or a blood-sucking convention? Dixton looked around for Pepper but it was an impossible task to try and select individuals from a hoard of coffin inhabitants. Back home in Dublin people seemed to dress up as priests and nuns for these parties.

'At least you're the only werewolf,' Nathalie consoled him.

'Yes I suppose there is that,' he sighed through his new-found pelt and examined the programme. The main events were scheduled for the bar with live music all night after the banquet. Outside, in the East Court, a marquee had been erected and this was set up as a casino with roulette tables and blackjack (Dixton made a mental note to get to this).

'At midnight a Strauss Ball will take place in the Dining Hall with a thirty piece orchestra,' Nathalie read aloud from the schedule. 'Oh Dixton, isn't that wonderful?'

'Eh yes, fairly wonderful all right, let's go to the bar, I'm roasting in this suit.'

Nathalie took his arm and they manouvered their way into the main building. Dixton plonked his head down on the bar counter.

'Two glasses of wine please Pickford.'

'Any particular type?' Pickford proffered the wine list.

'Yes, white, cool and cheap.'

They managed to get two seats near the window which looked out into the East Court. Couples streamed past the window heading in for the banquet. Dixton shook his head at the unimaginative choice of costumes.

'How could so many of them choose the same outfit?'

'Maybe they don't all have innovative girlfriends,' Nathalie smiled.

Dixton put his arms around her and teed up for a kiss.

'Ah, there you are,' Pepper's voice cut across the romantic moment. He was dressed as an Arab and was clutching a pint of beer.

'Let me guess,' said Dixton, 'you're an Arabian nightmare?'

'Oh, shut up Dixton, this was the only costume left in the whole bloody shop. It was either this or nothing.'

'Where's Heather?' Nathalie smiled. 'We're dying to meet her.'

'Well, she's dying of food poisoning in Edinburgh and can't make it. She phoned the Porters' Lodge this afternoon.' Pepper was evidently quite disappointed. The gong sounded for dining.

'Never mind Pepper,' Nathalie took his arm, 'you can spend the evening with us.'

'Yes Pepper, do cheer up, we might even win some money on the tables later on.' They climbed the stairs to the Dining Hall. Pepper eyed up women left, right and centre. (The old boyho.)

'I heard about the punt,' Nathalie said as they found their placenames.

'Yes a bloody disaster, this whole week's been a disaster,' Pepper moaned.

'What made it sink?' Nathalie asked.

'We're not a hundred percent sure,' said Dixton.

'No, but we have a pretty good idea,' Pepper said tucking into the fruit cocktail starter.

'Speaking of the punt, look who's coming this way,' Dixton warned. It was Bernard and Zinowsky with two women in tow. Both men were dressed as Dracula. The women were pretty, suprisingly enough.

'Ah,' Bernard sneered, 'the swine are out in force.'

'Shove off,' Pepper countered.

'Have you dried off yet?' Zinowsky tried to make a joke.

'I see you didn't need to hire a mask,' Dixton swiped.

Zinowsky's face dropped as he got the dig. He edged forward but Bernard held him back. Pepper stood up ready to face them.

'Never mind them Mike,' Bernard soothed, 'let's not waste any time on these losers, we'll leave them to drown their sorrows, they've probably got that sinking feeling.'

Zinowsky roared laughing and Pepper and Dixton were reminded of the cyclists on the tow-path the other day.

'I suppose you think you're so bloody smart, wrecking the punt like that.' Dixton tried to provoke them as they turned to go.

'You had it coming you . . .' Zinowsky belowed. There was a fierce glance from Bernard at Zinowsky which said it all. Zinowsky stopped embarrassedly in mid-sentence. He'd obviously said too much. Any

215

doubts they might have had about the cause of the accident were now gone. The party of Bernard et al moved off. Pepper turned to Dixton.

'It was them, at least we know that for definite now.'

After dinner they adjourned to the Common Room downstairs where Professor Lynn was busy decanting the vintage port for the members of the Port and Stilton Society.

'To University College Hall,' they toasted. The port was like honey with a kick. Dixton noticed Jack and Penny canoodling in the corner of the room. This was what Cambridge was really about: friendship and alcohol. He spirited Nathalie out into the West Court for a romantic kiss under the moonlight after removing the werewolf's head. (Otherwise people might have got the wrong idea. This was the life.)

The roulette table was being manned by Jack. A large crowd had gathered in the temporary gambling den after dinner and wagered monopoly money in the hope of winning bottles of wine.

'Fancy your chances Dixton?' Jack grinned.

'No problem.' Dixton placed all of his tokens on black. Jack spun the wheel. It was red. Oh well. Jack laughed as he scooped up the tokens.

'Let me try,' said Nathalie. There was a loud hum of voices. Dixton edged back and let Nathalie in to his place. He stood behind her in his costume and could only watch as she won three bottles of wine on the trot.

'See, I *am* lucky,' she smiled as they emerged from the marquee.

Dixton looked around.

'Where's Pepper?'

'I don't know. When we came down after the meal he went to the bar and said he'd follow us.'

'Well I'm going to go to my room and change. This suit is killing me.'

'OK,' she smiled, 'I'll see you upstairs at the Strauss Ball, it begins in a few minutes.' They parted at the door to the Porters' Lodge.

It was like escaping from prison getting out of the werewolf costume. Dixton straightened his shirt up and put on a tie. He grabbed a tweed jacket from behind the door and put it on as he walked across the court. This was more like it. His breathing system returned to normal after the contraints of the fur and he felt that he could finally begin to enjoy himself. Pepper had seemed fairly down in the mouth during the meal. Despite his disapproval of Pepper's philandering, he sympathised with his situation. A Ball without a woman was like a Christmas without a tree. He liked the sound of that, it certainly sounded profound. He wondered if he might have a future as a writer of slogans for greeting cards. He opened the door into the main building and was met with a wall of metal noise. He looked at the event programme. "Credible Overcoat" from Nottingham were the band. They sounded like nails in a blender. Maybe he was getting old. The lyrics blasted into his inner ear as he passed the door. *My old man stays dread all day and says he lives for the pens . . ."* (at least that's what it sounded like). God they were awful.

Nathalie was leaning against one of the pillars swaying in time to the orchestra. Dixton hated dancing. He had to admit though that she looked fabulous and he was almost tempted to shelve his hatred of dancing for a while. He didn't get a chance to consider one way or the other because as soon as Nathalie saw him she took his hand and led him to the centre of the dance floor. There were four or five other couples dancing. Dixton recognised Dr Hagar the senior tutor and his wife presumably, and also Rose from the secretarial office. She smiled at him over her partners shoulder and he wondered how Sanjra was getting on.

'That's it Dixton, one two three four, one two three four.'

Nathalie guided him around the floor in a slow waltz.

'It's no good. I'll never get the hang of it,' he protested.

'Of course you will, you're doing fine, one two three . . .'

Then Dixton spotted Pepper. He wasn't sure at first, mainly because he didn't imagine Pepper was a keen waltzer, but also because he thought he recognised the girl he was dancing with and for some reason they seemed an unusual couple. The main barrier to recognition however was that they were stuck into each other snogging like a pair who had missed the dinner altogether. Dixton manoeuvered Nathalie around so he could watch them over her shoulder. Who was that girl? Whoever she was Pepper certainly had been fairly quick off the mark. The set ended and Dixton waved across the dance floor at Pepper, but Pepper didn't notice him. He was too busy. Suddenly a figure flew across the room in Pepper's direction as the Orchestra prepared for another set. It was Zinowsky. Dixton remembered where he'd seen the girl before; she was with Zinowsky at dinner. It looked like a fight might break out but there were too many staff and other people around so Zinowsky was hardly likely to risk anything. Dixton couldn't hear what was being said but it was quite obvious even without sub-titles what was going on. There was an exchange of some sort between Pepper and Zinowsky, then the American took the girl to one side and spoke to her rather heatedly. While this was going on Pepper was waving very obviously at her over Zinowsky's shoulder. Finally Zinowsky left the Dining Hall.

217

Pepper and the girl stepped back onto the dance floor and, within a few seconds, were once again exploring each others tonsils. Dixton and Nathalie left the floor and sat down.

'Did you see that?' he exclaimed.

'How could I? You kept my back to them so you could watch over my shoulder,' smiled Nathalie.

'Oh did I? Sorry, look it's just that. . .' he went on to explain to her what had happened.

'Well I'm glad to see Pepper has cheered up,' Nathalie laughed mischieviously as the dance ended and Pepper led his dancing partner across the room towards them.

'Hi Dixton, Nathalie,' Pepper grinned, 'this is . . .?' he hesitated.

'Clodagh,' she smiled.

'Ah yes, Clodagh,' Pepper agreed. God he was some operator.

'Did you see his face?' Pepper grinned.

'From what I could see he looked completely crazy,' Dixton said switching on the electric hand-dryer. Pepper zipped himself up and washed his hands then splashed some water on his face.

'Oh well, sod him, it's no more than he deserves,' Pepper turned the nozzle on the dryer upwards and blasted his face with warm air.

'I'm surprised she abandoned him,' Dixton said.

'Sex appeal, pure sex appeal, I can't keep them away Dixton.'

'I thought he was going to hit you at one stage.'

'Not at all, too many people around, anyway I'd sort him out.' Pepper flicked his hair in front of the mirror.

'Yeah right,' Dixton laughed, 'Like you sorted him out when he chased you after you flooded his room.'

'Tactics, Dixton, tactics.'

'Rubbish.'

'We'd better get back to the girls, they've probably finished the bottle of wine.' Dixton reached for the door but didn't get a chance to open it as someone pushed it from the other side. Pepper was still fixing his hair but Dixton recognised the newcomer to the toilet facility.

'Ah, the very men,' smirked the Praelector.

Dixton and Pepper looked at each other.

'Robin Hood,' said Pepper.

'I beg your pardon?' Dr Winston held the door open with one arm and blocked their way.

'The "very men",' Pepper smiled, 'Robin Hood and his very men.'

'I don't know whether you think you're being funny, or clever, but let me assure you that you are neither Mr Pepper. I was going to summon you to my office but I suppose now is as good an opportunity as any.'

'I beg your pardon?' Dixton said.

'The College punt,' announced the Praelector as though he were about to produce it from a hat.

'It sank,' Pepper and Dixton spoke in unison.

'I *know* what happened to it,' the Praelector spoke slowly and patronisingly, 'what I want to know is why did it sink?'

'Because it became full with water and was unable to maintain it's bouyant equilibrium?' Pepper suggested unhelpfully.

'Wipe that smile off your face Mr Pepper, the punt sank because of the negligence of yourelf and Mr Larkin.' he smiled viciously at Dixton.

'But, but the . . .' Dixton began.

'Save your excuses, Mr Larkin. College property has been damaged and this time there is no doubt as to the connection between you and that damage. Both of you are responsible for it and you shall pay for it. It may be too late to have you sent down but mark my words, if the punt is not replaced at your expense then I shall have no hesitation in approaching your respective families at the graduation and asking them personally to pay for the damage you have caused. That is of course, if either of you graduate at all.'

'In fairness Praelector I think that . . .' Pepper tried to defend them.

'I'm not interested in what you think Mr Pepper. Pay for the punt or suffer the consequences of your actions.' The Praelector turned on his heel and left the Gents having only used the facilities in a metaphorical sense.

'Jesus,' said Dixton.

'Jesus is right,' echoed Pepper. 'Let's worry about him when the hangovers have cleared.' He pulled the door towards him and they stepped out into the corridor.

'Do you think he knows something?' Dixton ventured.

'How do you mean?'

'About our results, you know all that stuff about "if either of you graduate"?'

'Nonsense, he doesn't know anything, he's just trying to scare us.'

'I wonder.'

Dixton was very worried. He'd managed to forget about the results being out the following day. They walked back along the corridor to the bar and as various Draculas passed them, Dixton wondered if the werewolf outfit wasn't perhaps indicative of an overall picture. Maybe he didn't fit in here. Maybe he would fail. Maybe the Praelector did know more than they thought. Perhaps there was a real world going side by side with his own which he'd completely overlooked or been thrown out of without even knowing it. He heard Aunt Sheila's voice from all those years ago when he lived in fear of school reports – "The Christmas exams will reveal all". Funny, she seemed to say that even during the summer.

Dixton had often wondered what had become of the tutor from Hell, Miss Hindley. He'd presumed that the reference from Feldman had kept her quiet but at the same time she had been a little too quiet since his one and only meeting with her all those months ago. The Disciplinary Committee would have been requesting reports from her he supposed but oddly enough she had not contacted Dixton all year since their meeting. Stan the Porter filled him in when Dixton clandestinely brought him a pint from the bar to the Porters' Lodge. He was still on duty.

'Thanks Dixton, you're a lifesaver. Now about that Hindley woman, you'll never guess where she is now?'

'Where?'

'The maternity wing at Addenbrookes Hospital.'

'You're joking Stan?'

'Not a word of it.' He slurped his pint. 'Some archaelogist from King's College apparently.'

'Got more than he bargained for there,' Dixton smiled.

'So did she,' grinned Stan, 'triplets.'

'No way?'

Dixton wondered if he should write a letter to Miss Hindley inquiring whether, as her tutorial student, the college authorities might hold him, in some bizzare way, vicariously liable for the whole thing. If she thought she had problems before well she'd probably revised her thinking quite recently!

It was ten to two in the morning and the last band in the bar were packing up their gear. A Scottish traditional group, they'd been a definite improvement on "Credible Overcoat".

'I'd better go soon,' Clodagh was totally trashed. Her evening dress looked less than regal and her speech was reasonably slurred.

'I'll get you a taxi,' offered Pepper. Dixton and Nathalie exchanged glances, both amazed at Pepper's gentlemanlike display. It was a situation you might expect someone, less sexually active than Pepper, to exploit to the full. Perhaps the impending exam results were beginning to get to him. Pepper was still wearing his Arab outfit and was nursing the remnants of a pint of Guinness. Dixton looked around the bar. Snogging couples were scattered liberally on the available couchspace.

He saw Niall the vet exit out into the East Court holding hands with a tall gorgeous lady in a red dress with a black jacket draped across her shoulders. Andy Chalmers formed half of one of the snogging couples, good for him. There was debris from the Ball everywhere. Pepper went to phone a cab.

'Are you coming back to Clopton Way?' Nathalie asked. Dixton nodded and felt that he was the luckiest person in the whole world regardless of what the results were tomorrow. Or rather today. Jesus it was today already.

'I'll get the werewolf,' he said.

'Oh yes I nearly forgot about that,' said Nathalie, 'I've got to take him back to the shop tomorrow.'

'A werewolf?' Clodagh revived momentarily, 'you have a were-wolf?'

'Well, not really,' Dixton began to explain but changed his mind.

'Yes we do have a werewolf but only until the morning.'

'Oh right.' Clodagh was satisfied with the explanation, like a child who is more concerned with the fruits of Santa Claus' visit than the plausibility of his getting down every chimney in the world inside twenty four hours.

'Back in a minute or two,' said Dixton.

The Court was dark and quiet. Although it was still quite warm a cold dawn was on its way. Some couples were heading for the car-park and the marquee was like a silenced white turtle. Dixton walked across the grass to E block. The main door was locked, blow, he only had a key to his room. He'd have to go around to the back door. He remembered someone saying earlier that week that the main doors would be locked at midnight on the night of the Ball. There were tons of strangers around and there was always a danger of people wandering into the blocks and disturbing the people who weren't actually attending the Ball.

'Hello Dixton,' Herve was going into his own block. 'Did you enjoy the Ball?'

'Great stuff, Herve, your hard work paid off no end.'

'Glad you enjoyed it, goodnight.'

As Dixton passed the back of F block he noticed a light on in Pepper's room. As he passed he thought he saw something move in the room between a chink in the curtains. He retraced his steps and saw a shape inside the room. 'That's strange,' he thought, 'Pepper couldn't have come back from the phone that quickly.' He entered F Block. Pepper's door was slightly ajar.

'Pepper?' he called edging the door open. No reply. He went into the room. A figure was lurking behind the door.

'Zinowsky, what the fuck are you doing here?'

The fat American didn't reply but a quick glance at the bed revealed all; Pepper's Blue's Blazer had been cut to ribbons and lay tattered on the duvet. Zinowsky held a pair of scissors in his hand.

'You bastard.' Dixton lunged forward. Zinowsky squared up to him and pointed the scissors menacingly at Dixton.

'What are you going to do about it?' he sneered.

'I'm going to rip your head off your shoulders.' (Dixton couldn't think of anything better to say but he had grave doubts as to how he'd be able to carry out the threat.)

'You couldn't fight your way out of a paper bag,' Zinowsky laughed.

Dixton tried to imagine the scenario before deciding that he'd be well able for that kind of thing. He began to get quite worried however about the situation in hand.

'Look you stupid ape,' Dixton stalled, 'first you sink our punt and now this, what are you trying to achieve? I'm sure that . . .'

'Shut up,' snarled Zinowsky, 'I'm going to leave this room and you're not going to stop me.'

Dixton was incensed. He wasn't going to let this dick walk out of Pepper's room without doing something. Zinowsky moved towards the door, Dixton stood in his way. If this guy's IQ was one point higher he'd be a plant.

'Get out of my way,' Zinowsky grabbed Dixton's jacket and threw him against the wall. Dixton lashed out and punched him in the mouth. Blood dribbled from the corner of Zinowsky's mouth like in the films. Zinowsky wiped the blood with the back of his hand, looked at it and then announced.

'You're going to be very sorry you did that.' He threw the scissors on the floor and went for Dixton.

'I presume you mean "you" plural will be sorry.' An Arab entered the room behind Zinowsky. Zinowsky turned and looked from face-to-face and then made a lunge for the door to try to escape. Pepper stuck out his leg and helped Zinowsky out into the corridor where he crashed into the fire extinguisher and lay in a heap on the floor.

'Are you OK, Dixton?' Pepper asked.

'I'm fine.'

'Will we find out how sorry we're going to be?' Pepper nodded in Zinowsky's direction. He was just beginning to pick himself up off the floor.

'Bloody right,' answered Dixton. Sunken punts, torn Blue's Blazers, broken fountains, stolen bikes, near misses, dressing downs, savage

Aunts and God knows what else flashed before Dixton's eyes. The exam results would be known in a couple of hours and then his fate would be sealed one way or another. Well Fate could eye herself up in the vitrine of human endeavour wearing her most unfortunate blouse, but she'd bloody well have to wait. There were more important things to be done first.

EPILOGUE

The multicoloured hat rose above the crowd like an outside elevator on a glass building.

'Madam, please sit down,' someone whispered authoritatively but there was no stopping Aunt Sheila. She levelled the camera at the front of the Mall and began to snap furiously. She'd worked herself up to this occasion and no-one was going to deprive her of it. Dixton caught Pepper's questioning glance as he turned to avoid his aunt's attentions and signalled back, "yes, that's her". Dixton had feared this day might not come ever so he was prepared to let his aunt have her reward for her lavish investment of money and prayers.

The parade of graduating Lupin Hall students shuffled up the aisle towards the podium where the Vice Chancellor was doing the honours, ably assisted by a plethora of attendant academics all decked out in their finery. A crier called the names out and the candidates stepped forward to receive their pieces of paper. An academic soup kitchen.

'Sanjra Klintra.'

They shuffled forward another couple of inches. Dixton felt as if he were on the balcony watching all of this dispassionately but no, it was real, he'd made it. A second class honours grade two degree was an excellent return for the work he hadn't done. Well done that old guy with the beard and gown. Dixton's stomach lurched as he remembered that it was in this very room that he'd made a balls of the Remedies and Restitution paper. Now here he was, a month later, collecting a degree (an honours degree) from Cambridge. Aunt Sheila was in her element about the whole thing.

'Dixton, the power of prayer, what did I tell you?' she'd gushed as she enveloped him in her houndstooth overcoat at the railway station.

'Well, I suppose it's not too bad,' he'd replied. There was nothing like underplaying success; it was the only way to really overstate the thing. In actual fact he was over the bloody moon. The Judge had gripped his hand firmly and somberly as though in a gesture of welcoming him into the real world. In fact everyone had an inflated view of Dixton's achievement and Dixton was anxious not to rock the boat.

'It was tough but it was worth it.' He looked the Judge in the eye and spoke in an unassuming voice. Conceit at it's best. It was amazing how the whole thing had worked out. He was thoroughly pleased with himself.

'Bernard Rainford.'

Now there was a surprise. Dixton looked around and caught Pepper's smirk. God it was so un-Christian to take pleasure in the failure of others but there you are. A pass degree in Land Economy for Bernard. No honours, no Ferrari. It was poetic justice really. For the entire year he'd waged a sneaky war against Dixton and Pepper. Andy Chalmers was convinced that Bernard had been responsible for tipping off the police about the stolen bicycles in an attempt to get Dixton and Pepper into trouble. Of course they had no proof but anything was possible. Bernard passed Dixton on his way back from the podium and gave him a filthy look. Dixton smiled smarmily and adjusted the shoulder of his gown bearing the extra buttons to indicate honours. Pepper of the honours geology degree coughed significantly behind him.

'Dixton Larkin.'

He walked to the podium. There was a flurry of activity as his scroll was handed over. As he turned to walk back to the end of the Hall, Aunt Sheila jumped up again and started with her "ack ack" camera. Her fruity hat lopped to one side while his aunt persisted in photographing her investment despite millions of filthy looks from people who thought they knew better.

'Go and get some refreshments for the Judge and myself.' Aunt Sheila had no intention of wading across the Senate House garden herself in the blazing sunshine in search of a drink. Dixton was happy to oblige, his Aunt was really draining when she was in peak form like this. Since her arrival the previous morning he'd been with her during every waking moment. She insisted on seeing every single college and was tireless in her search for postcards. Everything photographable was snapped with the enthusiasm of woodworm in a coffin. Dixton's abiding memory of this tour of Cambridge would always be of his aunt clearing a queue of twenty people at a cash dispensing machine out of the way so she could get a proper photo of Trinity. Give his aunt an inch and she'd park a car on it. He squeezed past a vast lady who was scoffing canapes. There was an unexpected clearing on the other side of her and the Zinowsky family were trying to oganise more drink for themselves. Zinowsky's dad looked exactly like his stupid son. Tweedle Dum and Tweedle Dumber. They were so alike that as Dixton retreated back past the lady with the canapes, the only way he could tell them apart was because of Zinowsky junior's crutches. He'd certainly picked the wrong blazer shredding victim on the night of the Ball.

'Three glasses of wine please.' He found a space at the long drinks table which ran the length of one side of the Senate House garden. It was a long way to battle for one measly drink each. Put off by the prospect of a return trip after one drink, he downed a glass in one.

'Oh, sorry, one more please.' The waiter looked at the empty glass and smirked. Dixton embarked on the return journey with three full glasses. There were flowery hats everywhere and his aunt's was by no means the most repulsive. Thinking of flowers reminded him that Laura the bedder had given him a bunch of roses for his room the day of the results. He resolved to buy her a present before he left Cambridge. Someone tugged his sleeve from behind when he was halfway through the crowd.

'Oh hello Sanjra, how are you getting on?' Dixton wasn't sure whether or not to allude to Bernard's poor performance. Sanjra was unperturbed.

'Things are really great Dixton.'

'Pleased with the results?'

'Definitely. I see my notes helped you in EU Law' he grinned.

'Did they what?' smiled Dixton taking a slurp out of the glass nearest to his mouth. 'Thanks ever so much.'

'Think nothing of it Dixton. I got some even better news this morning.'

'Oh yes?'

'I had an interview for a lecturing post in Leeds and I got the job. In the end I didn't need any help from anyone,' Sanjra beamed.

'I'd hug you if I didn't have these glasses in my hands.' This was fabulous stuff. 'I've got to get back to my aunt I'm afraid.'

'OK see you,' Sanjra said, 'Oh, I think maybe Jack is organising a "Grantchester Run" for tomorrow evening.'

'Excellent,' thought Dixton. His aunt would be gone by then.

'You took your time Dixton,' said Aunt Sheila handing the Judge one of the glasses and getting stuck into her own.

'We thought we'd take ourselves back to the hotel for the afternoon' the Judge spoke, 'give us a chance to sort ourselves out before this big dinner at Lupin Hall,' he winked at Dixton. Great, he'd be able to psyche himself up for the meal. He was dreading the prospect of the Praelector getting the chance to meet his aunt. His aunt, as if reading his mind, chimed in.

'I'm looking forward to meeting this Dr Winston who sent us the tickets, is he around?'

'I don't think so,' Dixton looked around perfunctorily. He wondered where Pepper was.

'Perhaps you'd get us another drink,' his aunt suggested, 'these glasses seem rather small.' Dixton smiled to himself.

'Of course Aunt Sheila.'

'Do you need a hand?' offered the Judge.

'Oh no, I'm fine on my own.' Dixton turned to face the jungle of parents and graduates.

He'd progressed about thirty yards when his way was blocked by a stocky figure. Dixton was looking down at the ground trying to negotiate his way so it wasn't until he'd said "excuse me" twice and the figure failed to move that he looked up and saw who it was.

'Ah hello Larkin,' grimaced the Praelector, 'I'm looking forward to meeting your aunt.'

'My aunt?' Dixton stalled. 'I'm not sure I know what you mean.'

'I think you know very well what I mean Larkin. You may have fluked a pass in the exams . . .'

'I may have fluked a pass but I thoroughly deserved the honours,' Dixton grinned back into the fat little face.

'There is still the outstanding matter of the college punt to be paid for and I intend collecting the money to replace it from your aunt if necessary and also from Mr Pepper's parents.'

This was war. There was every indication that the Praelector was, though ignorant and boorish, a man of his word.

'Well I don't know if . . .' Dixton began but the Praelector continued his threats.

'I wonder if your aunt knows that you were nearly sent down from Cambridge, that you assaulted a fellow student, that your attendance at lectures was atrocious and that you have been the most difficult student ever to darken the doors of Lupin Hall and what's more I'm sure she'd be very interested to know that . . .'

'I really don't think that there's anything to be gained by this sort of animosity, Praelector, perhaps . . .' Dixton tried diplomacy but his adversary was intent on all out war. He was terrified his aunt would overhear.

'Shut up Larkin, I've had it up to here with you all year. You are anathema to Cambridge, you are an out of place ne'er-do-well who has managed to avoid your responsibilities but however much you may think you've got away with it you're in for a very nasty shock.' Dr Winston snarled and a number of people were now nervously eavesdropping on their confrontation. The Praelector continued.

'You are going to pay for the damage to the college punt and I am going to inform your aunt about your behaviour over the last year. At the very least she should be given the opportunity to assess your abuse of her money and her trust for herself, now if you don't mind.' Dr

Winston attempted to sidestep Dixton.

It was one of those moments which define an entire lifetime. Dixton's heart went into overdrive at the prospect of a denouement on the scale threatened. He knew his aunt well enough to know that an intrusion of this nature would totally wreck the occasion for her. His entire future relationship with her depended on the success of this day. He could face his pillow that night as the legitimate graduate who had repaid her kindness with academic success abroad or as the rat of a nephew who had gambled her dreams in foreign sewers. He recalled the battle he'd endured at the hands of the Praelector during the past year. Surely this kind of antipathy could be sorted out with a handshake and a smile? He remembered that debate, when he'd offered his hand in friendship to the Praelector and had been virtually spat at. Now this bastard was going to tip off his aunt and ruin his life. Something inside Dixton snapped. It was now or never. He blocked the Praelector's way and glared at him.

'Look, you little weasel,' Dixton exploded. An old lady nearby dropped her cream bun and the Praelector stepped on it as he took in the insult. He looked completely taken aback. Dixton continued.

'I've had just about enough of being fucked around by you. You've done nothing all year but try to implicate me in every sort of disaster you can concoct and I know that if you had your way I would have been thrown out.' The Praelector opened his mouth but Dixton didn't give him a chance to rev up.

'I know that you don't like me or Johnny Pepper. Well we don't like you, but we can live with that. I'm also sure that the college authorities would be very interested to know that Dr Winston, "Praelector and Keeper of the Morals" has a criminal conviction. I wonder how long you'd last before the Disciplinary Board yourself on that one?' (Good old filing room in the CPS.)

If he'd kicked the Praelector between the legs while telling him at the same time that he had just missed winning the California State Lottery and had only days to live, he couldn't have made more of an impression. The Praelector reddened from the socks up and sank back into his tatty second-hand suit. He looked like a man caught in a cheese-grater. They just stood there facing each other in the crowd on the Senate House lawn, each silently contemplating the situation, though with different coloured faces.

'Feel free to talk to my aunt. Her name is Sheila.' Dixton finished him off by stepping aside. The Praelector obviously decided that this wasn't going to be his moment, he turned on his heel (which wasn't easy given the crowd and the conditions underfoot) and stole away into the midday sunshine. Dixton needed a drink.

'Jesus, that's incredible.' For the first time Dixton could remember Pepper was impressed.

'I know, I couldn't believe it myself. I was so furious at him that I decided what had I to lose?'

'It certainly paid off.' Pepper signalled the barman for another two pints of Guinness.

'I'm bloody glad too, I was terrified he'd get to Aunt Sheila.'

'Oh well, "all's well", and all that,' Pepper grinned.

'It was certainly a close thing,' said Dixton, 'I mean if he'd spilled the beans to Aunt Sheila, any goods I had on him would have been useless.'

'Would you actually have told the college authorities about him?'

'Probably not.' Dixton felt that you had to draw the line at snitching per se, even executive snitching. The barman brought over the pints. Pepper rummaged in his pockets.

'No, no this is on me, or rather, on the Judge.' Dixton took a wad of new notes out of his inside pocket and peeled one off. (He had always thought you had to be a cattle dealer to do that.)

'How do you get on with him?' Pepper asked.

'Really well, I think he thinks I'm respectable now.'

'Have you mentioned Nathalie to them?'

'Well I broached the subject over lunch. I thought she'd go bananas but none of it.'

'How do you mean?'

'Well the Judge said "She sounds like a lovely girl".'

'And your Aunt?'

'She started off on this kick about France being the "Daughter of the Catholic Church" and how she'd love to visit Paris again.'

'So what do you think?' Pepper slurped his pint.

'Well they'll meet her tonight at Lupin. Are your parents going?'

'Yeah, they're spending the afternoon mooching around the town and I'm picking them up at eight in the geology department car.'

Dixton looked around the pub. They were the only customers in the entire place which probably wasn't surprising at half three in the afternoon. They seemed to have spent the year in various pubs. The Bit and Bridle was the best of them. He remembered Bernard's face that morning in the Senate House. It prompted a query which was more rhetorical than anything else.

'It was poetic justice really Bernard doing so badly in the exams.'

Pepper looked down into his pint and then up at Dixton. There was a glint in his eye which suggested subterfuge.

'What? What is it Pepper? You know something, don't you?'

Pepper grinned mischievously.

'Well I suppose I can tell you now.'

'Tell me what?'

'Well,' Pepper took a drink, 'you remember the essay Sanjra, I mean Rose, typed?'

'Yeah, the one you delivered? You did deliver it didn't you?' Dixton said worriedly.

'Oh I delivered it all right,' Pepper smirked.

'What? Did you hand it all in? You didn't hide a few pages or something did you?' Dixton was breathless with inquiry.

'Oh I handed it in all right, I just added to it that's all.'

'What do you mean? Did you write on it or. . .?'

'I increased it's value you might say.'

'Come on Pepper, what did you do? Tell me.' Dixton was dying to know. Pepper finished off the pint and grinned across the table.

'I stuck a twenty pound note to the front of the essay with a paper clip and re-sealed the envelope.'

'Jesus Christ, Pepper,' Dixton was stunned, 'anything could have happened.'

'The way I look at it,' Pepper continued, 'that boy Rainford deserves the best education money can buy.'

The two friends exploded into their drinks.

'What are you going to do now Pepper?'

'A friend of mine in Copenhagen said he could get us a job in a restaurant there for the summer if we've nothing better to do.' Pepper gestured to the barman for another two pints.

'Sounds like good fun. What about long term though? What are you going to do after the summer?'

'God I don't know, back to Belfast maybe, some cushy insurance job or I might try and turn professional.'

'With women?' Dixton quipped.

'No, with golf you bastard. I suppose I'd better find out what Clara is up to. We might get married or something. I've really not given the future a whole lot of thought. What about you?'

'Same here, no real plans.'

'And Nathalie?'

'Well she's the one definite feature in my future. I wouldn't mind going to France towards the end of the summer. If we go to Denmark I'm sure she'd come and visit. She's quite keen to visit Dublin too.

Depends on how the job scene is for her next year when she qualifies. At least she's into final year now.'

'Do you have to go to the Bar now or what? Do you have to be a solicitor first?'

'I'm not sure if I even want to practice as a lawyer. McInnes says he'll get me into the CPS if I qualify but I don't know that I'd like to live here forever.'

'Who wants to live forever?' grinned Pepper.

'You know what I mean.'

'Of course I do. Cheers fellow honours graduate.' They clinked glasses, and not for the first or last time.

It was all so vague, this future business. Who was it who said that life is what happens when you're busy making other plans? He'd never dreamed he'd get into Cambridge and now here he was leaving it with a degree. Fucking incredible. Fate lurked around every corner tarting herself up in unfortunate garb but you never knew when the fashions would change or the price of old clothes would go through the roof. He wasn't sure what he'd do next but there was a notice in the foyer of Lupin Hall about a five year Doctorate of Law in Quebec. It was some environmental rubbish sponsored by a chemical firm, no doubt as a PR exercise. He'd miss Nathalie though if he went too far away. The Bar was of course still an option. He'd not yet managed to solve the big questions such as how thermos flasks know whether to keep something hot or cold. He still had no idea what the Hawks Club was but what of it? The jobs market was now, in a comforting way, further away than ever before. The possibility of becoming an academic would have to be explored too before any sleeves actually had to be rolled up. God knows where he'd be in twelve months time, even twelve weeks, but who cared?

Through the window the summer sun cast a beam of happy light on the varnished pine table where two pints were settling. The warm river hummed through Grantchester on its inexorable journey past the Bit and Bridle and on into middle England while the breeze whispered encouragement through the trees. It was all over in one sense but in another more real way it was only beginning.

Dixton Larkin still couldn't believe his luck.

THE END

I only know that you may lie
Day-long and watch the Cambridge sky,
And flower-lulled in sleepy grass,
Hear the cool lapse of hours pass,
Until the centuries blend and blur
In Grantchester, in Grantchester. . . .

Rupert Brooke, *The Old Vicarage, Grantchester 1912*